A RED HERRING WITHOUT MUSTARD

For eleven-year-old Flavia de Luce, an audience with a gypsy fortune-teller at the Bishop's Lacey village fête is just a bit of fun. Until the old woman sees (or claims to see) a vision of Flavia's mother, Harriet, who died on a mountain side in Tibet when Flavia was a baby. 'She is trying to come home,' the old woman intones, chilling them both. With only her faithful bicycle, Gladys, and her precocious powers of deduction to help her, Flavia starts down a dark and twisting road to the truth.

A RED HERRING
WITHOUT MUSTARD

A Red Herring Without Mustard

by

Alan Bradley

Magna Large Print Books
Long Preston, North Yorkshire,
BD23 4ND, England.

British Library Cataloguing in Publication Data.

Bradley, Alan
    A red herring without mustard.

    A catalogue record of this book is
    available from the British Library

    ISBN   978-0-7505-3612-7

First published in Great Britain in 2011 by Orion Books
an imprint of The Orion Publishing Group Ltd.

Published in Large Print 2012 by arrangement with
Orion Publishing Group

Magna Large Print is an imprint of Library Magna Books Ltd.

Printed and bound in Great Britain by
T.J. (International) Ltd., Cornwall, PL28 8RW

For John and Janet Harland

...a cup of ale without a wench, why, alas,
'tis like an egg without salt or a red herring
without mustard.

THOMAS LODGE AND ROBERT GREENE
A Looking Glasse,
for London and Englande (1592)

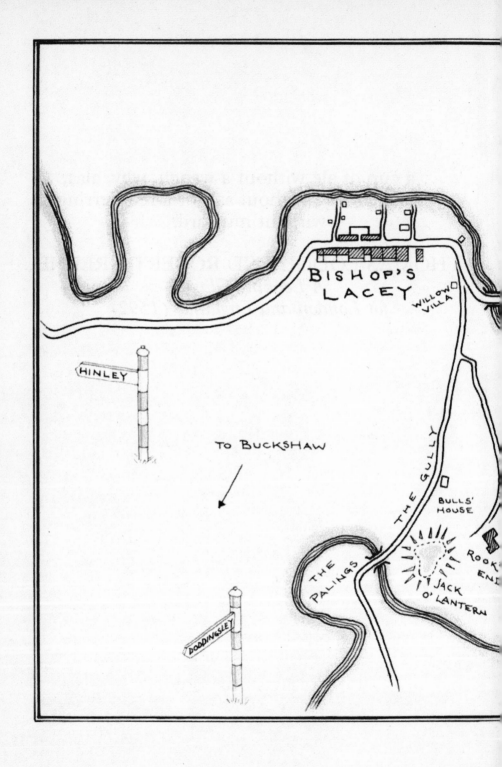

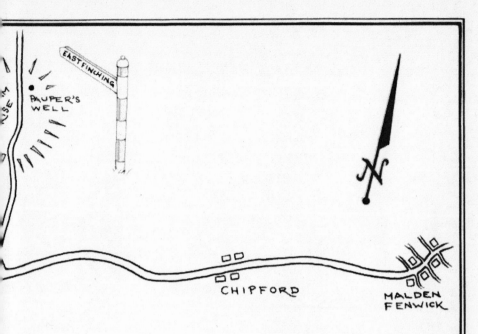

EAST FINCHING

PAUPER'S WELL

CHIPFORD

MALDEN FENWICK

RIVER EFON

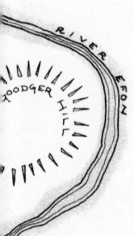

GOODGER HILL

BISHOP'S LACEY
& Environs

~NOT TO SCALE~

FdL

ONE

'You frighten me,' the Gypsy said. 'Never have I seen my crystal ball so filled with darkness.'

She cupped her hands around the thing, as if to shield my eyes from the horrors that were swimming in its murky depths. As her fingers gripped the glass, I thought I could feel ice water trickling down inside my gullet.

At the edge of the table, a thin candle flickered, its sickly light glancing off the dangling brass hoops of the Gypsy's earrings, then flying off to die somewhere in the darkened corners of the tent.

Black hair, black eyes, black dress, red-painted cheeks, red mouth, and a voice that could only have come from smoking half a million cigarettes.

As if to confirm my suspicions, the old woman was suddenly gripped by a fit of violent coughing that rattled her crooked frame and left her gasping horribly for air. It sounded as though a large bird had somehow become entangled in her lungs and was flapping to escape.

'Are you all right?' I asked. 'I'll go for help.'

I thought I had seen Dr. Darby in the church-yard not ten minutes earlier, pausing to have a word or two at each stall of the church fête. But before I could make a move, the Gypsy's dusky hand had covered mine on the black velvet of the tabletop.

'No,' she said. 'No ... don't do that. It happens

all the time.'

And she began to cough again.

I waited it out patiently, almost afraid to move.

'How old are you?' she said at last. 'Ten? Twelve?'

'Eleven,' I said, and she nodded her head wearily as though she'd known it all along.

'I see – a mountain,' she went on, almost strangling on the words, 'and the face – of the woman you will become.'

In spite of the stifling heat of the darkened tent, my blood ran cold. She was seeing Harriet, of course!

Harriet was my mother, who had died in a climbing accident when I was a baby.

The Gypsy turned my hand over and dug her thumb painfully into the very center of my palm. My fingers spread – and then curled in upon themselves like the toes of a chicken's severed foot.

She took up my left hand. 'This is the hand you were born with,' she said, barely glancing at the palm, then letting it fall and picking up the other. '...and this is the hand you've grown.'

She stared at it distastefully as the candle flickered. 'This broken star on your Mount of Luna shows a brilliant mind turned in upon itself – a mind that wanders the roads of darkness.'

This was not what I wanted to hear.

'Tell me about the woman you saw on the mountain,' I said. 'The one I shall become.'

She coughed again, clutching her coloured shawl tightly about her shoulders, as though wrapping herself against some ancient and invisible winter wind.

16

'Cross my palm with silver,' she demanded, sticking out a grubby hand.

'But I gave you a shilling,' I said. 'That's what it says on the board outside.'

'Messages from the Third Circle cost extra,' she wheezed. 'They drain the batteries of my soul.'

I almost laughed out loud. Who did this old hag think she was? But still, she seemed to have spotted Harriet beyond the veil, and I couldn't let scepticism spoil even half a chance of having a few words with my dead mother.

I dug for my last shilling, and as I pressed the coin into her hand, the Gypsy's dark eyes, suddenly as bright as a jackdaw's, met mine.

'She is trying to come home,' she said. 'This ... woman ... is trying to come home from the cold. She wants you to help her.'

I leapt to my feet, bashing the bottom of the table with my bare knees. It teetered, then toppled to one side as the candle slid off and fell among a tangle of dusty black hangings.

At first there was a little wisp of black smoke as the flame turned blue, then red, then quickly orange. I looked on in horror as it spread along the drapery.

In less time than it takes to tell, the entire tent was in flames.

I wish I'd had the presence of mind to throw a wet cloth over the Gypsy's eyes and lead her to safety, but instead I bolted – straight through the circle of fire that was the entranceway – and I didn't stop until I reached the coconut pitch, where I stood panting behind a canvas drape, trying to catch my breath.

Someone had brought a wind-up gramophone to the churchyard, from which the voice of Danny Kaye was singing 'I've Got a Lovely Bunch of Coconuts', made nauseously tinny by the throat of the machine's painted horn.

I looked back at the Gypsy's tent just in time to see Mr. Haskins, St. Tancred's sexton, and another man whom I didn't recognise heave a tub of water, apples and all, onto the flames.

Half the villagers of Bishop's Lacey, or so it seemed, stood gaping at the rising column of black smoke, hands over mouths or fingertips to cheeks, and not a single one of them knowing what to do.

Dr. Darby was already leading the Gypsy slowly away towards the St. John's Ambulance tent, her ancient frame wracked with coughing. How small she seemed in the sunlight, I thought, and how pale.

'Oh, there you are, you odious little prawn. We've been looking for you everywhere.'

It was Ophelia, the older of my two sisters. Feely was seventeen, and ranked herself right up there with the Blessed Virgin Mary, although the chief difference between them, I'm willing to bet, is that the BVM doesn't spend twenty-three hours a day peering at herself in a looking glass while picking away at her face with a pair of tweezers.

With Feely, it was always best to employ the rapid retort: 'How dare you call me a prawn, you stupid sausage? Father's told you more than once it's disrespectful.'

Feely made a snatch at my ear, but I side-stepped her easily. By sheer necessity, the lightning dodge had become one of my specialties.

18

'Where's Daffy?' I asked, hoping to divert her venomous attention.

Daffy was my other sister, two years older than me, and at thirteen already an accomplished co-torturer.

'Drooling over the books. Where else?' She pointed with her chin to a horseshoe of trestle tables on the churchyard grass, upon which the St. Tancred's Altar Guild and the Women's Institute had joined forces to set up a jumble sale of secondhand books and assorted household rubbish.

Feely had seemed not to notice the smoking remnants of the Gypsy's tent. As always, she had left her spectacles at home out of vanity, but her inattentiveness might simply have been lack of interest. For all practical purposes, Feely's enthusiasms stopped where her skin ended.

'Look at these,' she said, holding a set of black earrings up to her ears. She couldn't resist showing off. 'French jet. They came from Lady Trotter's estate. Glenda says they were quite fortunate to get a tanner for them.'

'Glenda's right,' I said. 'French jet is nothing but glass.'

It was true: I had recently melted down a ghastly Victorian brooch in my chemical laboratory, and found it to be completely silicaceous. It was unlikely that Feely would ever miss the thing.

'English jet is so much more interesting,' I said. 'It's formed from the fossilised remains of monkey-puzzle trees, you see, and–'

But Feely was already walking away, lured by the sight of Ned Cropper, the ginger-haired potboy at the Thirteen Drakes who, with a certain

19

muscular grace, was energetically tossing wooden batons at the Aunt Sally. His third stick broke the wooden figure's clay pipe clean in two, and Feely pulled up at his side just in time to be handed the teddy bear prize by the madly blushing Ned.

'Anything worth saving from the bonfire?' I asked Daffy, who had her nose firmly stuck in what, judging by its spotty oxidised pages, might have been a first edition of *Pride and Prejudice*.

It seemed unlikely, though. Whole libraries had been turned in for salvage during the war, and nowadays there wasn't much left for the jumble sales. Whatever books remained unsold at the end of the summer season would, on Guy Fawkes Night, be carted from the basement of the parish hall, heaped up on the village green, and put to the torch.

I tipped my head sideways and took a quick squint at the stack of books Daffy had already set aside: *On Sledge and Horseback to Outcast Siberian Lepers*, Pliny's *Natural History*, *The Martyrdom of Man*, and the first two volumes of the *Memoirs of Jacques Casanova* – the most awful piffle. Except perhaps for Pliny, who had written some ripping stuff about poisons.

I walked slowly along the table, running a finger across the books, all of them arranged with their spines upwards: Ethel M. Dell, E. M. Delafield, Warwick Deeping...

I had noticed on another occasion that most of the great poisoners in history had names beginning with the letter *C*, and now here were all of these authors beginning with a *D*. Was I on to something? Some secret of the universe?

20

I squeezed my eyes shut and concentrated: Dickens ... Doyle ... Dumas ... Dostoyevsky – I had seen all of them, at one time or another, clutched in Daffy's hands.

Daffy herself was planning to become a novelist when she was older. With a name like Daphne de Luce, she couldn't fail if she tried!

'Daff!' I said. 'You'll never guess–'

'Quiet!' she snapped. 'I've told you not to speak to me when I'm reading.'

My sister could be a most unpleasant porpoise when she felt like it.

It had not always been this way. When I was younger, for instance, and Father had recruited Daffy to hear my bedtime prayers, she had taught me to recite them in Pig Latin, and we had rolled among the down-filled pillows, laughing until we nearly split.

'Od-gay ess-blay Ather-fay, Eely-fay, and Issis-may Ullet-may. And Ogger-day, oo-tay!'

But over the years, something had changed between my sisters and me.

A little hurt, I reached for a volume that lay on top of the others: *A Looking Glasse, for London and Englande*. It was a book, I thought, that would appeal to Feely, since she was mad about mirrors. Perhaps I would purchase it myself, and store it away against the unlikely day when I might feel like giving her a gift, or a peace offering. Stranger things had happened.

Riffling through its pages, I saw at once that it was not a novel, but a play-full of characters' names and what each of them said. Someone named Adam was talking to a clown:

21

'...*a cup of ale without a wench, why, alas, 'tis like an egg without salt or a red herring without mustard.*'

What a perfect motto for a certain someone, I thought, glancing across to where Ned was now grazing away at my sister's neck as she pretended not to notice. On more than one occasion I'd seen Ned sitting at his chores in the courtyard of the Thirteen Drakes with a tankard of ale – and sometimes Mary Stoker, the landlord's daughter – at his elbow. I realised with an unexpected shock that without either ale or a female within easy reach, Ned was somehow incomplete. Why hadn't I noticed that before? Perhaps, like Dr. Watson on the wireless in *A Scandal in Bohemia,* there are times that I see, but do not observe. This was something I needed to think about.

'Your handiwork, I suppose?' Daffy said suddenly, putting down a book and picking up another. She gestured towards the small knot of villagers who stood gawking at the smoking ruins of the Gypsy's tent. 'It has Flavia de Luce written all over it.'

'Sucks to you,' I said. 'I was going to help carry your stupid books home, but now you can jolly well lug them yourself.'

'Oh, do stop it!' she said, clutching at my sleeve. 'Please desist. My heartstrings are playing Mozart's *Requiem,* and a fugitive tear is making its way to my right eye, even as we speak.'

I wandered away with a careless whistle. I'd deal with her insolence later.

'Ow! Leave off, Brookie! You're 'urtin' me.'

The whining voice was coming from somewhere behind the shove ha'penny booth and, when I recognised it as belonging to Colin Prout, I stopped to listen.

By flattening myself against the stone wall of the church and keeping well back behind the canvas that draped the raffle booth, I could eavesdrop in safety. Even better, I was pleased to find that I had an unexpectedly clear view of Colin through the gaps in the booth's raw lumber.

He was dancing at the end of Brookie Harewood's arm like a great spectacled fish, his thick eyeglasses knocked askew, his dirty blond hair a hayrick, his large, damp mouth hanging open, gasping for air.

'Leave off. I didn't do nothin'.'

With his other hand, Brookie took hold of the seat of Colin's baggy trousers and swiveled him round to face the smoking remains of the Gypsy's tent.

'Who did that, then, eh?' he demanded, shaking the boy to accentuate his words. 'Where there's smoke, there's fire. Where there's fire, there's matches. And where there's matches, there's Colin Prout.'

''Ere,' Colin said, trying to ram a hand into his pocket. 'Count 'em! You just count 'em, Brookie. Same number as I had yesterday. Three. I ain't used a one.'

As Brookie released his grip, Colin fell to the ground, rolled over on his elbows, dug into his trouser pocket, and produced a box of wooden matches, which he waved at his tormentor.

Brookie raised his head and sniffed the air, as if

23

for guidance. His greasy cap and India rubber boots, his long moleskin coat and, in spite of the hot summer weather, a woollen scarf that clung like a scarlet serpent to his bulldog neck made him look like a rat catcher out of Dickens.

Before I could even wonder what to do, Colin had scrambled to his feet, and the two of them had ambled away across the churchyard, Colin dusting himself off and shrugging elaborately, as though he didn't care.

I suppose I should have stepped out from behind the booth, admitted I was responsible for the fire, and demanded that Brookie release the boy. If he refused, I could easily have run for the vicar, or called for any one of the other able-bodied men who were within earshot. But I didn't. And the simple reason, I realised with a little chill, was this: I was afraid of Brookie Harewood.

Brookie was Bishop's Lacey's riffraff.

'Brookie Harewood?' Feely had sniffed, the day Mrs. Mullet suggested that Brookie be hired to help Dogger with weeding the garden and trimming the hedges at Buckshaw. 'But he's a remittance man, isn't he? Our lives wouldn't be worth tuppence with him hanging about the place.'

'What's a remittance man?' I asked when Feely had flounced from the kitchen.

'I don't know, luv, I'm sure,' Mrs. M had replied. 'His mother's that lady as paints over in Maiden Fenwick.'

'Paints?' I had asked. 'Houses?'

'Houses? Bless you! No, it's pitchers she paints. The gentry on 'orseback and that. P'raps she'll even paint you someday in your turn. You and

24

Miss Ophelia and Miss Daphne.'

At which I had let out a snort and dashed from the room. If I were to be painted in oils, shellacked, and framed, I would be posed in my chemical laboratory and nowhere else.

Hemmed in by beakers, bell jars, and Erlenmeyer flasks, I would be glancing up impatiently from my microscope in much the same way as my late great-uncle Tarquin de Luce is doing in his portrait, which still hangs in the picture gallery at Buckshaw. Like Uncle Tar, I would be visibly annoyed. No horses and gentry for me, thank you very much.

A light pall of smoke still hung over the churchyard. Now that most of the onlookers had wandered off, the charred and smoldering remains of the Gypsy's tent were clearly visible beside the path. But it wasn't so much the scorched circle in the grass that interested me as what had been hidden behind it: a brightly painted Gypsy caravan.

It was butter yellow with crimson shutters, and its lath-work sides, which sloped gently outwards beneath a rounded roof, gave it the look of a loaf of bread that has puffed out beyond the rim of the baking pan. From its spindly yellow wheels to its crooked tin chimney, and from its arched cathedral windows to the intricately carved wooden brackets on each side of the door, it was something that might have come rumbling out of a dream. As if to perfect the scene, an ancient, swaybacked horse was grazing in a picturesque manner among the leaning gravestones at the far corner of the churchyard.

It was a Romany cob. I recognised it at once

from photographs I had seen in *Country Life*. With its feathered feet and tail, and a long mane that overhung its face (from beneath which it peered coyly out like Veronica Lake), the cob looked like a cross between a Clydesdale and a unicorn.

'Flavia, dear,' said a voice behind me. It was Denwyn Richardson, the vicar of St. Tancred's. 'Dr. Darby would be most obliged if you'd run in and fetch a fresh pitcher of lemonade from the ladies in the kitchen.'

My ruffled glance must have made him feel guilty. Why is it that eleven-year-old girls are always treated as servants?

'I'd go for it myself, you see, but the good doctor feels that the poor lady may well be put off by my clerical collar and so forth and, well...'

'Happy to, Vicar,' I said cheerily, and I meant it. Being the Lemonade Bearer would give me access to the St. John's Ambulance tent.

Before you could say 'snap!' I had loped into the parish hall kitchen ('Excuse me. Medical emergency!'), made off with a frosty jug of iced lemonade, and was now in the dim light of the first-aid tent, pouring the stuff into a cracked tumbler.

'I hope you're all right,' I said, handing it to the Gypsy. 'Sorry about the tent. I'll pay for it, of course.'

'Mmmm,' Dr. Darby said. 'No need. She's already explained that it was an accident.'

The woman's awful red-rimmed eyes watched me warily as she drank.

'Dr. Darby,' the vicar said, sticking his head through the flaps of the tent like a turtle, so that his dog collar wouldn't show, 'if you can spare a moment ... it's Mrs. Peasley at the skittles pitch. She's come all over queer, she says.'

'Mmmm,' the doctor said, snapping shut his black bag. 'What you need, my old gal,' he said to the Gypsy, 'is a good rest.' And to me: 'Stay with her. I shan't be long.

'Never rains,' he remarked to no one in particular on his way out.

For the longest time I stood awkwardly staring at my feet, trying to think of something to say. I dared not look the Gypsy in the eye.

'I'll pay for the tent,' I repeated. 'Even though it *was* an accident.'

That set her off coughing again and it was evident, even to me, that the fire had taken its toll on her already shaky lungs. I waited, helpless, for the gasping to subside.

When at last it did, there was another long, unnerving silence.

'The woman,' the Gypsy said at last. 'The woman on the mountain. Who was she?'

'She was my mother.' I said. 'Her name was Harriet de Luce.'

'The mountain?'

'Somewhere in Tibet, I think. She died there ten years ago. We don't often speak of it at Buckshaw.'

'Buckshaw means nothing to me.'

'It's where I live. South of the village,' I said with a vague wave of my hand.

'Ah!' she said, fixing me with a piercing look. 'The big house. Two wings folded back.'

'Yes, that's it,' I said. 'Not far from where the river loops round.'

27

'Yes,' the woman said. 'I've stopped there. Never knew what the place was called.'

Stopped there? I could hardly believe it.

'The lady let my *rom* and me camp in a grove by the river. He needed to rest–'

'I know the spot!' I said. 'It's called the Palings. All elder bushes and–'

'Berries,' she added.

'But wait!' I said. 'The lady? There's been no lady at Buckshaw since Harriet died.'

The Gypsy went on as though I'd said nothing.

'A beautiful lady she was, too. Bit like you,' she added, peering at me closely, 'now that I see you in the light.'

But then her face darkened. Was it my imagination, or was her voice growing stronger as she spoke.

'Then we got turned out,' she said angrily. 'They said we wasn't wanted there no more. 'Twas the summer Johnny Faa died.'

'Johnny Faa?'

'My *rom*. My husband. Died in the middle of a dusty road, clutching at his chest, like, and cursing the *Gajo* – the Englishman – that had turned us out.'

'And who was that?' I asked, already fearing the answer.

'Never asked his name. Straight as a ramrod on two sticks, the devil!'

Father! I was sure of it! It was Father who, after Harriet's death, had run the Gypsies off his estate.

'And Johnny Faa, your husband ... he died because of it, you say?'

The Gypsy nodded, and I could see by the sadness in her eyes that it was true.

'Because he needed to rest?'

'Needed to rest,' she repeated in a whisper, 'and so do I.'

And that was when it came to me. Before I could change my mind I had blurted out the words.

'You can come back to Buckshaw. Stay as long as you like. It will be all right ... I promise.'

Even as I said it I knew that there would be a great flaming row with Father, but somehow that didn't matter. Harriet had once given these people refuge and my blood would hardly allow me to do otherwise.

'We'll park your caravan at the Palings,' I said, 'in the bushes. No one even needs to know you're there.'

Her black eyes scanned my face, darting quickly from side to side. I held out my hand to her for encouragement.

'Mmmm. Go on, old girl. Take her up on it. Spot of rest would do you a world of good.'

It was Dr. Darby, who had slipped quietly back into the tent. He shot me an eighth of a wink. The doctor was one of Father's oldest friends, and I knew that he, too, could already foresee the coming battle. He had viewed the field and weighed the risks even before he spoke. I wanted to hug him.

He placed his black bag on the table, rummaged in its depths, and extracted a corked bottle.

'Take as required for cough,' he said, handing it to the Gypsy. She stared at it dubiously.

'Go on,' he urged, 'take it. It's wicked bad luck to refuse a licensed practitioner, you know.

'I'll help with the horse,' he volunteered. 'Used to have one meself.'

Now he was putting on the old country doctor routine and I knew that, medically speaking, we were in the clear.

Knots of people stared as the doctor shepherded us towards the caravan. In no time at all he had the Gypsy's horse in harness and the two of us settled on the wooden ledge that served as both doorstep and driving seat.

The old woman made a clucking noise and the villagers gave way on both sides as the caravan jerked into motion and began to rumble slowly along the churchyard path. From my high vantage point I looked down into the many upturned faces, but Feely's and Daffy's were not among them.

Good, I thought. They were most likely in one of the stalls stuffing their stupid faces with scones and clotted cream.

TWO

We lumbered through the high street, the sound of the horse's hooves echoing loudly on the cobbles.

'What's his name?' I asked, pointing at the ancient animal.

'Gry.'

'Gray?'

'Gry. "Horse" in the Romany tongue.'

I tucked that odd bit of knowledge away for

30

future use, looking forward to the time when I would be able to trot it out in front of my know-it-all sister, Daffy. Of course she would pretend that she knew it all along.

It must have been the loud clatter of our passage that brought Miss Cool, the village postmistress, scurrying to the front of her confectionery shop. When she spotted me seated beside the Gypsy, her eyes widened and her hand flew to her mouth. In spite of the heavy plate-glass windows of the shop and the street between us, I could almost hear her gasp. The sight of Colonel Haviland de Luce's youngest daughter being carried off in a Gypsy caravan, no matter how gaily it was painted, must have been a terrible shock.

I waved my hand like a frantic dust mop, fingers spread ludicrously wide apart as if to say 'What jolly fun!' What I wanted to do, actually, was to leap to my feet, strike a pose, and burst into one of those 'Yo-ho for the open road!' songs they always play in the cinema musicals, but I stifled the urge and settled for a ghastly grin and an extra twiddle of the fingers.

News of my abduction would soon be flying everywhere, like a bird loose in a cathedral. Villages were like that, and Bishop's Lacey was no exception.

'We all lives in the same shoe,' Mrs. Mullet was fond of saying, 'just like Old Mother 'Ubbard.'

A harsh cough brought me back to reality. The Gypsy woman was now bent over double, hugging her ribs. I took the reins from her hands.

'Did you take the medicine the doctor gave you?' I asked.

31

She shook her head from side to side, and her eyes were like two red coals. The sooner I could get this wagon to the Palings, and the woman tucked into her own bed, the better it would be.

Now we were passing the Thirteen Drakes and Cow Lane. A little farther east, the road turned south towards Doddingsley. We were still a long way from Buckshaw and the Palings.

Just beyond the last row of cottages, a narrow lane known to locals as the Gully angled off to the right, a sunken stony cutting that skirted the west slope of Goodger Hill and cut more or less directly cross country to the southeast corner of Buckshaw and the Palings. Almost without thinking, I hauled on the reins and turned Gry's head towards the narrow lane.

After a relatively smooth first quarter mile, the caravan was now lurching alarmingly. As we went on, bumping over sharp stones, the track became more narrow and rutted. High banks pressed in on either side, so steeply mounded with tangled outcroppings of ancient tree roots that the caravan, no matter how much it teetered, could not possibly have overturned.

Just ahead, like the neck of a great green swan, the mossy branch of an ancient beech tree bent down in a huge arc across the road. There was scarcely enough space to pass beneath it.

'Robber's Roost,' I volunteered. 'It's where the highwaymen used to hold up the mail coaches.'

There was no response from the Gypsy: she seemed uninterested. To me, Robber's Roost was a fascinating bit of local lore.

In the eighteenth century, the Gully had been

the only road between Doddingsley and Bishop's Lacey. Choked with snow in the winter, flooded by icy runoffs in spring and fall, it had gained the reputation, which it still maintained after two hundred years, of being rather an unsavoury, if not downright dangerous, place to hang about.

'Haunted by history,' Daffy had once told me as she was inking it onto a map she was drawing of 'Buckshaw & Environs.'

With that sort of recommendation, the Gully should have been one of my favorite spots in all of Bishop's Lacey, but it was not. Only once had I ventured nearly its whole length on Gladys, my trusty bicycle, before a peculiar and unsettling feeling at the nape of my neck had made me turn back. It had been a dark day of high, gusty winds, cold showers, and low scudding clouds, the kind of day...

The Gypsy snatched the reins from my hands, gave them a sharp tug. 'Hatch!' she said gruffly, and pulled the horse up short.

High on the mossy branch a child was perched, its thumb jammed firmly into its mouth.

I could tell by its red hair it was one of the Bulls.

The Gypsy woman made the sign of the cross and muttered something that sounded like 'Hilda Muir.'

'Ja!' she added, flicking the reins, 'Ja!' and Gry jerked the caravan back into motion. As we moved slowly under the branch, the child let down its legs and began pounding with its heels on the caravan's roof, creating a horrid hollow drumming noise behind us.

If I'd obeyed my instincts, I'd have climbed up

33

and at the very least given the brat a jolly good tongue-lashing. But one look at the Gypsy taught me that there were times to say nothing.

Rough brambles snatched at the caravan as it jolted and lurched from side to side in the lane, but the Gypsy seemed not to notice.

She was hunched over the reins, her watery eyes fixed firmly on some far-off horizon, as if only her shell were in this century, the rest of her escaped to a place far away in some dim and misty land.

The track broadened a little and a moment later we were moving slowly past a decrepit picket fence. Behind the fence were a tumbledown house that seemed to be hammered together from cast-off doors and battered shutters, and a sandy garden littered with trash which included a derelict cooker, a deep old-fashioned pram with two of its wheels missing, a number of fossilised motorcars, and, strewn everywhere, hordes of empty tins. Clustered here and there around the property stood sagging outbuildings – little more than makeshift lean-tos thrown together with rotten, mossy boards and a handful of nails.

Over it all, arising from a number of smoking rubbish heaps, hung a pall of grey acrid smoke which made the place seem like some hellish inferno from the plates of a Victorian illustrated Bible. Sitting in a washtub in the middle of the muddy yard was a small child, which jerked its thumb from its mouth the instant it saw us and broke into a loud and prolonged wailing.

Everything seemed to be coated with rust. Even the child's red hair added to the impression that we had strayed into a strange, decaying land where oxidation was king.

Oxidation, I never tire of reminding myself, is what happens when oxygen attacks. It was nibbling away at my own skin at this very moment and at the skin of the Gypsy seated beside me, although it was easy to see that she was much further gone than I was.

From my own early chemical experiments in the laboratory at Buckshaw, I had verified that in some cases, such as when iron is combusted in an atmosphere of pure oxygen, oxidation is a wolf that tears hungrily at its food: so hungrily, in fact, that the iron bursts into flames. What we call fire is really no more than our old friend oxidation working at fever pitch.

But when oxidation nibbles more slowly – more delicately, like a tortoise – at the world around us, without a flame, we call it rust and we sometimes scarcely notice as it goes about its business consuming everything from hairpins to whole civilisations. I have sometimes thought that if we could stop oxidation we could stop time, and perhaps be able to–

My pleasant thoughts were interrupted by an ear-piercing shriek.

'Gypsy! Gypsy!'

A large, redheaded woman in a sweat-stained cotton housedress came windmilling out of the house and across the yard towards us. The sleeves of her cardigan were rolled up above her raw-boned elbows as if for battle.

'Gypsy! Gypsy! Clear off!' she shouted, her face as red as her hair. 'Tom, get out here! That

Gypsy's at the gate!'

Everyone in Bishop's Lacey knew perfectly well that Tom Bull had cleared off ages ago and that he would not likely be back. The woman was bluffing.

''Twas you as stole my baby, and don't tell me you didn't. I seen you hangin' round here that day and I'll stand up in any court o' law and say so!'

The disappearance of the Bulls' baby girl several years earlier had been a seven-day wonder, but the unsolved case had gradually crept to the back pages of the newspapers, then faded from memory.

I glanced at the Gypsy to see how she was bearing up under the ravings of her howling accuser. She sat motionless on the driving ledge, staring straight ahead, numb to the world. It was a response that seemed to spur the other woman to an even greater frenzy.

'Tom, get yourself out here ... and bring the axe!' the woman screeched.

Until then, she had seemed hardly to notice me, but now my gaze had become suddenly entangled with hers, and the effect was dramatic.

'I know you!' she shouted. 'You're one of them de Luce girls from over at Buckshaw, ain't you? I'd rec'nise them cold blue eyes anywhere.'

Cold blue eyes? Now, here was something worth thinking about. Although I had often been frozen in my tracks by Father's icy stare, I had never for an instant thought of possessing such a deadly weapon myself.

I realised, of course, that we were in a dangerous situation, the sort of predicament that can turn nasty in a flash. It was obvious that the Gypsy woman was beyond counting upon. For all practical purposes I was on my own.

'I'm afraid you're mistaken,' I said, lifting my chin and narrowing my eyes to achieve the greatest effect. 'My name is Margaret Vole, and this is my great-aunt Gilda Dickinson. Perhaps you've seen her in the cinema? *The Scarlet Cottage? Queen of the Moon?* But of course, how foolish of me: you wouldn't recognise her in this Gypsy costume, would you? Or in her heavy makeup? I'm sorry, I'm afraid I didn't catch your name, Miss...'

'B-Bull,' the woman stammered, slightly taken aback. '*Mrs.* Bull.'

She stared at us in utter astonishment, as if she couldn't believe her eyes.

'Lovely to meet you, Mrs. Bull,' I said. 'I wonder if you might offer us assistance? We're thoroughly lost, you see. We were to have joined the cine crew hours ago at Malden Fenwick. We're both of us quite hopeless when it comes to directions, aren't we, Aunt Gilda?'

There was no response from the Gypsy.

The redheaded woman had already begun to poke damp strands of hair back into position.

'Damn fools, whoever you are,' she said, pointing. 'There's no turning round hereabouts. Lane's too narrow. Straight on to Doddingsley you'll have to go, then back by way of Tench.'

'Thanks awfully,' I said in my best village-twit voice, taking the reins from the Gypsy and giving them a flick.

'Ya!' I cried, and Gry began to move at once.

We had gone about a quarter of a mile when

37

suddenly the Gypsy spoke.

'You lie like one of us,' she said.

It was hardly the sort of remark I should have expected. She must have seen the puzzled look on my face.

'You lie when you are attacked for nothing ... for the colour of your eyes.'

'Yes,' I said. 'I suppose I do.' I had never really thought of it in this way.

'So,' she said, suddenly animated, as if the encounter with Mrs. Bull had warmed her blood, 'you lie like us. You lie like a Gypsy.'

'Is that good?' I asked. 'Or bad?'

Her answer was slow in coming.

'It means you will live a long life.'

The corner of her mouth twitched, as if a smile was about to escape, but she quickly suppressed it.

'In spite of the broken star on my Mount of Luna?' I couldn't resist asking.

Her creaking laugh caught me by surprise.

'Mumbo jumbo. Fortune-teller's rubbish. You weren't taken in by it, were you?'

Her laughter set off another round of coughing, and I had to wait until she regained her breath.

'But ... the woman on the mountain ... the woman who wants to come home from the cold...'

'Look,' the Gypsy woman said wearily – as if she were unaccustomed to speaking – 'your sisters put me up to it. They tipped me off about you and Harriet. Slipped me a couple of bob to scare the daylights out of you. No more to it than that.'

I felt my blood freeze. It was as though the faucet that feeds my brain had suddenly switched from hot to cold. I stared at her.

'Sorry if I hurt you,' she went on. 'I never meant to...'

'It makes no difference,' I said with a mechanical shrug. But it did. My mind was reeling. 'I'm sure I shall find a way of repaying them.'

'Maybe I can help,' she said. 'Revenge is my specialty.'

Was she pulling my leg? Hadn't the woman just admitted that she was a fraud? I looked deeply into her black eyes, searching for a sign.

'Don't stare at me like that. It makes my blood itch. I said I was sorry, didn't I? And I meant it.'

'Did you?' I asked rather haughtily.

'Spare us the pout. There's enough lip in the world without you adding to it.'

She was right. In spite of my turning them down, the corners of my mouth flickered, then began to rise. I laughed and the Gypsy laughed with me.

'You put me in mind of that creature that was in the tent just before you. Regular thundercloud. Told her there was something buried in her past; told her it wanted digging out – wanted setting right. She went white as the garden gate.'

'Why, what did you see?' I asked.

'Money!' she said with a laughing snort. 'Same as I always see. Couple of quid if I played my cards right.'

'And did you?'

'Pfah! A bloomin' shilling she left me – not a penny more. Like I said, she went all goosey when I told her that. Scampered out of my pitch as if she'd sat on a thistle.'

We rode along in silence for a while, and I realised that we had almost reached the Palings.

To me, the Palings was like some lost and forgotten corner of Paradise. At the southeast angle of the Buckshaw estate, beneath a spreading tent of green and leafy branches, the river, as though twirling in its skirts, swept round to the west in a gentle bend, creating a quiet glade that was almost an island. Here, the east bank was somewhat higher than the west; the west bank more marshy than the east. If you knew precisely where to look among the trees, you could still spot the pretty arches of the little stone bridge, which dated from the time of the original Buckshaw, an Elizabethan manor house that had been put to the torch in the 1600s by irate villagers who made the wrong assumptions about our family's religious allegiances.

I turned to the Gypsy, eager to share my love of the place, but she seemed to have fallen asleep. I watched her eyelids carefully to see if she was shamming, but there wasn't so much as a flicker. Slumped against the frame of the caravan, she gave off the occasional wheeze, so that I knew she was still breathing.

In rather an odd way I found that I resented her easy slumber. I was simply itching to reel off for her, like a tour guide, some of the more fascinating bits of Buckshaw's history. But for now, I should have to keep them to myself.

The Palings, as we called it, had been one of the haunts, in his latter days, of Nicodemus Flitch, a former tailor who, in the seventeenth century, had founded the Hobblers, a religious sect named for the peculiar shackled gait they adopted as they paced out their prayers. The Hobblers' beliefs seemed to be based largely on such novel ideas as that heaven was handily located six miles above the earth's surface, and that Nicodemus Flitch had been appointed personally by God as His mouthpiece and, as such, was licensed to curse souls to eternity, whenever he felt like it.

Daffy had told me that once, when Flitch was preaching at the Palings, he had called down God's wrath upon the head of a heckler, who fell dead on the spot – and that if I didn't fork over the tin of liquorice allsorts that Aunt Felicity had sent me for my birthday, she would bring the same curse crashing down upon my head.

'And don't think I can't,' she had added ominously, tapping a forefinger on the book that she'd been reading. 'The instructions are right here on this page.'

The heckler's death was a coincidence, I had told her, and most probably due to a stroke or a heart attack. He would likely have died anyway, even if he'd decided to stay home in bed on that particular day.

'Don't bet on it,' Daffy had grumbled.

In his later years Flitch, driven from London in disgrace, and steadily losing ground to the more exciting religious sects such as the Ranters, the Shakers, the Quakers, the Diggers, the Levellers, the Sliders, the Swadlers, the Tumblers, the Dunkers, the Tunkers, and yes, even the Incorrupticolians, had made his way to Bishop's Lacey, where at this very bend in the river he had begun baptising converts to his weird faith.

Mrs. Mullet, after glancing over each of her shoulders and dropping her voice to a furtive whisper, had once told me that Nicodemus Flitch's strange brand of religion was still said to be practised in the village, although nowadays strictly behind closed doors and drawn curtains.

'They dips their babies by the 'eels,' she said, wide-eyed. 'Like Killies the 'Eel in the River Stynx, my friend Mrs. Wailer says 'er Bert told 'er. Don't you 'ave nothin' to do with them 'Obblers. They'll 'ave your blood for sausages.'

I had grinned then and I smiled now as I re-called her words, but I shivered, too, as I thought of the Palings, and the shadows that swallowed its sunshine.

My last visit to the glade had been in spring when the clearing was carpeted with cowslips – 'paigles', Mrs. Mullet called them – and prim-roses.

Now the grove would be hidden by the tall elder bushes that grew along the river's bank. It was too late in the season to see, and to inhale the delicious scent of, the elder flowers. Their white blossoms, like a horde of Japanese parasols, would have turned brown and vanished with the rains of June. Perhaps more cheerful was the thought that the purplish-black elderberries which took their place would soon be hanging in perfectly arranged clusters, like a picture gallery of dark bruises.

It was at the Palings, in the days of the early numbered Georges, that the river Efon had been diverted temporarily to form the ornamental lake and feed the fountains whose remnants dotted the lawns and terraces at Buckshaw. At the time of its construction, this marvel of subterranean hydraulic engineering had caused no end of hard

42

feelings between my family and the local land-owners, so that one of my ancestors, Lucius de Luce, had subsequently become known as 'Leaking de Luce' to half the countryside. In his portrait, which still hangs in our picture gallery at Buckshaw, he seems rather bored, overlooking the northwest corner of his lake, with its folly, its fountains, and the – now long gone – Grecian temple. Lucius is resting the bony knuckles of one hand on a table, upon which are laid out a compass, a pocket watch, an egg, and a piece of gadgetry meant for surveyors, called a theodolite. In a wooden cage is a canary with its beak open. It is either singing or crying for help.

My cheerful musings were interrupted by a barking cough.

'Pull up,' the Gypsy said, snatching the reins from my hands. Her brief nap must have done her some good, I thought. In spite of the cough, there was now more colour in her dusky cheeks and her eyes seemed to burn more brightly than ever.

With a clucking noise to Gry and a quick ease that showed her familiarity with the place, she steered the caravan off the narrow road, under a leafy overhang, and onto the little bridge. Moments later, we had come to a stop in the middle of the glade.

The Gypsy climbed heavily down from her seat and began unfastening Gry's harness. As she saw to her old horse, I took the opportunity to glory in my surroundings.

Patches of poppies and nettles grew here and there, illuminated by the downward slanting bars of the afternoon sun. Never had the grass seemed so green.

Gry had noticed it, too, and was already grazing contentedly upon the long blades.

The caravan gave a sudden lurch, and there was a sound as though someone had stumbled.

I jumped down and raced round the other side.

It was evident at once that I had misread the Gypsy's condition. She had crumbled to the ground, and was hanging on for dear life to the spokes of one of the tall wooden wheels. As I reached her side, she began to cough again, more horribly than ever.

'You're exhausted,' I said. 'You ought to be lying down.'

She mumbled something and closed her eyes.

In a flash I had climbed up onto the wagon's shafts and opened the door.

But whatever I had been expecting, it wasn't this.

Inside, the caravan was a fairy tale on wheels. Although I had no time for more than a quick glance round, I noticed an exquisite cast-iron stove in the Queen Anne style, and above it a rack of blue-willow chinaware. Hot water and tea, I thought – essentials in all emergencies. Lace curtains hung at the windows, to provide first-aid bandages if needed, and a pair of silver paraffin lamps with red glass chimneys swung gently from their mounts for steady light, a bit of heat, and a flame for the sterilising of needles. My training as a Girl Guide, however brief, had not been entirely in vain. At the rear, a pair of carved wooden panels stood half-open, revealing a roomy bunk bed that occupied nearly the whole width of the caravan.

Back outside, I helped the Gypsy to her feet, throwing one of her arms across my shoulder.

'I've folded the steps down,' I told her. 'I'll help you to your bed.'

Somehow, I managed to shepherd her to the front of the caravan where, by pushing and pulling, and by placing her hands upon the required holds, I was at last able to get her settled. During most of these operations, she seemed scarcely aware of her surroundings, or of me. But once tucked safely into her bunk, she appeared to revive somewhat.

'I'm going for the doctor,' I said. Since I'd left Gladys parked against the back of the parish hall at the fête, I realised I'd have to hoof it later, from Buckshaw back into the village.

'No, don't do that,' she said, taking a firm grip on my hand. 'Make a nice cup of tea, and leave me be. A good sleep is all I need.'

She must have seen the sceptical look on my face.

'Fetch the medicine,' she said. 'I'll have just a taste. The spoon's with the tea things.'

First things first, I thought, locating the utensil among a clutter of battered silverware, and pouring it full of the treacly looking cough syrup.

'Open up, little birdie,' I said with a grin. It was the formula Mrs. Mullet used to humour me into swallowing those detestable tonics and oils with which Father insisted his daughters be dosed. With her eyes fixed firmly on mine (was it my imagination, or did they warm a little?), the Gypsy opened her mouth dutifully and allowed me to insert the brimming spoon.

45

'Swallow, swallow, fly away,' I said, pronouncing the closing words of the ritual, and turning my attention to the charming little stove. I hated to admit my ignorance: I hadn't the faintest idea how to light the thing. You might as well ask me to stoke up the boilers on the *Queen Elizabeth*.

'Not here,' the Gypsy said, spotting my hesitation. 'Outside. Make a fire.'

At the bottom of the steps, I paused for a quick look round the grove.

Elder bushes, as I have said, were growing everywhere. I tugged at a couple of branches, trying to tear them loose, but it was not an easy task. *Too full of life*, I thought; *too springy*. After something of a tug-of-war, and only by jumping vigorously on a couple of the lower branches, was I able to tear them free at last.

Five minutes later, at the center of the glade, I had gathered enough twigs and branches to have the makings of a decent campfire.

Hopefully, while muttering the Girl Guide's Prayer ('Burn, blast you!'), I lit one of the matches I had found in the caravan's locker. As the flame touched the twigs, it sizzled and went out. Another did the same.

As I am not noted for my patience, I let slip a mild curse.

If I were at home in my chemical laboratory, I thought, *I would be doing as any civilised person does and using a Bunsen burner to boil water for tea: not messing about on my knees in a clearing with a bundle of stupid green twigs.*

It was true that, before my rather abrupt departure from the Girl Guides, I had learned to

46

start campfires, but I'd vowed that never again would I be caught dead trying to make a fire-bow from a stick and a shoestring, or rubbing two dry sticks together like a demented squirrel.

As noted, I had all the ingredients of a roaring fire – all, that is, except one.

Wherever there are paraffin lamps, I thought, *paraffin can not be far away.* I let down the hinged side panel of the caravan and there, to my delight, was a gallon of the stuff. I unscrewed the cap of the tin, splashed a bit of it onto the waiting firewood, and before you could say 'Baden-Powell', the teakettle was at a merry boil.

I was proud of myself. I really was.

'Flavia, the resourceful,' I was thinking. 'Flavia, the all-round good girl.'

That sort of thing.

Up the steep steps of the caravan I climbed, tea in hand, balancing on my toes like a tightrope walker.

I handed the cup to the Gypsy and watched as she sipped at the steaming liquid.

'You were quick about it,' she said.

I shrugged humbly. No need to tell her about the paraffin.

'You found dry sticks in the locker?' she asked.

'No,' I said, 'I...'

Her eyes grew wide with horror, and she held out the cup at arm's length.

'Not the bushes! You didn't cut the elder bushes?'

'Why, yes,' I said modestly. 'It was no trouble at all, I–'

The cup flew from her hands with a clatter, and

47

scalding tea went flying in all directions. She leapt from the bunk with startling speed and shrank herself back into the corner.

'Hilda Muir!' she cried, in an eerie and desolate wail that rose and fell like an air-raid siren. 'Hilda Muir!' She was pointing to the door. I turned to look, but no one was there.

'Get away from me! Get out! Get out!' Her hand trembled like a dead leaf.

I stood there, dumbfounded. What had I done?

'Oh, God! Hilda Muir! We are *all* dead!' she groaned. 'Now we are *all* dead!'

THREE

Seen from the rear, at the edge of the ornamental lake, Buckshaw presented an aspect seldom seen by anyone other than family. Although the tall brick wall of the kitchen garden hid some parts of the house, there were two upper rooms, one at the end of each wing, that seemed to rise up above the landscape like twin towers in a fairy tale.

At the southwest corner was Harriet's boudoir, an airless preserve that was kept precisely as it had been on that terrible day ten years ago when news of her tragic death had reached Buckshaw. In spite of the Italian lace that hung at its windows, the room inside was a curiously sanitised preserve as if, like the British Museum, it had a team of silent gray-clad scrubbers who came in the night to sweep away all signs of pass-

48

ing time, such as cobwebs or dust.

Although I thought it unlikely, my sisters believed that it was Father who was the keeper of Harriet's shrine. Once, hiding on the stairs, I had overheard Feely telling Daffy, 'He cleans in the night to atone for his sins.'

'Bloodstains and the like,' Daffy had whispered dramatically.

Far too agog for sleep, I had lain in bed for hours, open-eyed and wondering what she meant.

Now, at the southeast corner of the house, the upstairs windows of my chemical laboratory reflected the slow passage of the clouds as they drifted across the dark glass like fat sheep in a blue meadow, giving no hint to the outside world of the pleasure palace that lay within.

I looked up at the panes happily, hugging myself, visualising the array of gleaming glassware that awaited my pleasure. The indulgent father of my great-uncle Tarquin de Luce had built the laboratory for his son during the reign of Queen Victoria. Uncle Tar had been sent down from Oxford amidst some sort of scandal that had never been quite fully explained – at least in my presence – and it was here at Buckshaw that he had begun his glorious, if cloistered, chemical career.

After Uncle Tar's death, the laboratory was left to keep its secrets to itself: locked and forgotten by people who were more concerned with taxes and drainage than with cunningly shaped vessels of glass.

Until I came along, that is, and claimed it for my own.

I wrinkled my nose in pleasure at the memory.

As I approached the kitchen door, I felt proud of myself to have thought of using the least conspicuous entrance. With Daffy and Feely forever scheming and plotting against me, one could never be too careful. But the excitement of the fête and the moving of the Gypsy's caravan to the Palings had caused me to miss lunch. Right now, even a slice of Mrs. Mullet's stomach-churning cabbage cake would probably be bearable if taken with a glass of ice-cold milk to freeze the taste buds. By this late in the afternoon Mrs. M would have gone home for the day, and I would have the kitchen to myself.

I opened the door and stepped inside.

'Got you!' said a grating voice at my ear, and everything went dark as a sack was pulled over my head.

I struggled, but it did no good. My hands and arms were useless, as the mouth of the sack was tied tightly about my thighs.

Before I could scream, my assailants – of whom I was quite sure there were two, judging by the number of hands that were grabbing at my limbs – turned me head over heels. Now I was upside down, standing on my head, with someone grasping my ankles.

I was suffocating, fighting for breath, my lungs filled with the sharp earthy smell of the potatoes that had recently occupied the sack. I could feel the blood rushing to my head.

Damn! I should have thought sooner of kicking them. Too late now.

'Make all the noise you want,' hissed a second voice. 'There's no one here to save you.'

With a sinking feeling I realised that this was true. Father had gone up to London to a philatelic auction, and Dogger had gone with him to shop for secateurs and boot polish.

The idea of burglars inside Buckshaw was unthinkable.

That left Daffy and Feely.

In an odd way I wished it had been burglars.

I recalled that in the entire house there was only one doorknob that squeaked: the door to the cellar stairs.

It squeaked now.

A moment later, like a shot deer, I was being hoisted up onto the shoulders of my captors and roughly borne, headfirst, down into the cellars.

At the bottom of the stairs they dumped me heavily onto the flagstones, banging my elbow, and I heard my own voice shrieking with pain as it came echoing back from the vaulted ceilings – followed by the sound of my own ragged breathing.

Someone's shoes shifted in the grit not far from where I lay sprawled.

'Pray silence!' croaked a hollow voice, which sounded artificial, like that of a tin robot.

I let out another shriek, and I'm afraid I might even have whimpered a little.

'Pray silence!'

Whether it was from the sudden shock or the clammy coldness of the cellars I could not be certain, but I had begun to shiver. Would they take this as a sign of weakness? It is said that in certain small animals it is instinctive when in danger to play dead, and I realised that I was one of them.

51

I took shallow breaths and tried not to move a muscle.

'Free her, Garbax!'

'Yes, O Three-Eyed One.'

It sometimes amused my sisters to slip suddenly into the roles of bizarre alien creatures: creatures even more bizarre and alien than they were already in everyday life. Both of them knew it was a trick that for some reason I found particularly upsetting.

I had already learned that sisterhood, like Loch Ness, has things that lurk unseen beneath the surface, but I think it was only now that I realised that of all the invisible strings that tied the three of us together, the dark ones were the strongest.

'Stop it, Daffy. Stop it, Feely!' I shouted. 'You're frightening me.'

I gave my legs a couple of convincing froglike kicks, as if I were on the verge of a seizure.

The sack was suddenly whisked away, spinning me round so that I now lay facedown upon the stones.

A single candle, stuck to the top of a wooden cask, flickered fitfully, its pale light sending dark shapes dancing everywhere among the stone arches of the cellar.

As my eyes became accustomed to the gloom, I saw my sisters' faces looming grotesquely in the shadows. They had drawn black circles round their eyes and their mouths with burnt cork, and I understood instantly the message that this was intended to convey: 'Beware! You are in the hands of savages!'

Now I could see the cause of the distorted

robot voice I had heard: Feely had been speaking into the mouth of an empty cocoa tin.

'French jet is nothing but glass,' she spat, chucking the tin to the floor where it fell with a nerve-wracking clatter. 'Your very words. What have you done with Mummy's brooch?'

'It was an accident,' I whined untruthfully.

Feely's frozen silence lent me a bit of confidence.

'I dropped it and stepped on it. If it were real jet it mightn't have shattered.'

'Hand it over.'

'I can't, Feely. There was nothing left but little chips. I melted them down for slag.'

Actually, I had hit the thing with a hammer and reduced it to black sand.

'Slag? Whatever do you want with slag?'

It would be a mistake to tell her that I was working on a new kind of ceramic flask, one that would stand up to the temperatures produced by a super-oxygenated Bunsen burner.

'Nothing,' I said. 'I was just mucking about.'

'Oddly enough, I believe you,' Feely said. 'That's what you pixie changelings do best, isn't it? Muck about?'

My puzzlement must have been evident on my face.

'Changelings,' Daffy said in a weird voice. 'The pixies come in the night and steal a healthy baby from its crib. They leave an ugly shriveled changeling like you in its place, and the mother desolate.'

'If you don't believe it,' Feely said, 'go stand in front of a looking glass.'

'I'm not a changeling,' I protested, my anger

rising. 'Harriet loved me more than she did either of you two morons!'

'Did she?' Feely sneered. 'Then why did she used to leave you sleeping in front of an open window every night, hoping that the pixies would bring back the real Flavia?'

'She didn't!' I shouted.

'I'm afraid she did. I was there. I saw. I remember.'

'No! It's not true.'

'Yes, it is. I used to cling to her and cry, "Mummy! Mummy! Please make the pixies bring back my baby sister."'

'Flavia? Daphne? Ophelia?'

It was Father!

His voice came at parade-square volume from the direction of the kitchen staircase, amplified by the stone walls and echoing from arch to arch.

All three of our heads snapped round just in time to see his boots, his trousers, his upper body, and finally his face come into sight as he descended the stairs.

'What's the meaning of this?' he asked, peering round at the three of us in the near-darkness. 'What have you done to yourselves?'

With the backs of their hands and their forearms, Feely and Daffy were already trying to scrub the black markings from their faces.

'We were only playing Prawns and Trivets,' Daffy said before I could answer. She pointed accusingly at me. 'She gives us jolly good whatfor when it's her turn to play the Begum, but when it's ours she always...'

Well done, Daff, I thought. I couldn't have concocted a better spur-of-the-moment excuse myself.

'I'm surprised at you, Ophelia,' Father said. 'I shouldn't have thought...'

And then he stopped, unable to find the required words. There were times when he seemed almost – what was it ... *afraid?* ... of my oldest sister.

Feely rubbed at her face, smearing her cork makeup horribly. I nearly laughed out loud, but then I realised what she was doing. In a bid for sympathy, she was spreading the stuff to create dark, theatrical circles under her eyes.

The vixen! Like an actress applying her makeup onstage, it was a bold and brazen performance, which I couldn't help admiring.

Father looked on in thrall, like a man fascinated by a cobra.

'Are you all right, Flavia?' he said at last, not budging from his position on the third step from the bottom.

'Yes, Father,' I said.

I was going to add 'Thank you for asking' but I stopped myself just in time. I didn't want to overdo it.

Father looked slowly from one of us to another with his sad eyes, as if there were no words left in the world from which to choose.

'There will be a parley at seven o'clock,' he said at last. 'In the drawing room.'

With a final glance at each of us, he turned and trudged slowly up the stairs.

'The thing of it is,' Father was saying, 'you girls

55

just don't seem to understand...'

And he was right: we no more understood his world than he did ours.

His was a world of confetti: a brightly colored universe of royal profiles and scenic views on sticky bits of paper; a world of pyramids and battleships, of rickety suspension bridges in far-flung corners of the globe, of deep harbours, lonely watchtowers, and the heads of famous men. In short, Father was a stamp collector, or a 'philatelist', as he preferred to call himself, and to be called by others.

His every waking moment was spent in peering through a magnifying lens at paper scraps in an eternal search for flaws. The discovery of a single microscopic crack in a printing plate, which had resulted in an unwanted hair on Queen Victoria's chin, could send him into raptures.

First would come the official photograph, and elation. He would bring out of storage, and set up on its tripod in his study, an ancient plate camera with a peculiar attachment called a macroscopic lens, which allowed him to take a close-up of the specimen. This, when developed, would produce an image large enough to fill an entire page of a book. Sometimes, as he fussed happily over these operations, we would catch snatches of *H.M.S. Pinafore* or *The Gondoliers* drifting like fugitives through the house.

Then would come the written paper which he would submit to *The London Philatelist* or such-like, and with it would come a certain crankiness. Every morning Father would bring to the break-fast table reams of writing paper which he would

56

fill, page after laborious page, with his minuscule handwriting.

For weeks he would be unapproachable, and would remain so until such time as he had scribbled the last word – and more – on the topic of the queen's superfluous whisker.

Once, when we were lying on the south lawn looking up into the blue vault of a perfect summer sky, I had suggested to Feely that Father's quest for imperfections was not limited to stamps, but was sometimes expanded to include his daughters.

'Shut your filthy mouth!' she'd snapped.

'The thing of it is,' Father repeated, bringing me back to the present, 'you girls don't appear to understand the gravity of the situation.'

Mainly he meant me.

Feely had ratted, of course, and the story of how I had vaporised one of Harriet's dreadful Victorian brooches had come tumbling out of her mouth as happily as the waters of a babbling brook.

'You had no right to remove it from your mother's dressing room,' Father said, and for a moment his cold blue stare was shifted to my sister.

'I'm sorry,' Feely said. 'I was going to wear it to church on Sunday to impress Dieter. It was quite wrong of me. I should have asked permission.'

It was quite wrong of me? Had I heard what I thought I'd heard, or were my ears playing hob with me? It was more likely that the sun and the moon should suddenly dance a jolly jig in the heavens than that one of my sisters should apologise. It was simply unheard of.

57

The Dieter Feely had mentioned was Dieter Schrantz, of Culverhouse Farm, a former German prisoner of war who had chosen to remain behind in England after the armistice. Feely had him in her sights.

'Yes,' Father said. 'You should have.'

As he turned his attention to me, I could not help noticing that the folds of skin at the outer corners of his hooded eyes – those folds that I so often thought of as making him look so aristocratic – were hanging more heavily than usual, giving him a look of deeper sadness than I had ever seen.

'Flavia,' he said in a flat and weary voice that wounded me more than a pointed weapon.

'Yes, sir?'

'What is to be done with you?'

'I'm sorry, Father. I didn't mean to break the brooch. I dropped it and stepped on it by accident, and it just crumbled. Gosh, it must have been very old to be so brittle!'

He gave an almost imperceptible wince, followed instantly by one of those looks that meant I had touched upon a topic that was not open for discussion. With a long sigh he shifted his gaze to the window. Something in my words had sent his mind fleeing to safety beyond the hills.

'Did you have an enjoyable trip up to London?' I ventured. 'To the philatelic exhibition, I mean?'

The word 'philatelic' drew him back quickly.

'I hope you found some decent stamps for your collection.'

He let out another sigh: this one frighteningly like a death rattle. 'I did not go to London to buy

58

stamps, Flavia. I went there to sell them.'

Even Feely gasped.

'Our days at Buckshaw may be drawing to a close,' Father said. 'As you are well aware, the house itself belonged to your mother, and when she died without leaving a will...'

He spread his hands in a gesture of helplessness that reminded me of a stricken butterfly.

He had deflated so suddenly in front of us that I could scarcely believe it.

'I had hoped to take her brooch to someone whom I know...'

For quite a few moments his words did not register.

I knew that in recent years the cost of maintaining Buckshaw had become positively ruinous, to say nothing of the taxes and the looming death duty. For years Father had managed to keep 'the snarling taxmen', as he called them, at bay, but now the wolves must be howling once again on the doorstep.

There had been hints from time to time of our predicament, but the threat had always seemed unreal: no more than a distant cloud on a summer horizon.

I remembered that for a time, Father had pinned his hopes on Aunt Felicity, his sister who lived in Hampstead. Daffy had suggested that many of his so-called 'philatelic jaunts' were, in fact, calls upon Aunt Felicity to touch her for a loan – or to beg her to fork over whatever remained of the family jewels.

In the end, his sister must have turned him down. Just recently, and with our own ears, we had heard her tell him he must think about selling his philatelic collection. 'Those ridiculous postage stamps,' she had called them, to be precise.

'Something will turn up,' Daffy remarked brightly. 'It always does.'

'Only in Dickens, Daphne,' Father said. 'Only in Dickens.'

Daffy had been reading *David Copperfield* for the umpteenth time. 'Boning up on pawnshops,' she had answered when I asked her why.

Only now did it occur to me that Father had intended to take Harriet's brooch – the one I had destroyed – to a pawnbroker.

'May I be excused?' I asked. 'I'm suddenly not feeling well.'

It was true. I must have fallen asleep the instant my head touched the pillow.

Now, hours later, I was suddenly awake. The hands of my alarm clock, which I had carefully dabbed with my own formulation of phosphorescent paint, told me that it was several minutes past two in the morning.

I lay in bed watching the dark shadows of the trees as they twitched restlessly on the ceiling. Ever since a territorial dispute between two of my distant ancestors had ended in a bitter stalemate – and a black line painted in the middle of the foyer – this wing of the house had remained unheated. Time and the weather had taken their toll, causing the wallpaper of nearly every room – mine was mustard yellow with scarlet worms – to peel away in great sheets which hung in forlorn flaps, while the paper from the ceilings hung down in great loose swags whose contents were probably best not thought about.

Sometimes, especially in winter, I liked to pretend that I lived beneath an iceberg in an Arctic sea; that the coldness was no more than a dream, and that when I awoke, there would be a roaring fire in the rusty fireplace and hot steam rising from the tin hip-bath that stood in the corner behind the door.

There never was, of course, but I couldn't really complain. I slept here by choice, not by necessity. Here in the east wing – the so-called 'Tar' wing – of Buckshaw, I could work away to my heart's content until all hours in my chemical laboratory. Since they faced south and east, my windows could be ablaze with light and no one outside would see them – no one, that is, except perhaps the foxes and badgers that inhabited the island and the ruined folly in the middle of the ornamental lake, or perhaps the occasional poacher whose footprints and discarded shell casings I sometimes found in my rambles through the Palings.

The Palings! I had almost forgotten.

My abduction at the kitchen door by Feely and Daffy, my subsequent imprisonment in the cellars, my shaming at the hands of Father, and finally my fatigue: all of those had conspired to make me put the Gypsy clean out of my mind.

I leapt from my bed, somewhat surprised to find myself still fully clothed. I *must* have been tired!

Shoes in hand, I crept down the great curving staircase to the foyer, where I stopped to listen in the middle of that vast expanse of black-and-white tiling. To an observer in one of the galleries

61

above, I must have looked like a pawn in some grand and Gothic game of chess.

A pawn? Pfah, Flavia! Admit it: surely something more than a pawn!

The house was in utter silence. Father and Feely, I knew, would be dreaming their respective dreams: Father of perforated bits of paper and Feely of living in a castle built entirely of mirrors in which she could see herself reflected again and again from every possible aspect.

Upstairs, at the far end of the west wing, Daffy would still be awake, though, goggling by candlelight, as she loved to do, at the Gustave Doré engravings in *Gargantua and Pantagruel*. I had found the fat calf-bound volume hidden under her mattress while rifling her room in search of a packet of chewing gum that an American serviceman had given to Feely, who had come across him sitting on a stile one morning as she was walking into the village to post a letter. His name was Carl, and he was from St. Louis, in America. He told her she was the spitting image of Elizabeth Taylor in *National Velvet*. Feely, of course, had come home preening and hidden the gum, as she always does with such tributes, in her lingerie drawer, from which Daffy had pinched it. And I in my turn from her.

For weeks afterwards it was 'Carl-this' and 'Carl-that' with Feely prattling endlessly on about the muddy Mississippi, its length, its twists and bends, and how to spell it properly without making a fool of oneself. We were given the distinct impression that she had personally conceived and executed the formation of that great river, with

God standing helplessly on the sidelines, little more than a plumber's assistant.

I smiled at the thought.

It was at that precise instant that I heard it: a metallic *click*.

For a couple of heartbeats, I stood perfectly still, trying to decide from which direction it had come.

The drawing room, I thought, and immediately began tiptoeing in that direction. In my bare feet, I was able to move in perfect silence, keeping an ear out for the slightest sound. Although there are times when I have cursed the painfully acute sense of hearing I've inherited from Harriet, this was not one of them.

As I moved at a snail's pace along the corridor, a crack of light suddenly appeared beneath the drawing-room door. *Who could be in there at this time of night?* I wondered. Whoever it was, it certainly wasn't a de Luce.

Should I call for help, or tackle the intruder myself?

I seized the knob, turned it ever so slowly, and opened the door: a foolhardy action, I suppose, but after all, I *was* in my own home. No sense in letting Daffy or Feely take all the credit for catching a burglar.

Accustomed to the darkness, my eyes were somewhat dazzled by the light of an ancient paraffin lamp that was kept for use during electrical interruptions, and so at first I didn't see anyone there. In fact, it took a moment for me to realise that someone – a stranger in rubber boots – was crouched by the fireplace, his hand on one of the brass firedogs that had been cast into the shape of foxes.

The whites of his eyes flashed as he looked up into the mirror and saw me standing behind him in the open doorway.

His moleskin coat and his scarlet scarf flared out as he came to his feet and spun quickly round.

'Crikey, gal! You might have given me a heart attack!'

It was Brookie Harewood.

FOUR

The man had been drinking. I noticed that at once. Even from where I stood I could detect the smell of alcohol – that and the powerful fishy odour that accompanies a person who wears a creel with as much pride as another might wear a kilt and sporran.

I closed the door quietly behind me.

'What are you doing here?' I asked, putting on my sternest face.

Actually, what I was thinking was that Buck-shaw, in the small hours of the morning, was becoming a virtual Paddington Station. It wasn't more than a couple of months since I had found Horace Bonepenny in a heated nocturnal argument with Father. Well, Bonepenny was now in his grave, and yet here was another intruder to take his place.

Brookie raised his cap and tugged at his fore-lock – the ancient signal of submission to one's better. If he were a dog, it would be much the same thing as prostrating himself and rolling over to expose his belly.

'Answer me, please,' I said. 'What are you *doing* here?'

He fiddled a bit with the wicker creel on his hip before he replied.

'You caught me fair and square, miss,' he said, shooting me a disarming smile. I noticed, much to my annoyance, that he had perfect teeth.

'But I didn't mean no harm. I'll admit I was on the estate hoping to do a bit of business rabbit-wise. Nothing like a nice pot of rabbit stew for a weak chest, is there?'

He knocked his rib cage with a clenched fist and forced a cough that, since I had done it so often myself, didn't fool me for an instant. Neither did his fake gamekeeper dialect. If, as Mrs. Mullet claimed, Brookie's mother was a society artist, he had probably been schooled at Eton, or some such place. The grubbing voice was meant to gain him sympathy. That, too, was an old trick. I had used it myself, and because of that, I found myself resenting it.

'The Colonel's no shooter,' he went on, 'and all the world knows that for a fact. So where's the harm in ridding the place of a pest that does no more than eat your garden and dig holes in your shrubbery? Where's the harm in that, eh?'

I noticed that he was repeating himself – almost certainly a sign that he was lying. I didn't know the answer to his question, so I remained silent, my arms crossed.

'But then I saw a light inside the house,' he went

on. ' "*Hullo!*" I said to myself, *"What's this, then, Brookie? Who could be up at this ungodly hour?"* I said. *"Could someone be sick?"* I know the Colonel doesn't use a motorcar, you see, and then I thought, *"What if someone's needed to run into the village to fetch the doctor?"'*

There was truth in what he said. Harriet's ancient Rolls-Royce – a Phantom II – was kept in the coach house as a sort of private chapel, a place that both Father and I went – though never at the same time, of course – whenever we wanted to escape what Father called 'the vicissitudes of daily life.'

What he meant, of course, was Daffy and Feely – and sometimes me.

Although Father missed Harriet dreadfully, he never spoke of her. His grief was so deep that Harriet's name had been put at the top of the Buckshaw Blacklist: things that were never to be spoken of if you valued your life.

I confess that Brookie's words caught me off guard. Before I could frame a reply he went on: 'But then I thought, *"No, there's more to it than that. If someone was sick at Buckshaw there'd be more lights on than one. There'd be lights in the kitchen – someone heating water, someone dashing about..."'*

'We might have used the telephone,' I protested, instinctively resisting Brookie's attempt to spin a web.

But he had a point. Father loathed the telephone, and allowed it to be used only in the most extreme emergencies. At two-thirty in the morning, it would be quicker to cycle – or even run! – into Bishop's Lacey than to arouse Miss Runciman at the telephone exchange and ask her to ring up the sleeping Dr. Darby.

By the time *that* tedious game of Button, Button, Who's Got the Button had been completed, we might all of us be dead.

As if he were the squire and I the intruder, Brookie, his rubber-booted feet spread wide and his hands clasped behind him, had now taken up a stance in front of the fireplace, midway between the two brass foxes that had belonged to Harriet's grandfather. He didn't lean an elbow on the mantel, but he might as well have.

Before I could say another word, he gave a quick, nervous glance to the right and to the left and dropped his voice to a husky whisper: *"But wait, Brookie, old man,"* I thought. *"Hold on, Brookie, old chum. Mightn't this be the famous Grey Lady of Buckshaw that you're seeing?"* After all, miss, everyone knows that there's sometimes lights seen hereabouts that have no easy explanation.'

Grey Lady of Buckshaw? I'd never heard of such an apparition. How laughably superstitious these villagers were! Did the man take me for a fool?

'Or is the family spectre not mentioned in polite company?'

Family spectre? I had the sudden feeling that someone had tossed a bucket of ice water over my heart.

Could the Grey Lady of Buckshaw be the ghost of my mother, Harriet?

Brookie laughed. 'Silly thought, wasn't it?' he went on. 'No spooks for me, thank you very much! More likely a housebreaker with his eye on the Colonel's silver. Lot of that going on nowadays, since the war.'

'I think you'd better go now,' I said, my voice trembling. 'Father's a light sleeper. If he wakes up and finds you here, there's no telling what he'll do. He sleeps with his service revolver on the night table.'

'Well, I'll be on my way, then,' Brookie said casually. 'Glad to know the family's come to no harm. We worry about you lot, you know, all of us down in the village. No telling what can happen when you're way out here, cut off, as it were...'

'Thank you,' I said. 'We're very grateful, I'm sure. And now, if you don't mind–'

I unlocked one of the French doors and opened it wide.

'Good night, miss,' he said, and with a grin he vanished into the darkness.

I counted slowly to ten – and then I followed him.

Brookie was nowhere in sight. The shadows had swallowed him whole. I stood listening for a few moments on the terrace, but the night was eerily silent.

Overhead, the stars twinkled like a million little lanterns, and I recognised the constellation called the Pleiades, the Seven Sisters, named for the family of girls in Greek mythology who were so saddened by their father's fate – he was the famous Atlas who was doomed to carry the heavens on his shoulders – that they committed suicide.

I thought of the rain-swept afternoon I had spent in the greenhouse with Dogger, helping him cut the eyes from a small mountain of potatoes, and listening to a tale that had been handed down by word of mouth for thousands of years.

'What a stupid thing to do!' I said. 'Why would they kill themselves?'

'The Greeks are a dramatic race,' Dogger had answered. 'They *invented* the drama.'

'How do you know all these things?'

'They swim in my head,' he said, 'like dolphins.' And then he had lapsed into his customary silence.

Somewhere across the lawn an owl hooted, bringing me back with a start to the present. I realised that I was still holding my shoes in my hand. What a fool I must have looked to Brookie Harewood!

Behind me, except for the paraffin lamp that still burned in the drawing room, Buckshaw was all in darkness. It was too early for breakfast and too late to go back to bed.

I stepped back into the house, put on my shoes, and turned down the wick. By now, the Gypsy woman would be rested and be over her fright. With any luck, I could manage an invitation to a Gypsy breakfast over an open campfire. And with a bit more luck, I might even find out who Hilda Muir was, and why we were all dead.

I paused at the edge of the Palings, waiting for my eyes to become accustomed to the deeper gloom among the trees.

A wooded glade in darkness is an eerie place, I thought; *a place where almost anything could happen.*

Pixies ... Hilda Muir ... the Grey Lady of Buckshaw...

I gave myself a mental shake. *'Stop it, Flavia!'* a voice inside me said, and I took its advice.

The caravan was still there: I could see several stars and a patch of the Milky Way reflected in one of its curtained windows. The sound of munching somewhere in the darkness told me that Gry was grazing not far away.

I approached the caravan slowly.

'Hel-lo,' I sang, keeping the tone light, in view of the Gypsy's earlier frame of mind. 'It's me, Flavia. Knock-knock. Anyone at home?'

There was no reply. I waited a moment, then made my way round to the back of the caravan. When I touched its wooden side to steady myself, my hand came away wet with the cold dew.

'Anyone here? It's me, Flavia.' I gave a light rap with my knuckles.

There was a faint glow in the rear window: the sort of glow that might be given off by a lamp turned down for the night.

Suddenly something wet and horrid and slobbering touched the side of my face. I leapt back, my arms wind-milling.

'Cheeses!' I yelped.

There was a rustling noise and a hot breath on the back of my neck, followed by the sweet smell of wet grass.

Then Gry was nuzzling at my ear.

'Creekers, Gry!' I said, spinning round. 'Creekers!'

I touched his warm face in the darkness and found it oddly comforting: much more so than I should ever have guessed. I touched my forehead to his, and for a few moments as my heart slowed

70

we stood there in the starlight, communicating in a way that is far older than words.

If only you could talk, I thought. *If only you could talk.*

'Hel-lo,' I called again, giving Gry's muzzle one last rub and turning towards the caravan. But still, there was no reply.

The wagon teetered a bit on its springs as I stepped onto the shafts and clambered up towards the driving seat. The ornamental door handle was cold in my hand as I gave it a twist. The door swung open – it had not been locked.

'Hello?'

I stepped inside and reached for the paraffin lamp that glowed dully above the stove. As I turned up the wick, the glass shade sprang to light with a horrid sticky red brilliance.

Blood! There was blood everywhere. The stove and the curtains were splattered with the stuff. There was blood on the lampshade – blood on my hands.

Something dripped from the ceiling onto my face. I shrank back in revulsion – and perhaps a little fright.

And then I saw the Gypsy – she was lying crumpled at my feet: a black tumbled heap lying perfectly still in a pool of her own blood. I had almost stepped on her.

I knelt at her side and took her wrist between my thumb and forefinger. *Could that thin stirring possibly be a pulse?*

If it was, I needed help, and needed it quickly. Mucking about would do no good.

I was about to step out onto the driving seat

71

when something stopped me in my tracks. I sniffed the air, which was sharp with the coppery, metallic smell of blood.

Blood, yes – but something more than blood. Something out of place. I sniffed again. What could it be?

Fish! The caravan reeked of blood and fish!

Had the Gypsy woman caught and cooked a fish in my absence? I thought not; there was no sign of a fire or utensils. Besides, I thought, she had been too weak and tired to do so. And there had certainly been no fishy smell about the caravan when I left it earlier.

I stepped outside, closed the door behind me, and leapt to the ground.

Running back to Buckshaw for help was out of the question. It would take far too long. By the time the proper people had been awakened and Dr. Darby summoned, the Gypsy might well be dead – if she wasn't already.

'Gry!' I called, and the old horse came shuffling towards me. Without further thought, I leapt onto his back, flung my arms round his neck, and gave his ribs a gentle kick with my heels. Moments later we were trotting across the bridge, then turning north into the leafy narrowness of the Gully.

In spite of the darkness, Gry kept up a steady pace, as if he were familiar with this rutted lane. As we went along, I learned quickly to balance on his bony spine, ducking down as overhanging branches snatched at my clothing, and wishing I'd been foresighted enough to bring a sweater. I'd forgotten how cold the nights could be at the end of summer.

On we trotted, the Gypsy's horse outdoing himself. Perhaps he sensed a hearty meal at the end of his journey.

Soon we would be passing the tumbledown residence of the Bulls, and I knew that we would not pass unnoticed. Even in broad daylight there were seldom travelers in the narrow lane. In the middle of the night, the unaccustomed sound of Gry's hooves on the road would surely be heard by one of the half-wild Bull family.

Yes, there it was: just ahead of us on the right. I could smell it. Even in the dark I could see the grey curtain of smoke that hung about the place. Spotted here and there about the property, the embers of the smouldering rubbish tips glowed like red eyes in the night. In spite of the lateness of the hour, the windows of the house were blazing with light.

No good begging for help here, I thought. Mrs. Bull had made no bones about her hatred of the Gypsy.

Seizing a handful of Gry's thick mane, I tugged at it gently. As if he had been trained from birth to this primitive means of control, the old horse slowed to a shamble. At the change of pace, one of his hooves struck a rock in the rutted road.

'Shhh!' I whispered into his ear. 'Tiptoe!'

I knew that we had to keep moving. The Gypsy woman needed help desperately, and the Bulls' was not the place to seek it.

A door banged as someone came out into the yard – on the far side of the house, by the sound of it.

Gry stopped instantly and refused to move. I

wanted to whisper into his ear to keep going, that he was a good horse – a remarkable horse – yet I hardly dared breathe. But Gry stood as motionless in the lane as if he were a purebred pointer. Could it be that a Gypsy's horse knew more about stealth than I did? Had years of travelling the unfriendly roads taught him more low cunning than even I possessed?

I made a note to think more about this when we were no longer in peril.

By the sound of it, the person in the yard was now rummaging through a lot of old pots, muttering to themselves whenever they stopped the clatter. The light from the house, I knew, would cast me into deeper darkness. Better, though, to make myself smaller and less visible than a rider on horseback.

I waited until the next round of banging began, and slipped silently to the ground. Using Gry as a shield, I kept well behind him so that my white face would not be spotted in the darkness.

When you're in a predicament time slows to a crawl. I could not begin to guess how long we stood rooted to the spot in the lane; it was probably no more than a few minutes. But almost immediately I found myself shifting my weight uneasily from foot to foot and shivering in the gloom while Gry, the old dear, had apparently fallen asleep. He didn't move a muscle.

And then the racket stopped abruptly.

Had the person in the garden sensed our presence? Were they lying in wait – ready to spring – on the far side of the house?

More time leaked past. I couldn't move. My

heart was pounding crazily in my chest. It seemed impossible that whoever was in the Bulls' garden could fail to hear it.

They must be keeping still … listening, as I was.

Suddenly there came to my nostrils the sharp reek of a safety match; the unmistakeably acrid odour of phosphorus reacting with potassium chlorate. This was quickly followed by the smell of a burning cigarette.

I smiled. Mrs. Bull was taking a break from her brats.

But not for long. A door banged and a dark shape fluttered across behind one of the closed curtains.

Before I could talk myself out of it I began moving along the lane – slowly at first, and then more quickly. Gry walked quietly behind me. When we reached the trees at the far edge of the property, I scrambled up onto his back and urged him on.

'Dr. Darby's surgery,' I said. 'And make it snappy!'

As if he understood.

The surgery was situated in the high street, just round the corner from Cow Lane. I lifted the knocker – a brass serpent on a staff – and pounded at the door. Almost instantly, or so it seemed, an upstairs window flew open with a sharp wooden groan and Dr. Darby's head appeared, his grey, wispy hair tousled from sleeping.

'The bell,' he said grumpily. 'Please use the bell.'

I gave the button a token jab with my thumb, and somewhere in the depths of the house a muted buzzing went off. 'It's the Gypsy woman,' I called up to him. 'The one from the fête. I think someone's tried to kill her.'

The window slammed shut.

It couldn't have been more than a minute before the front door opened and Dr. Darby stepped outside, shrugging himself into his jacket. 'My car's in the back,' he said. 'Come along.'

'But what about Gry?' I asked, pointing at the old horse, which stood quietly in the street.

'Bring him round to the stable,' he said. 'Aesculapius will be glad of his company.'

Aesculapius was the ancient horse that had pulled Dr. Darby's buggy until about ten years ago, when the doctor had finally caved in to pressure from patients and purchased a tired old bull-nosed Morris – an open two-seater that Daffy referred to as 'The Wreck of the Hesperus.'

I hugged Gry's neck as he sidled into the stall with an almost audible sigh.

'Quickly,' Dr. Darby said, tossing his bag into the back of the car.

A few moments later we were veering off the high street and into the Gully.

'The Palings, you said?'

I nodded, hanging on for dear life. Once, I fancied I caught Dr. Darby stealing a glance at my bloody hands in the dim light of the instrument panel, but whatever he might have been thinking, he kept it to himself.

We rocketed along the narrow lane, the Morris's headlamps illuminating the green tunnel of the trees and hedgerows with bounces of brightness. We sped past the Bulls' place so quickly that I almost missed it, although my mind did manage to register the fact that the house was now in total darkness.

As we shot across the little stone bridge and into the grove, the Morris nearly became airborne, then bounced heavily on its springs as Dr. Darby brought it to a skidding halt just inches from the Gypsy's caravan. Even in the dark his knowledge of Bishop's Lacey's lanes and byways was remarkable, I thought.

'Stay here,' he barked. 'If I need you, I'll call.' He threw open the driver's door, walked briskly round the caravan, and was gone.

Alone in the darkness, I gave an involuntary shiver.

To be perfectly honest, my stomach was a bit queasy. I don't mind death, but injury makes me nervous. It would all depend upon what Dr. Darby found inside the caravan.

I shifted restlessly in the Morris, trying to sift through these rather unexpected feelings. Was the Gypsy woman dead? The thought that she might be was appalling.

Although Death and I were not exactly old friends, we did have a nodding acquaintance. Twice before in my life I had encountered corpses, and each one had given me–

'Flavia!' The doctor was at the caravan's door. 'Fetch a screwdriver. It's in the tool kit in the boot.'

A screwdriver? What kind of–

It was perhaps just as well that my speculations were interrupted.

'Quickly. Bring it here.'

At any other time I might have balked at his insolence in ordering me about like a lackey, but I bit my tongue. In fact, I even forgave him a little.

As Dr. Darby began loosening the screws of the door hinges, I couldn't help thinking what remarkably strong hands he had for an older man. If he hadn't used them to save lives, he might have made a wizard carpenter.

'Unscrew the last few,' he said. 'I'll take the weight of the door. That's it ... good girl.'

Even without knowing what we were doing, I was his willing slave.

As we worked, I caught glimpses of the Gypsy beyond, in the caravan's interior. Dr. Darby had lifted her from the floor to her bed where she lay motionless, her head wrapped in surgical gauze. I could not tell if she was dead or alive and it seemed awkward to ask.

At last the door came free of the frame, and for an instant, Dr. Darby held it in front of him like a shield. The image of a crusader crossed my mind.

'Easy now – put it down here.'

He manoeuvred the heavy panel carefully onto the caravan's floor, where it fit with not an inch to spare between the stove and the upholstered seats. Then, plucking two pillows from the bed, he placed them lengthwise on the door, before wrapping the Gypsy in a sheet and ever so gently lifting her from the bunk onto the makeshift stretcher.

Again I was struck with his compact strength. The woman must have weighed almost as much as he did.

'Quickly now,' he said. 'We must get her to the hospital.'

So! The Gypsy *was* alive. Death had been thwarted – at least for now.

Pulling a second sheet from the bed, Dr. Darby tore it into long strips, which he worked swiftly into position under the door, then round and round the Gypsy, fastening the ends with a series of expert knots.

He had positioned her so that her feet were closest to the empty door frame, and now I watched as he eased past her and leapt to the ground outside.

I heard the Morris's starter grind – and then engage. The motor roared and moments later I saw him backing his machine towards the caravan.

Now he was clambering back aboard.

'Take this end,' he said, pointing to the Gypsy's feet. 'It's lighter.'

He scrambled past me, seized the end of the door that lay beneath her head, and began sliding it towards the doorway.

'Into the offside seat,' he said. 'That's it ... easy now.'

I had suddenly seen what he was trying to do, and as Dr. Darby lifted the head of the door, I guided its foot down into the space between the passenger's seat and the instrument panel.

With surprisingly little struggle, our task was finished. With the Gypsy jutting up at a rigid angle, the little Morris looked like an oversized woodworking plane; the Gypsy herself like a mummy lashed to a board.

79

It isn't the neatest of arrangements, I remember thinking, *but it will do.*

'You'll have to stay here,' Dr. Darby said, wedging himself in behind the steering wheel. 'There's not room for the three of us in the old bus. Just stay put and don't touch anything. I'll send the police as soon as I'm able.'

What he meant, of course, was that I was in far less physical danger if I remained in one spot, rather than risking the possibility of flushing out the Gypsy's attacker by walking home alone to Buckshaw.

I gave the doctor a halfhearted thumbs-up. More than that would have been out of place.

He let in the clutch and the car, with its weird cargo, began teetering slowly across the grove. As it crept over the humpbacked bridge, I had my last glimpse of the Gypsy, her face dead white in the light of a sudden moon.

FIVE

Now I was truly alone.

Or was I?

Not a leaf stirred. Something went *plop* in the water nearby, and I held my breath. An otter, perhaps? Or something worse?

Could the Gypsy's attacker still be here in the Palings? Still hiding ... still watching ... from somewhere in the trees?

It was a stupid thought, and I realised it instantly. I'd learned quite early in life that the mind loves nothing better than to spook itself with outlandish stories, as if the various coils of the brain were no more than a troop of roly-poly Girl Guides huddled over a campfire in the darkness of the skull.

Still, I gave a little shiver as the moon slipped behind a cloud. It had been cool enough when I'd first come here with the Gypsy, chilly when I'd ridden Gry into the village for Dr. Darby, and now, I realised, I was beastly cold.

The lights of the caravan glowed invitingly, warm patches of orange in the blue darkness. If a wisp of smoke had been floating up from the tin chimney, the scene might have been one of those frameable tear-away prints in the weekly magazines: A *Gypsy Moon*, for instance.

It was Dr. Darby who had left the lamp burning. Should I scramble aboard and turn it out?

Vague thoughts of saving paraffin crossed my mind, and even vaguer thoughts of being a good citizen.

Saints on skates! I was looking for an excuse to get inside the caravan and have a jolly good gander at the scene of the crime. Why not admit it?

'Don't touch anything,' Dr. Darby had said. Well, I wouldn't. I'd keep my hands in my pockets.

Besides, my footprints were already everywhere on the floor. What harm would a few more do? Could the police distinguish between two sets of bloody footprints made less than an hour apart? *We shall see,* I thought.

Even as I clambered up onto the footboard I realised that I should have to work quickly. Having arrived at the hospital in Hinley, Dr. Darby would soon be calling the police – or instructing someone else to call them.

There wasn't a second to waste.

A quick look round showed that the Gypsy lived a frugal life indeed. As far as I could discover, there were no personal papers or documents, no letters, and no books – not even a Bible. I had seen the woman make the sign of the cross and it struck me as odd that a copy of the scriptures should not have its place in her travelling home.

In a bin beside the stove, a supply of vegetables looked rather the worse for wear, as if they had been snatched hastily from a farmer's field rather than purchased clean from a village market: potatoes, beets, turnips, onions, all jumbled together.

I shoved my hand into the bin and rummaged around at the bottom. Nothing but clay-covered vegetables.

I don't know what I was looking for, but I would if I found it. If I were a Gypsy, I thought, the bottom of the veggie bin would have been high on my list of hiding places.

But now my hands were thoroughly covered not only with dried blood, but also with soil. I wiped them on a grubby towel that hung on a nearby nail, but I could see at once that this would never do. I turned to the tin basin, took down a rose-and-briar ewer from the shelf, and poured water over my filthy hands, one at a time. Bits of earth and caked blood turned it quickly to a muddy red.

A goose walked over my grave and I shuddered slightly. Red blood cells, I remembered from my chemical experiments, were really not much more

82

than a happy soup of water, sodium, potassium, chloride, and phosphorus. Mix them together in the proper proportions, though, and they formed a viscous liquid jelly: a jelly with mystic capabilities, one that could contain in its scarlet complexities not just nobility but also treachery.

Again I wiped my hands on the towel, and was about to chuck the contents of the basin outside onto the grass when it struck me: *Don't be a fool, Flavia! You're leaving a trail of evidence that's as plain to see as an advert on a hoarding!*

Inspector Hewitt would have a fit. And I had no doubt it would be he – four in the morning or not – who responded to the doctor's call.

If questioned about it later, Dr. Darby would surely remember that I hadn't washed or wiped the blood from my hands in his presence. And, unless caught out by the evidence, I could hardly admit to disobeying his orders by re-entering the caravan after he had gone.

Like a tightrope walker, I teetered my way down the shafts of the wagon, the basin held out in front of me at arm's length like an offering.

I made my way to the river's edge, put down the basin, and undid my laces. The ruin of another pair of shoes would drive Father into a frenzy.

I waded barefoot into the water, wincing at the sudden coldness. Closer to the middle, where the sluggish current was even slightly stronger, would be the safest place to empty the basin; closer in might leave telltale residue on the grassy bank, and for the first time in my life I offered up a bit of thanks for the convenience of a shortish skirt.

Knee-deep in the flowing water, I lowered the

basin and let the current wash away the telltale fluids. As the clotted contents combined with the river and floated off to God-knows-where, I gave a sigh of relief. The evidence – at least this bit of it – was now safely beyond the recall of Inspector Hewitt and his men.

As I waded back towards the riverbank, I stepped heavily on a submerged stone and stubbed my toe. I nearly went face-first into the water, and only a clumsy windmilling of my arms saved me. The basin, too, acted as a kind of counterweight, and I arrived breathless, but upright, at the riverbank.

But wait! The towel! The prints of my dirty and bloody hands were all over the thing.

Back to the caravan I dashed. As I had thought it would be, the towel was stained with a pair of remarkably clear Flavia-sized handprints. Rattling good luck I had thought of it!

One more trip to the river's edge; one more wade into the chilly water, where I scrubbed and rinsed the towel several times over, grimacing as I wrung it out with a series of surprisingly fierce twists. Only when the water that dribbled back into the river was perfectly clear in the moonlight did I retrace my steps to the bank.

With the towel safely back on its nail in the caravan, I began to breathe normally. Even if they analysed the cotton strands, the police would find nothing out of the ordinary. I gave a little snort of satisfaction.

Look at me, I thought. *Here I am behaving like a criminal.* Surely the police would never suspect me of attacking the Gypsy. Or would they?

Wasn't I, after all, the last person to be seen in her company? Our departure from the fête in the Gypsy's caravan had been about as discreet as a circus parade. And then there had been the set-to in the Gully with Mrs. Bull, who I suspected would be only too happy to fabricate evidence against a member of the de Luce family.

What was it she had said? *'You're one of them de Luce girls from over at Buckshaw.'* I could still hear her raw voice: *'I'd rec'nise them cold blue eyes anywhere.'*

Harsh words, those. What grievance could she possibly have against us?

My thoughts were interrupted by a distant sound: the noise of a motorcar bumping its bottom on a stony road. This was followed by a mechanical grinding as it shifted down into a lower gear.

The police!

I leapt to the ground and made for the bridge. There was enough time – but just barely – to assume the pose of a faithful lookout. I scrambled up onto the stone parapet and arranged myself as carefully as if I were sitting for a statue of Wendy, from *Peter Pan:* seated primly, leaning slightly forward in eager relief, palms pressed flat to the stone for support, brow neatly furrowed with concern. I hoped I wouldn't look too smarmy.

Not a minute too soon. The car's headlamps were already flashing between the trees to my left, and seconds later, a blue Vauxhall was chuddering to a stop at the bridge.

Fixed in the spotlight of the powerful beams, I turned my head slowly to face them, at the same

85

time lifting my hand ever so languidly, as if to shield my eyes from their harsh and unrelenting glare.

I couldn't help wondering how it looked to the Inspector.

There was an unnerving pause, rather like the one that occurs between the time the houselights go down, but before the orchestra strikes up the first notes of the overture.

A car door slammed heavily, and Inspector Hewitt came walking slowly into the converging beams of light.

'Flavia de Luce,' he said in a flat, matter-of-fact voice: too flat to be able to tell if he was thrilled or disgusted to find me waiting for him at the scene of the crime.

'Good morning, Inspector,' I said. 'I'm very happy to see you.'

I was half hoping that he would return the compliment but he did not. In the recent past I had assisted him with several baffling investigations. By rights he should be bubbling over with gratitude – but was he?

The Inspector walked slowly to the highest point in the middle of the humpbacked bridge and stared off towards the glade where the caravan was parked.

'You've left your footprints in the dew,' he said.

I followed his gaze, and sure enough: lit by the low angle of the Vauxhall's headlamps, and although Dr. Darby's footprints and the tyre tracks left by his car had already lightened somewhat, the impressions of my every step lay black and fresh in the wet, silvery grass of the glade,

86

leading straight back to the caravan's door.

'I had to make water,' I said. It was the classic female excuse, and no male in recorded history had ever questioned it.

'I see,' the Inspector said, and left it at that.

Later, I would have a quick piddle behind the caravan for insurance purposes. No one would be any the wiser.

A silence had fallen, each of us waiting, I think, to see what the other would say. It was like a game: first one to speak is the Booby.

It was Inspector Hewitt.

'You've got goose-bumps,' he said, looking at me attentively. 'Best go sit in the car.'

He had already reached the far side of the bridge before he turned back. 'There's a blanket in the boot,' he said, and then vanished in the shadows.

I felt my temper rising. Here was this man – a man in an ordinary business suit, without so much as a badge on his shoulder – dismissing me from the scene of a crime that I had come to think of as my very own. After all, hadn't I been the first to discover it?

Had Marie Curie been dismissed after discovering polonium? Or radium? Had someone told *her* to run along?

It simply wasn't fair.

A crime scene, of course, wasn't exactly an atom-shattering discovery, but the Inspector might at least have said 'Thank you.' After all, hadn't the attack upon the Gypsy taken place within the grounds of Buckshaw, my ancestral home? Hadn't her life likely been saved by my

87

horseback expedition into the night to summon help?

Surely I was entitled to at least a nod. But no–

'Go and sit in the car,' Inspector Hewitt had said, and now – as I realised with a sinking feeling that the law doesn't know the meaning of the word 'gratitude' – I felt my fingers curling slowly into involuntary fists.

Even though he had been on the scene for no more than a few moments, I knew that a wall had already gone up between the Inspector and myself. If the man was expecting co-operation from Flavia de Luce, he would bloody well have to work for it.

SIX

The nerve of the man!

I resolved to tell him nothing.

In the glade, across the humpbacked bridge, I could see his shadow moving slowly across the curtained window of the caravan. I imagined him stepping carefully between the bloodstains on the floor.

To my surprise the light was extinguished, and moments later the Inspector came walking back across the bridge.

He seemed surprised to see me standing where he had left me. Without a word, he walked to the boot, took out a tartan blanket, and wrapped it round my shoulders.

I yanked the thing off and handed it back to him. To my surprise, I noticed that my hands were shaking.

'I'm not cold, thank you very much,' I said icily.

'Perhaps not,' he said, wrapping the blanket round me once again, 'but you're in shock.'

In shock? Fancy that! I've never been in shock before. This was entirely new and uncharted territory.

With a hand on my shoulder and another on my arm, Inspector Hewitt walked me to the car and held open the door. I dropped into the seat like a stone, and suddenly I was shaking like a leaf.

'We'd better get you home,' he said, climbing into the driver's seat and switching on the ignition. As a blast of hot air from the car's heater engulfed me, I wondered vaguely how it could have warmed up so quickly. Perhaps it was a special model, made solely for the police ... something intentionally designed to induce a stupor. Perhaps...

And I remember nothing more until we were grinding to a stop on the gravel sweep at Buckshaw's front entrance. I had no recollection whatever of having been driven back through the Gully, along the high street, past St. Tancred's, and so to Buckshaw. But here we were, so I must have been.

Dogger, surprisingly, was at the door – as if he had been waiting up all night. With his prematurely white hair illuminated from behind by the lights of the foyer, he seemed to me like a gaunt Saint Peter at the pearly gates, welcoming me home.

'I could have walked,' I said to the Inspector. 'It

was no more than a half mile.'

'Of course you could,' Inspector Hewitt said. 'But this trip is at His Majesty's expense.'

Was he teasing me? Twice in the recent past the Inspector had driven me home, and upon one of those occasions he had made it clear that when it came to petrol consumption the coffers of the King were not bottomless.

'Are you sure?' I asked, oddly fuddled.

'Straight out of his personal change purse.'

As if in a dream, I found myself plodding heavily up the steps to the front door. When I reached the top, Dogger fussed with the blanket round my shoulders.

'Off to bed with you, Miss Flavia. I'll be along with a hot drink directly.'

As I trudged exhausted up the curving staircase, I could hear quiet words being exchanged between Dogger and the Inspector, but could not make out a single one of them.

Upstairs, in the east wing, I walked into my bedroom and without even removing His Majesty's tartan blanket, fell facedown onto my bed.

I was gazing at a cup of cocoa on my night table.

As I focused on the thick brown skin that had formed upon its surface like ice on a muddy pond, something at the root of my tongue leapt like a little goat and my stomach turned over. There are not many things that I despise, but chiefest among them is skin on milk. I loathe it with a passion.

Not even the thought of the marvellous chemical change that forms the stuff – the milk's proteins churned and ripped apart by the heat of boiling, then reassembling themselves as they cool into a jellied skin – was enough to console me. I would rather eat a cobweb.

Of course by now the cocoa would be as cold as ditch water. For various complicated reasons reaching back into my family's past, Buckshaw's east wing was, as I have said, unheated, but I could hardly complain. I occupied this part of the house by choice, rather than by necessity. Dogger must have–

Dogger!

In an instant the whole of the previous day's events came storming into my consciousness like a wayward crash of thunder, and like those fierce sharp bolts of lightning that are said to strike upwards from the earth to the sky, so did these thoughts arrive in curiously reversed order: first, Inspector Hewitt and Dr. Darby, the Gully, and then the blood – the blood! – my sisters, Daffy and Feely, the Gypsy and Gry, her horse, and finally the church fête – all of these tumbling in upon one another in tattered but nevertheless sharply etched detail.

Had I been hit by lightning? Was that why I felt so curiously electrified: like a comb rubbed with tissue paper?

No, that wasn't it – but something in my mind was evading itself.

Oh, well, I thought, *I'll turn, over and go back to sleep.*

But I couldn't manage it. The morning sun streaming in at the windows was painful to look at, and my eyes were as gritty as if someone had pitched a bucket of sand into them.

Perhaps a bath would buck me up. I smiled at the thought. Daffy would be dumbstruck if she knew of my bathing without being threatened. 'Filthy Flavia,' she called me, at least when Father wasn't around.

Daffy herself loved nothing better than to subside into a steaming tub with a book, where she would stay until the water had gone cold.

'It's like reading in one's own coffin,' she would say afterwards, 'but without the stench.'

I did not share her enthusiasm.

A light tapping at the door interrupted these thoughts. I wrapped myself tightly in the tartan blanket and, like a penguin, waddled across the room.

It was Dogger, a fresh cup of steaming cocoa in his hand.

'Good morning, Miss Flavia,' he said. He did not ask how I was feeling, but nonetheless, I was aware of his keen scrutiny.

'Good morning,' I replied. 'Please put it on the table. Sorry about the one you brought last night. I was too tired to drink it.'

With a nod, Dogger swapped the cups.

'The Colonel wishes to see you in the drawing room,' he said. 'Inspector Hewitt is with him.'

Blast and double blast! I hadn't had time to think things through. How much was I going to tell the Inspector and how much was I going to keep to myself?

To say nothing of Father! What would he say when he heard that his youngest daughter had been out all night, wading around in the blood of a Gypsy he had once evicted from his estate?

Dogger must have sensed my uneasiness.

'I believe the Inspector is inquiring about your health, miss. I shall tell them you'll be down directly.'

Bathed and rigged up in a ribboned dress, I came slowly down the stairs. Feely turned from a mirror in the foyer in which she had been examining her face.

'Now you're for it,' she said.

'Fizz off,' I replied pleasantly.

'Half the Hinley Constabulary on your tail and still you have time to be saucy to your sister. I hope you won't expect a visit from me when you're in the clink.'

I swept past her with all the dignity I could muster, trying to gather my wits as I walked across the foyer. At the door of the drawing room, I paused to form a little prayer: 'May the Lord bless me and keep me and make His face to shine upon me; may He fill me with great grace and lightning-quick thinking.'

I opened the door.

Inspector Hewitt came to his feet. He had been sitting in the overstuffed armchair in which Daffy was usually lounging sideways with a book. Father stood in front of the mantelpiece, the dark side of his face reflected in the mirror.

'Ah, Flavia,' he said. 'The Inspector was just telling me that a woman's life has been saved by your prompt action. Well done.'

Well done?... Well done?

Was this my father speaking? Or was one of the Old Gods merely using him as a ventriloquist's dummy to deliver to me a personal commendation from Mount Olympus?

But no – Father was a most unlikely messenger. Not once in my eleven years could I recall him praising me, and now that he had done so, I hadn't the faintest idea how to respond.

The Inspector extracted me from a sticky situation.

'Well done, indeed,' he said. 'They tell me that in spite of the ferocity of the attack, she's come out of it with no more than a fractured skull. At her age, of course...'

Father interrupted. 'Dr. Darby rang up to express his commendations, Flavia, but Dogger told him you were sleeping. I took the message myself.'

Father on the telephone? I could hardly believe it! Father only allowed 'the instrument,' as he called it, to be kept in the house with the express understanding that it be used only in the direst of emergencies: the Apocalypse, for instance.

But Dr. Darby was one of Father's friends. In due course, I knew, the good doctor would be sternly lectured on his breach of household standing orders, but ultimately would live to tell the tale.

'Still,' Father said, his face clouding a little, 'you're going to have to explain what you were doing wandering round the Palings in the middle of the night.'

'That poor Gypsy woman,' I said, changing the subject. 'Her tent burned down at the fête. She had nowhere to go.'

As I talked, I watched Father's face for any sign

of balking. Hadn't he, after all, been the one who had driven Johnny Faa and his wife from the Buckshaw estate? Had he forgotten the incident? He was almost certainly not aware that his actions had caused the Gypsy's husband to fall dead in the road, and I wasn't about to tell him.

'I thought of the vicar's sermon, the one about Christian charity—'

'Yes, yes, Flavia,' Father said. 'Most commendable.'

'I told her she could camp in the Palings, but only for one night. I knew that you'd—'

'Thank you, Flavia, that's quite enough.'

'—approve.'

Poor Father: outflanked, outgunned, and outwitted. I almost felt sorry for him.

He crooked a forefinger and touched the angled joint to each side of his clipped moustache in turn: right and then left – a kind of suppressed, nervous preening that had probably been practised by military officers since time immemorial. I'd be willing to bet that if Julius Caesar had a moustache he knuckled it in precisely the same way.

'Inspector Hewitt would like a word with you. Because it concerns confidential information about individuals with whom I am not acquainted, I shall leave you alone.'

With a nod to the Inspector, Father left the room. I heard the door of his study open, and then close, as he sought refuge among his postage stamps.

'Now then,' the Inspector said, flipping open his notebook and unscrewing the cap of his Biro.

95

'From the beginning.'

'I couldn't sleep, you see,' I began.

'Not *that* beginning,' Inspector Hewitt said without looking up. 'Tell me about the church fête.'

'I'd gone into the Gypsy's tent to have my fortune told.'

'And did you?'

'No,' I lied.

The last thing on earth I wanted to share with the Inspector was the woman on the mountain – the woman who wanted to come home from the cold. Nor did I care to tell him about the woman that I was in the process of becoming.

'I knocked her candle over, and before I knew it, I ... I...'

Much to my surprise, my lower lip was trembling at the recollection.

'Yes, we've heard about that. The vicar was able to provide us with a very good account, as was Dr. Darby.'

I gulped, wondering if anyone had reported how I'd hidden behind a pitch as the Gypsy's tent burned to ashes.

'Poor girl,' he said tenderly. 'You've had quite a series of shocks, haven't you?'

I nodded.

'If I'd had any idea of what you'd already been through, I'd have taken you to the hospital directly.'

'It's all right,' I said gamely. 'I'll be all right.'

'Will you?' the Inspector asked.

'No,' I said, struggling with tears.

And suddenly it all came pouring out: from the fête to the Palings, not forgetting the seething

96

Mrs. Bull; from my frankly fabricated tale of awakening in the night to fret about the Gypsy woman's welfare to my discovery of her lying in a pool of her own blood in the caravan, I left out not a single detail.

Except Brookie Harewood, of course.

I was saving him for myself.

It was a magnificent performance, if I do say so. As I had been forced to learn at a very young age, there's no better way to mask a lie – or at least a glaring omission – than to wrap it in an emotional outpouring of truth.

During it all, Inspector Hewitt's Biro fairly flew over the pages, getting every scrap of it down for the record. *He must have studied one of the short-hand methods,* I thought idly as he scribbled. Later, he would expand these notes into a longer, neater, more legible form.

Perhaps he would dictate them to his wife, Antigone. I had met her not long before at a puppet show in the parish hall. Would she remember me?

In my mind I could see her seated at a typewriter at the kitchen table in their tastefully decorated cottage, her back ramrod straight in a position of perfect posture, her fingers hovering eagerly over the keys. She would be wearing hooped earrings, and a silk blouse of oyster gray.

'Flavia de Luce?' she would be saying, her large, dark eyes looking up at her husband. 'Why, isn't she that charming girl I met at St. Tancred's, dear?'

Inspector Hewitt's eyes would crinkle at the corners.

'One and the same, my love,' he would tell her, shaking his head at the memory of me. 'One and

97

the same.'

We had reached the end of my statement, the point at which the Inspector himself had arrived upon the scene in the Palings.

'That will do for now,' he said, flipping closed his notebook and shoving it into the inside pocket of his jacket. 'I've asked Sergeant Graves to come round later to take your fingerprints. Quite routine, of course.'

I wrinkled my brow, but secretly I couldn't have been more delighted. The dimpled detective sergeant with his winks and grins had come to be one of my favorites among the Hinley Constabulary.

'I expect they'll be all over everything,' I said helpfully. 'Mine and Dr. Darby's.'

'And those of the Gypsy woman's attacker,' he might have added, but he did not. Rather, he stood up and stuck his hand out to be shaken, as formally as if he were being received at a royal garden party.

'Thank you, Flavia,' he said. 'You've been of great assistance ... as always.'

As always? Was the Inspector twitting me?

But no – his handshake was firm and he looked me straight in the eye.

I'm afraid I smirked.

SEVEN

'Dogger!' I said. 'They're coming to take my fingerprints!'

Dogger looked up from the vast array of silverware he was polishing on the kitchen table. For just a moment his face was a complete blank, and then he said, 'I trust they will be returned to you in good order.'

I blinked. Was Dogger making a joke? I hoped desperately that he was.

Dogger had suffered the most awful privations in the Far East during the war. His mind now seemed sometimes to consist of no more than a crazy tangle of broken suspension bridges joining the past with the present. If he had ever made a joke before, I had never heard of it. This, then, could be a momentous occasion.

'Oh! Ha ha ha.' I laughed too loudly. 'That's very good, Dogger. Returned to me in good order... I must remember to tell that one to Mrs. Mullet.'

I had no intention whatever of sharing this precious moment with our cook, but sometimes flattery does not know when to stop.

Dogger formed a faint smile as he returned a fish fork to the cutlery chest and selected another. The de Luce silverware was kept in a dark folding cabinet which, when opened, presented a remarkable array of fish forks, toddy ladles, mote spoons, marrow scoops, lobster picks, sugar nips, grape shears, and pudding trowels, all arranged in steps, like so many silvery salmon leaping up the stony staircase of a whisky-colored stream somewhere in Scotland.

Dogger had lugged this heavy box to the kitchen table for the ritual cleaning of the cutlery, a seemingly endless task that occupied a great deal of his time, and one that I never tired of watching.

Mrs. Mullet loved to tell about how, as a child, I had been found on top of the table playing with the dolls I had contrived by clothing a family of sterling silver forks in folded napkins. Their identical faces – long noses and round cheeks – were just barely suggested by the engraved *D L* on the top of each handle, and required a great leap of the imagination to make them out at all.

'The Mumpeters,' I had called them: Mother Mumpeter, Father Mumpeter, and the three little Mumpeter girls, all of whom – even though they were burdened with three or four legs each – I had made to walk and dance and sing gaily upon the tabletop.

I could still remember Grindlestick, the three-legged waif I had fashioned from a pickle fork (which Father referred to as a trifid), who performed the most amazing acrobatics until I jammed one of her legs in a crack and broke it off.

'Better than the 'ippodrome, it were,' Mrs. M would tell me as she wiped away a tear of laughter. 'Poor little tyke.'

I still don't know if she meant Grindlestick or me.

Now, as I watched him at his work, I wondered if Dogger had known about the Mumpeters. It was likely that he did, since Mrs. Mullet, when it came to gossip, was equalled only by the *News of the World*.

I knew that there would never be a better time to dig for information: Mrs. M was away from her usual post in the kitchen and Dogger seemed to be at a peak of alertness. I took a deep breath and plunged directly in: 'I found Brookie Harewood in the drawing room last night,' I said. 'Actually, it was past two in the morning.'

Dogger finished polishing a grapefruit knife, then put it down and aligned it perfectly with its mates on a strip of green baize.

'What was he doing?' he asked.

'Nothing. Just standing by the fireplace. No, wait! He was crouched down, touching one of the firedogs.'

These fire irons had belonged to Harriet, and although they had different faces, each was that of a wily fox. Harriet had used them as the main characters in the bedtime stories she'd invented for Daffy and Feely: a fact of which they never tired of reminding me.

To be perfectly truthful, I bitterly resented the fact that my mother had spun so many tales of the make-believe world for my sisters but not for me. She had died before I was old enough to receive my due.

'Which of the two irons was he touching?' Dogger asked, already halfway to his feet.

'The Sally Fox,' I said. 'The one on the right.'

Sally Fox and Shoppo were the names Harriet had given to the cunning pair, who had gone jauntily adventuring through an imaginary world

– a world that had been lost with Harriet's death. From time to time, Feely and Daffy, trying to resuscitate the warm and happy feeling of bygone days, had made up their own tales about the two crafty foxes, but in recent years they had, for some reason, stopped trying. Perhaps they had grown too old for fairy tales.

I followed as Dogger walked from the kitchen through to the foyer and made for the drawing room in the west wing.

He paused for a moment, listening at the door, then seemed to vanish through its panels like a wisp of smoke, as so many of the older servants are able to do.

He went straight to the Sally Fox, regarding her as solemnly as if he were a priest come to administer the last rites. When he had finished, he moved a few feet to his left and repeated the same performance with Shoppo.

'Most odd,' he said.

'Odd?'

'*Most* odd. This one,' he said, pointing to the Sally Fox, 'has been missing for several weeks.'

'Missing?'

'It was not here yesterday. I did not inform the Colonel because I knew he would worry. At first I thought I might have misplaced it myself during one of my – my...'

'Reveries,' I suggested.

Dogger nodded. 'Thank you,' he said.

Dogger suffered occasional terrors during which his very being was snatched away for a while by unseen forces and hurled into some horrid abyss. At such times his soul seemed to be replaying old atrocities, as he was once more thrown into the company of his dear old comrades-in-arms, their restless spirits dragged back from death by his love for them.

'A month ago it was Shoppo: here one day, gone the next. And then he reappeared. I thought I must be imagining things.'

'Are you sure, Dogger?'

'Yes, Miss Flavia – quite sure.'

I thought for a moment of telling him I had taken the firedogs, but I couldn't bring myself to mouth the lie. There was something in Dogger that demanded truth.

'Perhaps Daffy borrowed them for one of her drawing sessions.'

Daffy's occasional pencil sketches usually began well enough but then, quite often, took a spectacularly wrong turn. The Virgin Mary would suddenly sprout buck teeth, for instance, or an impromptu cartoon of Father seated at the dinner table would turn into a man with no eyes. Whenever this happened, Daffy would set the drawing aside and go back to her reading. For weeks afterwards we would keep finding, stuffed into the crevices of the chesterfield and under the cushions of the drawing-room chairs, the pages she had ripped from her sketchbook.

'Perhaps,' Dogger said. 'Perhaps not.'

I think it was at that moment, without realising it, that I began to see the solution to the puzzle of the fire irons.

'Is Mrs. Mullet here today?'

I knew perfectly well that she was but I hadn't seen her in the kitchen.

'She's outside having a word with Simpkins, the milk-float man. Something about a wood chip in the butter.'

I'd have to wait until Dogger put away the cutlery before I tackled Mrs. M.

I wanted to be alone with her.

'Them tradesmen don't give a flick,' Mrs. Mullet said disgustedly, her arms white to the elbows with flour. 'Really, they don't. One day it's a fly in the clotted cream, and the next it's a – well, you really don't want to know, dear. But one thing's as clear as dishwater. If you lets 'em get away with it, there's never any tellin' what they'll bring round next time. Keep quiet about a toothpick in today's butter and next thing you know you'll be findin' a doorknob in the cottage cheese. I don't like it, dear, but it's the way of the world.'

How on earth, I wondered, could I bring the conversation around from tradesmen to Brookie Harewood without seeming to do so?

'Perhaps we should eat more fish,' I suggested. 'Some of the fishermen in the village sell it fresh from their creels. Brookie Harewood, for instance.'

Mrs. Mullet looked at me sharply. 'Hmph! Brookie Harewood! He's no more than a poacher. I'm surprised the Colonel hasn't run him off the Palings. Them are *your* fish he's sellin' at the cottage gates.'

'I suppose he has to earn a living.'

'Livin'?' She bristled, giving the great mound of bread dough an extra pummel. 'He don't need to make a livin' no more than Grace's goose. Not with that mother of his over in Maiden Fenwick

104

sendin' him reg'lar checks to stay away. He's a layabout, plain and simple, that one is, and a rascal to boot.'

'A remittance man?' I asked.

Daffy had once told me about the black-sheep son of our neighbours, the Blatchfords, who was paid to keep well away in Canada. 'Two pounds ten shillings per mile per year,' she said. 'He lives in the Queen Charlotte Islands to maximise his pension.'

'Mittens man or not, he's no good, and that's a fact,' said Mrs. Mullet. 'He's managed to get in with a bad lot.'

'Colin Prout?' I suggested, thinking of the way Brookie had bullied the boy at the fête.

'Colin Prout's no more than Brookie Harewood's spare fingers, or so I've 'eard. No, I was talkin' about Reggie Pettibone an' that lot what 'as the shop in the 'igh street.'

'The antiques place?'

Pettibone's Antiques & Quality Goods was just a few doors west of the Thirteen Drakes. Although I had passed it often, I had never been inside.

Mrs. Mullet sniffed.

'Antiques, my sitter!' she exclaimed. 'Sorry, dear, but that's 'ow I feels about it. That Reggie Pettibone give us two pounds six and three last year for a table me and Alf bought new at the Army and Navy when first we was married. Three weeks later we spots it in 'is window with silver knobs and fifty-five guineas on it! And a sign what says "Georgian Whist Table by Chippendale." We knew it was ours because Alf reckernised the burn mark on the leg where 'e raked it with an 'ot

105

poker whilst 'e was tryin' to fish out a coal what 'ad popped out of the grate and rolled under it when our Agnes was just a mite.'

'And Brookie's in with Pettibone?'

'I should say he is. Thick as thieves. Tight as the jaws off a nutcracker, them two.'

'What does his mother think of that, I wonder?'

'Pfaw!' Mrs. Mullet said. 'A fat lot she cares about 'im. 'Er with 'er paints and brushes! She does the 'orses and 'ounds crowd, you know – that lot o' swells. Charges 'em a pretty penny, too, I'll wager. Brookie and 'is under'anded ways 'as brought 'er nothin' but shame. To my mind, she don't rightly care what 'e gets 'isself up to so long as 'e keeps clear of Malden Fenwick.'

'Thank you, Mrs. M,' I said. 'I enjoy talking to you. You always have such interesting stories to tell.'

'Mind you, I've said nothing,' she said in an undertone, raising a finger. 'My lips are sealed.'

And in rather an odd way, there was truth in what she said. Since I first came into the room I had been waiting for her to ask me about the Gypsy, or why the police had turned up at Buckshaw, but she had done neither. Was it possible she didn't know about either of these events?

It seemed unlikely. Mrs. M's recent chin-wag at the kitchen door with the milk-float man was likely to have resulted in more swapping of intelligence than a chin-wag between Lord Haw-Haw and Mata Hari.

I was already across the kitchen with my hand on the door when she said it: 'Don't go wandering too far off, dear. That nice officer – the one

106

with the dimples – will be round soon to 'ave your fingerprints.'

Curse the woman! Was she eavesdropping from behind every closed door at Buckshaw? Or was she truly clairvoyant?

'Oh, yes,' I replied lamely. 'Thanks for reminding me, Mrs. M. I'd almost forgotten about him.'

The doorbell rang as I came through the passage beneath the stairs. I put on a sprint but Feely beat me to it.

I skidded to a stop on the foyer's chequerboard tiles just as she swung open the front door to reveal Detective Sergeant Graves standing on the doorstep, small black box in hand and his jaw already halfway to the ground.

I have to admit that Feely had never looked more beautiful: from her salmon-coloured silk blouse to her sage green mohair sweater (both of which, as I knew from my own snooping expeditions, she had pinched from Harriet's dressing room), from her perfect honey-colored hair to her sparkling blue eyes (having, of course, left her black-rimmed spectacles, as she always did, stuffed behind the pillows on the chesterfield), she was a close-up from a Technicolor cinema film.

She had planned this, the hag!

'Sergeant Graves, I presume?' she said in a low, husky voice – one I had never heard her use before. 'Come in. We've been expecting you.'

We? What in the old malarkey was she playing at?

'I'm Flavia's sister, Ophelia,' she was saying, extending a coral-encrusted wrist and a long white

107

hand that made the Lady of Shalott's fingers look like meathooks.

I could have killed her!

What right did Feely have to insert herself, without so much as a by-your-leave, between me and the man who had come to Buckshaw expressly to take my fingerprints? It was unforgiveable!

Still, I mustn't forget that I'd had more than one daydream in which the chipper little sergeant married my older sister and lived in a flower-choked cottage where I would be able to drop in for afternoon tea and happy professional chats about criminal poisoners.

Sergeant Graves had finally recovered enough of his wits to say 'Yes,' and bumble his way into the foyer.

'Would you like a cup of tea and a biscuit, Sergeant?' Feely asked, managing to suggest in her tone that the poor dear was overworked, dog-tired, and malnourished.

'I *am* quite thirsty, come to think of it,' he managed with a bashful grin. 'And hungry,' he added.

Feely stepped back and ushered him towards the drawing room.

I followed like a neglected hound.

'You may set up your gear here,' Feely told him, indicating a Regency table that stood near a window. 'How dreadfully trying the life of a police officer must be. All firearms and criminals and hobnail boots.'

Sergeant Graves had the good grace not to slug her. In fact, he seemed to be enjoying himself.

'It *is* a hard life, Miss Ophelia,' he said, 'at least most of the time.'

His dimpled grin suggested that this was one of the easier moments.

'I'll ring for Mrs. Mullet,' Feely said, reaching for a velvet pull that hung near the mantelpiece, and which probably hadn't been used since George the Third was foaming at the mouth. Mrs. M would have kidney failure when the bell in the kitchen went off right above her head.

'What about the dabs?' I asked. It was a term I had picked up from Philip Odell, the private eye on the wireless. 'Inspector Hewitt will be dead keen on having a squint at them.'

Feely laughed a laugh like a tinkling silver bell. 'You must forgive my little sister, Sergeant,' she said. 'I'm afraid she's been left alone too much.'

Left alone? I almost laughed out loud! What would the sergeant say if I told him about the Inquisition in the Buckshaw cellars? About how Feely and Daffy had trussed me up in a smelly potato sack and flung me onto the stony floor?

'Dabs it is, then,' said the sergeant, opening the clasps and flinging open his kit. 'I suppose you'll be wanting to have a dekko at the chemicals and so forth,' he added, giving me a wink.

If I'd had my way, he'd have been sanctified on the spot: *Saint Detective Sergeant Graves*. Come to think of it, I didn't even know his given name, but now was not the time to ask.

'This,' he said, extracting the first of two small glass bottles, 'is fingerprint powder.'

'Mercury-based, I assume? Fine enough to give good definition to the loops and whorls, and so on?'

This, too, I had learned from Philip Odell. It

109

had stuck in my mind because of its chemical connection.

The sergeant grinned and pulled out the second bottle, this one darker than the first.

'Go on,' he said. 'See if you can guess this one.'

Guess? I thought. *The poor deluded man!*

'Graphite-based,' I said. 'More coarse than the mercury, but shows up better on certain surfaces.'

'Top marks!' the sergeant said.

I turned away as if to wipe a bit of grit from my eye and stuck out my tongue at Feely.

'But surely these are for dusting?' I protested. '... and not needed for recording prints?'

'Right enough,' the sergeant said. 'I just thought you'd be interested in seeing the tools of the trade.'

'Oh, I am indeed,' I said quickly. 'Thank you for the thought.'

I did not suppose it would be polite to mention that I had upstairs in my chemical laboratory enough mercury and graphite to supply the needs of the Hinley Constabulary until well into the next century. Great-uncle Tar had been, among many other things, a hoarder.

'Mercury,' I said, touching the bottle. 'Fancy that!'

Sergeant Graves was now removing from its protective padding a rectangular sheet of plain glass, followed in quick succession by a bottle of ink and a roller.

Deftly he applied five or six drops of the ink to the surface of the glass, then rolled it smooth until the plate was uniformly covered with the black ooze.

'Now then,' he said, taking my right wrist, and spreading my fingers until they were just hovering above the glass, 'relax – let me do the work.'

With no more than a slight pressure, he pushed my fingertips down and into the ink, one at a time, rolling each one from left to right on the ball of my fingertip. Then, moving my hand to a white card, which was marked with ten squares – one for each finger – he made the prints.

'Oh, Sergeant Graves!' Feely said. 'You must take mine, too!'

'Oh, Sergeant Graves! You must take mine, too!'

I could have swatted her.

'Happy to, Miss Ophelia,' he said, taking up her hand and dropping mine.

'Better ink the glass again,' I said, 'otherwise you might make a bad impression.'

The sergeant's ears went a bit pink, but he soldiered on. In no time at all he had recoated the glass with a fresh film, and was taking up Feely's hand as if it were some venerable object.

'Did you know that, in the Holy Land, they have the fingerprints of the angel Gabriel?' I asked, trying desperately to regain his attention. 'At least they used to. Dr. Robert Richardson and the Earl of Belmore saw them at Nazareth. Remember, Feely?'

For nearly a week – before our recent set-to – Daffy had been reading aloud to us at the breakfast table from an odd volume of the doctor's *Travels along the Mediterranean and Parts Adjacent,* and some of its many wonders were still fresh in my mind.

'They also showed him the Virgin Mary's

Kitchen, at the Chapel of the Incarnation. They still have the cinders, the fire irons, the cutlery–'

Something in the back room of my brain was thinking about our own fire irons: the Sally Fox and Shoppo firedogs that had once belonged to Harriet.

'That will be quite enough, thank you, Flavia,' Feely said. 'You may fetch me a rag to wipe my fingers on.'

'Fetch it yourself,' I flung at her, and stalked from the room.

Compared with my life, Cinderella was a spoiled brat.

EIGHT

Alone at last!

Whenever I'm with other people, part of me shrinks a little. Only when I am alone can I fully enjoy my own company.

In the kitchen garden, I grabbed my faithful old BSA Keep-Fit from the greenhouse. The bicycle had once belonged to Harriet, who had called her *l'Hirondelle,* 'the Swallow': a word that reminded me so much of being force-fed cod-liver oil with a gag-inducing spoon that I had renamed her 'Gladys.' Who, for goodness' sake, wants to ride a bicycle with a name that sounds like a sickroom nurse?

And Gladys was much more down-to-earth than *l'Hirondelle:* an adventurous female with Dunlop

112

tyres, three speeds, and a forgiving disposition. She never complained and she never tired, and neither, when I was in her company, did I.

I pedalled southeast from Buckshaw, wobbling slowly along the edge of the ornamental lake. To my left was a somewhat flat expanse called the Visto which had been cleared by Sir George de Luce in the mid-nineteenth century to serve as what he described in his diary as a 'coign of vantage': a grassy green plain across which one was supposed to contemplate the blue enfolding hills.

In recent times, however, the Visto had been allowed to become little more than an overgrown cow pasture: a place where nettles ran riot and the contemplator's clothing was at risk of being ripped to tatters. It was here that Harriet had kept *Blithe Spirit,* her de Havilland Gypsy Moth, which she had flown regularly up to London to meet her friends.

All that remained now of those happy days were the three iron rings, still rusting somewhere among the weeds, to which *Blithe Spirit* had long ago been tethered.

Once, when I had asked Father how Buckshaw looked from the air, he had gone all tight around the temples.

'Ask your aunt Felicity,' he'd said gruffly. 'She's flown.'

I'd made a mental note to do so.

From the Visto an overgrown path ran south, crossing here and there long-abandoned lawns and hedges, which gave way eventually to copses and scrub. I followed the narrow track, and soon arrived at the Palings.

The Gypsy's caravan was as I had left it, although the ground bore signs of many 'hobnail boots,' as Feely had called them.

Why was I drawn back here? I wondered. Was it because the Gypsy had been under my protection? I had, after all, offered her sanctuary in the Palings and she had accepted. If amends were to be made, I would make them on my own – not because I was made to do so by a sense of shame.

Gry was grazing contentedly near the elders at the far side of the grove. Someone had brought him back to the Palings. They had even thought to bring a bale of fresh hay to the clearing, and he was making short work of it. He looked up at me without curiosity and then went back to his food.

'Who's a good boy, then?' I asked him, realising, even as I said it, that these were words to be used in addressing a parrot.

'Good Gry,' I said. 'Splendid horse.'

Gry paid not the slightest attention.

Something fastened to one of the tree trunks near the bridge caught my eye: a white wooden panel about six feet from the ground. I walked round the other side for a closer look.

Police Investigation – No Admittance by Order – Hinley Constabulary

The signboard was facing east – away from Buckshaw. Obviously it was meant to deter those hordes of the idly curious who flock to places where blood has been shed like crows to a winter oak.

I was, after all, on my own property. I could hardly be trespassing. Besides, I could always claim that I hadn't seen the thing.

I put a foot carefully onto one of the caravan's shafts and, waving my arms for balance like an aerialist, made my way slowly, heel to toe, up the slope to the driving board. To my surprise, the door had been replaced.

I paused to prepare myself – took a deep breath – then opened the door and stepped inside.

The blood had been cleaned up – I saw that at once. The floor was newly scrubbed and the sharp clean smell of Sunlight soap still hung in the air.

It wasn't dark inside the caravan, but neither was it light. I took a step towards the rear and froze in my tracks.

Someone was lying on the bed!

Suddenly my heart was pounding in a frenzy, and my eyes felt as if they were about to pop out of their sockets. I hardly dared breathe.

In the gloom of the drawn curtains I could see that it was a woman – no, not a woman – a girl. A few years older than me, perhaps. Her hair was raven black, her complexion tawny, and she was wrapped in a shapeless garment of black crepe.

As I stood motionless, staring at her face, her dark eyes opened slowly – and met mine.

With a quick, powerful spring she leapt from the bed, snatching something from a shelf, and I suddenly found myself wedged sharply against the wall, my arm twisted behind my back and a knife at my throat.

'Let go! You're hurting me!' I managed to squeeze the words out through the pain.

'Who are you? What are you doing here?' she hissed. 'Tell me before I slit your gullet.'

115

I could feel the knife's blade against my wind-pipe.

'Flavia de Luce,' I gasped.

Damn it all! I was beginning to cry.

I caught a glimpse of myself in the mirror: her arm beneath my chin ... my bulging eyes ... the knife – the knife!

'That's a butter knife,' I croaked in desperation.

It was one of those moments that might later seem amusing, but it wasn't now. I was trembling with fear and anger.

I felt my head jerk as she pulled back to look at the blade, and then I was being pushed away.

'Get out of here,' she said roughly. 'Get away – now before I take the razor to you.'

I didn't need a second invitation. The girl was obviously mad.

I stumbled towards the door and jumped to the ground. I grabbed Gladys and was halfway to the trees when–

'Wait!'

Her voice echoed in the glade.

'Did you say your name was Flavia? Flavia de Luce?'

I did not reply, but stopped at the edge of the grove, making sure that I kept Gry between us as a makeshift barrier.

'Please,' she said. 'Wait. I'm sorry. I didn't know who you were. They told me you saved Fenella's life.'

'Fenella?' I managed, my voice shaking, still hollowed out by fear.

'Fenella Faa. You brought the doctor to her ... here ... last night.'

116

I must have looked a perfect fool as I stood there with my mouth open like a goldfish. My brain needed time to catch up as the girl flip-flopped suddenly from holding a blade at my throat to being sorry. I was not accustomed to apologies, and this one – probably the first I had ever received in my life – caught me off guard.

'Who are you?' I asked.

'Porcelain,' she said, jumping down from the caravan. 'Porcelain Lee – Fenella's my gram.'

She was coming towards me through the grass, her arms extended in biblical forgiveness.

'Let me hug you,' she said. 'I need to thank you.'

I'm afraid I shrank back a little.

'Don't worry, I won't bite,' she said, and suddenly she was upon me, her arms enfolding me in a tight embrace, her chin resting sharply on my shoulder.

'Thank you, Flavia de Luce,' she whispered in my ear, as if we had been friends forever. 'Thank you.'

Since I was still half expecting a dagger to be plunged between my shoulder blades, I'm afraid I did not return her hug, which I received in stiff silence, rather like one of the sentries at Buckingham Palace pretending he doesn't notice the liberties being taken by an excessively affectionate tourist.

'You're welcome,' I managed. 'How is she? Fenella, I mean.'

Using the Gypsy's first name did not come easily to me. In spite of the fact that Daffy and I have always referred to our own mother as

Harriet (only Feely, who is older, seems to have the right to call her Mummy), it still felt excessively saucy to call a stranger's grandmother by her given name.

'She'll be all right, they think. Too early to tell. But if it hadn't been for you–'

Tears were beginning to well up in her dark eyes.

'It was nothing,' I said uncomfortably. 'She needed help. I was there.'

Was it really that simple? Or did something deeper lie beneath?

'How did you hear – about this?' I asked, waving at the glade.

'The coppers tracked me down in London. Found my name and all that on a scrap of paper in her handbag. I begged a ride off a bloke with a lorry in Covent Garden, and he brought me as far as Doddingsley. I walked the rest of the way. Got here no more than an hour ago.'

Four gold stars to Inspector Hewitt and his men, I thought. Searching the caravan for Fenella Faa's handbag had never crossed my mind.

'Where are you staying? At the Thirteen Drakes?'

'Blimey!' she said in a feigned Cockney accent. 'That's a larf, that is!'

I must have looked offended.

'I couldn't rub two shillings together if my life depended on it,' she said, waving her hands expansively at the grove. 'So I expect right here is where I'll stay.'

'Here? In the caravan?'

I looked at her aghast.

'Why not? It's Fenella's, isn't it? That means it's

118

as good as mine. All I have to do is find out who's the nob that owns this bit of green, and–'

'It's called the Palings,' I said, 'and it belongs to my father.'

Actually it didn't: it belonged to Harriet, but I didn't feel that I needed to explain our family's legal difficulties to a semi-ragamuffin stranger who had just threatened my life.

'Coo!' she said. 'I'm sorry. I never thought.'

'But you can't stay here,' I went on. 'It's a crime scene. Didn't you see the sign?'

''Course I did. Didn't you?'

I chose to ignore this childish response. 'Whoever attacked your gram might still be hanging about. Until the police find out who and why, it isn't safe to be here after dark.'

This was a part, but not all, of the truth.

Every bit as important as Porcelain's physical safety was the sudden gnawing need I felt to make amends to the family of Fenella Faa: to correct an old wrong committed by my father. For the first time in my life I found myself seized by hereditary guilt.

'So you'll have to stay at Buckshaw,' I blurted.

There! I'd done it. I'd made the leap. But even as I spoke, I knew that I would soon regret my words.

Father, for instance, would be furious.

Even when his beloved Harriet had invited the Gypsies to stay at Buckshaw, Father had driven them off. If she had failed, I didn't stand a chance.

Perhaps that was why I did it.

'My father's quite eccentric,' I said. 'At least, he has some odd ideas. He won't allow guests at

119

Buckshaw, other than his own sister. I'll have to sneak you in.'

Porcelain seemed quite alarmed at the thought. 'I don't want to make trouble.'

'Nonsense,' I said, sounding like Aunt Felicity, the Human Steamroller. 'It will be no trouble at all. Nobody ever comes into the east wing. They won't even know you're there.

'Bring your things,' I ordered.

Until that moment I hadn't noticed how haggard Porcelain was looking. With her black crepe dress and the black circles under her eyes, she looked like someone made up for a masquerade party: 'The Grim Reaper as a Young Woman.'

'I've nothing,' she said. 'Just what you see.' She tugged apologetically at her heavy hem. 'This is Fenella's,' she said. 'I had to wash out my own things in the river this morning, and they aren't dry.'

Wash out her things? Why would she need to do that? Since it didn't seem to be any of my business, I didn't ask – perhaps I could find an excuse to bring it up later.

'Off we go, then,' I said, trying to sound cheerful. 'Buckshaw awaits.'

I picked up Gladys and wheeled her along beside me. Porcelain trudged a few steps behind, her eyes downcast.

'It isn't awfully far,' I said, after a while. 'I expect you'll be happy to get some sleep.'

I turned and saw her nodding in response, but she did not speak. She shuffled along behind me, drained, and not even the ornamental dolphins of the Poseidon fountain made her take her eyes

120

from the ground.

'These were made in the eighteenth century,' I told her, 'so they're rather elderly. They used to spout water from their mouths.'

Again a nod.

We were taking a shortcut across the Trafalgar Lawn, an abandoned series of terraces that lay to the southeast of the house. Sir George de Luce, who planned it as a tribute to Admiral Nelson and his victory over the Spanish, which had taken place some forty years earlier, had laid it out at about the same time as the Visto.

By the simple expedient of tapping into Lucius 'Leaking' de Luce's earlier and extensive subterranean waterworks, Sir George had planned to activate his glorious fountained landscape as a surprise for his bride.

And so he had begun on a work of landscape architecture that would rival or even surpass the spectacle of the ornamental lake, but speculation during the Railway Mania had scotched his fortunes. With most of his capital gone, what had been planned as a noble avenue of fountains, with Buckshaw as its focal point, had been abandoned to the elements.

Now, after a century of rain and snow, sun and wind, and the nocturnal visits of the villagers who came at night to steal stone for their garden walls, the Trafalgar Lawn and its statues were like a sculptor's scrapyard, with various bits of stone cherubs, mossy Tritons, and sea nymphs jutting up out of the ground here and there like stone swimmers from a shipwreck waiting to be rescued from a sea of earth.

Only Poseidon had survived, lounging with his net atop a crumbling base, brooding in marble over his broken family, his three-pronged trident like a lightning rod, sticking up towards whatever might be left of the ancient Greek heavens.

'Here's old Poseidon,' I said, turning to haul Gladys up yet another set of crumbled steps. 'His photograph was in *Country Life* a couple of years ago. Rather splendid, isn't he?'

Porcelain had come suddenly to a dead stop, her hand covering her mouth, her hollowed-out eyes staring upwards, as wide and as dark as the pit. Then she let out a cry like a small animal.

I followed her gaze, and saw at once the thing that had frozen her in her tracks.

Dangling from Poseidon's trident, like a scarecrow hung on a coat hook, was a dark figure.

'It's Brookie Harewood,' I said, even before I saw his face.

NINE

One of the Trident's tines had pierced Brookie's long moleskin coat at the neck, and he swung slightly in the breeze, looking rather casual in his flat cap and scarlet scarf, as if he were enjoying one of the roundabouts at an amusement pier.

For a moment, I thought he might have fallen. Perhaps in an excess of alcoholic high spirits he'd been attempting to scale the statue. Perhaps he had slipped from Poseidon's head and fallen onto the trident.

That idea was short-lived, however. I saw almost at once that his hands were tied behind his back. But that wasn't the worst of it.

As I came round full front-on, the sun glinted brightly on something that seemed to be projecting from Brookie's mouth.

'Stay here,' I told Porcelain, even though I could see that there wasn't a chance of her moving.

I leaned Gladys against the lower of the three seashell bowls that comprised the fountain, then climbed up her tubular frame until finally I was standing on her seat, from which point I could get a knee up onto the rough stone rim.

The bowl of the thing was filled with a disgusting broth of black water, dead leaves, and mould, the result of a century of neglect, and it smelled to high heaven.

By standing on the rim, I was able to clamber up onto the fountain's middle bowl, and finally the highest one. I was now level with Brookie's knees, staring up into his unseeing eyes. His face was a horrid fish-belly white.

He was quite dead, of course.

After the initial shock of realising that someone I had spoken to just hours before was no longer in the land of the living, I began to feel oddly excited.

I have no fear of the dead. Indeed, in my own limited experience I have found them to produce in me a feeling that is quite the opposite of fear. A dead body is much more fascinating than a live one, and I have learned that most corpses tell better stories. I'd had the good fortune of seeing several of them in my time; in fact, Brookie was my third.

As I teetered on the edge of the sculptured stone seashell, I could see clearly what it was that had glinted in the sun. Projecting from one of Brookie's nostrils – not his mouth – was an object that first appeared to be a round silver medallion: a flat, perforated disk with a handle attached. On the end of it was suspended a single drop of Brookie's blood.

The image punched out of the disk was that of a lobster, and engraved on the handle was the de Luce monogram.

DL.

It was a silver lobster pick – one of the set that belonged to Buckshaw.

The last time I'd seen one of these sharp-pointed utensils, Dogger had been rubbing it with silver polish at the kitchen table.

The business end of the thing, I recalled, ended in two little tines that stuck out like the horns on a snail's head. These prongs, which had been designed to pry the pink meat from the cracks and crevices of a boiled lobster, were now lodged firmly somewhere deep in Brookie Harewood's brain.

Death by family silver, I thought, before I could turn off that part of my mind.

A little moan from below reminded me that Porcelain was still there.

Her face was nearly as white as Brookie's, and I saw that she was trembling.

'For God's sake, Flavia,' she said in a quavering voice, 'come down – let's get out of here. I think

124

I'm going to throw up.'

'It's Brookie Harewood,' I said, and I think I offered up a silent prayer for the repose of the poacher's soul.

Protect him, O Lord, and let heaven be bountifully supplied with trout streams.

The thought of trout reminded me of Colin Prout. I'd almost forgotten the boy. Would Colin breathe a sigh of relief when he heard that his tormentor was dead? Or would he grieve?

Brookie's mother would be in the same quandary. And so I realised, would almost everyone in Bishop's Lacey.

I put one foot on Poseidon's knee and hauled myself up by his muscular elbow. I was now slightly above Brookie and looking down at something that had caught my eye. In the notch between two of the trident's prongs was a shiny spot the size of a sixpence, as if someone had given the bronze a bit of a polish with a rag.

I memorised the shape of the thing, then began to climb down slowly, taking great care not to touch Brookie's body.

'Come on,' I said to Porcelain, giving her arm a shake. 'Let's get out of here before they think one of us did it.'

I did not tell her that the back of Brookie's skull was a bloody mess.

We paused for a moment behind one of the rose hedges which, at this time of year, were in their second bloom. From the direction of the kitchen garden came the sound of Dogger scraping old soil from flowerpots with a trowel. Mrs. Mullet, I knew, had probably gone for the day.

'Stay here,' I whispered, 'while I scout things out.'

Porcelain seemed barely to have heard me. White with fright and fatigue, she stood stock-still among the roses like one of Buckshaw's statues, over which someone, as a joke, had flung an old black dress.

I flitted, invisibly I hoped, across the grass and the gravelled drive to the kitchen door. Flattening myself against it, I pressed my ear to the heavy wood.

As I've said, I had inherited from Harriet an almost freakish sense of hearing. Any clatter of pots and pans or the hum of conversation would be instantly audible. Mrs. Mullet talked constantly to herself as she worked, and even though I guessed she had gone for the day, one could never be too careful. If Feely and Daffy were planning another ambush, surely their giggles and their tittering would give them away.

But I could hear nothing.

I opened the door and stepped into an empty kitchen.

My first priority was to get Porcelain into the house and stick her safely away in a place where her presence would be unsuspected. That done, I would call the police.

The telephone at Buckshaw was kept out of sight in a small cupboard in the narrow passageway that connected the foyer with the kitchen. As I have said, Father loathed 'the instrument,' and all of us at Buckshaw were forbidden to use the thing.

As I tiptoed along the passage, I heard the

unmistakable sound of shoe leather on tiles. It was Father, most likely. Daffy and Feely's shoes were more feminine, and made a softer, more shuffling sound.

I ducked into the telephone cubicle and quietly pulled the door shut. I would sit on the little Oriental bench in the darkness and wait it out.

In the foyer, the footsteps slowed – and stopped. I held my breath.

After what seemed like two and a half eternities, they moved away, towards the west wing and Father's study, I thought.

At that instant – right at my elbow! – the telephone rang ... then rang again.

A few moments later, the footsteps returned, advancing towards the foyer. I picked up the receiver and pressed it tightly against my chest. If the ringing stopped suddenly, Father would think that the caller had rung off.

'Hello? Hello?' I could hear a tinny voice saying to my breastbone. 'Are you there?'

Outside, in the foyer, the footsteps stopped – and then retreated.

'Are you there? Hello? Hello?' the muffled voice was now shouting, rather irately.

I put the receiver to my ear and whispered into the mouthpiece. 'Hello? Flavia de Luce speaking.'

'Constable Linnet here, at Bishop's Lacey. Inspector Hewitt has been attempting to get in touch with you.'

'Oh, Constable Linnet,' I breathed in my best Olivia de Havilland voice. 'I was just about to ring you. I'm so glad you called. The most awful thing has just happened at Buckshaw!'

That chore done, I beat a rapid retreat to the rosebushes.

'Come on,' I said to Porcelain, who was standing precisely as I had left her. 'There's no time to waste!'

In less than a minute, we were creeping stealthily up the wide staircase of Buckshaw's east wing.

'Blimey,' Porcelain said when she saw my bedroom. 'It's like a bloomin' parade square!'

'And every bit as cold,' I replied. 'Climb under the quilt. I'll go fix a hot water bottle.'

A quick trip next door to my laboratory, five minutes with a Bunsen burner, and I had filled a red rubber bag with boiling water, ready to shove in under Porcelain's feet.

I hoisted a corner of my mattress and pulled out a box of chocolates I'd nicked from the kitchen doorstep, where Ned, the smitten potboy, was forever leaving tributes to Feely. Since Miss Snotrag never knew they'd arrived, she could hardly miss them, could she? I reminded myself to tell Ned, the next time I saw him, how much his gift had been appreciated. I just wouldn't tell him by whom.

'Help yourself,' I said, ripping the cellophane from the box. 'They may not be as fresh as the flowers in May, but at least they're not crawling with maggots.'

Ned's budget could only afford chocolates that had been left in the shop window for a quarter century or more.

Porcelain stopped with a vanilla cream halfway

to her mouth.

'Go ahead,' I told her. 'I was teasing.'

Actually I wasn't, but there was no point in upsetting the girl.

Meaning to close the drapes, I went to the window, where I paused to have a quick look outside. There was no one in sight.

Beyond the lawns, I could see one corner of the Visto, and to the south – Poseidon! I'd completely forgotten that I could see the fountain from my bedroom window.

Was it possible that–? I rubbed my eyes and looked again.

Yes! There he was – Brookie Harewood, from this distance, no more than a dark doll hanging from the sea god's trident. I could easily slip back for another look before the police turned up. And if they *did* arrive while I was at the scene, I'd tell them that I'd been waiting for them; keeping an eye on Brookie, making sure that nothing was touched. And so forth.

'You look exhausted,' I said, turning to Porcelain.

Her eyelids were already flickering as I drew the drapes.

'Sleep tight,' I said, but I don't think she heard me.

The doorbell rang as I came down the stairs. Rats! Just when I thought I was alone. I counted to ten and opened the door – just as the bell rang again.

Inspector Hewitt was standing there, his finger still on the button, a slightly embarrassed look on his face, as if he were a small boy who'd been

129

caught playing Knock-Knock-Run.

They certainly don't believe in letting the grass grow under their feet, I thought. It had been less than ten minutes since I'd spoken to Constable Linnet.

The Inspector seemed a little taken aback to see me at the door.

'Ah,' he said. 'The ubiquitous Flavia de Luce.'

'Good afternoon, Inspector,' I said, in a butter-wouldn't-melt-in-her-heart voice. 'Won't you come in?'

'Thank you, no,' he replied. 'I understand there's been another ... incident.'

'An incident,' I said, falling into the game. 'It's Brookie Harewood, I'm afraid. The quickest way to the Trafalgar Lawn is through here,' I added, pointing towards the east. 'Follow me and I'll show you.'

'Hold on,' Inspector Hewitt said. 'You'll do no such thing. I want you to keep completely out of this. Do you understand, Flavia?'

'It *is* our property, Inspector,' I said, just to remind him that he was talking to a de Luce.

'Yes, and it's *my* investigation. So much as one of your fingerprints at the scene and I'll have you up on charges. Do you understand?'

What insolence! It didn't deserve an answer. I could have said 'My fingerprints are already at the scene, Inspector,' but I didn't. I spun on my heel and slammed the door in his face.

Inside, I quickly clapped my ear to the panel and listened for all I was worth.

Although it sounded like a dry chuckle, the sound I heard must really have been a little cry of dismay from the Inspector at having so foolishly lost the services of a first-rate mind.

Damn and blast the man! He'd regret his high-handed manner. Oh yes he would – he'd regret it!

Up the stairs I flew to my chemical laboratory. I unlocked the heavy door, stepped into the room, and almost instantly relaxed as a deep feeling of peace came over me.

There was something special about the place: the way in which the light fell so softly through the tall leaded casement windows, the warm brass glow of the Leitz microscope that had once belonged to Uncle Tar and was now so satisfyingly mine, the crisp – almost eager – shine of the laboratory's glassware, the cabinets filled with neatly labelled bottles of chemicals (including some quite remarkable poisons), and the rows upon rows of books – all of these lent to the room something I can only describe as a sense of sanctuary.

I took one of the tall laboratory stools and lifted it onto a counter near the windows. Then, from the bottom drawer of the desk – which, because it contained his diaries and documents, I still thought of as being Uncle Tar's – I removed a pair of German binoculars. Their lenses, I had learned from one of the books in his library, had been made from a special sand found only in the Thuringian Forest near the village of Martinroda, in Germany, which, because of its aluminum oxide content, produced an image of remarkable clarity. Which was precisely what I needed!

With the binoculars hung round my neck, I used a chair to climb up onto the countertop, then scaled the stool, where I teetered uneasily atop my improvised observation tower, my head

131

almost touching the ceiling.

Using one hand to steady myself against the window frame, and the binoculars pressed to my eyes with the other, I used whatever fingers were left to turn the focusing knob.

As the hedges surrounding the Trafalgar Lawn sprang into sharp detail, I realised that the view from the laboratory, and from this angle, should be much better than the one I'd had from my bedroom window.

Yes – there was Poseidon, gazing out upon his invisible ocean, oblivious to the dark bundle dangling from his trident. But now I had a good view of the entire fountain.

With distance collapsed by the powerful lenses, I could also see Inspector Hewitt as he came into view from behind the fountain, raised a hand to shield his eyes from the sun, and stood gazing up at Brookie's body. He pursed his lips and I could almost hear in my mind the little whistle that escaped him.

I wondered if he knew he was being watched.

The image in the binoculars faded suddenly, was restored – and then faded again. I took the glasses away from my eyes and realised that a sudden cloud had blotted out the sun. Although it was too far to the west for me to actually see it, I could tell by the darkness that had fallen on the landscape that we were in for a storm.

I raised the binoculars again just in time to see that the Inspector was now looking directly at me. I gasped – then realised that it was a trick of the optics; of course he couldn't see me. He must be looking up at the storm clouds that were gathering over Buckshaw.

He turned away, then turned again, and now it appeared as if he was talking to somebody, and so he was. As I looked on, Detective Sergeant Woolmer came round the base of the fountain carrying a heavy kit, closely followed by Dr. Darby and Detective Sergeant Graves. *They must all have come in the same car,* I thought, *and driven round by way of the Gully and the Palings.*

Before you could say Jack Robinson, Sergeant Woolmer had set up his folding tripod and attached the heavy police camera. I marvelled at how deftly his stubby fingers handled the delicate controls, and how quickly he managed to take his initial exposures.

There was a sudden, blinding flash of lightning, followed almost instantly by an ear-splitting clap of thunder, and I nearly toppled off the stool. I let the binoculars fall free to dangle round my neck, and slapped both hands against the windowpanes to regain my balance.

What was it Daffy had once told me during a summer downpour?

'Stay away from windows during a thunderstorm, you silly moke.'

Now here I was, with lightning licking at the transom, pinned against the glass like a butterfly to a card in the Natural History Museum.

'Even if the lightning misses you,' she'd added, 'the breath will be sucked from your lungs by the sound of the thunder, and you'll be turned inside out like a red sock.'

The lightning flashed again and the thunder roared, and now the rain was coming down in

133

sweeping sheets, pounding on the roof like the roll of kettledrums. A sudden wind had sprung up, and the trees in the park pitched wildly in its gusts.

Actually it was quite exhilarating. *Daffy be damned,* I thought. If I practised a bit, I could even come to love the thunder and the lightning.

I straightened up, adjusted my balance, and raised the glasses to my eyes.

What I saw was like a scene from Hell. In the watery green light, blown by the wind and illuminated by erratic flashes of lightning, the three policemen were removing Brookie's body from the trident. They had looped a rope under his armpits, and were lowering him slowly, almost tenderly to the ground. Towering above them in the rain, Poseidon, like a monstrous stone Satan with his pitchfork at the ready, still stared out across his watery world as if he were bored stiff with the antics of mere humans.

Inspector Hewitt reached out to touch the rope and ease the body's descent, his hair plastered flat against his forehead by the rain, and for a moment, I had the feeling that I was watching some horrific passion play.

And perhaps I was.

Only when Sergeant Woolmer had fetched a bit of tarpaulin from his kit and covered Brookie's body did the men seem to think of sheltering themselves. Although it provided precious little protection, Dr. Darby held his black medical bag above his head and stood there motionless, looking miserable in the rain.

Inspector Hewitt had unfolded a small transparent raincoat and slipped it on over his saturated clothing. It seemed like something that a chambermaid might wear, and I wondered if his lovely wife, Antigone, had slipped it into his pocket for emergencies such as this.

Sergeant Woolmer stood stolid in the downpour, as if his bulk were protection enough against the wind and rain, while Sergeant Graves, who was the only one of the four small enough to do so, had tucked himself comfortably under the lowest bowl of the fountain on the downwind side, where he squatted as dry as a duck.

Then suddenly, as quickly as it had begun, the storm was over. The dark cloud was now drifting off to the east as the sun reappeared and the birds renewed their interrupted songs.

Sergeant Woolmer removed the waterproof covering with which he had draped his camera, and began photographing the fountain from every imaginable angle. As he began his close-ups, an ambulance came into view, teetering its way across the rough ground between the Palings and the Trafalgar Lawn.

After a few words with the driver, Dr. Darby helped shift Brookie's shrouded body onto a stretcher, then climbed into the passenger's seat.

As the ambulance bumped slowly away, swerving to avoid the half-buried statuary, I noticed that a rainbow had appeared. An eerie yellow light had come upon the landscape, making it seem like some garish painting by a madman.

On the far side of the Trafalgar Lawn, at the edge of the trees, something moved. I swivelled a bit and refocused quickly, just in time to see a figure vanish into the wood.

Another poacher, I thought, *watching the police; not wanting to be seen.*

I made a slow sweep of the tree trunks, but whoever had been there was gone.

I found the ambulance again with the binoculars, and watched until it vanished behind a distant hedge. When it was lost to view, I climbed down from the stool and locked up the laboratory.

If I wanted to search Brookie's digs before the police got there, I'd have to get cracking.

TEN

The only problem was this: I hadn't the faintest idea where Brookie lived.

I could have made another visit to the telephone closet, I suppose, but in Buckshaw's foyer I was risking an encounter with Father, or worse – with Daffy or Feely. Besides, it seemed most unlikely that a ne'er-do-well such as Brookie would be listed in the directory.

Rather than risk being caught, I slipped stealthily into the picture gallery, which occupied nearly the entire ground floor of the east wing.

An army of de Luce ancestors gazed down upon me as I passed, in whose faces I recognised, uncomfortably, aspects of my own. *I wouldn't have liked most of them,* I thought, *and most of them wouldn't have liked me.*

I did a cartwheel just to show them that I didn't care.

Still, because the old boy deserved it, I gave Uncle Tar's portrait a brisk Girl Guide salute, even though I'd been drummed out of that organisation, quite unfairly I thought, by a woman with no sense of humour whatsoever. *'Honestly, Miss Pashley,'* I'd have told her, had I been given half a chance, *'the ferric hydroxide was only meant to be a joke.'*

At the far end of the gallery was a box room which, in Buckshaw's glory days, had been used for the framing and repair of the portraits and landscapes that made up my family's art collection.

A couple of deal shelves and the workbench in the room were still littered with dusty tins of paint and varnish whose contents had dried out at about the same time as Queen Victoria, and from which brush handles stuck up here and there like fossilised rats' tails.

Everyone but me seemed to have forgotten that this room had a most useful feature: a sashed window that could be raised easily from both inside and out – and all the more so since I had taken to lubricating its slides with lard pinched from the pantry.

On the outside wall, directly below the window casing and halfway to the ground, a brick had half crumbled away – its slow decay encouraged somewhat, I'll admit, by my hacking at it with one of Dogger's trowels: a perfect foothold for anyone who wished to leave or get back into the house without attracting undue attention.

As I scrambled out the window and climbed to the ground, I almost stepped on Dogger, who was on his knees in the wet grass. He got to his feet, lifted his hat, and replaced it.

'Good afternoon, Miss Flavia.'

'Good afternoon, Dogger.'

'Lovely rain.'

'Quite lovely.'

Dogger glanced up at the golden sky, then went on with his weeding.

The very best people are like that. They don't entangle you like flypaper.

Gladys's tyres hummed happily as we shot past St. Tancred's and into the high street. She was enjoying the day as much as I was.

Ahead on my left, a few doors from the Thirteen Drakes, was Reggie Pettibone's antiques shop. I was making a mental note to pay it a visit later when the door flew open and a spectacled boy came hurtling into the street.

It was Colin Prout.

I swerved to avoid hitting him, and Gladys went into a long shuddering slide.

'Colin!' I shouted as I came to a stop. I had very nearly taken a bad tumble.

But Colin had already crossed the high street and vanished into Bolt Alley, a narrow, reeking passage that led to a lane behind the shops.

Needless to say, I followed, offering up fresh praise for the invention of the Sturmey-Archer three-speed shifter.

Into the lane I sped, but Colin was already disappearing round the corner at the far end. A few seconds more, having taken a roughly circular route, and he would be back in the high street.

I was right. By the time I caught sight of him again, he was cutting into Cow Lane, as if the hounds of Hell were at his heels.

Rather than following, I applied the brakes.

Where Cow Lane ended at the river, I knew, Colin would veer to the left and follow the old towpath that ran behind the Thirteen Drakes. He would not risk going to ground anywhere along the old canal for fear of being boxed in behind the shops.

I turned completely round and went back the way I'd come, making a broad sweeping turn into Shoe Street, where Miss Pickery, the new librarian, lived in the last cottage. I braked, dismounted, and, leaning Gladys against her fence, climbed quickly over the stile and crept into position behind one of the tall poplars that lined the towpath.

Just in time! Here was Colin hurrying towards me, and all the while looking nervously back over his shoulder.

'Hello, Colin,' I said, stepping directly into his path.

Colin stopped as if he had walked into a brick wall, but the shifting of his pale eyes, magnified like oysters by his thick lenses, signalled that he was about to make a break for it.

'The police are looking for you, you know. Do you want me to tell them where you are?'

It was a bald-faced lie: one of my specialties.

'N-n-n-no.'

His face had gone as white as tissue paper, and I thought for a moment he was going to blubber. But before I could tighten the screws, he blurted

139

out: 'I never done it, Flavia! Honest! Whatever they think I done, I didn't.'

In spite of his tangle of words I knew what he meant. 'Didn't do what, Colin? What is it you haven't done?'

'Nothin'. I 'aven't done nothin'.'

'Where's Brookie?' I asked casually. 'I need to see him about a pair of fire irons.'

My words had the desired effect. Colin's arms swung round like the vanes on a weathercock, his fingers pointing north, south, west, east. He finally settled on the latter, indicating that Brookie was to be found somewhere beyond the Thirteen Drakes.

'Last time I seen him 'e was unloading 'is van.'

His van? Could Brookie have a van? Somehow the idea seemed ludicrous – as if the scarecrow from *The Wizard of* Oz had been spotted behind the wheel of a Bedford lorry – and yet...

'Thanks awfully, Colin,' I told him. 'You're a wonder.'

With a scrub at his eyes and a tug at his hair, he was over the stile and up Shoe Street like a whirling dervish. And then he was gone.

Had I just made a colossal mistake? Perhaps I had, but I could hardly carry out my inquiries with someone like Colin drooling over my shoulder.

Only then did a cold horror of an idea come slithering across my mind. What if–

But no, if there'd been blood on Colin's clothing, I'd surely have noticed it.

As I walked back to retrieve Gladys, I was taken with a rattling good idea. In all of Bishop's Lacey there were very few vans, most of which were known to me on sight: the ironmonger's, the butcher's, the electrician's, and so forth. Each one had the name of its owner in prominent letters on the side panels; each was unique and unmistakeable. A quick ride up the high street would account for most of them, and a strange van would stand out like a sore thumb.

And so it did.

A few minutes later I had pedalled a zigzag path throughout the village without any luck. But as I swept round the bend at the east end of the high street, I could hardly believe my eyes.

Parked in front of Willow Villa was a disreputable green van that, although its rusty panels were blank, had Brookie Harewood written all over it.

Willow Villa was aptly named for the fact that it was completely hidden beneath the drooping tassels of a giant tree, which was just as well since the house was painted a hideous shade of orange. It belonged to Tilda Mountjoy, whom I had met under rather unhappy circumstances a few months earlier. Miss Mountjoy was the retired Librarian-in-Chief of the Bishop's Lacey Free Library where, it was said, even the books had lived in fear of her. Now, with nothing but time on her hands, she had become a freelance holy terror.

Although I was not anxious to renew our acquaintance, there was nothing for it but to open her gate, push my way through the net of dangling fronds, squelch through the mosses underfoot, and beard the dragon in her den.

My excuse? I would tell her that, while out bicycling, I had been overcome with a sudden faintness.

141

Seeing Brookie's van, I thought that perhaps he would be kind enough to load Gladys into the rear and drive me home. Father, I was sure, would be filled with eternal gratitude, etc., etc., etc.

Under the willow's branches, lichens flourished on the doorstep and the air was as cool and dank as a mausoleum.

I had already raised the corroded brass knocker, which was in the shape of the Lincoln Imp, when the door flew open and there stood Miss Mountjoy – covered with blood!

I don't know which of us was the most startled to see the other, but for a peculiar moment we both of us stood perfectly still, staring wide-eyed at each other.

The front of her dress and the sleeves of her gray cardigan were soaked with the stuff, and her face was an open wound. A few fresh drops of scarlet had already plopped to the floor before she lifted a bloody handkerchief and clapped it to her face.

'Nosebleed,' she said. 'I get them all the time.'

With her mouth and nose muffled by the stained linen, it sounded as if she had said 'I give them all the twine,' but I knew what she meant.

'Gosh, Miss Mountjoy,' I blurted. 'Let me help you.'

I seized her arm and before she could protest, steered her towards the kitchen through a dark hallway lined with heavy Tudor sideboards.

'Sit down,' I said, pulling out a chair, and to my surprise, she did.

My experience with nosebleeds was limited but practical. I remembered one of Feely's birthday parties at which Sheila Foster's nose had erupted

142

on the croquet lawn and Dogger had stanched it with someone's handkerchief dipped in a solution of copper sulfate from the greenhouse.

Willow Villa, however, didn't seem likely to have a supply of Blue Vitriol, as the solution was called, although I knew that, given no more than half a teacup of dilute sulphuric acid, a couple of pennies, and the battery from Gladys's bicycle lamp, I could whip up enough of the stuff to do the trick. But this was no time for chemistry.

I grabbed for an ornamental iron key that hung from a nail near the fireplace and clapped it to the back of her neck.

She let out a shriek, and came halfway out of the chair.

'Easy now,' I said, as if talking to a horse (a quick vision of clinging to Gry's mane in the darkness came to mind). 'Easy.'

Miss Mountjoy sat rigid, her shoulders hunched. Now was the time.

'Is Brookie here?' I said conversationally. 'I saw his van outside.'

Miss Mountjoy's head snapped back and I felt her stiffen even more under my hand. She slowly removed the bloody handkerchief from her nose and said with perfect cold clarity, 'Harewood will never set foot in this house again.'

I blinked. Was Miss Mountjoy merely stating her determination, or was there something more ominous in her words? Did she know that Brookie was dead?

As she twisted round to glare at me, I saw that her nosebleed had stopped.

I let the silence lengthen, a useful trick I had

143

picked up from Inspector Hewitt.

'The man's a thief,' she said at last. 'I should never have trusted him. I don't know what I was thinking.'

'Can I bring you anything, Miss Mountjoy? A glass of water? A damp cloth?'

It was time to ingratiate myself.

Without a word I went to the sink and wetted a hand towel. I wrung it out and gave it to her. As she wiped the blood from her face and hands, I looked away discreetly, taking the opportunity to examine the kitchen.

It was a square room with a low ceiling. A small green Aga crouched in the corner and there was a plain, scrubbed deal table with a single chair: the one in which Miss Mountjoy was presently sitting. A plate rail ran round two sides of the room, upon which were displayed an assortment of blue and white plates and platters – mostly Staffordshire, by the look of them: village greens and country scenes, for the most part. I counted eleven, with an empty space about a foot and a half in diameter where a twelfth plate must once have hung.

Filtered through the willow branches outside, the weak green light that seeped in through the two small windows above the sink gave the plates a weird and watery tint, which reminded me of what the Trafalgar Lawn had looked like after the rain: after the taking down of Brookie's body from the Poseidon fountain.

At the entrance to the narrow passage through which we had entered the kitchen was a chipped wooden cabinet, on top of which was a cluster of identical bottles, all of them medicinal-looking.

Only as I read their labels did the smell hit me. *How odd,* I thought: the sense of smell is usually lightning fast, often speedier than that of sight or hearing.

But now there was no doubt about it. The whole room – even Miss Mountjoy herself – reeked of cod-liver oil.

Perhaps until that moment the sight of Miss Mountjoy's nosebleed and her blood-splattered clothing had overwhelmed my sense of smell. Although I had first noticed the fishy odour when I saw her dripping blood at the door, and again when I had applied the cold key to the nape of her neck, my brain must have labelled the fact as not immediately important, and tucked it away for later consideration.

My experience of cod-liver oil was vast. Much of my life had been spent fleeing the oncoming Mrs. Mullet, who, with uncorked bottle and a spoon the size of a garden spade, pursued me up and down the corridors and staircases of Buckshaw – even in my dreams.

Who in their right mind would want to swallow something that looked like discarded engine oil and was squeezed out of fish livers that had been left to rot in the sun? The stuff was used in the tanning of leather, and I couldn't help wondering what it would do to one's insides.

'Open up, dearie,' I could hear Mrs. Mullet calling as she trundled after me. 'It's good for you.'

'No! No!' I would shriek. 'No acid! Please don't make me drink acid!'

And it was true – I wasn't just making this up. I had analysed the stuff in my laboratory and found it to contain a catalogue of acids, among them oleic, margaric, acetic, butyric, fellic, cholic, and phosphoric, to say nothing of the oxides, calcium and sodium.

In the end, I had made a bargain with Mrs. M: she would allow me to take the cod-liver oil alone in my room at bedtime, and I would stop screaming like a tortured banshee and kicking at her ankles. I swore it on my mother's grave.

Harriet, of course, had no grave. Her body was somewhere in the snows of Tibet.

Happy to be relieved of a difficult and unwanted task, Mrs. Mullet had pretended to be scandalised, but cheerfully handed over both spoon and bottle.

My mind came snapping back to the present like a rubber ball on an elastic string.

'Trouble with antiques, was it?' I heard myself say. 'You're not alone in that, Miss Mountjoy.'

Although I almost missed it, her rapid glance upwards, towards the spot where the missing plate had hung, told me I had hit the bull's-eye.

She saw me following her gaze.

'It was from the time of Hongwu, the first Ming emperor. He told me he knew a man–'

'Brookie?' I interrupted.

She nodded.

'He said he knew someone who could have the piece assessed discreetly, and at reasonable cost. Things have been difficult since the war, you see, and I thought of–'

'Yes, I know, Miss Mountjoy,' I said. 'I understand.'

With Father's financial difficulties, and the

146

blizzard of past-due accounts that arrived with every postal delivery being the subject of much idle chitchat in Bishop's Lacey, there was no need for her to explain her own poverty.

Her look formed a bond between us. 'Partners in debt,' it seemed to say.

'He told me the railway had broken it. He'd packed the plate in straw, he said, and put it in a barrel, but somehow – he'd taken out no insurance, of course, trying to keep expenses down – trying not to burden me with additional – and then–'

'Someone spotted it in an antiques shop,' I blurted.

She nodded. 'My niece, Julia. In Pimlico. She said, "Auntie, you'll never guess what I saw today: the mate to your Ming!"'

'She was standing right there where you are, and just as you did, she looked up and saw the empty space on the shelf. "Oh, Auntie!' she said. "Oh, Auntie."

'We tried to get the plate back, of course, but the man said he had it on consignment from an MP who lived in the next street. Couldn't give out names because of confidentiality. Julia was all for going to the police, but I reminded her that Uncle Jamieson, who brought the piece into the family, was not always on the up-and-up. I'm sorry to have to tell you that story, Flavia, but I've always made it a point to be scrupulously honest.'

I nodded and gave her a little look of disappointment. 'But Brookie Harewood,' I said. 'How did *he* come to get his hands on the plate?'

'Because he's my tenant. He lives in my coach

house, you see.'

Brookie? Here? In Miss Mountjoy's coach house? This was news to me.

'Oh, yes,' I said. 'Of course he does. I'd forgotten. Well, then, I'd better be getting along. I think you'd best lie down for a while, Miss Mountjoy. You're still quite pale. A nosebleed takes so much out of one, doesn't it? Iron, and so forth. You must be quite worn out.'

I led her to the little parlour I had seen at the front of the house and helped her recline on a horsehair settee. I covered her with an afghan, and left her clutching at it with white fingers.

'I'll see myself out,' I said.

ELEVEN

Like an actor in the pantomime muddling his way out from behind the curtains, I pushed aside the hanging willow branches and stepped out from the green gloom and into the blinding glare of the sun's spotlight.

Time was running out. Inspector Hewitt and his men were probably minutes away and my work was hardly begun.

Since Brookie's van was directly in front of me, I'd begin there. I glanced quickly up and down the Street. There was no one in sight.

One of the van's windows was rolled all the way down: obviously just as Brookie had left it. Here was a bit of luck!

148

Father was always going on about the importance of carrying a handkerchief at all times, and for once he was right. Opening the door would leave my fingerprints on the nickel-plated handle. A clean bit of linen was just the ticket.

But the handle wouldn't budge, although it did give off an alarming groan that hinted of extensive rust beneath. One thing that I didn't need was to have a van door fall off and go clattering into the street.

I stepped up onto the running board (another metallic groan) and used my elbows to lever myself into position. With my stomach on the bottom of the window frame, I was able to hinge the top half of my body into the van, leaving my legs and feet sticking straight out in the air for balance.

With the handkerchief wrapped round my hand, I pressed on the glove compartment's release button, and when it popped open, reached inside and pulled out a small packet. It was, as I thought it might be, the registration papers for the van.

I almost let out a cheer! Now I would find out Brookie's real address, which I somehow doubted would be Willow Villa.

Edward Sampson, the document said. *Rye Road, East Finching.*

I knew well enough where East Finching was: it lay about five miles by road to the north of Bishop's Lacey.

But who was Edward Sampson? Other than being the owner of the van from which my bottom was probably projecting like a lobster's claw from a trap – I hadn't the faintest idea.

I shoved the papers back into the glove com-

149

partment and pushed home the panel.

Now for the coach house.

'Come along, Gladys,' I said, taking her from where she had been waiting. No sense having my presence detected by leaving her parked in plain view.

Because of the peculiar shape of Miss Mountjoy's property, the coach house was located at the end of a hedge-lined L-shaped lane that ran along one side and across the back. I tucked Gladys out of sight behind a box hedge and proceeded on foot.

As I approached the building, I could see that the term 'coach house' was no more than a courtesy title. In fact, it was almost a joke.

The building was square, with bricks on the bottom floor and boards on the top. The windows were coated with the kind of opaque film that tells of neglect and cobwebs; the kind of windows that watch you.

The door had once been painted, but had blistered away to reveal grey, weathered wood that matched the unpainted boards of the upper storey.

I wrapped my hand in the handkerchief and tried the latch. The door was locked.

The first-floor windows were too high to gain entry, and the tangle of ivy on a broken trellis too fragile to climb. A rickety ladder leaned wearily against the wall, too dangerous to be pressed into service. I decided to try round the back.

I had to be careful. Only a sagging wooden fence and a narrow walkway separated the rear of the coach house from Miss Mountjoy's overhanging willow tree: I'd have to crouch and run, like a commando on the beach.

At the end of the fence, on the left side of the walkway, was a wire compound attached to the coach house, from which issued, as I approached, an excited clucking. Inside the compound, there was a cage no more than two feet high – rather less, in fact – and in it was the biggest rooster I had ever seen: so large that he had to strut about his cage with stooped shoulders.

As soon as he saw me the bird made for the wires that separated us, fluttering up towards my face with a frightening rustle of wings. My first instinct was to take to my heels – but then I saw the pleading look in his marmalade eye.

He was hungry!

I took a handful of feed from a box that was nailed to the framework of the cage and tossed it through the mesh. The rooster fell upon the stuff like a wolf upon Russian travellers, his comb, as red as paper poppies, bobbing busily up and down as if it were driven by steam.

As he feasted, I noticed a hatch on the far side of the cage that opened into the coach house. It was no more than rooster-sized, but it would do.

Throwing a couple more handfuls of feed to distract the bird, I turned to the wire fence. It was only about seven feet high, but too far to leap up and grasp the upper frame. I tried to swarm up the mesh, but my shoes could find no grip.

Undefeated, I sat down and removed my shoes and socks.

When I come to write my autobiography, I must remember to record the fact that a chicken-wire fence *can* be scaled by a girl in bare feet, but only by one who is willing to suffer the tortures of the damned to satisfy her curiosity.

As I climbed, my toes stuck through the hexagons of the wire mesh, each strand like the blades of a cheese cutter. By the time I reached the top, my feet felt as if they belonged to Scott of the Antarctic.

As I dropped to the ground on the inside of the enclosure the rooster made a lunge for me. Since I hadn't thought to bring a pocketful of feed to appease the famished bird, I was at his mercy.

He threw himself at my bare knees and I made a dive for the hatchway.

It was a tight fit, and I could only squirm my way painfully through the opening as the enraged bird pecked furiously at my legs – but moments later I was inside the coach house: still inside a wired partition, but inside.

And so was the rooster, who had followed me in, and was now flinging himself upon me like an avenging fury.

Seized by a sudden inspiration, I squatted, caught the bird's eye, then with a loud hissing, rose up suddenly to my full height, weaving my head and flicking my tongue in and out like a king cobra.

It worked! In his feeble rooster brain, some age-old instinct whispered a sudden, wordless tale of terror that involved a chicken and a snake, and taking to his heels, he shot out through the hatch like a feathered cannonball.

I poked my fingers through the mesh and rotated the strip of wood that served as a latch, then stepped into the corridor.

152

I suppose my mind had been filled with images of dusty box stalls, of shrivelled harnesses hanging from wooden pegs, of currycombs and benches, and perhaps a long-abandoned phaeton carriage lurking in some dim corner. Perhaps I was thinking of our own coach house at Buckshaw.

But whatever the case, I was totally unprepared for what I saw.

Beneath the low, beamed ceiling of what had once been a stable, couches upholstered in green and pink silk were jammed together like buses in Piccadilly Circus. Cameo jars and vases – some of them surely Wedgwood – stood here and there on tables whose old wood managed to glow even in the dim light. Carved cabinets and elaborately inlaid tables receded into the shadows, while nearby horse stalls overflowed with Royal Albert ewers and Oriental screens.

The place was a warehouse – and, I thought, no ordinary one at that!

Against one wall, almost hidden by a massive sideboard, was an exquisitely carved Georgian chimneypiece, in front of which, half-unrolled, was a rich and elaborate carpet. Something very much like it had been pointed out to me on more than one occasion by Feely's friend and toady, Sheila Foster, who managed to drag their carpet into even the most casual conversation: 'The Archbishop of Canterbury was down for the weekend, you know. As he was pinching my cheek, he dropped a crumb of his Dundee cake on our dear old Aubusson.'

I had just stepped forward to have a closer look at the thing when something caught my eye: a gleam in a dark corner by the chimneypiece. I sucked in my breath, for there in Miss Mountjoy's coach house stood Sally Fox and Shoppo – Harriet's brass fire irons!

What on earth–? I thought. *How can this be?*

I had seen the firedogs just hours before in the drawing room at Buckshaw. Brookie Harewood couldn't possibly have crept back into the house and stolen them because Brookie was dead. But who else could have brought them here?

Could it have been Colin Prout? Colin was, after all, Brookie's puppet, and I had found him hanging about the neighbourhood just minutes ago.

Did Colin live here with Brookie? Miss Mountjoy had referred to Brookie as her tenant, which surely meant that he lived here. I hadn't seen any sign of a kitchen or sleeping quarters, but perhaps they lay somewhere beyond the vast expanse of furniture or upstairs on the first floor.

As I retraced my steps to the central corridor, a car door slammed in the lane outside.

Crackers! It could well be Inspector Hewitt.

I ducked down and waddled my way towards a window, where I pressed myself flat against the back of a massive ebony armoire, round which I could peek out without being seen.

But it was not Inspector Hewitt who was coming towards the door: it was a walking bulldog. The man's shirtsleeves were rolled to his elbows, revealing arms that, except for their excessive hairiness, might have been a pair of Christmas hams, His shirt, open at the neck, revealed a forest of black, springy chest hair, and his fists

154

clenched and unclenched as he strode purposefully towards the door.

Whoever he was, it was clear that he was unhappy. The man was powerful enough to tear me open like a packet of cigarettes. I couldn't let him find me here.

It was unnerving to work my way back through the maze of furniture. Twice I startled at a movement close by, only to find that it was a reflection of myself in an uncovered mirror.

The man was already opening the door as I reached the caged cubicle. I slipped inside – thank goodness for bare feet and straw on the floor! – then lowered myself to hands and knees, then flat on my face, and began to crawl through the narrow hole to the outside.

The rooster was on me like a champion fighting cock. As I crawled, I tried to keep my hands up to protect my face, but the bird's spurs were razor sharp. Before I was even halfway through, my wrists were bleeding.

Up the wire wall I swarmed, the rooster throwing himself again and again at my feet and legs. There was no time even to think of what the wire mesh was doing to my toes. At the top, I threw myself over the wooden bar and dropped heavily to the ground.

'Who's there?' Inside the coach house, the man's voice sounded as if he was no more than a few feet away. But unless he got down on his belly and crawled, he could not follow me – could not even see me in the outside pen.

He would have to return to his car, then come round behind the coach house in the lane.

155

I heard his footsteps retreating on the wooden floor.

Again I made a crouching scuttle along the crumbling fence – but wait: I'd forgotten my shoes and socks!

Back again I went to retrieve them, my breath now coming in quick painful gasps. Once more along the fence and I ducked behind the hedge where I had left Gladys.

Just in time. I froze behind the box hedge – trying not to breathe – as the human bulldog went lumbering past.

'Who's there?' he demanded again, and I heard the rooster throw himself at the wire mesh with a wild crowing.

A few more coarse oaths and my pursuer was gone. I cannot bring myself to record his exact words, but will keep them in mind against the day I can put them to good use.

I waited for a minute or two to be sure, then dragged Gladys from behind the hedge and set off for home.

As I pedalled along I did my best to look like a respectable English girl out for a bracing bicycle ride in the fresh air.

But somehow I doubted that my charade would convince anyone: my hands and face were filthy, my wrists and ankles were bleeding, my knees were scraped to the bone, and my clothing would have to be tossed in the dustbin.

Father would not be amused.

And what if, in my absence, they had discovered Porcelain in my bedroom? What if she had awakened and wandered downstairs? Or into

Father's study!

Although I had never before cringed on a bicycle, I cringed.

'I caught her crawling in at one of the windows of the picture gallery,' Feely said. 'Like a common housebreaker. Can you imagine? I'd gone there to study the Maggs painting of Ajax, and–'

Maggs was a ruffian painter who had lived in the vicinity of Bishop's Lacey during the Regency, and Ajax a horse that had been bought on a whim by one of my ancestors, Florizel de Luce. Ajax had rewarded his new owner by going on to win enough races that Florizel was able to have himself elected to a rotten borough.

'Thank you, Ophelia,' Father said.

Feely cast down humble eyes and drifted out the door, where she would sit on the chair in the hallway to eavesdrop comfortably upon my humiliation.

'Do you know what day it is, Flavia?' Father began.

'Sunday,' I said without hesitation, although yesterday's fête at St. Tancred's seemed as far removed in time as the last ice age.

'Precisely,' Father said. 'And what have we done on Sundays since time immemorial?'

'Gone to church,' I replied like a trained macaw.

Church! I'd forgotten all about it.

'I'd thought to let you lie in this morning to recover from that nasty business in the Palings. Next thing I know, there's an inspector at the door and you're wanted for fingerprinting.

'Now I'm informed that there's a dead body on

157

the Trafalgar Lawn and that you're nosing about the village asking impertinent questions.'

'Miss Mountjoy?' I ventured.

Give a little, learn a lot. That was going to be my Motto of the Month. I would have to remember to jot it down in my notebook.

But wait! How could Miss Mountjoy have known about the body on the lawn? Unless–

'Miss Mountjoy,' Father confirmed. 'She telephoned to ask if you'd got home safely.'

The old harpy! She must have got up from her settee and been peering out through the trailing seaweed fronds of the willow tree, spying on my encounters with the rooster and the bulldog-man.

'How very kind of her,' I said. 'I must remember to send her a card.'

I'd send her a card, all right. It would be the Ace of Spades, and I'd mail it anonymously from somewhere other than Bishop's Lacey. Philip Odell, the detective on the wireless, had once investigated such a case, and it had been a cracking good story – one of his best adventures.

'And your dress!' Father went on. 'What have you done to your dress?'

My dress? Hadn't Miss Mountjoy described to him fully what she'd seen?

Hold on! – perhaps she hadn't after all. Perhaps Father was still unaware of what had taken place at the coach house.

God bless you, Miss Mountjoy! I thought. *May you live forever in the company of those saints and martyrs who refused to tell them where the church plate was buried.*

But wasn't Father going to remark upon my

158

cuts and abrasions?

Apparently not.

And it was at that moment, I think, it began to dawn upon me – truly dawn upon me – that there were things that were never mentioned in polite company no matter what; that blue blood was heavier than red; that manners and appearances and the stiff upper lip were all of them more important, even, than life itself.

'Flavia,' Father repeated, fighting to keep from wringing his hands, 'I asked you a question. What have you done to your dress?'

I looked down at myself as if noticing the damage for the first time.

'My dress?' I said, smoothing it down and making sure he had a good view of my bloodied wrist and knees. 'Oh, I'm sorry, Father. It's nothing. I had a bit of a prang with my bicycle. Jolly bad luck, but still – I'll rinse it out at once and mend it myself. It'll be a piece of cake.'

My acute hearing detected the sound of a coarse snicker in the hallway.

But I'd like to believe that what I saw in Father's eyes was pride.

TWELVE

Porcelain was sleeping the sleep of the dead. I had worried in vain.

I stood looking down at her as she lay on my bed in much the same position as when I had left her. The dark swatches under her eyes seemed to have lightened, and her breathing was almost imperceptible.

Two seconds later there was a flurry of furious motion and I was pinned to the bed with Porcelain's thumbs pressing into my windpipe.

'Fiend!' I thought she hissed.

I struggled to get free but I couldn't move. Bright stars were bursting in my brain as I clawed at her hands. I wasn't getting enough oxygen. I tried to pull away.

But I was no match for her. She was bigger and stronger than me, and already I could feel myself becoming languid and uncaring. How easy it would be to give in...

But no!

I stopped trying to fight her hands and instead took hold of her nose with my thumb and forefinger. With my last remaining strength I gave it a most vicious twist.

'Flavia!'

She seemed suddenly surprised to see me – as if we were old friends who had met unexpectedly in front of a lovely Vermeer in the National Gallery.

Her hands withdrew themselves from my throat, but still I couldn't seem to breathe. I rolled off the bed and onto the floor, seized with a fit of coughing.

'What are you doing?' she demanded, looking round in puzzlement.

'What are *you* doing?' I croaked. 'You've crushed my windpipe!'

'Oh, God!' she said. 'How awful. I'm sorry, Flavia really I am. I was dreaming I was in Fenella's caravan and there was some horrid ... beast! ... standing over me. I think it was–'

'Yes?'

She looked away from me. 'I ... I'm sorry. I can't tell you.'

'I'll keep it to myself. I promise.'

'No, it's no good. I mustn't.'

'All right, then,' I said. 'Don't. In fact, I forbid you to tell me.'

'Flavia–'

'No,' I said, and I meant it. 'I don't want to know. Let's talk about something else.'

I knew that if I bided my time, whatever it was that Porcelain was withholding would come spilling out like minced pork from Mrs. Mullet's meat grinder.

Which reminded me that I hadn't eaten for ages.

'Are you hungry?' I asked.

'Starving. You must have heard my tummy rumbling.'

I hadn't, but I pretended I had, and nodded wisely.

'Stay here. I'll bring something from the kitchen.'

Ten minutes later I was back with a bowl of food nicked from the pantry.

'Follow me.' I said, 'Next door.'

Porcelain looked round wide-eyed as we entered my chemical laboratory. 'What is this place? Are we supposed to be in here?'

'Of course we are,' I told her. 'It's where I do my experiments.'

161

'Like magic?' she asked, glancing around at the glassware.

'Yes,' I said. 'Like magic. Now then, you take these...'

She jumped at the *pop* of the Bunsen burner as I put a match to it.

'Hold them over the flame,' I said, handing her a couple of bangers and a pair of nickel-plated test tube clamps. 'Not too close – it's exceedingly hot.'

I broke six eggs into a borosilicate evaporating dish and stirred them with a glass rod over a second burner. Almost immediately the laboratory was filled with mouthwatering aromas.

'Now for toast,' I said. 'You can do two slices at a time,' I said. 'Use the tongs again. Do both sides, then turn them inside out.'

By necessity, I had become quite an accomplished laboratory chef. Once, just recently, when Father had banished me to my room, I had even made myself a spotted dick by steaming suet from the larder in a wide-neck Erlenmeyer flask. And because water boils at only 212 degrees Fahrenheit, while nylon doesn't melt until it is heated to 417 degrees, I had verified my theory that one of Feely's precious stockings would make a perfect pudding bag.

If there's anything more delicious than a sausage roasted over an open Bunsen burner, I can't imagine what it might be – unless it's the feeling of freedom that comes of eating it with the bare fingers and letting the fat fall where it may. Porcelain and I tore into our food like cannibals after a missionary famine, and before long there

162

was nothing left but crumbs.

As two cups of water came to the boil in a glass beaker, I took down from the shelf where it was kept, alphabetically, between the arsenic and the cyanide, an apothecary jar marked *Camellia sinensis*.

'Don't worry,' I said. 'It's only tea.'

Now there fell between us one of those silences that occur when two people are getting to know each other: not yet warm and friendly, but neither cold nor wary.

'I wonder how your gram is doing?' I said at last. 'Fenella, I should say.'

'Well enough, I expect. She's a hard old bird.'

'Tough, you mean.' Her answer had surprised me.

'I mean hard.'

She deliberately let go of the glass test tube she'd been toying with and watched it shatter on the floor.

'But she'll not be broken,' she said.

I begged to differ but I kept my mouth shut. Porcelain had not seen her grandmother, as I had, sprawled in a pool of her own blood.

'Life can kill you, but only if you let it. She used to tell me that.'

'You must have loved her awfully,' I said, realising even as I spoke that I made it sound as if Fenella were already dead.

'Yes, sometimes very much,' Porcelain said reflectively, '–and sometimes not at all.'

She must have seen my startled reaction.

'Love's not some big river that flows on and on forever, and if you believe it is, you're a bloody

163

fool. It can be dammed up until nothing's left but a trickle...'

'Or stopped completely,' I added.

She did not reply.

I let my gaze wander out the window and across the Visto and I thought about the kinds of love I knew, which were not very many. After a while I thought about Brookie Harewood. Who had hated him enough to kill him, I wondered, and hang him from Poseidon's trident? Or had Brookie's death come about through fear rather than hate?

Well, whatever the case, Brookie would be laid out on a wheeled trolley in Hinley by now, and someone – his next of kin – would have been asked to identify the body.

As an attendant in a white coat lifted the corner of a sheet to reveal Brookie's dead face, a woman would step forward. She would gasp, clap a handkerchief to her mouth, and quickly turn her head away.

I knew how it was done: I'd seen it in the cinema.

And unless I missed my bet, the woman would be his mother: the artist who lived in Maiden Fenwick.

But perhaps I was wrong: Perhaps they would spare a mother the grief. Perhaps the woman who was stepping forward was just a friend. But no – Brookie didn't seem the type to have ladies as friends. Not many women would fancy spending their nights sneaking about the countryside in rubber boots and handling dead fish.

I was so wrapped up in my thoughts that I hadn't heard Porcelain begin speaking.

164

'–but never in summer,' she was saying. 'In summer she'd chuck all that and take to the roads with Johnny Faa, and not a penny between them. Like a couple of kids, they were. Johnny was a tinker when he was younger, but he'd given it up for some reason he would never explain. Still, he made friends easily enough, and his way with a fiddle meant that he spoke every language under the sun. They lived on whatever Fenella could get by telling the fortunes of fools.'

'I was one of those fools,' I told her.

'Yes,' Porcelain said. She was not going to spare my feelings.

'Did you travel with them?' I asked.

'Once or twice when I was younger. Lunita didn't much like me being with them.'

'Lunita?'

'My mother. She was their only child. Gypsies like large families, you know, but she was all they had. Their hearts were broken in half when she ran off with a *Gajo* – an Englishman from Tunbridge Wells.'

'Your father?'

Porcelain nodded sadly. 'She used to tell me my father was a prince – that he rode on the back of a pure white horse that was faster than the wind. His jacket was of spun gold and his sleeves of finest silk. He could talk to the birds in their own language and make himself invisible whenever the fancy took him.

'Some of that was true – he was specially good at the invisible dodge.'

As Porcelain spoke, there appeared in my mind a thought as sudden and as uninvited as a shoot-

165

ing star in the night sky: would I trade my father for hers?

I brushed it away.

'Tell me about your mother,' I said, perhaps a little too eagerly.

'There's little enough to tell. She was on her own. She couldn't go home, if you can call it that, because Fenella and Johnny – mostly Fenella – wouldn't have her. She'd me to care for, and she hadn't a friend in the world.'

'How awful,' I said. 'How did she manage?'

'By doing the only thing she knew. She had the gift of the cards, so she told fortunes. Sometimes, when things got bad, she would send me to Fenella and Johnny for a while. They cared for me well enough, but when I was with them they never asked about Lunita.'

'And you never told them.'

'No. But when the war came, things were different. We'd been living in a frightful old bed-sitter in Moorgate, where Lunita told fortunes behind a bedsheet strung up across the room. I was only four at the time, so I don't remember much about it in those days, apart from a spider that lived in a hole in the bathroom wall.

'We'd been there for, oh, I think about four years, so I must have been eight when one day a sign went up in the window of the empty house next door, and the landlady told Lunita that the place was being turned into a servicemen's club.

'Suddenly she was making more money than she knew what to do with. I think she felt guilty about all the Canadians, the Americans, the New Zealanders, and the Australians – even the Poles

166

– that came flocking in their uniforms to our rooms to have their cards turned. She didn't want anyone to think she was profiting by the war.

'I'll never forget the day I found her weeping in the W.C. "Those poor boys!" I remember her sobbing. "They all ask the same question: *Will I go home alive?*"'

'And what did she tell them?'

'You will go home in greater glory than ever you came.' She told them all the same, every one of them: half-a-crown a time.'

'That's very sad,' I said.

'Sad? No, not sad. Those were the best days of our lives. We just didn't realise it at the time.

'There was one particular officer that was always hanging round the club: tall bloke with a little blond moustache. I used to see him in the street, coming and going. Never had much to say, but he always seemed to be keeping an eye out for something. One day, just for a lark, Lunita invited him in and told his fortune. Wouldn't take a penny for it because it happened to be a Sunday.

'Within a day or two she was working for MI-something. They wouldn't tell her what, but it seemed that whatever she'd seen in his cards, she'd hit the nail on the head.

'Some boffin in Whitehall was trying to work out what Hitler's next move was going to be, and he'd heard through the grapevine about the Gypsy who spread the cards in Moorgate.

'They invited Lunita straightaway to lunch at the Savoy. At first, it might have been no more than a game. Maybe they wanted word to get about that they were desperate enough to pin their hopes on a Gypsy.

'But again, the things she told them were so close to the top-secret truth that they couldn't believe their ears. They'd never heard anything like it.

'At first, they thought she was a spy, and they had a scientist from Bletchley Park come up to London to interrogate her. He was hardly through the door before she told him he was lucky to be alive: that an illness had saved his life.

'And it was true. He'd just been attached to the Americans as a liaison officer when a sudden attack of appendicitis had kept him from taking part in a rehearsal for D-day – Exercise Tiger, it was called. The thing had been badly botched – hundreds killed. It was all hushed up, of course. Nobody knew about it at the time.

'Needless to say, the bloke was flabbergasted. She passed the test with flying colours, and within days – within hours – they had us set up in our own posh flat in Bloomsbury.'

'She must have remarkable powers,' I said.

Porcelain's body went slack. 'Had,' she said flatly. 'She died a month later. A V1 rocket in the street outside the Air Ministry. Six years ago. In June.'

'I'm sorry,' I said, and I was. At last we had something in common, Porcelain and I, even if it was no more than a mother who had died too young and left us to grow up on our own.

How I longed to tell her about Harriet – but somehow I could not. The grief in the room belonged to Porcelain, and I realised, almost at once, that it would be selfish to rob her of it in any way.

168

I set about cleaning up the shattered glass from the test tube she had dropped.

'Here,' she said. 'I should be doing that.'

'It's all right,' I told her. 'I'm used to it.'

It was one of those made-up excuses that I generally despise, but how could I tell her the truth: that I was unwilling to share with anyone the picking up of the pieces.

Was this a fleeting glimpse of being a woman? I wondered.

I hoped it was ... and also that it was not.

We were sitting on my bed, Porcelain with her back against the head, and I cross-legged at the foot.

'I expect you'll be wanting to visit your gram,' I said.

Porcelain shrugged, and I think I understood her.

'The police don't know you're here yet. I suppose we'd better tell them.'

'I suppose.'

'Let's leave it till the morning,' I told her. 'I'm too tired to think.'

And it was true: my eyelids felt as if they had been hung with lead sinkers. I was simply too exhausted to deal with the problems at hand. The greatest of these would be to keep secret Porcelain's presence in the house. The last thing I needed was to look on helplessly as Father drove away the granddaughter of Fenella and Johnny Faa.

Fenella was in hospital in Hinley and, for all I knew, she might be dead by now. If I was to get

169

to the bottom of the attack upon her at the Palings – and, I suspected, the murder of Brookie Harewood – I would have to attract as little attention as possible.

It was only a matter of time before Inspector Hewitt would be at the door, demanding details about how I had discovered Brookie's body. I needed time to review which facts I would tell him and which I would not. Or did I?

My mind was a whirl. *Heigh-ho!* I thought. *What jolly sport is the world of Flavia de Luce.*

Next thing I knew it was morning, and sunlight was pouring in through the windows.

THIRTEEN

I rolled over and blinked. I had been sprawled across the bottom of the bed, my head twisted painfully against the footboard. At the top of the bed, Porcelain was tucked in with my blanket pulled over her shoulders, her head on my pillow, sleeping away for all she was worth like some Oriental princess.

For a moment I felt my resentment rising, but when I remembered the tale she had told me last night, I let the resentment melt into pity.

I glanced at the clock and saw, to my horror, that I had overslept. I was late for breakfast. Father insisted that dishes at the table arrive and be taken away with military precision.

Taking great care not to awaken Porcelain, I

170

made a quick change of clothing, took a swipe at my hair with a brush, and crept down to breakfast.

Father, as usual, was immersed in the latest number of *The London Philatelist*, and seemed hardly to notice my arrival: a sure sign that another philatelic auction was about to take place. If our financial condition was as precarious as he claimed, he'd need to be sharp about current prices. As he ate, he made little notes on a napkin with the stub of a pencil, his mind in another world.

As I slipped into my chair, Feely fixed me with the cold and stony stare she had perfected by watching Queen Mary in the newsreels.

'You have a pimple on your face,' I said matter-of-factly as I poured milk on my Weetabix.

She pretended she didn't hear me, but less than a minute later I was gratified to see her hand rise automatically to her cheek and begin its exploration. It was like watching a crab crawl slowly across the seabed in one of the full-colored short subjects at the cinema: *The Living Ocean*, or something like that.

'Careful, Feely!' I said. 'It's going to explode.'

Daffy looked up from her book – the copy of *A Looking Glasse, for London and Englande* I had found at the fête. She'd picked it up herself, the swine!

I made a note to steal it later.

'What does it mean where it says "a red herring without mustard"?' I asked, pointing.

Daffy loved the slightest opportunity to show off her superior knowledge.

I had already reviewed in my mind what I knew

171

about mustard, which was precious little. I knew, for instance, that it contained, among other things, the acids oleic, erucic, behenic, and stearic. I knew that stearc acid was found in beef and mutton suet because I had once subjected one of Mrs. Mullet's greasy Sunday roasts to chemical analysis, and I had looked up the fact that erucic acid gets its name from the Greek word meaning 'to vomit.'

'Red herring, in the sixteenth and seventeenth centuries, was considered an inferior dish,' Daffy replied, with an especially withering look at me on the word 'inferior.'

I glanced over at Father to see if he was looking, but he wasn't.

'Nicholas Breton called it "a good gross dish for a coarse stomach,"' she went on, squirming and preening in her chair. 'He also said that old ling – that's another fish, in case you don't know – is like "a blew coat without caugnisaunce," which means a servant who doesn't wear his master's badge of arms.'

'Daphne, please...' Father said, without looking up, and she subsided.

I knew that they were referring – over my head, they thought – to Dogger. Warfare at Buckshaw was like that: invisible and sometimes silent.

'Pass the toast, please,' Daffy said, as quietly and politely as if she were addressing a stranger in an A.B.C. tea shop: as if the last eleven years of my life hadn't happened.

'They're having a new badminton court at Fosters',' Feely remarked suddenly to no one in particular. 'Sheila's going to use the old one to park her Daimler.'

172

Father grunted, but I could tell he was no longer listening.

'She's such a saucy stick,' Feely went on. 'She had Copley bring out little dishes of dessert onto the south lawn, but instead of ices she served snails – *escargots!* We ate them raw, like oysters, as the cinema stars do. It was ever so amusing.'

'You'd better be careful,' I said. 'The snail gatherers sometimes pick up leeches by mistake. If you swallow a leech, it will eat its way out of your stomach from the inside.'

Feely's face drained slowly, like a washbasin.

'There was something in *The Hinley Chronicle*,' I added helpfully, 'three weeks ago, if I remember correctly, about a man from St. Elfrieda's – not that far from here, really – who swallowed a leech and they had to–'

But Feely had scraped back her chair and fled.

'Are you provoking your sister again, Flavia,' Father asked, looking up from his journal, but leaving a forefinger on the page to mark his place.

'I was trying to discuss current events,' I said. 'But she doesn't seem much interested.'

'Ah,' Father said, and went back to reading about plate flaws in the 1840 tuppenny blue.

With Father present at the table, we were at least semi-civilised.

I made my escape with surprisingly little difficulty.

Mrs. Mullet was in the kitchen torturing the corpse of a chicken with a ball of butcher's twine.

'No good roastin' 'em 'less you truss properly,'

she said. 'That's what Mrs. Chadwick up at Norton Old Hall used to tell me, and she ought to know. She was the one that learned me – mind you that was back in the days of Lady Rex-Wells, long before you was born, dear. "Truss 'em up three-times-three," she used to say, "and you'll never have to rake out your oven." What are you laughin' at, miss?'

A nervous titter had escaped me as a sudden image – of being tied up in a similar way by my own flesh and blood – had flashed across my mind.

The very thought of it reminded me that I had not yet taken my revenge. Certainly, there had been my little leech joke, but that was a mere warm-up: no more than a prelude to vengeance. The fact was that I had simply been too busy.

As Mrs. M slid the doomed bird into the maw of the open Aga, I took the opportunity to pinch a pot of strawberry jam from the pantry.

'Three-times-three,' I said with an awful grimace and a horrid wink at Mrs. Mullet, as if I were giving the password of a secret society – one in which she and I were the only members. At the same time, I gave her a Winston Churchill 'V for Victory' sign with my right hand, to divert attention from the jam jar in my left.

Safely back upstairs, I opened the bedroom door as quietly as possible. There was no need to disturb Porcelain. I would leave a note telling her that I'd be back later, and that was all. No need to say where I was going.

But no note was necessary: The bed was perfectly made and Porcelain was gone.

Confound her! I thought. Hadn't she understood that she was to keep to my room and out of sight? I thought I had made that perfectly clear, but perhaps I hadn't.

Where was she now? Wandering the halls of Buckshaw – where she would surely be caught? Or had she returned to the caravan in the Palings?

I'd been intending to accompany her to the police station in Bishop's Lacey so that she could make her presence known to Constable Linnet. By being on the spot, I'd be not only doing my duty, but putting myself in the perfect position to overhear anything that passed between Porcelain and the police. PC Linnet would, in turn, inform his superiors in Hinley, who would pass the word to Inspector Hewitt. And I'd be the recipient of his grateful thanks.

It could have been so simple. Damn the girl!

Back through the kitchen I trudged with a second-degree wink to Mrs. Mullet and a muttered 'Three-times-three.'

Gladys was waiting by the garden wall and Dogger was in the greenhouse, intent upon his work.

But as I pedalled away, I was aware of his eyes upon my back.

Malden Fenwick lay to the east of Bishop's Lacey, not far beyond Chipford.

Although I had never been there before, the place had a familiar look: and no wonder. 'The Prettiest Village in England,' as it was sometimes called, had been photographed almost to distraction. Its Elizabethan and Georgian cottages, thatched and timbered, with their hollyhocks and diamond-paned windows, its duck pond and its tithe barn had appeared not just in hundreds of books and magazines, but as the setting for several popular films, such as *Honey for Sale* and *Miss Jenks Goes to War.*

'Trellis Terraces,' Daffy called it.

This was the place where Brookie Harewood's mother lived and had her studio, although I hadn't the faintest idea which of the cottages might be hers.

A green charabanc was parked in front of The Bull, its passengers spilling forth into the high street, cameras at the ready, fanning out in every direction with dangling arms, like a gaggle of gunfighters.

Several elderly villagers, caught out-of-doors in their gardens, began furtively fluffing up their hair or straightening their ties even as shutters began to click.

I parked Gladys against an ancient elm and walked round the coach.

'Good morning,' I said to a lady in a sun hat, as if I were helping to organise the tea. 'Welcome to Malden Fenwick. And where are *you* from?'

'Oh, Mel,' she said, turning to a man behind her, 'listen to her accent! Isn't she adorable? We're from Yonkers, New York, sweetheart. I'll bet you don't know where that is.'

As a matter of fact, I did: Yonkers was the home of Leo Baekeland, the Belgian chemist who had accidentally discovered *polyoxybenzylmethylenglycolanhydride,* better known as Bakelite, while working to produce a synthetic replacement for shellac which, until Baekeland came along, had

176

been made from the secretions of the lac beetle.

'Oh, yes,' I said. 'I think I've heard of Yonkers.'

I attached myself to Mel, who was busily arming his camera as he strolled off towards a wash-painted cottage, dragging along behind him, with slack bones and downcast eyes, a sulking daughter who looked fed up to the gills with transatlantic travel.

Shifting from foot to foot, I waited as he fired off a couple of shots of a white-haired woman in tweeds who was perched precariously on a ladder, deadheading a climbing rosebush.

As Mel wandered off in search of new memories, I lingered for a moment at the gate pretending to admire the garden and then, as if awakening from a partial trance, put on my best attempt at an American accent.

'Say,' I called out, pointing to the village green. 'Isn't this where whatsername lives? The painter lady?'

'Vanetta Harewood. Glebe Cottage,' the woman said cheerily, waving her secateurs. 'Last one on the right.'

It was so easy I was almost ashamed of myself.

So that was her name: 'Vanetta.' Vanetta Harewood. It certainly had the right ring to it for someone who painted the gentry with their hounds and horses.

Barging in on a freshly bereaved mother was not, perhaps, in the best of taste, but there were things I needed to know before the police knew them. I owed as much to Fenella Faa, and to a lesser degree, to my own family. Why, for instance, had I found Vanetta Harewood's son in

177

the drawing room at Buckshaw in the middle of the night, just before he was murdered?

I didn't expect his mother knew the answer to that, but mightn't she give me some scrap of information that would allow me to find it out for myself?

As the woman with the secateurs had said, Glebe Cottage was the last one on the right. It was twice the size of the others – as if two cottages had been shoved together end-to-end like dominos to form a larger one. Each half had its own front door, its own leaded window, and its own chimney; each half of the house was the mirror image of the other.

There was only one gate, though, and on it was a small brass plaque upon which was engraved: *Vanetta Harewood – Portraitist.*

My mind flew back to a spring evening upon which Daffy, during one of Father's compulsory literary evenings, had read aloud to us excerpts from Boswell's *The Life of Samuel Johnson, LL.D.*, and I remembered that Johnson had declared portrait painting to be an improper employment for a woman. 'Public practice of any art, and staring in men's faces, is very indelicate in a female,' he had said.

Well, I'd seen Dr. Johnson's face in the book's frontispiece, and I couldn't imagine anyone, male *or* female, wanting to stare into it for any length of time – the man was an absolute toad!

Behind the gate, the garden of Glebe Cottage was a mass of electric blue; the tall delphiniums in their second blooming seemed to stand on tiptoe behind the salvia, trying desperately to be

178

first to touch the sky.

Dogger had once told me that although delphiniums could be made to bloom again by cutting them down low after their first flowering, no honest gardener would dream of doing so, since it weakened the stock.

Whatever else she might be, Vanetta Harewood was not an honest gardener.

I touched my finger to the china doorbell button and gave it a jab. As I waited for someone to answer, I stepped back and stared up in an interested way at the sky, pursing my lips as if I were whistling carelessly. You never knew: someone might be peeking out from behind the curtains and it was important to look harmless.

I waited – then pushed the button again. There was a scurrying inside the house, followed by a grating noise directly behind the door, as if someone were moving a barricade of furniture.

As the door opened, I almost gasped aloud. Standing in front of me was a muscular woman in riding breeches and a lavender blouse. Her short gray hair lay tightly against her head like an aluminium helmet.

She screwed a tortoiseshell monocle into her eye and peered at me.

'Yes?'

'Mrs. Harewood?'

'No,' she said, and shut the door in my face.

Very well, then!

I remembered Father remarking once that if rudeness was not attributable to ignorance, it could be taken as a sure sign that one was speaking to a member of the aristocracy. I pushed the bell again. I would ask for directions.

But this time the door stayed closed, and the house behind it remained in silence.

But wait! The cottage had *two* front doors. I had simply chosen the wrong one.

I gave myself a knuckle on the head and walked to the other door. I raised the door knocker and gave it a gentle tap.

The door flew open instantly, and there stood Riding Breeches, glaring at me for all she was worth, though not through her monocle this time.

'May I speak to Mrs. Harewood?' I ventured. 'It's about–'

'No!' she said loudly. 'Go away!'

But before she could slam the door, a voice came from somewhere inside the house.

'Who is it, Ursula?'

'A girl selling something,' she called over her shoulder, and to me, 'Go away. We don't want any biscuits.'

I saw my opportunity and I took it.

'Mrs. Harewood,' I shouted. 'It's about Brookie!'

It was as if I had cast a spell and frozen time. For what seemed like forever, the woman at the door stood perfectly motionless, gaping at me as if she were a life-sized painted cutout from a picture book. She didn't even breathe.

'Mrs. Harewood – please! It's Flavia de Luce, from Bishop's Lacey.'

'Show her in, Ursula,' the voice said.

As I brushed past her and into the narrow hallway, Ursula didn't move a muscle.

'In here,' the voice said, and I moved towards it.

I suppose I was half expecting to find a decayed

180

Miss Haversham, clinging to her mouldy treasures in the curtained cave of her drawing room. What I found was altogether different.

Vanetta Harewood stood in a beam of sunlight at the bow window, and she turned to hold out her hands to me as I entered.

'Thank you for coming,' she said.

She looked, I thought, to be about forty-five. But surely she must be much older than that. How on earth could such a beautiful creature be the mother of that middle-aged layabout, Brookie Harewood?

She wore a smart dark suit with an Oriental silk at her neck, and her fingers were afire with diamonds.

'I must apologise for Ursula,' she said, taking my hand in hers, 'but she's fiercely protective of me. Perhaps too fiercely.'

I nodded dumbly.

'In my profession, privacy is paramount, you see, and now, with all this...'

She made a wide sweep of her hands to take in the entire world.

'I understand,' I said. 'I'm sorry about Brookie.'

She turned and took a cigarette from a silver box, lit it with a silver lighter that might have been a scale model of Aladdin's lamp, and blew out a long jet of smoke which, oddly enough, was also silver in the sunlight.

'Brookie was a good boy,' she said, 'but he did not grow up to be a good man. He had the fatal gift of making people believe him.'

I wasn't sure what she meant, but I nodded anyway.

181

'His life was not an easy one,' she said reflectively. 'Not as easy as it might seem.'

And then, quite suddenly– 'Now tell me, why have you come?'

Her question caught me by surprise. Why *had* I come?

'Oh, don't be embarrassed, child. If you're here to express your condolences, you have already done so, for which I thank you. You may leave, if you wish.'

'Brookie was at Buckshaw,' I blurted. 'I found him in the drawing room in the middle of the night.'

I could have cut out my tongue! There was no need for his mother to know this – no need at all, and even less for me to tell her.

But part of me knew that it was safe enough. Vanetta Harewood was a professional woman. She would no more want the midnight ramblings of her son brought to light than ... than I would.

'I am going to ask you a very great favor, Flavia. Tell the police if you must, but if you feel it isn't essential...'

She had walked back to the window, where she stood staring out into the past. 'You see, Brookie had his ... demons, if you will. If there is no need to make them public, then–'

'I won't tell anyone, Mrs. Harewood,' I said. 'I promise.'

She turned back to me and came across the room slowly. 'You're a remarkably intelligent girl, Flavia,' she said. And then, after thinking for a couple of seconds, she added, 'Come with me; there's something I wish to show you.'

Down a step we went, and then up another, into the part of the house whose door I had first knocked upon. Low timbered ceilings made her stoop more than once as we went from room to room.

'Ursula's studio,' she said, with a wave of a hand at a room that seemed full of twigs and branches.

'Basketry,' she explained. 'Ursula is a devotee of traditional crafts. Her willow baskets have taken prizes both here and on the Continent.

'To tell you the truth,' she went on, lowering her voice to a confidential whisper, 'the smell of her chemical preparations sometimes drives me out of the house, but then, it's all she has, poor dear.'

Chemical preparations? My ears went up like those of an old warhorse at the sound of the bugle.

'Mostly sulphur,' she said. 'Ursula uses the fumes to bleach the willow withies. They end up as white as polished bones, you know, but oh dear – the smell!'

I could foresee that I was going to have a late night poring over books in Uncle Tar's chemical library. Already my mind was racing ahead to the chemical possibilities of salicin ($C_{13}H_{18}O_7$) – which was discovered in willow bark in 1831 by Leroux – and good old sulphur (S). I already knew from personal experience that certain willow catkins, kept in a sealed box for several weeks, give off the most dreadful odour of dead fish, a fact which I had filed away for future use.

'Through here,' Mrs. Harewood said, ducking to keep her head from banging on an exceptionally low beam. 'Mind your head and watch your step.'

Her studio was a glorious place. Clear north light flooded in through the angled transom windows overhead, making it seem like a room suddenly stumbled upon in a forest glade.

A large wooden easel stood in the light, and on it was a half-finished portrait of Flossie, the sister of Feely's friend Sheila Foster. Flossie was sitting in a large upholstered chair, one leg curled under her, petting an enormous white Persian cat that nestled in her lap. The cat, at least, looked almost human.

Actually, Flossie didn't look that bad, either. She was not my favorite living person, but I didn't hold that against her. The portrait captured perfectly, in a way that even a camera can't, her air of highly polished dopiness.

'Well, what do you think?'

I looked around at the tubes of paints, the daubed rags, and the profusion of camel-hair brushes that jutted up all around me from tins, glasses, and bottles like reeds in a December marsh.

'It's a very nice studio,' I said. 'Is that what you wanted to show me?'

I pointed a finger at Flossie's portrait.

'Good heavens, no!' she said.

I had not noticed it before but at the far end of the studio, away from the windows, were two shadowy corners in which perhaps a dozen un-framed paintings were leaning with their faces against the wall, their paper-sealed backsides towards the room.

Vanetta (by now I was thinking of her as 'Van-etta,' rather than 'Mrs. Harewood') bent over them, shifting each one as if she were riffling through the record cards in a giant index file.

'Ah! Here it is,' she said at last, pulling a large canvas from among the others.

Keeping its back towards me, she carried the painting to the easel. After shifting Flossie to a nearby wooden chair, she turned it round and lifted it into place.

She stepped back without a word, giving me an unobstructed view of the portrait.

My heart stopped.

It was Harriet.

FOURTEEN

Harriet. My mother.

She is sitting on the window box of the drawing room at Buckshaw. At her right hand, my sister Ophelia, aged about seven, plays with a cat's cradle of red wool, its strands entangling her fingers like slender scarlet snakes. To Harriet's left, my other sister, Daphne, although she is too young to read, uses a forefinger to mark her place in a large book: *Grimm's Fairy Tales*.

Harriet gazes tenderly down, a slight smile on her lips, like a Madonna, at the white bundle which she holds supported in the crook of her left arm: a child – a baby dressed in a white, trailing garment of elaborate and frothy lace – could it be a baptismal gown?

I want to look at the mother but my eyes are

drawn repeatedly back to the child.

It is, of course, me.

'Ten years ago,' Vanetta was saying, 'I went to Buckshaw on a winter day.'

She was now standing behind me.

'How well I remember it. There had been a killing frost overnight. Everything was covered with ice. I rang up your mother and suggested that we leave it until another day, but she wouldn't hear of it. She was going away, she said, and she wanted the portrait as a gift for your father. She meant to give it to him as a surprise when she returned.'

My head was spinning.

'Of course, she never did,' she added softly, 'and frankly I've not since had the heart to hand it over to him, the poor man. He grieves so.'

Grieves? Although I had never thought about it in precisely this way, it was true. Father did grieve, but he did so in private, and mostly in silence.

'The painting, I suppose, belongs to him, since your mother paid me for it in advance. She was a very trusting person.'

Was she? I wanted to say. *I wouldn't know. I didn't know her as well as you did.*

Suddenly, I needed to get out of this place – to be outdoors again where I could breathe my own breath.

'I think you'd better keep it, Mrs. Harewood – at least for now. I wouldn't want to upset Father.'

Hold on! I thought. My whole life was given over to upsetting Father – or at least to going against his wishes. Why now was I filled with a sudden desire to comfort him, and to have him hug me?

Not that I would, of course, because in real life

we de Luces don't do that sort of thing.

But still, some unknowable part of the universe had changed, as if one of the four great turtles that are said to support the world on their backs had suddenly shifted its weight from one foot to another.

'I have to go now,' I said, backing, for some reason, towards the door. 'I'm sorry to hear about Brookie. I know he had lots of friends in Bishop's Lacey.'

Actually, I knew no such thing! Why was I saying this? It was as if my mouth were possessed, and I had no way of stopping its flow of words.

All I really knew about Brookie Harewood was that he was a poacher and a layabout – and that I had surprised him in his midnight prowling. That and the fact that he had claimed to have seen the Grey Lady of Buckshaw.

'Good-bye, then,' I said. As I stepped into the hallway, Ursula turned rapidly away and scuttled out of sight with a wicker basket in her hand. But not so quickly that I missed the look of pure hatred that she shot me.

As I bicycled westward towards Bishop's Lacey, I thought of what I had seen. I'd gone to Maiden Fenwick in search of clues to the behaviour of Brookie Harewood – surely it was he who had attacked Fenella Faa in the Palings, for who else could have been abroad at Buckshaw that night? But instead, I had come away with a new image of Harriet, my mother: an image that was not as happy as it might have been.

Why, for instance, did it gnaw at my heart so

187

much to see Feely and Daffy, like two contented slugs, secure and basking in her glow, while I lay helpless, wrapped up like a little mummy in white cloth; of no more interest than a bundle from the butcher?

Had Harriet loved me? My sisters were forever claiming that she did not: that, in fact, she despised me; that she had fallen into a deep depression after I was born – a depression that had, perhaps, resulted in her death.

And yet, in the painting, which must have been made just before she set out on her final journey, there was not a trace of unhappiness. Harriet's eyes had been upon *me* and the look on her face had shown, if anything, a trace of amusement.

Something about the portrait nagged at my mind: some half-forgotten thing that had tried to surface as I stood staring at the easel in Vanetta Harewood's studio. But what was it?

Hard as I tried, I couldn't think of it.

Relax, Flavia, I thought. *Calm down. Think about something else.*

I had long ago discovered that when a word or formula refused to come to mind, the best thing for it was to think of something else: tigers, for instance, or oatmeal. Then, when the fugitive word was least expecting it, I would suddenly turn the full blaze of my attention back onto it, catching the culprit in the beam of my mental torch before it could sneak off again into the darkness.

'Thought-stalking,' I called the technique, and I was proud of myself for having invented it.

I let my mind drift away towards tigers, and the first one that came to mind was the tiger in

188

William Blake's poem: the one that burned away with fearful symmetry in the forests of the night.

Once, when I was younger, Daffy had driven me into hysterics by wrapping herself in the tiger-skin rug from Buckshaw's firearm museum and creeping into my bedroom in the middle of the night, while reciting the poem in a deep and fearsome snarl: *'Tyger, tyger, burning bright...'.*

She had never forgiven me for throwing my alarm clock. She still had the scar on her chin.

And now I thought of porridge: in the winter, great steaming ladles of the stuff, grey, like lava dished from a volcano on the moon. Mrs. Mullet, under orders from Father–

Mrs. Mullet! Of course!

It was something she'd told me when I'd asked about Brookie Harewood. 'His mother's that woman as paints over in Maiden Fenwick.

'P'raps she'll even paint you in your turn,' Mrs. M had added. *'In your turn.'*

Which meant that Mrs. M knew about the portrait of Harriet! She must have been in on the secret sittings.

'Tiger!' I shouted. 'Tye-ger!'

My words echoed back from the hedgerows on either side of the narrow lane. Something ahead of me bolted for cover.

An animal, perhaps? A deer? No, not an animal – a human.

It was Porcelain. I was sure of it. She was still wearing Fenella's black crepe dress.

I brought Gladys to a skidding stop.

'Porcelain?' I called. 'Is that you?'

There was no answer.

189

'Porcelain? It's me, Flavia.'

What a foolish thing to say. Porcelain had hidden in the hedgerow *because* it was me. But why?

Although I couldn't see her, she was probably close enough to touch. I could feel her eyes upon me.

'Porcelain? What is it? What's the matter?'

The eerie silence lengthened. It was like one of those parlour séances when you're waiting for the dial on the Ouija board to move.

'All right,' I said at last, 'take your time. I'm sitting down and I'm not moving until you come out.'

There was another long wait, and then the bushes rustled and Porcelain stepped out into the lane. The look on her face suggested that she was on her way to the guillotine.

'What's the matter?' I asked. 'What's happened?'

As I took a step towards her, she moved away, keeping a safe distance between us.

'The police took me to see Fenella,' she said shakily. 'In the hospital.'

Oh, no! I thought. *She's died of her injuries. Let it not be true.*

'I'm sorry,' I said, taking another step. Porcelain fell back, raising her hands as if to fend me off.

'Sorry?' she said in a strange voice. 'What for? No!– Stay where you are!'

'Sorry for whatever's happened to Fenella. I did everything I could to help her.'

'For God's sake, Flavia,' Porcelain screamed, 'stop it! You bloody well tried to kill her, and you know you did. And now you want to kill me!'

Her words hit me like a body blow, knocking the

wind completely out of me. I couldn't breathe; my head was spinning, my mind was spinning, and there was a sound in my head like a swarm of locusts.

'I–'

But it was no good – I couldn't speak.

'Fenella told me all about it. You and your family have hated us for years. Your father drove Fenella and Johnny Faa off your estate and that's why Johnny died. You took her back to their old camping place so that you could finish the job, and you very nearly did, didn't you?'

'That's insane,' I managed. 'Why would I want to–'

'You were the only one that knew she was camped there.'

'Look, Porcelain,' I said. 'I know you're upset. I understand that. But if I wanted to kill Fenella, why would I bother going for Dr. Darby? Wouldn't I simply let her die?'

'I – I don't know. You're confusing me now. Maybe you wanted an excuse – just in case you hadn't killed her.'

'If I'd wanted to kill her, I'd have killed her,' I said, exasperated. 'I'd have kept at it until I was finished. I wouldn't have botched it. Do you understand?'

Her eyes widened, but I could see that I had made my point.

'And as for being the only one around that night, what about Brookie Harewood? He was roaming around at Buckshaw – I even caught him in our drawing room. Do you think I killed him, too? Do you think someone who weighs less

191

than five stone murdered Brookie – who probably weighs thirteen – and hung him up like a bit of washing from Poseidon's trident?'

'Well...'

'Oh, come off it, Porcelain! I don't think Fenella saw her attacker. If she had, she wouldn't have blamed it on me. She's badly injured and she's confused. She's letting her mind fill in the blanks.'

She stood there in the lane staring at me as if I were the cobra in a snake charmer's basket, and had suddenly begun to speak.

'Come on,' I said, getting Gladys ready to go. 'Hop on. We'll go back to Buckshaw and find some grub.'

'No,' she said. 'I'm going back to the caravan.'

'It isn't safe,' I said. Perhaps by presenting the nasty facts without varnish I could change her mind. 'Whoever bashed in Fenella's skull and stuck a lobster pick up Brookie's nostril is still wandering about. Come on.'

'No,' she said. 'I told you, I'm going back to the caravan.'

'Why? Are you afraid of me?'

Her answer came a little too quickly for my liking.

'Yes,' she said. 'I am.'

'All right, then,' I said softly. 'Be a fool. See if I care.'

I put a foot on a pedal and prepared to push off.

'Flavia–'

I turned and looked at her over my shoulder.

'I told Inspector Hewitt what Fenella said.'

Wonderful, I thought. *Just bloody wonderful.*

192

Someone once said that music has charms to soothe a savage breast – or was it 'beast'? Daffy would know for sure, but since I wasn't speaking to her, I could hardly ask.

But for me, music wasn't half as relaxing as revenge. To my way of thinking, the settling of scores has a calming effect upon the mind that beats music by a Welsh mile. The encounter with Porcelain had left me breathing noisily through my nose like a boar at bay and I needed time to simmer down.

Stepping through the door into my laboratory was like gaining sanctuary in a quiet church: the rows of bottled chemicals were my stained-glass windows, the chemical bench my altar. Chemistry has more gods than Mount Olympus, and here in my solitude I could pray in peace to the greatest of them: Joseph Louis Gay-Lussac (who, when he found a young assistant in a linen draper's shop surreptitiously reading a chemistry text which she kept hidden under the counter, promptly dumped his fiancée and married the girl); William Perkin (who had found a way of making purple dye for the robes of emperors without using the spit of molluscs); and Carl Wilhelm Scheele, who probably discovered oxygen, and – more thrilling even than that – hydrogen cyanide, my personal pick as the last word in poisons.

I began by washing my hands. I always did this in a ceremonial way, but today they needed to be dry.

I had brought with me to the laboratory an object that was normally strapped to Gladys's seat. Gladys had come fully equipped from the factory with a tyre repair kit, and it was this tin box with the name of Messrs. Dunlop on the lid that I now deposited on my workbench.

But first I closed my eyes and focused on the object of my attentions: my beloved sister, Ophelia Gertrude de Luce, whose mission in life is to revive the Spanish Inquisition with me as the sole victim. With Daffy's connivance, her recent torture of me in the cellars had been the last straw. And now the dreadful clock of revenge was about to strike!

Feely's great weakness was the mirror: when it came to vanity, my sister made Becky Sharp look like one of the Sisters of the Holy Humility of Mary – an order with which she was forever comparing me (unfavourably, I might add).

She was capable of examining herself for hours in the looking glass, tossing her hair, baring her teeth, toying with her pimples, and pulling down the outer corners of her upper eyelids to encourage them to droop aristocratically like Father's.

Even in church and already primped to the nines, Feely would consult a little mirror that she kept hidden inside *Hymns Ancient and Modern* so that she could keep an eye on her complexion while pretending to refresh her memory with the words to Hymn 573: *All Things Bright and Beautiful.*

She was also a religious snob. To Feely, the morning church service was a drama, and she its pious star. She was always off like a shot to be the first at the communion rail, so that in returning to our pew, she would be seen with her humble eyes downcast, her long white fingers cupped at her waist, by the maximum number of churchgoers.

These were the facts that had sifted through my mind as I planned my next move, and now the time had come.

With the little white Bible Mrs. Mullet had given me on my confirmation day in one hand and the tyre kit in the other, I headed for Feely's bedroom.

This was not as difficult as it might seem. By following a maze of dusty, darkened hallways, and keeping to the upper floor, I was able to make my way from Buckshaw's east wing towards the west, passing on my way a number of abandoned bedrooms that had not been used, since Queen Victoria had declined to visit in the latter years of her reign. She had remarked to her private secretary, Sir Henry Ponsonby, that she 'could not possibly find enough breath in such a wee dwelling.'

Now, behind their panelled doors, these rooms were like furniture morgues, inhabited only by sheet-covered bedsteads, dressers, and chairs which, because of the dryness of their bones, had been known sometimes to give off alarming cracking noises in the night.

All was quiet now, though, as I passed the last of these abandoned chambers, and arrived at the door that opened into the west wing. I put my ear to the green baize cloth, but all was silent on the other side. I opened the door a crack and peered through it into the hallway.

Again nothing. The place was like a tomb.

I smiled as the strains of Bach's *Jesu, Joy of Man's Desiring* came drifting up the west staircase: Feely was busy at her practice in the drawing room, and I knew that my work would not be disturbed.

I stepped into her bedroom and closed the door.

It was a room not totally unknown to me, since I often came here to filch chocolates and to have a good old rifle through her drawers. In design, it was much like my own: a great old barn of a place with high ceilings and tall windows; a place that seemed better suited to the parking of an aeroplane than the parking of one's carcass for a good night's sleep.

The greatest difference between this room and my own was that Feely's did not have damp paper hanging in bags from the walls and ceiling: bags that during heavy rainstorms would fill up with cold, dripping water that turned my mattress into a soggy swamp. On those occasions, I would be forced to abandon my bed and spend the night, wrapped in my dressing gown, in a mousy-smelling wing chair that stood in the one dry corner of the room.

Feely's bedroom, by contrast, was like something out of the cinema. The walls were covered with a delicate floral pattern (moss roses, I think) and the tall windows were bracketed with yards of lace.

A four-poster with embroidered curtains was dwarfed by the room, and stood almost unnoticed in a corner.

To the left of the windows, in pride of place, was a particularly fine Queen Anne dresser, whose curved legs were as slender and delicate as those of the ballet dancers in the paintings of Degas. Above it, on the wall, was fastened a monstrous dark-framed looking glass, too large by far for the dainty legs that stood beneath. The effect was rather Humpty Dumpty-ish: like an obscenely oversized head on a body with leprechaun legs.

I used Feely's hairbrush to prop open the Bible on the dresser top. From the tyre repair kit, I extracted a tin of magnesium silicate hydroxide, better known as French chalk. The stuff was meant to keep a freshly patched inner tube from sticking to the inside of the rubber tire, but this was not the application I had in mind.

I dipped one of Feely's camel-hair makeup brushes into the French chalk and, with one last glance at the Bible for reference, wrote a short message across the mirror's surface in bold letters: *Deuteronomy 28:27*.

That done, I pulled a handkerchief from my pocket and gently dusted away the words that I had written. I blew the excess chalk from where it had fallen on the dresser top, and wiped up the few traces that had drifted to the floor.

It was done! The rest of my plan was guaranteed.

It would unfold itself through the inexorable laws of chemistry, without my having to lift a finger.

When Feely next parked herself in front of the mirror and leaned in for a closer look at her ugly hide, the moisture of her warm breath would make visible the words that I had written on the glass. Their message would spring boldly into view:

Deuteronomy 28:27

Feely would be terror-stricken. She would run to look up the passage in the Bible. Actually, she might not: since it had to do with personal grooming, she might already have the verse off by heart. But if she did have to search it out, this is what she would find:

The LORD shall smite thee with the boils of Egypt, and with the emerods, and with the scurvy, and with the itch, whereof thou canst not be healed.

As if the boils weren't bad enough, 'emerods' were haemorrhoids, the perfect added touch, I thought.

And if I knew my sister, she wouldn't be able to resist reading the rest of the verse:

The LORD shall smite thee with madness, and with blindness, and with astonishment of heart; and thou shalt grope at noonday, as the blind gropeth in darkness, and thou shalt not prosper in thy ways: and thou shalt be only oppressed and spoiled alway, and there shall be none to save thee.

Feely would toss up her marmalade!

Having seen the message materialise before her very eyes, she'd believe it to be a telegram from God, and – by the Old Harry! – would *she* be sorry!

I could see it now: She'd fling herself down and grovel on the carpet, begging forgiveness for the rotten way she'd treated her little sister.

Later, she would appear at the dinner table, haunted, haggard, and shocked into silence.

I chortled as I skipped down the staircase. I could barely wait.

At the bottom, in the foyer, stood Inspector Hewitt.

198

FIFTEEN

The Inspector did not look happy.

Dogger, who had only just let him in, closed the door silently, and vanished in the way he does.

'You should think about opening an auxiliary police station here at Buckshaw,' I said affably, trying to cheer him up. 'It would certainly save on petrol.'

The Inspector was not amused.

'Let's have a chat,' he said, and I had the impression that he was not entirely attempting to put me at my ease.

'Of course. I am at your disposal.'

I was capable of being gracious when I felt like it.

'About your discovery at the fountain–' he began.

'Brookie Harewood, you mean? Yes, that was awful, wasn't it.'

The Inspector seemed startled.

Damn! Ten seconds into the game and I had already made a serious misstep.

'You know him, then?'

'Oh, everyone knows Brookie,' I said, recovering quickly. 'He's one of the village characters. At least – he was.

'Someone *you* knew?'

'I've seen him about. Here and there, you know. In the village. That sort of thing.'

I was sewing an invisible seam between truth and untruth, a skill of which I was especially proud. One of the tricks of the trade when doing this is to volunteer fresh information before your questioner has time to ask another. So I went on:

'I had returned to the Palings, you see, because I was worried about Gry. Gry is the name of the Gypsy woman's horse. I wanted to make sure he had food.'

This was not entirely true: Gry could have survived for weeks by nibbling the grass in the glade, but noble motives can never be questioned.

'Very commendable,' Inspector Hewitt said. 'I had asked Constable Linnet to lay on some hay.'

I had a quick vision of PC Linnet producing an egg in the straw, but I banished it from my mind to keep from grinning.

'Yes, I noticed that when I got there,' I said. 'And of course, I met Porcelain. She told me you had tracked her down in London.'

As I spoke, the Inspector produced a notebook, flipped it open, and began to write. I'd better watch my step.

'I didn't think she'd be safe in the caravan. Not with whoever attacked her gram still wandering about. I insisted she come back with me to Buckshaw, and it was on our way here that we came across the body.'

I didn't say 'Brookie's body' because I didn't want to seem too chummy with him, which could only lead to more questions about our prior acquaintance.

'What time was that?'

'Oh, let me see – you were here when I got up,

just around breakfast time – that was at about nine-thirty, I should say.'

The Inspector riffled back several pages in his notebook and nodded. I was on the right track.

'After that, Sergeant Graves came straightaway to take my fingerprints – ten-thirty – perhaps eleven?

'At any rate,' I went on, 'Constable Linnet should be able to tell you what time I called to report it, which couldn't have been much more than ten or fifteen minutes after we discovered the body in the fountain.'

I was stalling – treading water, delaying the time when he would inevitably ask about my so-called assault on Fenella. I decided to leap into the breach.

'Porcelain thinks I attacked her gram,' I said bluntly.

Inspector Hewitt nodded. 'Mrs. Faa is very disoriented. It often happens with injuries to the head. I thought I'd made that quite clear to the granddaughter, but perhaps I'd best have another word–'

'No!' I said. 'Don't do that. It doesn't matter.'

The Inspector looked at me sharply, then made another scribble in his notebook.

'Are you putting another *P* beside my name?'

It was a saucy question, and I was sorry as soon as I asked it. Once, during an earlier investigation, I had seen him print a capital *P* beside my name in his notebook. Maddeningly, he had refused to tell me what it meant.

'It's not polite to ask,' he said with a slight smile. 'One must never ask a policeman his secrets.'

'Why not?'

'For the same reason I don't ask you yours.'

How I adored this man! Here we were, the two of us, engaged in a mental game of chess in which both of us knew that one of us was cheating.

At the risk of repetition, how I adored this man!

And that had been the end of it. He had asked me a few more questions: whether I had seen anyone else about, whether I had heard the sound of a motor vehicle, and so forth. And then he had gone.

At one point I had wanted to tell him more, just to prolong the pleasure of his company. He'd have been thrilled to hear about how I had caught Brookie prowling about our drawing room, for instance, to say nothing about my visits to Miss Mountjoy and to Brookie's digs. I might even have confided in him what I'd found at Vanetta Harewood's house in Malden Fenwick.

But I hadn't.

As I stood musing in the foyer, the slight squeak of a shoe on tile caught my attention, and I looked up to find Feely staring down at me from the first-floor landing. She'd been there all along!

'Little Miss Helpful,' she sneered. 'You think you're so clever.'

I could tell by her attitude that she had not yet consulted her bedroom mirror.

'One tries to be of assistance,' I said, casually dusting a few stray smudges of French chalk from my dress.

'You think he likes you, don't you? You think a lot of people do – but they don't. No one likes you.

There may be a few who pretend to, but they don't – not really. It's such a pity you can't see that.'

Amplified by the panelling of the foyer, her voice came echoing all the way down from among the cherub-painted panels of the ceiling. I felt as if I were the prisoner at the bar, and she my accuser.

As always when one of my sisters turned on me, I felt a strange welling in my chest, as if some primeval swamp creature were trying to crawl out of my insides. It was a feeling I could never understand, something that lay beyond reason. What had I ever done to make them detest me so?

'Why don't you go torture Bach?' I flung back at her, but my heart was not really in it.

It always surprises me after a family row to find that the world outdoors has remained the same. While the passions and feelings that accumulate like noxious gases inside a house seem to condense and cling to the walls and ceilings like old smoke, the out-of-doors is different. The landscape seems incapable of accumulating human radiation. Perhaps the wind blows anger away.

I thought about this as I trudged towards the Trafalgar Lawn. If Porcelain chose to go on believing that I was the monster who had bashed in her grandmother's skull with – with what?

When I had found Fenella lying on the floor of the caravan, the inside of the wagon had been, except for the blood, as neat as a pin: no bloody weapon flung aside by her attacker: no stick, no stone, no poker. Which seemed odd.

Unless the weapon had some value, why would the culprit choose to carry it away?

Or had it been ditched? I'd seen nothing to suggest that it had.

Surely the police would have gone over the Palings with a microscope in search of a weapon. But had they found one?

I paused for a moment to stare up at the Poseidon fountain. Old Neptune, as the Romans called him, all muscles and tummy, was gazing unconcernedly off into the distance, like someone who has broken wind at a banquet and is trying to pretend it wasn't him.

His trident was still held up like a sceptre (he was, after all, the King of the Sea) and his fishnets lay in a tangle at his feet. There wasn't a trace of Brookie Harewood. It was hard to believe that, just hours ago, Brookie had dangled dead here – his body a gruesome addition to the sculpture.

But why? Why would his killer go to the trouble of hoisting a corpse into such a difficult position? Could it be a message – some bizarre form of the naval signal flag, for instance?

What little I knew about Poseidon had been gained from *Bullfinch's Mythology*, a copy of which was in the library at Buckshaw. It was one of Daffy's favourite books, but since there was nothing in it about chemistry or poisons, it didn't really interest me.

Poseidon was said to rule the waters, so it was easy enough to see why he was chosen to adorn a fountain. The only other waters within spitting distance of this particular Poseidon were the river Efon at the Palings and Buckshaw's ornamental lake.

Brookie had been hung from the trident much

like the way a shrike, or larder bird, impales a songbird on a thorn for later use – although it seemed unlikely, I thought, that Brookie's killer planned to eat him later.

Was it a warning, then? And if so, to whom?

I needed to have a few hours alone with my notebook, but now was not the time. There was Porcelain to deal with.

I wasn't finished with Porcelain. As a token of goodwill, I would not be put off by her childish behaviour – nor would I take offense. I would forgive her whether she liked it or not.

I can't claim that Gry was happy to see me arriving at the Palings, although he did look up for a moment from his grazing. A fresh bale of hay strewn nearby told me that Constable Linnet was on the job, but Gry seemed to prefer the green salad of weeds that grew along the river's edge.

'Hello!' I shouted to the caravan, but there was no answer. The delicate instrument that was the back of my neck told me, too, that the glade was deserted.

I didn't remember Porcelain locking the caravan when we left together, but it was locked now. Either she had returned and found the key, or somebody else had done so.

But someone had been here and – if I could believe my nose – quite recently.

Warmed by the sun, the wooden door was releasing an odour that did not belong here. As I would do in my laboratory with a chemical, I used my cupped fingers to scoop air towards my nostrils.

No doubt about it: a definite odour lingered

205

near the door of the caravan – an odour that most certainly had not been on the outside of the caravan before: the smell of fish.

The smell of the sea.

SIXTEEN

'You're in my light,' Daffy said.

I had intentionally planted myself between her book and the window.

It was not going to be easy to ask my sister for assistance. I took a deep breath.

'I need some help.'

'Poor Flavia!'

'Please, Daff,' I said, despising myself for begging. 'It's about that man whose body I found at the fountain.'

Daffy threw down her book in exasperation. 'Why drag me into your sordid little games? You know perfectly well how much they upset me.'

Upset her? Daff? Games?

'I thought you loved crime!' I said, pointing to her book. It was a collection of G.K. Chesterton's Father Brown mysteries.

'I do,' she said, 'but not in real life. The antics you get up to turn my stomach.'

This was news to me. I'd file it away for later use.

'And Father's almost as bad,' she added. 'Do you know what he said at breakfast yesterday, before you came down? "Flavia's found another

206

body." Almost as if he was proud of you.'

Father said that? I could hardly believe it.

The revelations were coming thick and fast! I should have thought of talking to Daffy sooner.

'It's true,' I said. 'I did. But I'll spare you the details.'

'Thank you,' Daffy said quietly, and I thought she might actually have meant it.

'Poseidon,' I said, taking advantage of the partial thaw. 'What do you know about Poseidon?'

This was throwing down the gauntlet. Daffy knew everything about everything, and I knew she couldn't resist showing off her uncanny power of recall.

'Poseidon? He was a cad,' she said. 'A bully and a cad. He was also a womaniser.'

'How can a god be a cad?'

Daffy ignored my question. 'He was what we would call nowadays the patron saint of sailors, and with jolly good reason.'

'Which means?'

'That he was no better than he ought to be. Now run along.'

Ordinarily I might have taken umbrage at being dismissed so high-handedly (I love that word, 'umbrage' – it's in *David Copperfield*, where David's aunt, Betsey Trotwood, takes umbrage at his being born), but I didn't – instead, I felt rather an odd sense of gratitude towards my sister.

'Thanks, Daff!' I said. 'I knew I could count on you.'

This was shovelling it on, but I was honestly pleased. And so, I think, was Daffy. As she picked up her book, I saw that the corners of her mouth were turned up by about the thickness of one of its pages.

I was half expecting to find Porcelain in my room, but of course she was gone. I had almost forgotten that she'd accused me of attempted murder.

I'd begin with her.

PORCELAIN (I wrote in my notebook) – *Can't possibly be her grandmother's attacker since she was in London at the time. Or was she? I have only her word for it. But why did she feel compelled to wash out her clothing?*

BROOKIE HAREWOOD – *Was likely killed by the same person who attacked Fenella. Or was he? Did Brookie attack Fenella? He was on the scene at the time.*

VANETTA HAREWOOD – *Why would she kill her own son? She paid him to keep away from her.*

URSULA ?– *I don't know her surname. She mucks about with bleaches and willow branches, and Vanetta Harewood said she was fiercely protective. Motive?*

COLIN PROUT – *was bullied by Brookie, but what could Colin have had against Fenella?*

MRS BULL – *threatened Fenella with an axe – claimed she'd been seen in the neighbourhood when the Bull baby vanished years ago.*

HILDA MUIR – *whoever she may be. Fenella had*

208

mentioned her name twice: once when we saw the Bull child perched in a tree in the Gully, and again when I cut the elder branches in the Palings. 'Now we are all dead!' Fenella had cried. Was Hilda Muir her attacker?

MISS MOUNTJOY – *was Brookie's landlady. But why would she want to kill him? The theft of an antique plate seems hardly a sufficient reason.*

I drew a line and under it wrote:

FAMILY

FATHER – *very unlikely (although he once drove Fenella and Johnny Faa off the Buckshaw estate).*

FEELY, DAFFY, DOGGER, and MRS MULLET – *no motive for either crime.*

But wait! What about that mysterious person whose fortune Fenella had told at the church fête? What was it she had said about her?

'*A regular thundercloud, she was.*' I could almost hear her voice. '*Told her there was something buried in her past ... told her it wanted digging out ... wanted setting right.*'

Had Fenella seen something in the crystal ball that had sealed her fate? Although I remembered that Daffy scoffed at fortune-tellers ('Mountebanks,' she called them), not everyone shared her opinion. Hadn't Porcelain, for instance, claimed that her own mother, Lunita, had such great gifts of second sight that the War Office had funded her crystal-gazing?

209

If Lunita had actually possessed such great powers, it wasn't too great a stretch of the imagination to guess that she had inherited them from Fenella, her mother.

But wait!

If Fenella and Lunita both had the power of second sight, would it be unreasonable to assume that Porcelain, too, might be able to see beyond the present?

Was that the real reason she was afraid of me? She had admitted that she was.

Could it be that Porcelain saw things in my past that I could not see myself?

Or was it that she could see into my future?

Too many questions and not enough facts.

My shoulders were seized by a shudder, but I shook it off and went on with my notes.

THE PALINGS

There is a feeling about this place that cannot be easily explained. To my ancestor, Lucius de Luce, it must have seemed like the Great Flood when the river was diverted to form the ornamental lake. Before that time, it had been no more than a quiet, isolated grove where Nicodemus Flitch and the Hobblers came for baptisms and beanfests. Later, the Gypsies had adopted it as a stopping-place in their travels. Harriet had encouraged this but after her death, Father had forbidden it. Why?

Another solid line, under which I wrote:

FISH

(1) When I surprised Brookie in the drawing room at Buckshaw, besides alcohol, he (or his creel) reeked of fish.

(2) There was also a fishy smell in the caravan when I found Fenella beaten on the floor. By the time I discovered Porcelain sleeping there the next morning this odour had vanished – but it had been there again today, this time on the outside of the caravan.
(Q): Can odours come and go? Like actors in a play?

(3) Miss Mountjoy smelled of fish, too – cod-liver oil, judging by the vast quantities of the stuff that she keeps about Willow Villa.

(4) Brookie was killed (I believe) by a lobster pick shoved up his nostril and into his brain. A lobster pick from Buckshaw. (Note: Lobster is not a fish, but a crustacean – but still…) His body was left hanging on a statue of Poseidon: the god of the sea.

(5) When we found him hanging, Brookie's face was fish-belly white – not that that means anything other than that he had been dangling from the fountain for quite a long time. Perhaps all night. Surely whoever had done this thing had done it during the hours of darkness, when there was little chance of being seen.

There are probably people abroad on the earth at this very moment who would be tempted to joke 'There's something fishy here.'

But I am not one of them.

211

As any chemist worth her calcium chloride knows, it's not just fish that smell fishy. Offhand, I could think of several substances that gave off the smell of deceased mackerel, among them propylamine.

Propylamine (which had been discovered by the great French chemist Jean-Baptiste Dumas) is the third of the series of alcohol radicals – which might sound like boring stuff indeed, until you consider this: when you take one of the alcohols and heat it with ammonia, a remarkable transformation takes place. It's like a game of atomic musical chairs in which the hydrogen that helps form the ammonia has one or more of its chairs (atoms, actually) taken by the radicals of the alcohol. Depending upon when and where the music stops, a number of new products, called amines, may be formed.

With a bit of patience and a Bunsen burner, some truly foul odours can be generated in the laboratory. In 1889, for instance, the entire city of Freiburg, in Germany, had to be evacuated when chemists let a bit of thioacetone escape. It was said that people even miles away were sickened by the odour, and that horses fainted in the streets.

How I wish I had been there to see it!

While other substances, such as the lower aliphatic acids, can be easily manipulated to produce every smell from rancid butter to a sweaty horse, or from a rotten drain to a goat's rugger boots, it is the lower amines – those ragged children of ammonia – that have a most unique and interesting characteristic: as I have said, they smell like rotten fish.

212

In fact, propylamine and trimethylamine could, without exaggeration, be given the title 'The Princes of Pong,' and I knew this for a fact.

Because she has given us so many ways of producing these smelly marvels, I know that Mother Nature loves a good stink as much as I do. I thought fondly of the time I had extracted trimethylamine (for another harmless Girl Guide prank) by distilling it with soda from a full picnic basket of Stinking Goosefoot *(Chenopodium olidum),* an evil-smelling weed that grew in profusion on the Trafalgar Lawn.

Which brought me back to Brookie Harewood.

One thing I was quite certain of was this: that the riddle of Brookie's death would be solved not by cameras, notebooks, and measuring tapes at the Poseidon fountain, but rather in the chemical laboratory.

And I was just the one to do it.

I was still thinking about riddles as I slid down the banister and landed in the foyer. Nursery rhyme riddles had been as much a part of my younger years as they had anyone else's.

Thirty white horses upon a red hill
Now they tramp, now they champ
Now they stand still.

'Teeth!' I would shout, because Daffy had cheated and whispered the answer in my ear.

That, of course, was in the days before my sisters began to dislike me.

Later came the darker verses:

213

One's joy, two's grief,
Three's marriage; four's a death.

The answer was 'magpies.' We had seen four of these birds land on the roof while having a picnic on the lawn, and my sisters had made me memorise the lines before they would allow me to dig into my dish of strawberries.

I didn't yet know what death was, but I knew that their verses gave me nightmares. I suppose it was these little rhymes, learned at an early age, that taught me to be good at puzzles. I've recently come to the conclusion that the nursery rhyme riddle is the most basic form of the detective story. It's a mystery stripped of all but the essential facts. Take this one, for instance:

As I was going to St. Ives
I met a man with seven wives.
Each wife had seven sacks
Each sack had seven cats
Each cat had seven kits.
Kits, cats, sacks, wives
How many were going to St. Ives?

The usual answer, of course, is 'one.' But when you stop to think about it, there's much more to it than that. If, for instance, the teller of the rhyme happened to be overtaking the man with the travelling menagerie, the actual number – including sacks – would be almost three thousand!

It all depends upon how you look at things.

Mrs. Mullet was having her tea at the window. I

214

helped myself to a digestive biscuit.

'The Hobblers,' I said, diving in with both feet. 'You said they'd have my blood for sausages. Why?'

'You keep clear o' them lot, miss, like I told you.'

'I thought they were extinct?'

'They smells just the same as everybody else. That's why you don't reck'nise 'em till somebody points 'em out.'

'But how can I keep clear of them if I don't know who they are?'

Mrs. M lowered her voice and looked over both shoulders. 'That Mountjoy woman, for one. God knows what goes on in 'er kitchen.'

'Tilda Mountjoy? At Willow Villa?'

I could hardly believe my good fortune!

'The very one. Why, it was no more than this morning I saw her in the Gully – headed for the Palings, she was, just as bold as brass. They still go there to do things with the water – poison it, for all I know.'

'But wait,' I said. 'Miss Mountjoy can't be a Hobbler – she goes to St. Tancred's.'

'To spy, most likely!' Mrs. Mullet snorted. 'She told my friend Mrs. Waller it was on account of the organ. The 'Obblers got no organs, you know – don't 'old by 'em. "I do love the sound of a good organ well played," she told Mrs. Waller, who told it to me. Tilda Mountjoy's an 'Obbler born and bred, as was 'er parents before 'er. It's in the blood. Don't matter whose collection plate she puts 'er sixpences in, she's an 'Obbler from snoot to shoes, believe you me.'

'You saw her in the Gully?' I asked, making mental notes like mad.

'With my own eyes. Since that Mrs. Ingleby come into her troubles I've been havin' to stretch my legs for eggs. All the way out to Rawlings, now, though I must say they're better yolks than Ingleby's. It's all in the grit, you know – or is it the shells? 'Course once I'm all the way out there, it makes no sense to go traipsin' all the way back round, does it? So it's into the Gully I go, eggs and all, and take a shortcut through the Palings. That's when I seen her, just by Bull's bonfires, she was – no more'n a stone's throw ahead of me.'

'Did she speak to you?'

'Ho! Fat chance of that, my girl. As soon as I seen who it was I fell back and sat on a bank and took my shoe off. Pretended I'd got a stone in it.'

Obviously, Mrs. M had been walking in the same direction as Miss Mountjoy, and was about to overtake her – just like the person who was walking to St. Ives.

'Good for you!' I said, clapping my hands together with excitement and shaking my head in wonder. 'What a super idea.'

'Don't say "super," dear. You know the Colonel doesn't like it.'

I made the motion of pulling a zipper across my lips.

'Oon ewdge?'

'Sorry, dear. I don't know what you're saying.'

I unfastened the zipper.

'Who else? The other Hobblers, I mean.'

'Well, I really shouldn't say, but that Reggie Pettibone, for one. His wife, too. Reg'lar stuffed hat, she thinks she is, at the Women's Institute, all Looey the Nineteenth, an' that.'

'Her husband owns the antiques shop?'

Mrs. Mullet nodded her head gloomily, and I knew she was reliving the loss of her Army and Navy table.

'Thank you, Mrs. M,' I said. 'I'm thinking of writing a paper on the history of Buckshaw. I shall mention you in the footnotes.'

Mrs. Mullet primped her hair with a forefinger as I walked to the kitchen door.

'You stay away from them lot, mind.'

SEVENTEEN

Like several of the shops in Bishop's Lacey, Pettibone's had a Georgian front with a small painted door squeezed in between a pair of many-paned bow windows.

I bicycled slowly past the place, then dismounted and strolled casually towards the shop, as if I had only just noticed it.

I put my nose to the glass, but the interior was too dim to see more than a stack of old plates on a dusty table.

Without warning, a hand came out of nowhere and hung something directly in front of my face – a hand-lettered cardboard sign.

CLOSED, it said, and the card was still swaying from its string as I made a dash for the door. I grabbed the knob, but at the same instant, the disembodied pair of hands seized it on the inside, trying desperately to keep it from turning – trying

217

to drive home the bolt before I could gain entry.

But luck was on my side. My hearty shove proved stronger than the hands that were holding it closed, and I was propelled into the shop's interior a little faster than I should have liked.

'Oh, thank you,' I said. 'I thought you might be closed. It's about a gift, you see, and–'

'We *are* closed,' said a cracked, tinny voice, and I spun round to find myself face to face with a peculiar little man.

He looked like an umbrella handle that had been carved into the shape of a parrot: beaked nose, white hair as tight and curly as a powdered wig, and red circles on each cheek as if he had just rouged them. His face was powder white and his lips too red for words.

He seemed to stand precariously on his tiny feet, swaying so alarmingly backwards and forwards that I had the feeling he was about to topple from his perch.

'We're closed,' he repeated. 'You must come back another time.'

'Mr. Pettibone?' I asked, sticking out a hand. 'I'm Flavia de Luce, from Buckshaw.'

He didn't have much choice.

'Pleased to meet you, I'm sure,' he said, taking two of my fingers in his miniature fist and giving them a faint squeeze. 'But we're closed.'

'It's my father, you see,' I went on breathlessly. 'Today's his birthday, and we wanted to – my sisters and I, that is – surprise him. He's expressed a great interest in something you have in your shop, and we'd hoped to – I'm sorry I'm so late, Mr. Pettibone, but I was folding bandages at

218

the St. John's Ambulance…'

I allowed my lower lip to tremble very slightly.

'And what is this … er … object?'

'A table,' I blurted. It was the first thing that came to mind, and a jolly good thing I'd thought of it. There must be dozens of tables in a place like this, and I'd be able to have a good old snoop round while searching for the right one.

'Could you … er … describe it?'

'Yes,' I said. 'Of course. It has four legs and – a top.'

I could see that he was unconvinced.

'It's for stamps, you see. Father's a philatelist, and he needs something he can spread his work on … under a lamp. His eyes are not quite what they used to be, and my sisters and I–'

He was edging me towards the door.

'Oh – just a minute. I think that's it,' I said, pointing to a rather sorry bit of furniture that was huddled in the gloom beneath an ormolu clock with plump-bellied pewter horses. By moving to touch it, I was six or eight feet deeper into the shop.

'Oh, no, this one's too dark. I thought it was mahogany. No – wait! It's this one over here.'

I had plunged well towards the back of the shop and into the shadows. With Pettibone bearing down upon me like a wolf upon the fold, I realised that I was now cut off from the door and freedom.

'What are you playing at?' he said, making a sudden grab for my arm. I leapt out of his reach.

Suddenly the situation had turned dangerous. But why? Was there something in the shop Pettibone didn't want me to see? Did he suspect that

219

I was on to his shady antiques dealings?

Whatever the cause of his aggressiveness, I needed to act quickly.

To my right, standing about a foot out from the wall, was a massive wardrobe. I slid behind it.

For a while, at least, I was safe. He was too big to squeeze behind the thing. I might not be able to come out, but I'd have a moment to plan my next move.

But then Pettibone was back with a broom. He shoved the bristles into my ribs – and pushed. I stood my ground.

Now he turned the broom around and began prodding at me furiously with the handle, like a man who has trapped a rat behind the kitchen cupboard.

'Ouch!' I cried out. 'Stop! Stop it! You're hurting me!'

Actually, he wasn't, but I couldn't let him know that. I was able to slip far enough along the wall that I was beyond reach of his broom.

As he came round the wardrobe to have a try from the other side, I slithered back to the far end.

But I knew I was trapped. This game of cat and mouse could go on all day.

Now the wardrobe had begun to move, its china casters squealing. Pettibone had put his shoulder to a corner and was shifting the thing out from the wall.

'Oh!' I shrieked. 'You're crushing me!'

The wall of wood stopped moving and there was a brief pause in his attack, during which I could hear him breathing heavily.

'Reginald!'

The voice – a woman's – cut through the shop like a falling icicle. I heard him mutter something.

'Reginald, come up here at once! Do you hear me?'

'Hello upstairs!' I shouted. 'It's Flavia de Luce.'

There was a silence, and then the voice said, 'Come up, Flavia. Reginald, bring the girl here.'

It was as if she'd said 'fetch.'

I slipped out from behind the wardrobe, rubbing my elbows, and shot him a reproachful look.

His eyes strayed to a narrow staircase at the side of the shop, and before he could change his mind, I moved towards it.

I could have made a break for the door, but I didn't. This could be my only chance at scouting out the place. 'In for a penny, in for a pound,' as Mrs. Mullet was fond of saying.

I put my foot on the first step and began my slow trudge upstairs to whatever fate awaited me.

The room at the top came as a complete surprise. Rather than the rabbit's warren of little cubicles I had imagined, the place was unexpectedly large. Obviously, all of the interior walls had been knocked out to form a spacious attic which was the same size as the shop beneath.

And what a contrast with the shop it was! There was no clutter up here: in fact, with one exception, the room was almost empty.

In the middle of the floor stood a great square bed hung with white linen, and in it, propped up by a wall of pillows, was a woman whose features might well have been chiselled from a block of ice. There was a faint bluish – or cyanotic – tinge to her face and hands which suggested, at first

221

glance, that she might be the victim of either carbon monoxide or silver poisoning, but as I stared, I began to see that her complexion was coloured not by poison, but by artifice.

Her skin was the colour of skimmed milk. Her lips, like those of her husband (I presumed that the parrot-man was her husband) were painted a startling red, and, as if she were a leftover star from the silent cinema, her hair hung down around her face in a mass of silver ringlets.

Only when I had taken in the details of the room and its occupant did I allow my attention to shift to the bed itself: an ebony four-poster with its posts carved into the shape of black angels, each of them frozen into position like a sentry in his box at Buckingham Palace.

Several mattresses must have been piled one atop the other to give the thing its height, and a set of wooden steps had been constructed at the bedside, like a ladder beside a haystack.

Slowly, the icy apparition in the bed lifted a lorgnette to her eyes and regarded me coolly through its lenses.

'Flavia de Luce, you say? One of Colonel de Luce's daughters – from Buckshaw?'

I nodded.

'Your sister Ophelia has performed for us at the Women's Institute. A remarkably gifted player.'

I should have known! This landlocked iceberg was a friend of Feely's!

Under any other circumstances, I'd have said something rude and stalked out of the room, but I thought better of it. The investigation of murder, I was beginning to learn, can demand great personal sacrifice.

Actually, the woman's words were true. Feely *was* a first-rate pianist, but there was no sense going on and on about it.

'Yes,' I said, 'she's quite talented.'

Until then I had been unaware that Reginald was close behind me, standing on the stairs just one or two steps from the top.

'You may go, Reginald,' the woman said, and I turned to watch him descend, in uncanny silence, to the shop below.

'Now then,' she said. 'Speak.'

'I'm afraid I owe you and Mr. Pettibone an apology,' I said. 'I told him a lie.'

'Which was?'

'That I'd come to buy a table for Father. What I really wanted was an opportunity to ask you about the Hobblers.'

'The Hobblers?' she said with an awkward laugh. 'Whatever makes you think I'd know anything about the Hobblers? They haven't existed since the days of powdered wigs.'

In spite of her denial, I could see that my question had caught her off guard. Perhaps I could take advantage of her surprise.

'I know that they were founded in the seventeenth century by Nicodemus Flitch, and that the Palings, at Buckshaw, have played an important role in their history, what with baptisms, and so forth.'

I paused to see how this would be received.

'And what has this to do with me?' she asked, putting down the lorgnette and then picking it up again.

'Oh, somebody mentioned that you belonged to that ... faith. I was talking to Miss Mountjoy, and she–'

True enough – I *had* been talking to Miss Mountjoy. As long as I didn't actually say that she'd told me, I'd be guilty of no great sin. Other than one of omission, perhaps. Feely was always going on and on about sins of commission and omission until your eyes were left spinning like fishing lures.

'Tilda Mountjoy,' she said, after a long pause. 'I see ... tell me more.'

'Well, it's just that I've been making a few notes about Buckshaw's history, you know, and as I was going through some old papers in Father's library, I came across some quite early documents.'

'Documents?' she demanded. 'What kind of documents?'

She was rising to the bait! Her thoughts were written on her face as clearly as if they were tattooed on her cheeks.

Old papers relating to Nicodemus Flitch and the Hobblers? she was thinking. *Now here's my opportunity to pull the rug out from under dear, dull-as-ditchwater old Tilda, and her longwinded papers in the* Hobblers' Historical Society Journal. *Former librarian be blowed! I'll show her what* real *research can bring to light.*

And so forth.

'Oh, just odd bits and pieces,' I said. 'Letters to one of my ancestors – Lucius de Luce – about this and that–

'Just a lot of names and dates,' I added. 'Nothing terribly interesting, I'm afraid.'

This was the cherry on the icing – but I would pretend to brush it off as worthless.

She was staring at me through her lenses like a bird-watcher who has unexpectedly come upon the rare spotted crake.

Now was the time to keep perfectly still. If my words hadn't primed the pump of curiosity, then nothing would.

I could almost feel the heat of her gaze.

'There's more,' she said. 'What is it? You're not telling me the whole truth.'

'Well,' I blurted, 'actually, I was thinking of asking if I might be allowed to convert to the Hobblers. We de Luces are not really Anglicans, you see – we've been Roman Catholics for ages, but – Feely was telling me that the Hobblers were non – non–'

'Nonconformists?'

'Yes, that's it – Nonconformists, and I thought that, since I'm a nonconformist myself ... well, why not join?'

There was a grain of truth in this: I remembered that one of my heroes, Joseph Priestley, the discoverer of oxygen, had once been the minister of a dissenting sect in Leeds, and if it was good enough for the esteemed Joseph–

'There's been a great deal of debate,' she said reflectively, 'about whether we're Nonconformists or Dissenters, what with our Reconstitution in 17–'

'Then you *are* a Hobbler!'

She stared at me long and hard, as if thinking. 'There are those,' she said, 'who work to preserve the foundations upon which their forefathers

225

built. It is not always easy in this day and age...'

'It doesn't matter to me,' I said. 'I'd give anything to be a Hobbler.'

And in a way it was true. I had visions of myself limping cheerily along a country lane, my arms outstretched for balance, teetering like a tightrope walker, as I veered crazily from hedge to hedge.

'I'm a Hobbler,' I would shout out to everyone as I stumped past.

As I was hobbling to St. Ives...

'Most interesting,' the woman was saying as I came back to reality. 'And is your father aware of your aspirations?'

'*No!*' I said, aghast. 'Please don't tell him! Father is very set in his ways and–'

'I understand,' she said. 'We shall let it be our little secret, then. No one but you and I shall know about any of this.'

Hey presto!

'Oh, *thank you,*' I breathed. 'I knew you'd understand.'

As she rattled on about the Act of Toleration, the Five Mile Act, the Countess of Huntingdon, and the Calvinist Connection, I took the opportunity to look around the room.

There wasn't much to see: the bed, of course, which, now that I had time to think about it, reminded me of the Great Bed of Ware in the Victoria and Albert Museum. In a far corner near a window was a small table with an electric ring and a small kettle, a Brown Betty teapot, a biscuit tin, and a single cup and saucer. Reginald Pettibone was evidently not in the habit of having

226

breakfast with his wife.

'Would you care for a biscuit?' she asked.

'No, thank you,' I said. 'I don't use sugar.'

It was a lie – but an excellent one.

'What an unusual child you are,' she said, and with a wave of the hand towards the tin, she added, 'Well, then, perhaps you won't mind fetching one for me. I have no such scruples.'

I went to the window and reached for the biscuit tin. As I turned, I happened to glance outside – down into the fenced area behind the shop's back door.

A rusty green van stood with its double doors open, and I knew instantly that it was the one I'd seen parked outside Willow Villa.

As I watched, a powerful man in shirtsleeves stepped into view from somewhere below. It was the bulldog man – the man who had almost caught me in the coach house!

Unless I was sadly mistaken, this would be Edward Sampson, of Rye Road, East Finching – whose name I had found on the papers in the glove compartment.

As I stood rooted to the spot, he reached into the back of the van and dragged out a couple of heavy objects. He turned and, perhaps feeling my eyes upon him, looked straight up at the window where I was standing.

My immediate reaction was to shrink back – to step away from the glass – but I found that I could not. Some remote part of my mind had already spotted a detail that was only now leaking slowly into my consciousness, and I'm afraid I let out a gasp.

The objects gripped in the hands of the bulldog man were Harriet's firedogs – Sally Fox and Shoppo!

EIGHTEEN

'What is it?' the woman asked. Her voice seemed to be coming from a very great distance.

'It's – it's–'

'Yes, dear ... what is it?'

It was the 'dear' that brought me snapping back. A 'dear' or 'dearie' to me is about as welcome as a bullet to the brain. I've had places reserved in the ha'penny seats of Hell for people who address me in this way.

But I bit my tongue.

'It's – just that you have such a smashing view from your window,' I said. 'The river ... Malplaquet Farm ... all the way to East Finching and the hills beyond. One would never suspect, walking in the high street, that such a–'

There was a floor-shaking crash from downstairs as some heavy object was dropped. A couple of muffled curses came drifting up through the floorboards.

'Reginald!' the woman shouted, and there was an awkward silence in the depths.

'Men!' she said, loudly enough to make herself heard downstairs. 'Windmills on legs.'

'I think I'd better go,' I said. 'They'll be expecting me at home.'

'Very well, dear,' she said. 'Run along, then. And don't forget about those letters. You may bring them whenever you're able.'

I did not tell her what I was thinking, but rather, gave a very small mock curtsy, then turned and made my way down the narrow stairs.

At the bottom, I glanced towards the back of the shop. Reginald Pettibone and the owner of the van stood staring at me from the shadows. Neither of them moved or spoke, but I knew, in the way we females are supposed to know, that they had been talking about me.

I turned my back on them and walked to the door, stopping only to write my initials casually in the dust that covered an ebony sideboard. I wasn't exactly afraid, but I knew how an animal trainer in a steel cage must feel when, for the first time, he turns his back on the fierce gaze of a pair of new tigers.

Although she didn't say so, Gladys seemed happy to see me. I had parked her against a tree across the high street from Pettibone's shop.

'There's dirty work at the crossroads,' I told her. 'I can feel it in my bones.'

I needed to get home at once to inspect the drawing-room hearth.

The trees were making late afternoon shadows as I cycled through the Mulford Gates and up the avenue of chestnuts. I'd soon be expected to put in an appearance at the dinner table, and I wasn't looking forward to it.

As I opened the kitchen door, the sound of a Schubert sonata came floating to my ears.

229

Success! I knew instantly that my psychic booby trap had been sprung.

Feely always played Schubert when she was upset, and the opening of the Piano Sonata in B Flat Major when she was especially distraught.

I could almost follow her thoughts as the piano's notes went flying past my ears like birds from a forest fire. At first there was the tightly controlled anger, with threats of rolling thunder (how I loved the thunder!), but when the full storm broke, Feely's fierce talent could still make me gasp with admiration.

I edged closer to the drawing room, the better to hear this remarkable outpouring of emotion. It was almost as good as reading her diary.

I had to be careful, though, that she didn't catch sight of me until dinner, when Father would be there to save my hide. If Feely so much as suspected that I was responsible for the spirit message on her mirror, there'd be buckets of blood on the carpet and entrails dangling from the chandeliers.

The drawing room would have to wait.

I did not realise how tired I had suddenly become until I was dragging myself up the stairs. It had been a long day, and it was far from over.

Perhaps, I thought, I would have a nap.

As I approached my laboratory, I came to an abrupt halt. The door was standing open!

I peered round the corner, and there stood Porcelain, still wearing Fenella's black dress, toasting a slice of bread over a Bunsen burner. I could hardly believe my eyes!

'Cheer-oh,' she said, looking up. 'Would you like some toast?'

As if she hadn't just recently accused me of bashing in her grandmother's brains.

'How did you get in?'

'I used your key,' she said, pointing. It was still inserted in the lock. 'I watched you hide it in the hollow bedpost.'

It was true. I had long before discovered Uncle Tar's secret hiding place for keys and other things he wanted to keep to himself. My bedroom had once been his, and over time all, or most, of its secrets had been revealed.

'You've got a bloody nerve,' I said. The thought of someone invading my laboratory made my skin crawl, as if an army of red ants were swarming up my arms, fanning out across my shoulders, and up the back of my neck.

'I'm sorry, Flavia,' she said. 'I know it wasn't you that attacked Fenella. I can't have been thinking straight. I was confused. I was tired. I came back to apologise.'

'Then you'd better get at it,' I said.

I was not going to be mollified – wasn't that the term Daffy had used when she'd said the same thing to me: 'mollified'? – with just a couple of token words. There are times when 'I'm sorry' is simply not enough.

'I'm sorry,' she said. 'I really am. It's all so upsetting. It's just too much.'

Suddenly she was in tears.

'First there was Fenella – now they won't let me see her, you know. They've got a constable in a chair watching the door to her room. Then there was that awful business of the man we found hanging from the fountain–'

'Brookie Harewood,' I said. I'd almost forgotten about Brookie.

'And now this latest body they've dug up in – what do you call it? – the Palings.'

'What?'

Another body? In the Palings?

'It's all too much,' she said, wiping her nose on her forearm. 'I'm going back to London.'

Before I could say another word, she dug into her pocket and pulled out a five-pound note.

'Here,' she said, prying open my fingers and pressing them closed upon the banknote. 'That's to feed Gry until Fenella's discharged from hospital. And…'

She looked straight into my eyes, still gripping my hand. Her lips were trembling. 'If she doesn't recover, he's yours. The caravan, too. I came here to tell you I'm sorry, and I've done it. And now I'm leaving.'

'Wait! What did you say about another body?'

'Ask your inspector friend,' she said, and turned towards the door.

I made a lunge for the key and slammed the door shut. We tussled for the doorknob, but I managed to grab the key, jam it into the inside lock, and give it a frantic twist.

'Hand it over. Let me out.'

'No,' I said. 'Not until you tell me what you saw in the Palings.'

'Come off it, Flavia. I'm not playing games.'

'Nor am I,' I told her, crossing my arms.

As I knew she would, she made a sudden snatch at the key. It was an old trick often used by Daffy and Feely, and I suppose I ought to have

232

been grateful for having learned it from them. Being ready for the next move, I was able to hold the key out, at arm's length, away from her.

And then she gave up. Just like that. I could see it in her eyes.

She brushed her hair away from her face and walked back to one of the laboratory tables, where she splayed her fingers out upon its surface, as if to keep from toppling over.

'I went back to the caravan to pick up my things,' she said, slowly and deliberately, 'and the police were there again. They wouldn't let me anywhere near it. They were lifting something out of a hole in the ground.'

'Lifting what?'

She was staring at me with something that might have been defiance.

'Believe me, it wasn't gold.'

'Tell me!'

'For God's sake, Flavia!'

I waved the key at her. 'Tell me.'

'It was a body. Wrapped in a carpet, or something – not very big. A child, I think. I only saw one of the feet ... or what was left of it.

'A bundle of old green bones,' she added.

She clapped her hand across her mouth and her shoulders heaved.

I waited patiently for more, but if there were any further interesting details, Porcelain was keeping them to herself.

We stared at each other for what seemed like a very long time.

'Fenella was right,' she said at last. 'There is a darkness here.'

I held out the key and she lifted it from my open palm with two fingers, as if it – or I – were contaminated.

Without a word, she unlocked the door and let herself out.

What was I supposed to feel? I wondered.

To be perfectly honest, I think I had been looking forward to having Porcelain dog my every step as I went about investigating the attack upon Fenella and the murder of Brookie Harewood. I had even thought of ways of giving her the slip, if necessary, as I traipsed about the village, digging up information. And perhaps I had too much anticipated sitting her down and patiently explaining the trail of clues, and the ways in which they pointed to the culprit – or culprits.

But now, by walking out, she had deprived me of all of that.

I was alone again.

As it was in the beginning, is now and ever shall be, world without end. Amen.

No one to talk to but myself.

Except Dogger, of course.

Dogger was sitting in the last shaft of sunlight in the garden. He had brought an old wooden chair from the greenhouse and, perched upon the edge of its seat, was hammering nails into the tin stripping that sealed the wooden tea chest that lay before him in the grass.

I lowered myself into the wheelbarrow that was standing nearby.

'They've found another body,' I said. 'At the Palings.'

Dogger nodded. 'I believe that's so, Miss Flavia.'

'It's the Bull baby, isn't it?'

Dogger nodded again and put down the hammer. 'I should be surprised if it weren't.'

'Did you hear about it from Mrs. Mullet?'

Although I knew it was not a done thing to inquire of one servant about another, there was no other way. I couldn't just ring up Inspector Hewitt and pump him for the details.

'No,' he said, preparing to drive home another nail. 'Miss Porcelain told me.'

'Porcelain?' I said, gesturing up towards the east wing – towards my bedroom window. 'You knew about Porcelain? That she was staying here?'

'Yes,' Dogger said, and left it at that.

After a few seconds I relaxed, and there fell between us another one of those luxurious silences that is part of most conversations with Dogger: silences so long and profound and golden that it seems irreverent to break them.

Dogger rotated the tea chest and began to apply stripping to another edge.

'You have very fine hands,' I said at last. 'They look as if they belong to a concert pianist.'

Dogger put down the hammer and examined both sides of each hand as if he had never seen them before.

'I can assure you that they are my own,' he said.

This time, there could be no doubt about it. Dogger *had* made a joke. But rather than laughing condescendingly, I did the right thing and nodded wisely, as if I knew it all along. I was learning that among friends, a smile can be better than a belly laugh.

'Dogger,' I said, 'there's something I need to know. It's about nosebleeds.'

I had the impression that he looked at me sharply – even though he hadn't.

'Are you having nosebleeds, Miss Flavia?'

'No,' I said. 'No – not at all. It's no one here at Buckshaw. Actually, it's Miss Mountjoy, at Willow Villa.'

And I described to him what I had seen in that dank kitchen.

'Ah,' Dogger said, and then fell silent. After a time, he spoke again – slowly – as if his words were being retrieved, one by one, from some deep well.

'Recurrent nosebleeds – epitaxis – may have many causes.'

'Such as?' I urged.

'Genetic predisposition,' he said. 'Hypertension – or high blood pressure ... pregnancy ... dengue – or breakbone – fever ... nasopharyngeal cancer ... adrenal tumour ... scurvy. ... certain diseases of the elderly, such as hardening of the arteries. It may also be symptomatic of arsenic poisoning.'

Of course! I knew that! How could I have forgotten?

'However,' Dogger went on, 'from what you've told me, it is none of these. Miss Mountjoy's nosebleeds are most likely brought on by the excessive consumption of cod-liver oil.'

'Cod-liver oil?' I must have said it aloud.

'I expect she takes it for her arthritis,' Dogger said, and went back to his hammering.

'Gaaak!' I said, making a face. 'I hate the smell of the stuff.'

But Dogger was not to be drawn out.

236

'Isn't it odd,' I plowed on, 'how nature puts the same pong in the liver of a fish as it does in a weed like the stinking goosefoot, and in the willow that grows by the water?'

'Stinking goosefoot?' Dogger said, looking up in puzzlement. And then: 'Ah, yes, of course. The methylamines. I'd forgotten about the methylamines. And then...'

'Yes?' I said, too quickly and too eagerly.

There were times when Dogger's memory, having been primed, worked beautifully for a short time, like the vicar's battered old Oxford which ran well only in the rain.

I crossed my fingers and my ankles and waited, biting my tongue.

Dogger removed his hat and stared into it as if the memory were hidden in its lining. He frowned, wiped his brow on his forearm, and went on hesitantly. 'I believe there were several cases reported in *The Lancet* in the last century in which a patient was recorded as exuding a fishy smell.'

'Perhaps he was a fisherman,' I suggested. Dogger shook his head.

'In neither case was the patient a fisherman, and neither had been known to be in contact with fish. Even after bathing, the piscine odour returned, often following a meal.'

'Of fish?'

Dogger ignored me. 'There was, of course, the tale in the *Bhagavad Ghita* of the princess who exuded a fishy odour...'

'Yes?' I said, settling back as if to hear a fairy tale. Somewhere in the distance, a harvesting machine clattered away softly at its work, and the

237

sun shone down. What a perfect day it was, I thought. 'But wait!' I said. 'What if his body were producing trimethylamine?'

This was such an exciting thought that I sprang out of the wheelbarrow.

'It would not be unheard of,' Dogger said, thoughtfully. 'Shakespeare might have been thinking of just such a complaint:

"What have we here? a man or a fish? dead or alive? A fish: he smells like a fish: a very ancient and fish-like smell."

A chill ran up my spine. Dogger had slipped into the loud and confident voice of an actor who has delivered these lines many and many a time before.

'*The Tempest*,' he said quietly. 'Act two, scene two, if I'm not mistaken. Trinculo, you'll recall, is speaking of Caliban.'

'Where do you dig up these things?' I asked in admiration.

'On the wireless,' Dogger said. 'We listened to it some weeks ago.'

It was true. At Buckshaw, Thursday evenings were devoted to compulsory wireless listening, and we had recently been made to sit through an adaption of *The Tempest* without fidgeting.

Other than the marvellous sound effects of the storm, I didn't remember much about the play, but obviously Dogger did.

'Is there a name for this fishy condition?' I asked.

'Not to the best of my knowledge,' he said. 'It is exceedingly rare. I believe...'

238

'Go on,' I said, eagerly.

But when I looked up at Dogger, the light in his eyes had gone out. He sat staring at his hat, which he held clutched in his trembling hands as if he had never seen it before.

'I believe I'll go to my room now,' he said, getting slowly to his feet.

'It's all right,' I said. 'I think I will, too. A nice nap before dinner will do both of us good.'

But I'm not sure that Dogger heard me. He was already shambling off towards the kitchen door.

When he was gone, I turned my attention to the wooden tea chest he had been nailing shut. In one corner was pasted a paper label, upon which was written in ink:

*THIS SIDE UP – Contents – Silver Cutlery –
de Luce – Buckshaw*

Cutlery? Had Dogger packed the Mumpeters in this crate? Mother and Father Mumpeter? Little Grindlestick and her silver sisters?

Is that why he'd been polishing them?

Why on earth would he do such a thing? The Mumpeters were my childhood playthings, and the very thought of anyone–

But hadn't Brookie Harewood been murdered with one of the pieces from this set? What if the police–?

I walked round to the far side of the crate: the side that Dogger had turned away from me as I approached.

As I read the words that were stencilled in awful black letters on the boards, something vile

239

and sour rose up in my throat.

Sotheby's, New Bond Street, London, WC., it said.

Father was sending away the family silver to be auctioned.

NINETEEN

Dinner was a grim affair.

The worst of it was that Father had come to the table without *The London Philatelist.* Instead of reading, he insisted upon solicitously passing me the peas and asking, 'Did you have a nice day today, Flavia?'

It almost broke my heart.

Although Father had spoken several times of his financial troubles, they had never seemed threatening: no more than a distant shadow, really, like war – or death. You knew it was there but you didn't spend all day fretting about it.

But now, with the Mumpeters nailed up inside a crate, ready to be taken to the train for London and pawed over by strangers at the auction rooms, the reality of Father's predicament had hit home with the force of a typhoon.

And Father – the dear man – was trying to shield us from the reality by making bright table chatter.

I could feel the tears welling up in my eyes, but I dared not give in to them. It was fortunate that Daffy, who sat across from me, did not even once look up from her book.

240

To my left, at the far end of the table, Feely sat staring down into her lap, her face pale, her colourless lips pressed together into a tight, thin line. The dark circles under her eyes were like bruises, and her hair was lank and lifeless.

The only word to describe her was 'blighted.'

My chemical wizardry had worked!

The proof of it was the fact that Feely was wearing her spectacles, which told me, without a doubt, that she had spent the day staring in horror at the spirit message that had materialised upon her looking glass.

In spite of her occasional cruelty – or perhaps because of it – Feely was a pious sort, whose time was devoted to making bargains with this saint or that about the clarity of her complexion, or the way in which a random beam of sunlight would strike her golden hair as she knelt at the altar for communion.

Where I generally believed in chemistry and the happy dance of the atom, Feely believed in the supernatural, and it was that belief I had taken advantage of.

But what had I done? I hadn't counted on such utter devastation.

Part of my brain was telling me to leap up and run to her – to throw my arms around her neck and tell her that it was only French chalk – and not God – that had caused her misery. And then we would laugh together as we used to in the olden days.

But I couldn't: if I did, I should have to confess to my prank in front of Father, and I wanted to spare him any further grief.

Besides, Feely would more than likely stab me to death with whatever came to hand, snow white tablecloth or not.

Which made me think of Brookie Harewood. How odd! There hadn't been a word at the dinner table about murder. Or was it now *murders*, plural?

It was then, I think, that I noticed the cutlery. Instead of our usual silver utensils, I realised that each of our places had been set with the yellow-handled knives and forks that were kept in the kitchen for the use of the servants.

I could contain it no longer. I scraped my chair back from the table, mumbled something about being excused, and fled. By the time I reached the foyer, my tears were splashing about me like rain on the black-and-white chequerboard of the tiles.

I threw myself onto the bed and buried my face in the pillow.

How could revenge hurt so keenly? It didn't make any sense. It simply didn't. Revenge was supposed to be sweet – and so was victory!

As I lay there, flattened by misery, I heard the unmistakeable sound of Father's leather-soled shoes outside in the hall.

I could hardly believe my ears. Father in the east wing? This was the first time since I had moved into it that he had set foot in this part of the house.

Father came slowly into the room, shuffling a little, and I heard him pause. A moment later I felt the bed sink a little as he sat down beside me.

I kept my face pressed tightly into the pillow.

After what seemed like a very long time, I felt his hand gently touching my head – but only for a moment.

He did not stroke my hair, nor did he speak, and I was glad he didn't. His silence spared both of us the embarrassment of not knowing what to say.

And then he was gone, as quietly as he had come.

And I slept.

In the morning, the world seemed a different place.

I whistled in my bath. I even remembered to scrub my elbows.

It had come to me in the night, as if in a dream, that I must apologise to Feely. It was as simple as that.

In the first place, it would disarm her. In the second place, it would impress Father, if Feely had told him what I had done. And finally, it would make me feel all warm and self-righteous about doing the decent thing.

Besides, if I played my cards right, I could also pump Feely for information about Vanetta Harewood. I would not, of course, tell her about the lost portrait of Harriet.

It was the perfect solution.

There's nothing as beautiful as the sound of a piano in the next room. A little distance gives the instrument a heart – at least to my sensitive hearing, it does.

As I stood outside the drawing-room door, Feely was practising something by Rameau: *Les Sauvages,* I think it was called. It sometimes made me think of a moonlight glade – the Palings, perhaps – with a tribe of devils dancing in a circle like maniacs: so much more pleasing, I thought, than that sleepy old thing on the same topic by Beethoven.

I straightened my back and squared my shoulders. Feely was always telling me to square my shoulders, and I thought she'd be happy to see that I'd remembered.

The instant I opened the door, the music stopped and Feely looked up from the keyboard. She was learning to play without her spectacles, and she was not wearing them now.

I couldn't help noticing how beautiful she looked.

Her eyes, which I had expected to be like a pair of open coal holes, shone with a cold blue brilliance in the morning light. It was like being glared at by Father.

'Yes?' she said.

'I – I've come to say I'm sorry,' I told her.

'Then do so.'

'I just did, Feely!'

'No, you didn't. You made a statement of fact. You stated that you had come to say you're sorry. You may begin.'

This was going to be more humiliating than I thought.

'I'm sorry,' I said, 'for writing on your mirror.'

'Yes?'

I swallowed and went on. 'It was a mean and thoughtless trick.'

'It was indeed, you odious little worm.'

She got up from the piano bench and came

towards me – menacingly, I thought. I shrank back a little.

'Of course I knew at once that it was you. *Deuteronomy? The boils of Egypt? The emerods? The scurvy and the itch?* It had Flavia de Luce written all over it. You might just as well have signed the thing – like a painting.'

'That's not true, Feely. You were devastated. I saw the circles under your eyes at dinner!'

Feely threw her head back and laughed.

'Makeup!' she crowed. 'French chalk! Two can play at that game, you stupid moke. A bit of French chalk and a pinch of ashes from the grate. It took me all afternoon to get it just the right shade. You should have seen your face! Daffy said she almost had an accident trying not to laugh!'

My face began to burn.

'Didn't you, Daff?'

There was the sound of a wet snicker behind me, and I spun round to find Daffy coming through the doorway – blocking my route of escape.

'*"It was a mean and thoughtless trick,"*' she said, imitating me in a grating, falsetto, parrot voice.

She had been eavesdropping on my apology from outside in the hallway!

But now, rather than flying at her in fury, as I might have done even yesterday, I gathered up every last scrap of inner strength and attacked her with a new and untried tool: clear, cold calm.

'Who is Hilda Muir?' I asked, and Daffy stopped moving instantly, as if she had been frozen in a snapshot.

The appeal to a superior knowledge. And it worked!

By coming to one of my sisters in humility and keeping my temper with the other, I had gained in just a few minutes not one, but two new weapons.

'What?'

'Hilda Muir. She's something to do with the Palings.'

'Hilda Muir,' Fenella had said, when we'd first spotted Mrs. Bull in the Gully. *'Hilda Muir.'* She'd said it again when I brought the elder branches to the caravan. *'Now we are all dead!'*

'Who is Hilda Muir?' I asked again in my new and maddeningly calm voice.

'Hilda Muir? The Palings? You must mean the Hildemoer. She's not a person, you idiot. She's the spirit of the elder branches. She comes to punish people who cut her branches without first asking permission. You didn't cut any elder branches, did you?' (This with another wet snicker.)

Daffy must have seen the effect her words had on me. 'I truly hope you didn't. They sometimes plant them on a grave to indicate whether the dead person is happy in the next world. If the elder grows, all's well. If not–'

The next world? I thought. Hadn't Porcelain watched the police pull a baby's body from the very spot – or very near it – that I had cut the elder for firewood?

'The Hildemoer's a pixy,' Daffy went on. 'Don't you remember what we told you about the pixies? For heaven's sake, Flavia – it was only a couple of days ago. The pixies are the Old Ones – those horrid creatures who stole Harriet's precious baby and left *you* in its place.'

My mind was an inferno. I could feel the anger

246

rushing back like the Red Sea after the passage of the Israelites.

'I hope you didn't cut elder from someone's grave,' she went on. 'Because if you did–'

'Thank you, Daffy,' I said. 'You've been most informative.'

Without another word, I brushed past her and stalked out of the drawing room.

With the mocking laughter of my darling sisters still ringing in my ears, I fled down the echoing hall.

TWENTY

In the laboratory I locked the door and waited to see what my hands were going to do.

It was always like this. If I just relaxed and tried not to think too hard, the great god Chemistry would guide me.

After a time, although I'm not sure why, I reached for three bottles and placed them on the bench.

Using a pipette, I measured half an ounce of a clear liquid from the first of these into a calibrated test tube. From the second bottle I measured three ounces of another fluid into a small flask. I watched in fascination as I combined the two clear fluids with several ounces of distilled water, and before my eyes a reddish color appeared.

Presto chango! Aqua regia ... royal water!

The ancient alchemists gave it that name

because it is capable of dissolving gold, which they considered to be the king of metals.

I have to admit that manufacturing the stuff myself never fails to excite me.

Actually, aqua regia is more orange than red: the precise color of pomegranates, if I remember correctly. Yes, pomegranates – that was it.

I had once seen these exotic fruits in a shop window in the high street. Mr. Hughes, the greengrocer, had imported the things on a trial basis, but they had remained in his shop window until they blackened and caved in upon themselves like rotted puffballs.

'Bishop's Lacey's been't ready for pomegranates yet,' he had told Mrs. Mullet. 'We don't deserves 'em.'

I had always marvelled at the way in which three clear liquids – nitric acid, hydrochloric acid, and water – when combined could produce, as if by magic, colour – and not just any colour, but the colour of a flaming sunset.

The swirling shades of orange in the glass seemed to illustrate perfectly the thoughts that were swarming round and round, mixing in my mind.

It was all so confoundedly complicated: the attack upon Fenella, the gruesome death of Brookie Harewood, the sudden appearance and equally sudden disappearance of Porcelain, Harriet's firedogs turning up in not one but three different locations, the strange antiques shop of the abominable Pettibones, Miss Mountjoy and the Hobblers, Vanetta Harewood's long-lost portrait of Harriet, and underneath it all, like the rumble

248

of a stuck organ pipe, the constant low drone of Father's looming bankruptcy.

It was enough to make an archangel spit.

In its container, the aqua regia was growing darker by the minute, as if it, too, were waiting impatiently for answers.

And suddenly I saw the way.

Lighting a Bunsen burner, I set it beneath the flask. I would warm the acid gently before proceeding with the next step.

From a cupboard I took down a small wooden box upon the end of which Uncle Tar had pencilled the word 'platinum'; and slid open the lid. Inside were perhaps a dozen flat squares of the silvery-grey mineral, none larger than an adult's fingernail. I selected a piece that weighed perhaps a quarter of an ounce.

When the aqua regia had reached the proper temperature, I picked up the bit of platinum with a pair of tweezers and held it above the mouth of the flask. Aside from the hiss of the gas, the laboratory was so quiet that I actually heard the tiny *plop* as I let the platinum drop into the fluid.

For a moment, nothing happened.

But now the liquid in the flask was a darkening red.

And then the platinum began to writhe.

This was the part I liked best!

As if in agony, the bit of metal crept towards the glass wall of the flask, trying to escape the acids that were consuming it.

And suddenly *poof!* The platinum was gone.

I could almost hear the aqua regia licking its lips. *'More, please!'*

It wasn't that the platinum had not put up a noble fight, because it had. The important thing, I reminded myself, was this: *platinum cannot be dissolved by any one acid!*

No, platinum could *not* be dissolved by nitric acid alone, and it merely laughed a jolly 'ha-ha!' at hydrochloric acid. Only when the two combined could platinum be broken down.

There was a lesson here – two lessons, in fact.

The first was this: I was the platinum. It was going to take more than a single opponent to overcome Flavia Sabina de Luce.

What was left in the flask was bichloride of platinum, which in itself would be useful to test – in some future experiment, perhaps – for the presence of either nicotine or potassium. More to the point, though, was the fact that although the platinum chip had vanished, something new had been formed: something with a whole new set of capabilities.

And then quite suddenly, I caught a glimpse of my face reflected in the glassware, watching wide-eyed as the somewhat cloudy liquid in the flask, shifting uneasily, took on, perhaps, a tinge of sickly yellow, as if in the drifting mists of a Gypsy's crystal ball.

I knew then what I had to do.

'Aha! Flavia!' the vicar said. 'We missed you at church on Sunday.'

'Sorry, Vicar,' I told him, 'I'm afraid I rather overdid myself on Saturday, what with the fête and so forth.'

Since good works do not generally require

trumpeting, I did not feel it necessary to mention the assistance I had offered to Fenella. And as it turned out, I was right to hold my tongue, because the vicar quickly brought up the subject himself.

'Yes,' he said. 'Your father tells me you were allowed rather a luxurious Sabbath lie-in. Really, Flavia, it was most kind of you to play the Good Samaritan, as it were. *Most* kind.'

'It was nothing,' I said, with becoming modesty. 'I was happy to help.'

The vicar got to his feet and stretched. He had been snipping away with a pair of kitchen scissors at the tufts of grass growing round the wooden legs of the St. Tancred's signboard.

'God's work takes many strange forms,' he said, when he saw me grinning at his handiwork.

'I visited the poor soul in hospital,' he went on, 'directly after Morning Prayer.'

'You spoke to her?' I asked, astonished.

'Oh, dear, no. Nothing like that. I'm sure she wasn't even aware of my presence. Nurse Duggan told me that she hadn't regained consciousness – the Gypsy woman, of course, not Nurse Duggan – and that she – the Gypsy woman, I mean – had spent a restless night, crying out every now and then about something that was hidden. The poor thing was delirious, of course.'

Something hidden? What could Fenella have meant?

It was true that she had mentioned to me the woman whose fortune she had told just before mine: something about something that was buried in the past, but would that count as hidden? It was worth a try.

'It's too bad, isn't it?' I said, shaking my head. 'Hers was the most popular pitch at the fête – until the tent caught fire, that is. She was telling me how startled someone was – the person who went in just before me, I believe – when she happened to guess correctly something about her past.'

Had a little cloud drifted across the vicar's face?

'Her past? Oh, I should hardly think so. The person whose fortune was told immediately before yours was Mrs. Bull.'

Mrs. Bull? Well, I'll be blowed! I'd have been willing to take an oath that Mrs. Bull's first encounter with Fenella in several years had taken place in my presence, on Saturday, in the Gully – after the fête.

'Are you sure?' I asked.

'Quite sure,' the vicar said. 'I was standing near the coconut pitch talking to Ted Sampson when Mrs. Bull asked me to keep an eye on her tots for a few minutes. "I shan't be long, Vicar," she said. "But I must have my fortune read – make sure there are no more of these little blighters in my future."

'She was joking, of course, but still, it seemed a very odd thing to say, under the circumstances.' The vicar reddened. 'Oh, dear, I fear I've been indiscreet. You must forget my words at once.'

'Don't worry, Vicar,' I told him. 'I won't say a word.'

I went through the motions of sewing my lips shut with a needle and a very long piece of thread. The vicar winced at my grimaces.

'Besides,' I said, 'it's not the same as if the Bulls were your parishioners.'

252

'It *is* the same,' he said. 'Discretion is discretion – it knows no religious bounds.'

'Is Mrs. Bull a Hobbler?' I asked suddenly.

His brow wrinkled. 'A Hobbler? Whatever makes you think that? Dear me, that somewhat peculiar faith was, if I am not mistaken, suppressed in the late eighteenth century. There have been rumours, of course, but one mustn't–'

'Was it?' I interrupted. 'Suppressed, I mean?'

Could it be that the Hobblers had gone underground so effectively that their very presence in Bishop's Lacey was disbelieved by the vicar of St. Tancred's?

'Whatever her allegiances,' the vicar continued, 'we mustn't pass judgement upon the beliefs of others, must we?'

'I suppose not,' I said, just as the meaning of his earlier words struck home.

'Did you say you were talking to a Mr. Sampson? Mr. Sampson of East Finching?'

The vicar nodded. 'Ted Sampson. He still comes back to lend a hand with the tents and booths. He's been doing it man and boy for twenty-five years. He says it makes him feel close to his parents – they're both of them buried here in the churchyard, you understand. Of course he's lived in East Finching since he married a–'

'Yes?' I said. If I'd had whiskers they'd have been trembling.

'Oh dear,' the vicar said. 'I fear I've said too much. You must excuse me.'

He dropped to his knees and resumed his snipping at the grass, and I knew that our interview was at an end.

Gladys's tyres purred on the tarmac as we sped north towards East Finching. It was easy going at first, but then as the road rose up, fold upon fold, into the encircling hills, I had to lean on her pedals like billy-ho.

By the time I reached Pauper's Well at the top of Denham Rise, I was panting like a dog. I dismounted and, leaning Gladys against the stone casing of the well, dropped to my knees for a drink.

Pauper's Well was not so much a well as a natural spring: a place where the water gurgled up from some underground source, and had done so since before the Romans had helped themselves to an icy, refreshing swig.

Spring water, I knew, was a remarkable chemical soup: calcium, magnesium, potassium, iron, and assorted salts and sulphates. I grabbed the battered old tin cup that hung from a chain, scooped it full of the burbling water, and drank until I thought I could feel my bones strengthening.

With the water still dribbling down my chin, I stood up and looked out over the countryside. Behind me, spread out like a handkerchief for a doll's picnic, was Bishop's Lacey. Through it, this side of the high street, the river Efon wound its lazy way round the village before ambling off to the southwest and Buckshaw.

Now, almost two weeks into the harvest, most of the countryside had traded its intense summer green for a paler, greyish shade, as if Mother Nature had nodded off a little, and let the colours leak away.

In the distance, like a black bug crawling up the hillside, a tractor dragged a harrow across a farmer's field, the buzz of its engine coming clearly to my ears.

From up here, I could see the Palings to the south, a green oasis at a bend in the river. And there was Buckshaw, its stones glowing warmly in the sunlight, as if they had been cut from precious citrine and polished by a master's hand.

Harriet's house, I thought, although for the life of me I don't know why. Something was welling up in my throat. It must have been something in the well water. I took Gladys from her resting place and shoved off towards East Finching.

From this point on, the journey was all downhill. After a couple of jolly good pumps to get up speed, I put my feet up on the handlebars, and Gladys and I with the wind in our teeth came swooping like a harrier down the dusty road and into East Finching's high street.

Unlike its neighbours, Malden Fenwick and Bishop's Lacey, East Finching was not a pretty bit of Ye Olde England. No half-timbered houses here – no riot of flowers in cottage gardens. Instead, the word that came to mind was 'grubby.'

At least half the shops in the high street had boarded-up windows, while those that were apparently still in business had rather a sad and defeated look.

In the window of a tobacconist's shop on the corner, a crooked sign advertised: *Today's Papers.*

A bell above the door gave out a harsh jangle as I stepped inside, and a grey-haired man with old-fashioned square spectacles looked up from

255

his newspaper.

'Well?' he said, as if I had surprised him in his bath.

'Excuse me,' I said. 'I wonder if you can help me? I'm looking for Mr. Sampson – Edward Sampson. Could you tell me where he lives?'

'What you want with him, then? Selling biscuits, are you?'

His mouth broke into a ghastly grin, revealing three horrid teeth which appeared to be carved from rotted wood.

It was the same thing, more or less, that the abominable Ursula had said to me at Vanetta Harewood's door: a bad joke that was doing the rounds of the countryside, the way bad jokes do.

I held my tongue.

'Selling biscuits, are you?' he said again, like a music hall comic beating a joke to death.

'Actually, no,' I said. 'Mr. Sampson's parents are buried in St. Tancred's churchyard, in Bishop's Lacey, and we're setting up a Graves Maintenance Fund. It's the war, you see... We thought that perhaps he'd like to–'

The man stared at me sceptically over his spectacles. I was going to have to do better than this.

'Oh, yes – I almost forgot. I also bring thanks from the vicar and the ladies of the Women's Institute – and the Altar Guild – for Mr. Sampson's help with the fête on Saturday. It was a smashing success.'

I think it was the WI and the Altar Guild that did it. The tobacconist wrinkled his nose in disgust, hitched his spectacles a little higher, and jabbed his thumb towards the street.

'Yellow fence,' he said. 'Salvage,' and went back to his reading.

'Thank you,' I said. 'You're very kind.'

And I almost meant it.

The place was hard to miss. A tall wooden fence, in a shade of yellow that betrayed the use of war surplus aviation paint, sagged inwards and outwards along three sides of a large property.

It was evident that the fence had been thrown up in an attempt to hide from the street the ugliness of the salvage business, but with little effect. Behind its boards, piles of rusting metal scrap towered into the air like heaps of giant jackstraws.

On the fence tall red letters, painted by an obviously amateur hand, spelled out: SAMP-SON – SALVAGE – SCRAP IRON BOUGHT – BEST PRICES – MOTOR PARTS.

An iron rod leant against the double gates, holding them shut. I put my eye to the crack and peered inside.

Maddeningly, there wasn't much to see – because of the angle, my view was blocked by a wrecked lorry that had been overturned and its wheels removed.

With a quick glance up and down the street, I shifted the rod, tugged the gates open a bit, took a deep breath, and squeezed through.

Immediately in front of me, a sign painted in blood-red letters on the hulk of a pantechnicon said BEWARE OF THE DOC – as if the animal in question had gone for the artist's throat before he could finish the letter G.

I stopped in my tracks and listened, but there

was no sign of the beast. Perhaps the warning was meant simply to scare off strangers.

On one side of the yard was a good-sized Nissen hut which, judging by the tyre tracks leading to its double doors, was in regular use. To my right, like a row of iron oasthouses, the towering junk piles I had seen from outside the gates led away towards the back of the lot. Projecting from the closest heap – as if it had just crashed and embedded itself – was what surely must be the back half of a Spitfire, the red, white, and blue RAF markings as fresh and bright as if they had been applied just yesterday.

The fence had concealed the size of the place – it must have covered a couple of acres. Beyond the mountains of scrap, spotted here and there, scores of wrecked motorcars subsided sadly into the grass, and even at the back of the property, where the scrap gave way gradually to an orchard, blotches of coloured metal glinting among the trees signalled that there were bodies there, too.

As I moved warily along the gravel path between the heaps of broken machinery, hidden things gave off an occasional rusty *ping* as if they were trying to warm themselves enough in the sun to come back to life – but with little success.

'Hello?' I called, hoping desperately that there would be no answer – and there wasn't.

At the end of an L-shaped bend in the gravel was a brick structure: rather like a washhouse, I thought, or perhaps a laundry, with a round chimney rising up about thirty feet above its flat roof.

The windows were so coated with grime that even by rubbing with my fist, I could see nothing

258

inside. In place of a knob, the door was furnished with what looked like a homemade latch: something cobbled together from bits of iron fencing.

I put my thumb on the tongue of the thing and pressed it down. The latch popped up, the door swung open, and I stepped into the dim interior.

The place was unexpectedly bare. On one side was a large fire chamber whose open door revealed a bottom covered with cold ashes and cinders. On its side was mounted what appeared to be a motor-driven blower.

These things hadn't changed in four or five hundred years, I thought. Aside from the electric fan, there was little difference between this device and the crucibles of the alchemists that filled the pages of several vellum manuscripts in Uncle Tar's library.

In essence, this furnace was not unlike the gas crucible that Uncle Tar had installed in the laboratory at Buckshaw, but on a much larger scale, of course.

On the brick hearth in front of the furnace, beside a long steel ladle, lay several broken moulds: wooden chests that had been filled with sand into which objects had been pressed to make an impression – into which the molten iron had then been poured.

Dogs, by the look of them, I thought. *Spaniels indented in the sand to make a pair of doorstops.*

Or firedogs.

And I knew then, even though I had not yet had a chance to test them for authenticity, that it was here, in Edward Sampson's washhouse foundry, that copies of Sally Fox and Shoppo had been cast: the copies that were likely, at this very moment, standing in for the originals on the drawing-room hearth at Buckshaw.

But where were Harriet's originals? Were they the fire irons I had seen in Miss Mountjoy's coach house – the antiques warehouse in which Brookie Harewood kept his treasure? Or were they the ones I had seen in the hands of Sampson, the bull-dog man, at the back door of Pettibone's antiques shop? I shuddered at the very thought of it.

Still, I had already accomplished much of what I had come to do. All that remained was to search the Nissen hut for papers. With any luck, a familiar name might well pop up.

At that moment I heard the sound of a motor outside.

I glanced quickly round the room. Save for diving into the cold furnace, there was nowhere to hide. The only alternative was to dash out into the open and make a run for it.

I chose the furnace.

Thoughts of Hansel and Gretel crossed my mind as I pulled the heavy door shut behind me and crouched, trying to make myself as small as possible.

Another dress ruined, I thought – and another sad-eyed lecture from Father.

It was then that I heard the footsteps on the stone floor.

I hardly dared take a breath – the sound of it would be amplified grotesquely by the brick bee-hive in which I was huddled.

The footsteps paused, as if the person outside were listening.

They moved on ... then stopped again.

There was a metallic *CLANG* as something touched the door just inches from my face. And then, slowly ... so slowly that I nearly screamed from suspense ... the door swung open.

The first thing I saw was his boots: large, dusty, scarred from work.

Then the leg of his coveralls.

I raised my eyes and looked into his face. 'Dieter!'

It was Dieter Schrantz, the labourer from Culverhouse Farm – Bishop's Lacey's sole remaining prisoner of war, who had elected to stay in England after the end of hostilities.

'Is it really you?'

I began dusting myself off as I scrambled out of the furnace. Even when I had come out of my crouch and stood up straight, Dieter still towered above me, his blue eyes and blond hair making him seem like nothing so much as a vastly overgrown schoolboy.

'What are you doing here?' I asked, breaking out in a silly grin.

'Am I permitted to ask the same?' Dieter said, taking in the whole room with a sweep of his hand. 'Unless this place has become part of Buckshaw, I should say you're a long way from home.'

I smiled politely at his little joke. Dieter had something of a crush on my sister Feely, but aside from that, he was a decent enough chap.

'I was playing Solitaire Hare and Hounds,' I said, making up rules wildly and talking too fast. 'East Finching counts double for a compound name, and Sampson's scores a triple S – Sampson's, Salvage, and Scrap – see? I'd get an extra point for having someone with a biblical name, but today's not a Sunday, so it doesn't count.'

Dieter nodded gravely. 'Very complex, the English rules,' he said. 'I have never completely grasped them myself.'

He moved towards the door, but turned to see if I was following.

'Come on,' he said, 'I'm going your way. I'll give you a lift.'

I wasn't particularly ready to leave, but I knew that my nosing around was at an end. Who, after all, can carry out full-scale snoopage with a six-foot-something ex-prisoner of war dogging one's every footstep?

I blinked a bit as we stepped out into the sun. On the far side of the path, Dieter's old grey Ferguson tractor stood tut-tutting to itself, like an elephant that has stumbled by accident upon the elephant's graveyard: a little shocked, perhaps, to find itself suddenly among the bones of its ancestors.

After closing the gate, I climbed onto the hitch between the two rear wheels, and dragged Gladys up behind me. Dieter let in the clutch, and we were off, the Fergie's tall tyres sending up a spray of cinders that fell away behind us like dark fireworks.

We flew like the wind, basking in the September sunlight and drinking in the fresh autumn air, so it was only when we were halfway down the south slope of Denham Rise that the penny dropped.

My posterior was braced firmly against one of the Fergie's wings and my feet on the clanking

262

hitch. As we sped along, the ground beneath was just a rushing blur of greenish black.

But why, I thought suddenly, *would a farmer be so far from home with no trailer rumbling along behind; no plough, no harrow swaying in the rear?* It simply made no sense.

I felt my hackles beginning to rise.

'Who sent you?' I shouted above the whistling wind and the roar of the Fergie's engine.

'What?'

I knew from my own experience that he was stalling for time.

'What?' he said again, as if I hadn't heard him, which made me suddenly and inexplicably furious.

'It was Father, wasn't it?'

But even as the words came out of my mouth, I knew that I was wrong. There was no more chance that Father would telephone Dieter than that the Man in the Moon should ring up the rat catcher.

'Inspector Hewitt!'

I was clutching at straws. The Inspector was equipped with his own official transportation, and would never send a civilian on one of his errands.

Dieter shoved up the throttle in its quadrant and the tractor slowed. He pulled off into a small lay-by where a wooden platform was piled with milk containers.

He turned to me, not smiling.

'It was Ophelia,' he said.

'Feely?' I screeched. Had my sister sent Dieter to follow me? All day?

How dare she! How doubly-damned dare she!

This was an outrage.

That I should be thwarted – torn away – kidnapped, virtually, from an important investigation – by my own sister made me see red.

Bright red.

Without a word, I jumped down from the tractor's hitch, lifted Gladys onto the road, and set off walking down the hill, my head held high and my pigtails swaying.

When I got far enough away to remember it, I put one foot onto a pedal and mounted, shoving off shakily, but recovering enough to begin an offended but dignified coasting.

Moments later, I heard the tractor's engine rev up, but I did not look back.

Dieter pulled alongside, driving precisely to keep pace.

'She was worried about you,' he said. 'She wanted me to see that you were all right.'

Feely worried about me? I could hardy believe it. I could count on one finger the times she had treated me decently in the past couple of years.

'To spy on me, you mean,' I shot back.

It was a mean thing to say, but I said it. I quite liked Dieter, but the thought of him being under my sister's thumb made me livid.

'Come on, hop up,' Dieter said, bringing the tractor to a full stop. 'Your bicycle, too.'

'No, thank you very much. We prefer to be alone.'

I began pedalling to get ahead of the tractor. I suppose I could have pulled over and waited, then climbed aboard for a graciously accepted ride into the village.

But by the time I thought of it, I was already halfway up the high street.

I was disappointed not to find Dogger at work in the greenhouse. It was always such a pleasure to slip in, sit quietly down beside him, and fall into easy conversation, like two old gaffers on a bench beside the duck pond.

Second choice, when I wanted information, was Mrs. Mullet, but as I discovered when I stepped into the kitchen, she had already gone home for the day.

I'd have given anything to be able to pump Daffy about the Hobblers, but something kept me from asking any more of her. I still hadn't taken my revenge for her part in the cellar inquisition, even though I had already twice broken my injured silence to ask her about Poseidon and about Hilda Muir – or Hildemoer, to be more precise – and the pixies.

It seemed to me that you couldn't possibly win a war in which you were forever going over to the other side for advice. Also, fraternising – or whatever you call it when sisters do it – with the enemy diluted one's resolve to kick them in the teeth.

My head was fairly fizzing with information, and there had been little time to sort it all out.

Some of the more interesting points had already begun to come together in my mind, clustering and curdling in much the same way that silver chloride (good old $AgCl$) forms a sort of chemical cheese when a soluble chloride is added to silver nitrate.

Soluble! That was the word. Would I ever be

able to solve this complex tangle of puzzles?

One thing was immediately clear: I needed to know more – much, much more – about the Hobblers, and it was clear that no Hobbler of my immediate acquaintance was going to make my life easier by spilling the beans.

TWENTY-ONE

I awakened to the roar of water on the roof tiles and in the drains – the sound of Buckshaw in the rain.

Even before I opened my eyes, I could hear that the whole house had come alive in a way that it never did in dry weather – a deep, wet breathing in and out – as if, after a mad dash down the centuries, the tired old place had just thrown itself across the finish line.

There would be little winds in the corridors, I knew, and sudden cold drafts would spring up in out-of-the-way corners. In spite of its size, Buckshaw had all the comfort of a submarine.

I wrapped myself in my blanket and stumped to the window. Outside, the stuff was coming straight down, as if it were lines drawn with pencil and a ruler. It was not the kind of rain that was going to pass away quickly – we were in for hours of it.

Father acknowledged my presence at the breakfast table with a curt nod. At least he didn't try to make chipper conversation, I thought, and for that I offered up a little prayer of thanksgiving.

266

Feely and Daffy, as usual, were busily pretending that I didn't exist.

Rainy days cast a darker than usual pall over our morning meal, and today was no exception.

Our September breakfast menu had been in force for almost two weeks now, and the base of my tongue shrank back a little as Mrs. Mullet brought to the table what I thought of as our daily ration of T.O.A.D.

Toast
Oatmeal
Apple Juice
Dates

The dates, stewed and served with cold clotted cream, were another of Mrs. Mullet's culinary atrocities. They looked and tasted like something that had been stolen from a coffin in a midnight churchyard.

'Pass the dead man's,' Daffy would say, without looking up from her book, and Father would fix her with a flickering glare until the latest philatelic journal dragged his attention back to its pages – a time span of, usually, no more than about two and three-quarter seconds.

But today Daffy said nothing, her arm reaching out robotically and shovelling a few spoonfuls of the vile mess into her bowl.

Feely wasn't down yet, so I made a relatively easy escape.

'May I be excused, please?' I asked, and Father grunted.

Seconds later I was in the hall cupboard, fishing

267

out my bright yellow waterproof.

'When cycling in the rain,' Dogger had told me, 'being visible is more important than keeping dry.'

'You mean that I can always dry out, but I can't be brought back to life when I'm impaled on the horns of a Daimler,' I said, partly joking.

'Precisely,' Dogger had said with a perfect tiny smile, and gone back to waxing Father's boots.

It was still coming down like lances as I made a dash for the greenhouse, where I had left Gladys. Gladys didn't much like the rain, since it made her skirts muddy, but she never complained.

I had plotted my course to Rook's End with great care, avoiding both the Gully and the house of the dreaded Mrs. Bull.

As I pedalled along the road towards Bishop's Lacey in my yellow mackintosh, I remembered what Dogger had said about visibility. In spite of the mist that hung like tatters of grey laundry over the soaked fields, I could probably be seen for miles. And yet, in another sense, because I was only eleven years old, I was wrapped in the best cloak of invisibility in the world.

I thought of the time Mrs. Mullet had taken me to see *The Invisible Man*. We had gone on the bus to Hinley to replace an Easter dress that I had ruined during a particularly interesting – but failed – experiment involving both sulphuric and hydrochloric acids.

After a sickening hour in Fashions by Eleanor, a shop in the high street whose windows were bandaged over with paper banners in dreadful shades of pink and aqua– 'Latest Easter Frocks for Young Misses!' 'New From London!' 'Just in Time for Easter!' – Mrs. Mullet had taken pity on me and suggested a visit to a nearby A.B.C. tea shop.

There we had sat, for three quarters of an hour at a table in the window, watching people stroll by on the pavement outside. Mrs. M had become quite chatty and, forgetting perhaps that I wasn't her friend Mrs. Waller, had let slip several things that, although they were not important at the time, would probably come in handy when I was older.

After the tea and the pastries, with most of the afternoon still ahead of us ('You was a real trouper about the frock, dear – in spite of them two witches with their tapes and pins!'), Mrs. M had decided to treat me to the cinema she had spotted in the narrow street beside the tea shop.

Because Mrs. Mullet had seen it years before, she talked all the way through *The Invisible Man*, nudging me in the ribs as she explained it to me minute by minute.

''E can see them, like, but they can't see 'im.'

Although I was amused at the mad scientist's idea of injecting a powerful bleach to render himself invisible, what truly shocked me was the way he treated his laboratory equipment.

'It's just a fill-um, dear,' Mrs. Mullet said, as I gripped her arm during the smashing of the glassware.

But all in all, I thought, looking back on it, the entertainment had not been a success. Invisibility was nothing new to me. It was an art I had been forced to learn from the day I took my first step.

Visible and invisible: the trick of being present and absent at the same time.

'Yaroo!' I shouted to no one in particular as I

splashed past St. Tancred's and into the high street.

At the far end of the village, I turned south. Through the rain I could just make out in the distance the Jack-o'-Lantern, a skull-shaped formation of rock that overhung my destination, Rook's End.

I was now running parallel to and a half-mile due east of the Gully, and before many minutes had passed, I was gliding along the edge of one of the great lawns that stretched off in three directions.

I had been at Rook's End once before to visit Father's old schoolmaster, Dr. Kissing. On that occasion I had found him in the decaying solarium of the nursing home, and was not looking forward to setting foot in that particular mausoleum again today.

But much to my surprise, as I leapt off Gladys at the front door, there was the old gentleman himself sitting in a wheelchair beneath a large, gaily coloured umbrella that had been set up on the lawn.

He waved as I plodded towards him through the wet grass.

'Ha! Flavia!' he said. 'It can be no ill day which brings a young visitor to my gate.' Horace, of course – or was it Catullus?'

I grinned as if I knew but had forgotten.

'Hello, Dr. Kissing,' I said, handing over the packet of Players I had filched from Feely's lingerie drawer. Feely had bought the things to impress Dieter. But Dieter had joked her out of it. 'No, thank you,' he said when she offered him

270

the packet. 'They ruin the chest,' and she had put the cigarettes away unopened. Feely was uncommonly proud of her chest.

'Ah,' Dr. Kissing said, producing a box of matches as if from nowhere and striking one expertly as he was still opening the packet of cigarettes. 'How very kind of you to think of my one great weakness.'

He inhaled deeply, holding the smoke in his lungs for what seemed like an eternity. Then, letting it escape as he spoke, he gazed off into the distance, as if addressing someone else.

'Thus he ruins his Health, and his Substance destroys,
By vainly pursuing his fanciful Joys,
Till perhaps in the Frolick he meets with his Bane
And runs on the weapon by which he is slain.'

And runs on the weapon by which he was slain?

My blood chilled as he spoke the last line. Was he referring to his own smoking of cigarettes – or to the bizarre death of Brookie Harewood?

A conversation with Dr. Kissing was, I knew, a game of chess. There would be no shortcuts.

'The Hobblers,' I said, making the opening move.

'Ah, yes.' He smiled. 'The Hobblers. I knew you would ask me about the Hobblers. One should have been disappointed if you hadn't.'

Could Mr. or Mrs. Pettibone have told him of my interest? Somehow, it seemed unlikely.

'Surely you don't suspect that I am one of them?'

271

'No,' I said, struggling to keep up with him. 'But I knew that your niece—'

Until that very moment I had nearly forgotten that Dr. Kissing was Miss Mountjoy's uncle.

'My niece? You thought that Tilda was keeping me briefed on your...? Good lord, no! She tells me nothing – nor anyone else. Not even God himself knows what Tilda's left hand is doing nowadays.'

He saw my puzzlement.

'One needs look no farther than one's own hearth,' he said.

'Mrs. Mullet?'

Dr. Kissing coughed a wheezy cough – which reminded me uncomfortably of Fenella – and consoled himself by lighting another cigarette.

'It is common knowledge that you are situated, as it were, in close proximity to the estimable Mrs. Mullet. The rest is mere conjecture.

'One has not, of course,' he went on, 'communicated personally with the good woman,' he said. 'But I believe she *is* known far and wide for, ah—'

'Dishing the dirt,' I volunteered.

He made a little bow from his waist. 'Your descriptive powers leave me in the dust,' he said.

I could easily grow to love this man.

'I know about Nicodemus Flitch,' I told him, 'and how he brought his faith to Bishop's Lacey. I know that there are still a few practising Hobblers in the neighbourhood, and that they still gather occasionally at the Palings.'

'To conduct baptisms.'

'Yes,' I said. 'For baptisms.'

'A much more common practice in years gone by,' he said. 'There are nowadays few Hobblers

272

left of childbearing age.'

I tried to think of who they might be. Certainly not Tilda Mountjoy or Mrs. Pettibone.

'I believe poor Mrs. Bull was the last,' he said, and I noticed he was watching me out of the corner of his eye.

'Mrs. Bull?'

Was Mrs. Bull a Hobbler?

'Mrs. Bull, who lives in the Gully?' I asked. 'The one whose baby was taken by Gypsies?'

I couldn't help myself. Even though I didn't believe it, the fearful words slipped out before I could think.

Dr. Kissing nodded. 'So it is said.'

'But you don't believe it.'

I was in fine form now, catching every shade of the old man's meaning.

'I must confess that I don't,' he said. 'And I expect that you would like me to tell you why.'

I could only manage a stupid grin.

Although the rain was still beating down upon the umbrella with a monotonous drumming, there was a surprising stillness and a warmth beneath its protective cover. Across the lawn, the dreadful house that was Rook's End crouched like a giant stone toad. In one of its tall windows – in what had once perhaps been the ballroom – two old ladies, in outlandish and outdated costumes, were dancing a stately minuet. I had seen this pair on my last visit to Dr. Kissing, executing their timeless steps beneath the trees, and now they had obviously spotted me.

As I watched, the shorter of the two paused long enough to wave a gloved hand and the other,

273

seeing her partner's greeting, came almost to the glass and made a deep and elaborate curtsy.

By the time I brought my attention back to Dr. Kissing, he was lighting another cigarette.

'Until last year,' he said, watching the smoke vanish into the rain, 'I was still able to make my way to the top of the Jack-o'-Lantern. For a young man in tip-top physical condition, it is no more than a pleasant stroll, but for a fossil in a wheelchair, it is torture.

'But then, to an old man, even torture can be a welcome relief to boredom, so I often made the ascent out of nothing more than spite.

'From the summit, one can survey the terrain as if from the basket of a hot-air balloon. To the northwest, in the distance, is Greyminster School, scene of my greatest triumphs and my greatest failure. To the west, one has a clear view of the Palings, and behind it, Buckshaw, your ancestral home.

'It was at the Palings, incidentally, that I once asked the lovely Letitia Humphrey for her hand in holy matrimony – and it was at the Palings that Letitia had the jolly good sense to say no.'

'I'll bet she lived to regret it,' I said gallantly.

'She lived – but without remorse. Letitia went on to marry a man who made a fortune adulterating wheat flour with bone dust. I am given to understand that they made each other very happy.'

A cloud of tobacco smoke made his sigh suddenly visible in the damp air.

'Did *you* regret it?' I asked. It was not a polite question, but I wanted to know.

'Although I scale the Jack-o'-Lantern no more,'

he said, 'it is not entirely because of my in-
firmities, but rather because of the increasingly
great sadness that is visible from the summit – a
sadness which is not nearly so noticeable from
the lower altitudes.'

'The Palings?'

'There was a time when I loved to gaze down
upon that ancient crook in the river as if from the
summit of my years. In fact, I was doing so on
that day in April, two and a half years ago, when
the Bull baby disappeared.'

My mouth must have fallen open.

'From my vantage point, I saw the Gypsy leave
her encampment – and later, saw Mrs. Bull pushing the baby's perambulator along the Gully.'

'Hold on,' I said. 'Surely it was the other way
round?'

'It was as I have described. The Gypsy woman
hitched her horse and drove her caravan north
along the Gully. Sometime later, the Bull woman
appeared, wheeling her baby south towards the
Palings.'

'Perhaps the pram was empty,' I ventured.

'An excellent point,' Dr. Kissing said, 'except
for the fact that I saw her lift out the infant whilst
she retrieved its lost bottle from the blankets.'

'But then Fenella couldn't have kidnapped the
baby.'

'Very good, Flavia. As you may have perceived,
I've long ago come to that same conclusion.'

'But–'

'Why did I not inform the police?'

I nodded dumbly.

'I have asked myself that, again and again. And

275

each time I have answered that it was, in part, because the police never asked me. But that will hardly do, will it? There is also the undeniable fact that when one reaches a certain age, one hesitates to take on a new cargo of trouble. It is as if, having experienced a certain amount of grief in a lifetime, one is given pass-slip to hand in to the Great Headmaster in the Sky. Do you understand?'

'I think I do,' I said.

'That is why I have kept it to myself,' he said. 'But oddly enough, it is also the reason that I am now telling you.'

The silence between us was broken only by the sound of the falling rain.

Then suddenly, from across the lawn, there came a shout: 'Dr. Kissing! Whatever are you thinking?'

It was the White Phantom, the same nurse I had seen on my previous visit to Rook's End, now looking ludicrous in her white uniform and huge black galoshes as she came galumphing across the grass towards us through the falling rain.

'Whatever are you *thinking?*' she asked again as she stepped beneath the umbrella. I've observed that domineering people like the White Phantom often say everything twice, as though they're on a quota system.

'I am thinking, Nurse Hammond,' Dr. Kissing said, 'of the sad decline in English manners since the late war.'

His words were met with a silent sniff as she seized the handles of his wheelchair and shoved off rapidly with it across the lawn.

As she paused to open the conservatory door,

Dr. Kissing's words came floating back to my ears—

'Tally-ho, Flavia!'

It was a call to the hunt.

I waved like mad to show him that I had understood, but it was too late. He had already been wheeled indoors and out of sight.

TWENTY-TWO

I think there must be a kind of courage that comes from not being able to make up your mind.

Whether it was this or whether it was Gladys's willfulness I can't be sure, but there we were, suddenly swerving off the main road and into the Gully.

I had been going here and there about the village, avoiding the unpleasant Mrs. Bull in much the same way as a housefly avoids the folded newspaper. But the Gully was a shortcut home to Buckshaw, and there was no time like the present.

Although Gladys's black paint was now spattered with mud, she seemed as frisky as if she had just been curried with a bristled brush and wiped down to perfection. Her nickel handlebars, at least, glittered in the sun.

'You're enjoying this, aren't you, old girl?' I said, and she gave a little squeak of delight.

Would Mrs. Bull be standing guard at her gate? Would I have to pretend again to be Margaret Vole, niece of that fictional – but beloved – old character actress, Gilda Dickinson?

I needn't have worried. Mrs. Bull was nowhere in sight, although the hovering smoke from the rubbish heaps made it difficult to see much of the property.

Her redheaded boy – the one who had been perched in the branches when I rode through the Gully with Fenella – was now sitting in the ditch at the edge of the road, digging his way to China with a piece of cutlery.

I brought Gladys to a slithering stop and put both feet on the ground.

'Hello,' I said, stupidly. 'What's *your* name?'

It was not the most brilliant opening, but I wasn't accustomed to talking to children, and hadn't the faintest idea how to begin. It didn't matter anyway, because the little wretch ignored me and went on with his excavating.

It was difficult to judge his age, which might have been anywhere between four and seven. His large head wobbled uneasily atop a spindly body, giving the impression that one was looking at rather a large baby or a small adult.

'Timofey,' he said in a froggy croak, just as I was about to shove off.

'Timothy?'

There was another awkward pause, during which I shifted uneasily from foot to foot.

'Timofey.'

'Is your mother at home, Timofey?' I asked.

'Dunno – yes – no,' he said, giving me a wary sideways glance, and he returned to his digging, stabbing fiercely at the soil with his bit of table-ware.

'Digging for treasure, are you?' I asked, going all chummy. I leaned Gladys against a bank and climbed down into the ditch. 'Here, let me help.'

I casually worked my hand into my off-side pocket and closed my fingers around a stick of horehound.

With a quick darting motion, I reached down into the hole he was digging, and pretended to extract the sweet.

'Oh, Timofey!' I cried, clapping my hands. 'Look what you've found! Good boy! Timofey's found a sweet!' Although it jarred, I couldn't bring myself to call him by any name other than the one he called himself.

As I held out the horehound, he snatched it away from me with a lightning-fast movement and shoved it into his mouth.

'Preasure!' he said, gnawing nastily.

'Yes, treasure,' I cooed. 'Timofey's found buried treasure.'

With the horehound stick jutting out of the corner of his mouth like a sickroom thermometer, Timofey put down his digging implement and attacked the hole with his bare hands.

My heart gave a leap as my mind registered what now lay exposed in the dirt: the silver ... the prongs ... the figure of the lobster punched from the handle ... the de Luce monogram...

The child was digging with one of the de Luce lobster picks! But how could that be? Dogger had already shipped the silver to Sotheby's for auction and the only piece that had been overlooked, perhaps, was the one that had been used to put paid to Brookie Harewood. And that, unless I was sadly mistaken, had, until quite recently, been shoved up Brookie Harewood's nostril and into his brain. How could it possibly have made its way from there into the hands of an urchin grubbing in the Gully? Or could this be a copy?

'Here,' I said. 'Let me help you. I'm bigger. I can dig faster. Find more sweets.'

I made digging motions with my hands, scooping like a badger.

But Timofey snatched up the lobster pick, and was holding it away from me.

'Mime!' he said around the horehound. 'Mime! Timofey foumd it!'

'Good boy!' I said. 'Let's have a look.'

'No!'

'All right,' I said. 'I don't want to see it anyway.'

If there's anyone on earth who knows the ways of a child's mind, I thought, *it's me – Flavia de Luce –* for I had not so long ago been one myself.

As I spoke, I reached into my pocket and extracted another stick of horehound – this one, my last. I gazed at it fondly, held it up to the sunlight to admire its golden glow, smacked my lips–

'Give over!' the child said. 'I wants it!'

'Tell you what,' I told him. 'I'll trade you for that nasty digger. You don't want that old thing. It's dirty.'

I pulled a horrid face and went through the motions of retching, sound effects and all.

He grinned, and inserted the prongs of the lobster pick into one of his nostrils.

'No, Timofey!' I said in the most commanding voice I could summon. 'It's sharp – you'll hurt yourself. Give it here.

'At once!' I added sternly, putting on the voice of authority, as Father does when he wants to be instantly obeyed. I held out my hand and Timofey meekly laid the silver lobster pick across my lifeline – the very part of my hand that the Gypsy – Fenella – was it only three days ago? – had held in her own and told me that in it she saw darkness.

'Good boy,' I said, my head swimming as my fingers closed upon the murder weapon. 'Where did you get it?'

I handed him the horehound stick and he grabbed it greedily. I shoved my hand into my empty pocket, as if I were digging into a bottomless bag of sweets.

I locked my eyes with his, noticing, for the first time, the strange transparency of his irises. I would not look away, I thought – not until–

'Danny's mocket,' he said suddenly, his words oozing out around the sticky horehound.

Danny's mocket? Danny's *pocket,* of course! I was proud of myself.

But who was Danny? It couldn't be the baby – the baby wasn't old enough to have pockets. Did Mrs. Bull have an older son?

My mind was buzzing with possibilities as I shoved the lobster fork into my pocket. It was a mistake.

'Mam!' the child shrieked, 'Mam! Mam! Mam! Mam! Mam!' each cry louder and higher in pitch.

I scrambled out of the ditch and made for Gladys.

'Mam! Mam! Mam! Mam! Mam!'

The little rotter had been set off like a blasted alarm.

281

'You!' came a voice from out of the smoke, and suddenly Mrs. Bull was coming towards me, lumbering through the smouldering heaps like something out of a nightmare.

'You!' she shouted, her raw arms already extended, ready to seize me. Once she laid hands on me, I knew, I was done for. The woman was big enough to tear me apart like a bundle of rotten rags.

I grabbed at Gladys and pushed off, my feet slipping wildly from the pedals as I threw myself forward, trying to put on speed.

Oddly enough, I was thinking quite clearly. Should I try to divert her by shouting 'Fire!' and pointing at her house? Since the place was surrounded by smouldering rubbish heaps, it seemed both a good and a bad idea.

But it was no time for tactics – Mrs. Bull was bearing down upon me with alarming speed.

'Mam! Mam! Mam! Mam! Mam!' Timofey went on maddeningly from the ditch.

The woman's huge hands snatched at me as our paths intersected. I needed to get past her to be safe. If she managed to seize even so much as one of my sleeves, I was sunk.

'Yaroo!' The cry came out of me quite unexpectedly, but I recognised it at once. It was the battle cry of a savage – a fierce, fearless bellowing that rose up out of my ancestral lungs as if it had been lying in wait for centuries.

'Yaroo!' I let another fly just for pleasure. It felt good.

Mrs. Bull didn't stop – but she faltered – missed a step – and I shot past.

I looked back over my shoulder and saw the woman standing in the road, her fists shaking, her red face contorted with fury as she screamed: 'Tom, get yourself out here ... and bring the axe!'

I sat on the river's edge letting the water cool my feet. There was an unearthly silence in the Palings, and I shivered a little at the thought of the things that had happened within the past few days. First there had been the attack on Fenella, followed almost immediately by the death of Brookie Harewood. Then, too, Porcelain had told me, just before she'd cleared off, that the police had found the body of a baby – probably the Bulls' baby – right here in the grove. I suppose I should have felt sorry for the mother. She may have been mad with grief, for all I knew. Perhaps I should have taken my life in my hands and expressed my condolences.

But life is never easy, is it? If only one could make time run backwards, as it does in those short subjects at the cinema where dynamited factory chimneys fall upwards and restore themselves, and shattered bits of glass fly together to form a vase...

In such a world I could, if I wished, bicycle backwards up the Gully, dismount from Gladys, and give the woman a hug. I could tell her I was sorry they'd found the body of her baby buried here in the Palings, and that if there was anything I could do to help, she had only to ask.

I sighed.

Across the river and through the trees, not far from where Fenella's caravan was parked, I could see a mound of fresh soil. That must be the spot where the body had been found.

Other than the fact that she'd seen the baby's foot– 'Wrapped in a carpet, or something,' she had said, 'a bundle of old green bones' – Porcelain hadn't given me any more of the details. And it was too late now – Porcelain was gone.

I could hardly ask Inspector Hewitt about the discovery of the body, and until I had the opportunity to find out from Mrs. Mullet what the village was saying, I was on my own. I would wade across and have a look.

The river was not very deep here. The Hobblers, after all, had been coming to this spot for centuries to baptise their babies. The water was of just sufficient depth for a good old ducking, and I was no more than a hundred feet from the disturbed spot where the police had evidently made their gruesome find.

I hitched up the hem of my dress a couple of inches and started across.

Even a few feet out from the bank, the water grew noticeably colder on the bottom as I waded slowly towards the centre, my arms widespread for balance, taking great care not to lose my footing in the ever-strengthening current.

Soon I was at the halfway point – and then I was past it. The water level had receded to just below my knees when I stepped on something hard, stumbled, missed my footing, and went flailing tail-over-teakettle into the water. Total immersion.

'Oh, rat spit!' I said. I was furious with myself. Why hadn't I taken Gladys and walked her across the little bridge?

'Double rat spit!'

I scrambled to my feet and looked down at myself. My dress was completely soaked.

Father would be furious.

'Damn it all – dash it all, Flavia,' he would say, as he always did, and then would begin one of those silences between us that would last for several days until one of us forgot about my offense. 'Being at loggerheads,' Daffy called it, and now, as I stood knee-deep in the water, I tried to imagine that I had been suddenly transported to a cold, rushing river somewhere in the Canadian north woods, with the severed heads of the loggers bobbing past me in the current like bloated, grizzled apples.

But practicality brought me back to Bishop's Lacey. I knew that when I got home to Buck-shaw, I would have to sneak into the house, make my way upstairs, and rinse out the dress in the sink of my laboratory.

In the water, the little cloud of mud stirred up by my feet was clearing quickly.

It was odd – although I could easily see the tops of my feet on the river's bed, there were no stones in sight. And yet I had certainly tripped on some-thing hard. I had nearly broken a toe on the stupid thing. *As I had done before!*

I stood there for a moment, already feeling a chill in the September air.

Something in the water shifted: a bubble ... a ripple of water ... of light.

Slowly I bent at the waist and reached carefully into the river's depths.

A little deeper ... a little farther to the left. Although I couldn't see it, my fingers closed around something hard. I took a firm grip and

285

lifted it towards the surface.

As the object came up towards me through the water it became visible. It was eerie.

Hard ... transparent ... invisible in the water ... becoming visible as it came into the air.

A sudden sinking feeling told me that my heart already knew what the thing was before my head did, and both had already begun to pound as I realised that the object I was holding in my hands was Fenella's crystal ball – the ball with which some unknown person had bashed in her skull: the ball with which someone had tried to kill her.

The thing had been lying on the river bottom for days, its transparency making it invisible in the water even though it was in plain sight. No wonder the police had missed it!

Only if they had waded around in the shallows – and only then if they had stepped upon it by accident, as I had – would they have found the object of their search.

I would, of course, take it to Inspector Hewitt at once.

As I climbed the bank, I noticed that a silence had fallen upon the Palings, as if the birds were afraid to make even a peep.

The crystal ball was cold in my hands, refracting distorted images of earth, trees, and sky, its swirling colours like dye dropped into water.

If it hadn't been for the glass, I might have missed the flash of blue among the trees – a colour that didn't belong there.

I stopped in my tracks as if preoccupied. *Don't look directly at it,* I thought.

I twisted the hem of my dress uselessly, as if trying to wring it dry, then made a little hammock of the material in which to sling the crystal ball.

Would my wet hands leave fingerprints? Who knew? It was the best I could do.

'Blast it all!' I said loudly, more for effect than anything, but signalling that I thought I was alone.

With my peripheral vision, I could see that there was a swatch of colour among the bushes. By shifting my gaze slightly, I could see that it appeared to be a scarf – a flowered scarf.

Could it be one of the pixies Daffy and Feely had told me about – one of those malevolent water sprites that stole babies? Perhaps it was the very one that had taken Mrs. Bull's child! But no … pixies didn't exist. Or did they?

I let my eyes drift slowly to the right.

Quite abruptly, as if by magic, an image snapped into place. It was like one of those optical illusions in *The Girl's Own Annual* in which a silhouette of two faces in profile is suddenly seen to be an egg cup.

Grey hair … grey eyes, staring straight at me … a scarf at the throat … riding breeches – even the monocle hanging by a black cord round the neck.

It was Vanetta Harewood's companion, Ursula, standing motionless among the bushes, counting on the camouflage of stillness to keep me from spotting her – Ursula who gathered willow withies from the riverbank to twist into her dreadful baskets.

I let my eyes meet hers, then drift away, as if I hadn't seen her. I looked to her right – to her left – and finally above her, letting my mouth fall open slackly.

287

I scratched my head, and then, I'm afraid, my bottom.

'I'm coming, Gladys,' I shouted. 'It's only a squirrel.'

And with that, I made off across the bridge, muttering away to myself like the mad daughter of an eccentric squire.

Damn! I thought. I hadn't had a chance to examine the police diggings.

Still, my day had been remarkably productive. In my pocket was the silver de Luce lobster pick that I was quite sure had been used to put an end to Brookie Harewood, and cradled in my skirt, the crystal ball that was almost certainly the object with which Fenella had been bashed. After all, if it wasn't, then why would it have been tossed into the river?

An idea began to take shape.

Of course I would hand over these weapons at once to Inspector Hewitt – I had planned to do so all along, for various reasons.

But first, I wondered, was it possible to retrieve fingerprints from an object that had been immersed for days in running water?

TWENTY-THREE

I had climbed no more than a dozen stairs when Father's voice, from somewhere below me in the foyer, said, 'Flavia–'

Thwarted!

I stopped, turned, and came down one step out of respect. He was standing at the entrance to the west wing. 'My study, please.'

He turned and was gone.

I trudged down the steps and trailed along behind him, making a point of hanging well back.

'Close the door,' he said, and sat down at his desk.

This was serious. Father usually delivered his little lectures while standing at the window, gazing out into the grounds.

I perched on the edge of a chair, and tried to look attentive.

'I've had a call from Nurse Hammond on the–' He pointed in the general direction of the telephone, but could not bring himself to say the word. '...instrument. She tells me that you took Dr. Kissing out into the rain.'

The hag! I'd done no such thing.

'He wasn't in the rain,' I protested. 'He was sitting under an umbrella on the lawn, and he was already outside when I got there.'

'It makes no difference,' Father said, holding up a hand like a policeman directing traffic.

'But–'

'He's an old man, Flavia. He's not to be bothered with nonsensical intrusions upon his privacy.'

'But–'

'This gadding about the countryside must stop,' he said. 'You're making a confounded nuisance of yourself.'

A nuisance! Well!

I could have spat on his carpet.

'I've given this a great deal of thought recently,'

he said, 'and come to the conclusion that you have far too much time on your hands.'

'But–'

'Part of that is my own fault, I'll admit. You've not been provided with sufficient supervision and, as a result, your interests have become rather – unhealthy.'

'Unhealthy?'

'Consequently,' Father ploughed on, 'I've decided that you need to be more among people – more in the company of your peers.'

What was he talking about? On the one hand I was wandering about the village excessively, and now, on the other, I was in need of human companionship. It sounded like something you might say about a rogue sheepdog.

But before I could protest, Father took off his glasses, very deliberately folded their black, spidery arms across the lenses, and put them away in their hard-shelled case. It was a sign that the conversation was nearing its end.

'The vicar tells me that the choir is in need of several extra voices, and I've assured him that you'd be happy to pitch in. They've laid on an extra practice this evening at six-thirty sharp.'

I was so astonished I couldn't think of a single word to say.

Later, I thought of one.

'Don't dawdle,' Feely said, as we marched across the fields towards the church. She had been summoned to sit in, as she sometimes did, for Mr. Collicutt.

'Where's old Cockie, then,' I had asked, and

waited for the inevitable explosion. Feely, I think, was half in love with the handsome young man who had recently been appointed organist at St. Tancreds. She had even gone so far as to join the choir because of the superior view of his bobbing blond curls afforded by a seat in the chancel.

But Feely wasn't biting – in fact, she was strangely subdued.

'He's adjudicating the music festival in Hinley,' she said, almost as if I'd asked a civil question.

'Do, re, mi, fa, so-what?' I sang loudly, and intentionally off-key.

'Save it for the sinners,' Feely said pleasantly, and walked on in silence.

Half a dozen boys in Scout uniforms, all members of St. Tancred's choir, were shoving one another about in the churchyard, playing a rough game of football with someone's hat. One of them was Colin Prout.

Feely stuck her first and last fingers into her mouth and let out a surprisingly piercing and unladylike whistle. The game broke up at once.

'Inside,' Feely ordered. 'Hymns before horse-play.'

Since its scoutmaster and several of the boys were also members of the choir, the Scout troop would not meet until after choir practice.

There were a couple of anonymous groans and whispers, but the boys obeyed her. Colin tried to scuttle past, his eyes fixed firmly on the ground.

'Hoy, Colin,' I said, stepping in front of him to block his way. 'I didn't know you were a Scout.'

He put his head down, jammed his hands into the pockets of his shorts, and sidestepped me. I followed him into the church.

The older members of the choir had already taken their places, chatting away to one another as they awaited the arrival of the organist, the men on one side of the chancel, the women facing them, on the other.

Miss Cool, who was both Bishop's Lacey's postmistress and its confectioner, shot me a beaming smile, and the Misses Puddock, Lavinia and Aurelia, who owned the St. Nicholas Tea Room, gave me identical twiddles of their fingers.

'Good evening, choir,' Feely said. It was a tradition that dated back into the mists of Christian history.

'Good evening, Miss de Luce,' they responded, automatically.

Feely took her seat on the organ bench, and with no more than a 'Hymn number three hundred and eighty-three,' barked out over her shoulder, launched into the opening bars of 'We Plough the Fields and Gather,' leaving me scrambling to find the page in the hymnbook.

'We plough the fields and scatter,' we sang,

'the good seed on the land,
but it is fed and watered
by God's almighty hand;
He sends the snow in winter,
the warmth to swell the grain,
the breezes and the sunshine,
and soft refreshing rain.'

As I sang, I thought of Brookie's body dangling from Poseidon's trident in the downpour. There had been nothing soft or refreshing about that particular storm – in fact, it had been one hell of a cloudburst.

I looked across the chancel at Colin. He was singing with intense concentration, his eyes closed, his face upturned to the day's last light which was now seeping in through the darkening stained-glass windows. I'd deal with him later.

'He only is the Maker
of all things near and far;
He paints the wayside flower,
He lights the evening star;
the winds and waves obey Him–'

The organ screeched to a halt in the middle of a note, as if someone had strangled it.

'De Luce,' a voice was saying sourly, and I became aware that it was Feely's.

She was addressing me!

'The voice cannot emerge through a closed mouth.'

Heads turned towards me, and there were a couple of smiles and titters.

'Now then, again – from "the winds and waves obey Him–"'

She struck a leading note on the keyboard, and then the organ roared back to life and we were off again.

How dare she single me out in that manner? The witch! *Just you wait, Ophelia Gertrude de Luce ... just you bloody well wait!*

To me, the choir practice seemed to go on forever, perhaps because there's no joy in simply

293

mouthing the words – in fact, it's surprisingly hard work.

But at last it was over. Feely was gathering up her music and having a jolly old chin-wag with Cynthia Richardson, the vicar's wife, whose fan club did not count me among its members. I'd take the opportunity to slip away unnoticed and tackle Colin in the churchyard with a couple of interesting questions that had come to mind.

'Flavia–'

Drat!

Feely had broken off her conversation, and was bearing down upon me. It was too late to pretend I hadn't heard her.

She seized my elbow and gave it a furtive shake. 'Don't go sneaking off,' she said in an undertone, using her other hand to wave a cheery good-bye to Cynthia. 'Father will be here in a few minutes, and he has asked in particular that you wait.'

'Father here? Whatever for?'

'Oh, come off it, Flavia – you know as well as I do. It's cinema night, and Father was quite right – he said you'd try to dodge it.'

She was correct on both counts. Although I had since put it out of my mind, Father *had* announced suddenly several weeks earlier that we didn't get out enough as a family – a situation that he intended to rectify by subscribing to the vicar's proposed cinema series in the parish hall.

And sure enough – here was Father now with Daffy, at the church door, shaking hands with the vicar. It was too late to escape.

'Ah, Flavia,' the vicar said, 'thank you for adding your voice to our little choir of angels, as it

294

were. I was just telling your father how pleased I was to see Ophelia on the organ bench. She plays so well, don't you think? It's a treat to see her conducting the choir with such verve. "And a little child shall lead them," as the prophet Isaiah tells us ... not, of course, that Ophelia's a little child, dear me, no! – far from it. But come away, the Bijou Cinema awaits!'

As we strolled through the churchyard towards the parish hall, I noticed Colin flitting from gravestone to gravestone, engaged apparently in some elaborate game of his own invention.

'I worry about that boy,' I heard the vicar confiding to Father. 'He has no parents, and now, with Brookie Harewood no longer around, as it were, to look out for him – but I'm chattering – ah, here we are ... shall we go in?'

Inside, the parish hall was already uncomfortably warm. In preparation for the pictures, the blackout curtains had been drawn against the evening light, and the place was already filling with that humid fug that is generated by too many overheated bodies in a confined space.

I could distinguish quite clearly the many odours of Bishop's Lacey, among them the various scents and shaving lotions; of talcum powder (the vicar); of bergamot scent (the Misses Puddock), of rubbing alcohol (our neighbor Maximilian Brock); of boiled cabbage (Mrs. Delaney), of Guinness stout (Mr. Danby), and of Dutch pipe tobacco (George Carew, the village carpenter).

Since Miss Mountjoy, with her pervading odour of cod-liver oil, was nowhere in sight, I circulated slowly round the hall, sniffing unobtrusively for the slightest whiff of fish.

'Oh, hello, Mr. Spirling. It's nice to see you. (Sniff) How's Mrs. Spirling getting on with her crocheting? Gosh, it's such a lot of work, isn't it? I don't know where she finds the time.'

In the centre of the room, Mr. Mitchell, the proprietor of the photographer's shop in the high street, was grappling with writhing snakes of black cine film, trying to feed them into the maw of a projector.

I couldn't help but reflect that the last time I'd been in the parish hall, it had been on the occasion of Rupert Porson's final puppet performance – on this same stage – of *Jack and the Beanstalk. Poor Rupert,* I thought, and a delicious little shudder shook my shoulders.

But this was no time for pleasantries – I had to keep my nose to the grindstone, so to speak.

I rejoined Father, Daffy, and Feely just as the front row of houselights was being switched off.

I will not bother quoting the vicar's preliminary remarks about 'the growing importance of film in the education of our young people,' and so forth. He did not mention either Brookie's death or the attack upon Fenella, although this was perhaps neither the proper time or place to do so.

We were then plunged into a brief darkness, and a few moments later the first film flashed onto the screen – a black-and-white animated cartoon in which a chorus of horribly grinning cats in bowler hats bobbed up and down in unison, yowling 'Ain't We Got Fun?' to the music of a tinny jazz band.

Mercifully, it did not last long.

In the brief pause, during which the lights came up and the film was changed, I noticed that Mrs. Bull had arrived with Timofey and her toddler. If she saw me among the audience, she did not let on.

The next film, *Saskatchewan: Breadbasket of the World,* was a documentary that showed great harvesting machines creeping across the flat face of the Canadian prairies, then rivers of grain being poured into railway hopper cars, and the open hatches of waiting cargo ships.

At the end of it I craned my neck for a glimpse of Colin Prout – yes, there he was at the very back of the hall, returning my gaze steadily. I gave him a little wave, but he made no response.

The third film, *The Maintenance of Aero Engines: Part III,* must have been something left over from the war – a film that was being shown simply because it happened to be in the same box as the others. In the light reflected from the screen, I caught Father and Feely exchanging puzzled glances before settling down to look as if they were finding it terrifically instructive.

The final feature on the programme was a documentary called *The Versatile Lemon,* which, aside from the narrator's mentioning that lemons had once been used as an antidote to a multitude of poisons, was a crashing bore.

I watched it with my eyes shut.

The new moon was no more than a sliver of silver in the sky as we made our way homeward across the fields. Father, Daffy, and Feely had got slightly ahead, and I trudged along behind them, immersed in my own thoughts.

'Don't dawdle, Flavia,' Feely said, in a patient, half-amused voice that drove me crazy. She was putting it on for Father.

'Squid!' I said, warping the word into a sneeze.

TWENTY-FOUR

My sleep was torn by images of silver. A silver horse in a silver glade chewed silver grass with silver teeth. A silver Man in the Moon shone in the sky above a silver caravan. Silver coins formed a cross in a corpse's hand. A silver river glided.

When I awoke, my thoughts flew back at once to Fenella. Was she still alive? Had she regained consciousness? Porcelain claimed she had and the vicar said she hadn't.

Well, there was only one way to find out.

'Sorry, old girl,' I said to Gladys in the grey dishwater light of the early morning, 'but I have to leave you at home.'

I could see that she was disappointed, even though she managed to put on a brave face.

'I need you to stay here as a decoy,' I whispered. 'When they see you leaning against the greenhouse, they'll think I'm still in bed.'

Gladys brightened considerably at the thought of a conspiracy.

'If I look sharp, I can hare it cross-country and catch the first bus for Hinley this side of Oakshott Hill.'

At the corner of the garden, I turned, and mouthed the words, 'Don't do anything I wouldn't do,' and Gladys signalled that she wouldn't.

I was off like a shot.

Mist hung in the fields as I flew across the ploughed furrows, bounding gracefully from clod to clod. By catching the bus on a country road, I wouldn't be seen by anyone except those passengers who were already on board, none of whom would pose much risk of reporting me to Father, since they were all heading for destinations away from Bishop's Lacey.

Just as I climbed over the last fence, the Cottesmore bus hove into view, clattering and flapping its wings like a large, dishevelled bird as it came jolting towards me along the lane.

It stopped with a rusty sigh, and a tendril of steam drifted up from its nickel radiator cap.

'Board!' said Ernie, the driver. 'Step up. Step up. Mind your feet.'

I handed him my fare and slipped into a seat three rows from the front. As I had suspected, there were few other riders at this time of day: a pair of elderly women who huddled together at the rear, too much in the grip of their own gossip to pay me the slightest bit of attention, and a farm worker in overalls with a hoe, who stared sadly out of the window at the darkly misty fields. Sunrise would not be for another quarter of an hour.

The hospital at Hinley stood at the end of a steep street that rose up precariously from behind the market square, its windows staring down glumly onto the black cobbles, which were still wet from the night's rain. Behind the high wrought-iron gate, a porter's lodge bore a sign written in no-nonsense letters: *All Visitors Please Report.*

Don't loiter, something told me, and I took its advice.

To the left, an archway of stained stone led to a narrow passage in which a couple of square gas lamps flickered with a sickly light.

Hearses Only, it said on a discreet plaque, and I knew I was on the right track.

In spite of my trying to walk in silence, my footsteps echoed from the wet cobbles and the seeping brick walls. At its far end, I could see that the passage opened into a small courtyard. I paused to listen.

Nothing but the sound of my own breathing. I peered cautiously round the corner–

'Beck!' said a loud voice, almost at my ear. I shrank back and flattened myself against the wall.

'Beck, get yourself out here. Quench's man will be along directly, and we want to have her ready to hand over. You know as well as I do what happens when we keep them waiting.'

Ellis and Quench, I knew, was Hinley's largest and oldest undertaking firm, and was known far and wide for the shininess of its Rolls-Royce hearses and the gleam of its Daimler mourners' cars.

'When Ellis and Quench buries you, you're buried,' Mrs. Mullet had once told me. I could easily believe that they would not like to be kept waiting.

300

'Old Matron gets her knickers in a knot,' the voice went on, 'if we're not all shipshape and Bristol fashion on the loading dock. And when old Matron's not happy, I'm not happy, and when I'm not happy, you're not happy. Beck? Get yourself out here, will you?'

There came the sound of boots shuffling on the timbers of the dock, and then a voice – a surprisingly young voice; perhaps a boy's voice – said: 'Sorry, Mr. Martin. I forgot to tell you. They rang up about twenty minutes ago. Said they'd be round later. Had a call out to the Old Infirmary, they did.'

'Oh, they did, did they? The buggers! Think nothing of leaving the likes of us twisting in the wind, whilst they go larking about the countryside in their bloody Bentleys. Well, I'm going down to the boiler room for a cup of tea, Quench or no Quench. Matron's up on Anson Ward with the latest crop of nursing sisters. Poor wee things – I hope they remembered their asbestos uniforms!'

I waited until I heard the heavy doors close, then quickly, before I could think better of it, scrambled up onto the loading dock.

'Blast!' I said under my breath, as a sliver of wood pierced my knee. I pulled the thing out and shoved it into my pocket so as not to leave any evidence behind. I dabbed at the oozing blood a bit with my handkerchief, but there was no time for compresses. It would have to do.

I took a breath, pulled open the heavy door, and stepped into a dimly lighted corridor.

The floors were marble, and the walls were painted – brown for the first four feet, then a

301

ghastly green from there all the way up to the ceiling, which appeared to have been white-washed in another century.

On my right were three small cubicles, one of which was occupied by a wheeled cart, upon which lay a sheeted figure. It took no great stretch of the imagination to guess what lay beneath. This was the real thing: the genuine article!

I was dying to undo the buckles on the straps and have a peek under the sheet, but there wasn't time.

Besides, there was part of me that didn't want to know if the body was Fenella's.

Not just yet. Not in that way.

From where I stood, I could see the full length of the corridor, which stretched away from me into the distance. It seemed endless.

I began to move slowly, putting one foot in front of another: right foot ... left foot. On one side of the corridor was a double door marked 'Laundry.' From behind it came the muffled rumble of machinery and a woman laughing.

Left foot ... right foot ... toe to heel.

The next door was the kitchen: dishes clattering, voices chattering, and the powerful, clinging smell of greasy cabbage soup.

Soup for breakfast? I realised that I hadn't eaten since yesterday, and my stomach gave a heave.

For the next dozen paces, the walls were inexplicably moss green, and then, just as quickly, a queasy mustard yellow. Whoever had chosen the paint, I decided, wanted to ensure that anyone who wasn't sick when they entered the hospital jolly well would be before they left.

The next set of doors on the left, judging by the bracing whiff of formalin, belonged to the morgue. I gave a little shiver as I passed: not one of fear, but rather of delight.

Another room was marked 'X-Ray,' and beyond that point, open doors on both sides of the corridor, with room numbers on every one. In each room, someone was sleeping, or rolling over. Someone was snoring, someone moaned, and I thought I heard the sound of a woman crying.

These are the wards, I thought, *and there must be others on the first and second floors.*

But how could I find Fenella? Until then, I hadn't given it a moment's thought. How does one quickly find a needle in a haystack?

Certainly not by examining one straw at a time!

I had now arrived at a doorway that opened into a sort of large foyer, in the centre of which a woman wrapped in a black woollen sweater was staring intently at a spread of playing cards on her desk. She did not hear me come up beside her.

'Excuse me,' I said, 'but you can put the five of diamonds on the black six.'

The woman nearly fell out of her chair. She jumped to her feet and spun round to face me.

'Don't *ever*–'she said, her face going the colour of beetroot. 'Don't you *ever* dare–' Her fists clenched and unclenched spasmodically.

'I'm sorry if I startled you,' I said. 'I didn't mean to, really…'

'What are you doing here?' she demanded. 'No visiting until one-thirty this afternoon, and it's only just gone–' She shot a glance at her watch, an impossibly tiny lump strapped to her wrist.

303

'I'm waiting for my cousin,' I explained. 'She's just slipped in to bring our grandmother some...'

I took a deep breath and wracked my brains for inspiration, but the only thing that came to mind – to my nostrils, actually – was the nauseating odour still leaking from the kitchen down the corridor.

'Soup!' I said. 'We've brought our gram some soup.'

'Soup?' The woman's voice – and her eyebrows – went up into an inverted V. 'You've brought *soup? Here?* To a *hospital?*'

I nodded meekly.

'Who's your grandmother?' she demanded. 'What's her name? Is she a patient here?'

'Fenella Faa,' I said without hesitation.

'Faa? The Gypsy woman?' she asked, sucking in her breath.

I nodded dumbly.

'And your cousin, you say, has brought her *soup?*'

'Yes,' I said, pointing haphazardly. 'She went that way.'

'What's your name?' the woman asked, snatching up a typewritten list from her desk.

'Flavia,' I said. 'Flavia Faa.'

It was just implausible enough to be true. With a snort like a racehorse, the woman was off, down a wide corridor on the far side of the foyer.

I followed in her wake, but I don't think she noticed. Still, I kept well back, hoping she didn't turn round. I was in luck.

Without a backwards glance, she vanished into the second room but one on the left, and I heard the sound of curtains being swept open. I didn't stop, but continued on past the open door. A single glance revealed Fenella in the farthest bed, her head swathed in bandages.

I ducked down out of sight behind a draped cart that was parked against the wall.

'All right, come out of there!' I heard the woman say, followed by the *click* of a door being opened – probably the room's W.C.

There was a silence – then a low, muttered conversation. Was she talking to Fenella – or to herself?

The only word that came clearly to my ears was 'soup.'

Another brief silence, and then the sound of the woman's shoes went echoing away down the corridor.

I counted to three, then flitted like a bat into Fenella's room, closing the door behind me. A whiff of ether told me that this must be the surgical ward.

Fenella was lying motionless on her back, her eyes closed. So frail, she looked – as if the bedsheets had absorbed the last ounce of her juices.

'Hello,' I whispered. 'It's me, Flavia.'

There was no response. I reached out and took her hand.

Ever so slowly her eyes came open, fighting to focus.

'It's me, Flavia,' I said again. 'Remember?'

Her wrinkled lips pursed, and the tip of her tongue appeared. It looked like the head of a turtle emerging from its shell after a long winter at the bottom of the pond.

'The ... liar,' she whispered, and I grinned as

stupidly as if I had just been awarded first prize at the spring flower show.

Licking her lips feebly, Fenella turned her head towards me, her black eyes now suddenly fierce and imploring in their sunken sockets.

'Sret,' she said quite distinctly, giving my hand a squeeze.

'Sorry,' I said, 'I don't understand.'

'Sret,' she said again. 'Puff.'

A light went on at the back of my brain.

'Cigarette?' I asked. 'Is that what you're saying?'

She nodded. 'Sret. Puff.'

'I'm sorry,' I said, 'I don't smoke.'

Her eyes were fixed upon mine, imploring.

'Tell you what,' I said. 'I'll go find you one, but first, I need to ask you a couple of important questions.'

I didn't give her time to think.

'The first is this: do you really believe I did this to you? I'd die if you did.'

Her brows knitted. 'Did this?'

'Put you here – in the hospital. Please, Fenella, I need to know.'

I hadn't meant to call her by her given name – it just slipped out. It was that kind of moment. Daffy had once told me that knowing and using someone's name gave you power over them.

There was no doubt that, at least for now, I had power over this poor injured creature, even if it was only the power to withhold a cigarette.

'Please, Fenella!' I pleaded.

If this was power, I wanted no part of it. It felt dreadful.

Without taking her eyes from mine, she moved

306

her head slowly from side to side.

'No,' she whispered at last, replying to my question.

No? It was not the answer I was expecting. If Fenella didn't think I had attacked her, then Porcelain had lied!

'Who was it, then?' I demanded in a voice so rough that it surprised even me. Had that savage snarl issued from my throat?

'Who was it? Tell me who did this to you!'

For some inexplicable reason, I wanted to seize her and shake the answer out of her. This was a kind of anger I had never known before.

Fenella was terrified. I could see it in her fuddled eyes.

'The *Red Bull*,' she said, accenting each of the two words. 'It was ... the *Red Bull.*'

The Red Bull? That made no sense at all.

'What's going on here?'

The voice came from the doorway. I spun round and found myself face-to-face with a nursing sister. It wasn't just the white uniform and stockings that made her seem so intimating: the blue cape with its red lining and piping had turned her into a human Union Jack.

'Flavia?'

The familiar voice took me by surprise.

It was Flossie Foster, the sister of Feely's friend Sheila!

'Flossie? Is it really you?'

I'd forgotten that Flossie had gone in for nursing. It was one of those trifles that had been mentioned at the dinner table by Feely, somewhere between the salad and the sausage rolls, and put out of mind before the plates were cleared away.

'Of course it's me, you goose. What on earth are *you* doing here?'

'I ... ah ... came to visit a friend,' I said, making a sweeping gesture towards Fenella.

'But visiting hours aren't until this afternoon. If Matron catches you, she'll have your toes on toast.'

'Listen, Flossie,' I said. 'I need a favour. I need a cigarette, and I need it quickly.'

'Ha!' said Flossie, 'I should have known! Feely's little sister is a tobacco fiend!'

'It's not like that at all,' I said. 'Please, Flossie – I'll promise you anything.'

Flossie reached into her pocket and pulled out a packet of Du Mauriers and a monogrammed cloisonné lighter.

'Now light it,' I told her.

Surprisingly, she did as she was told, although a little furtively.

'We only smoke in the nursing sisters' tea room,' she said, handing me the cigarette. 'And only when Matron's not around.'

'It's not for me,' I said, pointing to Fenella. 'Give it to her.'

Flossie stared at me, 'You must be mad,' she said.

'Go ahead, give it to her ... or I'll tell Matron what you had in the hip flask at the vicar's garden party.'

I was only teasing, but before I could shoot her a grin, Flossie had inserted the cigarette between Fenella's dry lips.

'You're a beast,' she said. 'An absolutely horrid little beast!'

I could tell she wanted to slap me, as I gave her a triumphant smirk.

But instead, we both of us broke off to look at Fenella. Her eyes were closed, and smoke was rising from her mouth in a series of puffs, like smoke signals from an Apache campfire. They might well have been spelling out the word 'b-l-i-s-s.'

It was at that very moment that Matron barged into the room.

In her elaborate cocked hat and starched white bib, she looked like Napoleon – only much larger.

She sized up the situation at a glance.

'Nurse Foster, I'll see you in my office.'

'No, wait,' I heard myself saying. 'I can explain.'

'Then do so.'

'The nurse just stepped in to tell us that smoking is forbidden. It's nothing to do with her.'

'Indeed!'

'I heard you coming,' I said, 'and stuck my cigarette into that poor woman's mouth. It was stupid of me. I'm sorry.'

I snatched what was left of the cigarette from Fenella's lips and shoved it between my own. I took a deep drag and then exhaled, holding the thing between my second and third fingers in the Continental manner, as I had seen Charles Boyer do in the cinema, and all the while fighting down the urge to choke.

'Then how do you explain this?' Matron asked, picking up Flossie's lighter from Fenella's blanket, and holding it out accusingly towards me.

'It's mine,' I said 'The F is for Flavia. Flavia de

309

Luce. That's me.'

I thought I detected a nearly imperceptible squint – or was it more of a wince?

'Of the Buckshaw de Luces?'

'Yes,' I said. 'It was a gift from Father. He believes that the occasional cigarette fortifies one's lungs against vapours from the drains.'

The Matron didn't exactly gape, but she *did* stare at me as if I had suddenly sprouted a beak and tail feathers.

Then suddenly, and without warning, she pressed the lighter into my hands and wiped her fingers on her skirt.

There was the sound of professional shoe leather in the corridor, and Dr. Darby walked calmly into the room.

'Ah, Flavia,' he said. 'How nice to see you. This, Matron, is the young lady whose prompt action saved the life of Mrs. Faa.'

I stuck out a hand so quickly that the old dragon was forced to take it.

'Pleased to meet you, Matron,' I said. 'I've heard so much about you.'

TWENTY-FIVE

'How is she?' I asked. 'Fenella, I mean – really?'

'She'll do,' said Dr. Darby.

We were motoring home to Bishop's Lacey, the doctor's Morris humming happily along between the hedgerows like a sewing machine on holiday.

310

'Fractured skull,' he went on when I said nothing. 'Depressed occipital condylar fracture, as we quacks call it. Has quite a ring to it, doesn't it? Thanks to you, we were able to get her into the operating room in time to elevate the broken bit without too much trouble. I think she'll likely make a full recovery, but we shall have to wait and see. Are you all right?'

He hadn't missed the fact that I was sucking in great deep breaths of the morning air, in an attempt to clear my system of cigarette smoke and the horrid odours of the hospital. The formalin of the morgue hadn't been too bad – quite enjoyable, in fact – but the reek of cabbage soup from the kitchen had been enough to gag a hyena.

'I'm fine, thank you,' I said, with what I'm afraid was rather a wan smile.

'Your father will be very proud of you–' he went on.

'Oh, please don't tell him! Promise you won't!'

The doctor shot me a quizzical glance.

'It's just that he already has so much to worry about–'

As I have said, Father's financial distress was no secret in Bishop's Lacey, particularly to his friends, of whom Dr. Darby was one. (The vicar was the other.)

'I understand,' the doctor said. 'Then he shall not hear it from me.

'Still,' he added with a chuckle, 'the news is bound to get about, you know.'

I could think of nothing but to change the subject.

'I'm rather puzzled about something,' I said.

311

'The police took Fenella's granddaughter, Porcelain, to see her in the hospital. She claims Fenella told her it was me who bashed her on the head.'

'And did you?' the doctor asked slyly.

'Later,' I said, ignoring his teasing, 'the vicar told me that he, too, had paid a visit, but that Fenella had not yet regained consciousness. Which of them was telling the truth?'

'The vicar is a dear man,' Dr. Darby said. 'A very dear man. He brings me flowers from his garden now and then to brighten up my surgery. But if cornered, I would have to admit that sometimes, on the wards, we are forced to tell him fibs. Little lies in little white jackets. For the good of the patient, of course. I'm sure you understand.'

If there was one thing in the world that I understood above all others, it was withholding selected snippets of the truth. It would not be an exaggeration to say that I was an Exalted Grand Master of the craft.

I nodded my head modestly. 'He *is* very devoted to his work,' I said.

'As it happens, I was present when both the granddaughter and the vicar came to the hospital. Although the vicar didn't get as far as her room, Mrs. Faa was fully conscious at the time of his visit.'

'And Porcelain?'

'At the time of Porcelain's visit, she was not. The victims of skull fracture, you see, can slip in and out of consciousness as easily as you and I move from one room to another – an interesting phenomenon when you come right down to it.'

I was hardly listening. Porcelain had lied to me.

312

The witch!

There's nothing that a liar hates more than finding that another liar has lied to them.

'But why would she blame it on me?'

The words must have slipped out. I'd had no intention of thinking aloud.

'Ah,' said Dr. Darby. '"There are more things in heaven and earth, Horatio, than are dreamt of in your philosophy."' Meaning that people can behave strangely in times of great stress. She's a complicated young woman, your friend Porcelain.'

'She's no friend of mine!' I said rather abruptly.

'You took her in and fed her,' Dr. Darby said with an amused look. 'Or perhaps I misunderstood.'

'I felt sorry for her.'

'Ah. No more than sorry?'

'I wanted to like her.'

'Aha! Why?'

The answer, of course, was that I was hoping to make a friend, but I could hardly admit that.

'We always want to love the recipients of our charity,' the doctor said, negotiating a sharp bend in the road with a surprising demonstration of steering skill, 'but it is not necessary. Indeed, it is sometimes not possible.'

Suddenly I found myself wanting to confide in this gentle man – to tell him everything. But I could not.

The best thing for it when you feel tears coming on for no reason at all is to change the subject.

'Have you ever heard of the Red Bull?'

'The Red Bull?' he asked, swerving to avoid a terrier that had dashed out barking into the road.

313

'Which Red Bull did you have in mind?'

'Is there more than one?'

'There are many. The Red Bull at St. Elfrieda's is the first that comes to mind.'

A smile crept over his face, as if he was recalling a cosy evening of darts and a couple of pleasant pints of half-and-half.

'And?'

'Well, let me see ... there was the Red Bull on a Green Field, from *Kim,* which was the god of nine hundred devils ... the Red Bull of the Borgias, which was a flag, and was on a field of gold, not green ... the notorious Red Bull playhouse that burned in the Great Fire of London in 1666 ... there was the mythical Red Bull of England that met the Black Bull of Scotland in a fight to the death ... and, of course, in the days when priests practised medicine, they used to hand out the hair of a red bull as a cure for epilepsy. Have I missed any?'

Not one of these seemed likely to be the Red Bull that had attacked Fenella.

'Why do you ask?' he said, seeing my obvious puzzlement.

'Oh, no reason,' I said. 'It was just something I heard somewhere ... the wireless, perhaps.'

I could see that he didn't believe me, but he was gentleman enough not to press.

'Here's St. Tancred's,' I said. 'You can let me off at the churchyard.'

'Ah,' said Dr. Darby, applying the Morris's brakes. 'Time for a spot of prayer?'

'Something like that,' I said.

Actually, I needed to think.

Thinking and prayer are much the same thing anyway, when you stop to think about it – if that makes any sense. Prayer goes up and thought comes down – or so it seems. As far as I can tell, that's the only difference.

I thought about this as I walked across the fields to Buckshaw. Thinking about Brookie Harewood – and who killed him, and why – was really just another way of praying for his soul, wasn't it?

If this was true, I had just established a direct link between Christian charity and criminal investigation. I could hardly wait to tell the vicar!

A quarter mile ahead, and off to one side, was the narrow lane and the hedgerow where Porcelain had hidden in the bushes.

Almost without realising it, I found my feet taking me in that direction.

If her claim about Fenella had been a lie, she couldn't really have been afraid of me, as she had pretended. There must, then, have been some other reason for her ducking into the hedgerow – one that I had not thought about at the time.

If that was the case, she had successfully tricked me.

I climbed over the stile and into the lane. It had been just about here that she'd slipped into the shrubbery. I stood for a moment in silence, listening.

'Porcelain?' I said, the hair at the back of my neck rising.

Whatever had made me think that she was still here?

'Porcelain?'

There was no answer.

I took a deep breath, realising it could easily be my last. With Porcelain, you could always so quickly find yourself with a knife at your throat.

Another deep breath – this one for insurance purposes – and then I stepped into the hedgerow.

I could see at once that there was nobody hidden here. A slightly flattened area and a couple of trampled weeds indicated clearly where Porcelain had squatted the other day.

I crouched beneath the branches and wiggled myself into the same position that she must have assumed, putting myself in her shoes, looking out at the world as if from her eyes. As I did so, my hand touched something solid ... something hard.

It was shoved inside a little tent of weeds. I wrapped my fingers round the object and pulled it into view.

It was black and circular, perhaps a little over three inches in diameter, and was made of some dark, exotic wood – ebony, perhaps. Carved into its circumference were the signs of the zodiac. I ran my forefinger slowly across the carved image of a pair of fish lying head to tail: Pisces.

The last time I had seen this wooden ring was at the fête. It had been on the table in Fenella's tent, supporting her crystal ball.

There was little doubt that Porcelain had pinched the ball's base from the caravan, and was making off with it when I had surprised her in the lane.

But why? Was it a souvenir? Did it have some sentimental attachment?

Porcelain was simply infuriating. Nothing that

she did made any sense.

Finding the base reminded me that the ball itself, hidden safely away in plain sight among my laboratory glassware, was still awaiting careful study.

My intention had been to examine it for fingerprints, even though most traces had likely been washed away by immersion in the river. I remembered how Philip Odell, the wireless detective, had once pointed out to Inspector Hanley that the glandular secretions of the palms and fingers consisted primarily of water and water-soluble solids.

'So you see, Inspector,' he had said, *'Garvin's fatal mistake was in running his fingers through his hair. The barber had scented it with brilliantine containing bay oil, which, of course, is soluble in alcohol, but not in water. Even after a night at the bottom of the millstream, the fingerprints on the handle of the knife were still plain enough to put his villainous neck in a noose.'*

Philip Odell aside, I had my own ideas about underwater fingerprints. There was, for instance, a quite readily available household substance that would fix and harden any traces of residual grime that might be left by a killer's hands. Given time, I would do the laboratory work, write it up, and present it to Inspector Hewitt on a silver platter. He would, of course, take my paper home at once and show it to his wife, Antigone.

But there had been no time. The compulsory cinema night and choir practice at St. Tancred's, followed by my visit to Fenella in hospital, had robbed me of the opportunity to carry out the necessary research.

I would hurry home and begin at once.

I had no more than one foot out of the thicket when I heard the sound of an approaching motor. I ducked back into hiding, remembering to turn my face away as the thing swept past. By the time I judged it safe to come out again, the machine had vanished in the direction of Buckshaw.

I did not actually spot the Inspector's blue Vauxhall until I had already set foot between the griffins of the Mulford Gates. It was parked off to one side beneath the chestnuts, and he was leaning patiently against it, waiting.

Too late now to turn and bolt. I'd have to make the best of it,

'Oh, Inspector,' I said, 'I was just about to ring you up and tell you what I've found!'

I was aware that I was gushing, but I didn't seem to be able to help myself. I held the wooden base out to him at arm's length.

'This was in a thicket by the side of the lane. I think it's part of Fenella's crystal ball.'

He pulled a silk handkerchief from his breast pocket and took the wooden O from my hands.

'You shouldn't have touched it,' he said. 'You ought to have left it where it was.'

'I realise that,' I told him. 'But it was too late. I touched it before I saw it – without meaning to. It was hidden under some weeds. I'd just stepped into the bushes for a moment...'

The look on his face told me that I was skating on thin ice: I had already used the 'sudden call of nature' excuse, and it wouldn't bear repeating.

'You saw me, of course, didn't you? That's why you stopped and waited for me here.'

The Inspector ignored this neat bit of deduction.

'Get in, please,' he said, holding open the back door of the Vauxhall. 'It's time for a talk.'

Sergeant Graves turned round and shot me a quick, quizzical glance from the driver's seat, but he did not smile. Only then did I realise how much trouble I was in.

We drove to the front door of Buckshaw in silence.

It was my second full confession in as many days.

We were sitting in the drawing room – all of us, that is, except Father, who was standing at the window, staring out, as if his life depended on it, across the ornamental lake.

He had insisted that we all of us be present, and had summoned Feely and Daffy, both of whom had annoyingly come at once, and were now seated primly side by side on a flowered divan like a couple of toads come to tea.

'It is regrettable,' Inspector Hewitt was saying, 'that our investigation has been so badly compromised. Crime scenes disturbed ... evidence tampered with ... crucial information withheld ... I hardly know where to begin.'

He was talking about me, of course.

'I have tried to impress upon Flavia the seriousness of these matters, but with little success. Therefore, I'm afraid I'm going to insist, Colonel de Luce, that until such time as our work is complete, you keep her confined to Buckshaw.'

I couldn't believe my ears! Confined to Buckshaw? Why not have me transported to Australia and be done with it?

Well, so much for choir duty and future cinema nights. So much for Father's decree that we needed to get out more as a family.

Father mumbled something and shifted his gaze from the ornamental lake to the distant hills.

'That said,' the Inspector went on, 'we come to the real reason for our being here.'

Real reason? My heart sank as if it already knew something that I did not.

The Inspector brought out his notebook. 'A statement has been taken from a Miss Ursula Vipond, who says that she witnessed the removal from the river of what she described as...' He opened the notebook and flipped through a couple of pages. '...a glass sphere...'

My eyes widened.

'...by a child whose name she has reason to believe is Flavia de Luce.'

Confound the woman! I knew at once that this busybody could be none other than that troll, Ursula, who haunted Vanetta Harewood's cottage in Maiden Fenwick. I'd listed the odious creature in my notebook, but hadn't known her surname.

She'd been standing hidden among the bushes at the Palings, watching as I pulled Fenella's crystal ball from the river.

'Well?'

I could tell by his tone that the Inspector was becoming impatient.

'I was going to give it to you straightaway,' I said.

'Where is it?' he asked.

'In my laboratory. I'll go get it and–'

'No! Stay as you are. Sergeant Graves'll see to it.'

Surprised, the sergeant broke off gazing at

320

Feely and leapt to his feet.

'Just a moment, Sergeant,' she said. 'I'll show you the way.'

The traitor! The minx! Even with her little sister under attack, Ophelia could think of nothing but courtship.

'Wait,' I said. 'The laboratory is locked. I'll have to go fetch the key.'

Before anyone could think to stop me, I had swept past Feely and the sergeant, out the door, and was halfway down the hall.

The truth was that the key was in my pocket, but without turning me upside down and shaking me, they had no way of knowing that.

Up the stairs I dashed, taking them two at a time, as if all the demons of Hades were at my heels. Into the east wing I fled, and down the long corridor.

I fumbled at the lock of the laboratory, but something inside the mechanism seemed to be mucked up, as if–

I gave a fierce shove and the door flew open, propelling me almost into the arms of ... Porcelain!

TWENTY-SIX

'What are you doing here?' I hissed, my heart still pounding like a trip-hammer. 'I thought you were in London.'

'I might have been,' Porcelain said, 'but something made me come back to apologise.'

'You did that once before,' I said, 'and you botched it. I can live without another of your so-called apologies.'

'I know,' she said, 'and I'm sorry. I didn't tell you the truth about Fenella. She wasn't conscious when I went to the hospital. And she didn't tell me you'd attacked her. I made all of it up because I wanted to hurt you.'

'But why?'

'I don't know. I wish I did, but I don't.'

Suddenly she was in tears, sobbing as if her heart would break. Without thinking, I went to her, put my arms around her, and pulled her head against my shoulder.

'It's all right,' I said, even though it wasn't.

But something inside me had undergone a sudden shift, as if my interior furniture had been rearranged unexpectedly, and I knew, with a strange new calmness, that we would sort things out later.

'Wait here until I come back,' I said. 'Father's expecting me downstairs, and I mustn't keep him waiting.'

Which was true, as far as it went.

As I walked back into the drawing room, Sergeant Graves was still standing quite close to Feely, a look of disappointment on his face.

'I put it in this,' I explained, handing Inspector Hewitt a square cardboard box, 'so that there would be the least number of points in contact with the glass surface.'

I did not explain that, because it was precisely the right size, I had pinched the box from Feely's bedroom, nor did I mention that I had flushed a pound of Yardley's lavender bath salts down the toilet for want of a better place to put it on short notice.

The Inspector lifted the top flap gingerly and glanced inside.

'You'll find a ring of faint smudges on the glass,' I said. 'Most likely whatever's left of the fingerprints–'

'Thank you, Flavia,' he said in a flat voice, handing the box to Sergeant Graves.

'...and perhaps a few of mine,' I added.

'Take this straightaway to Sergeant Woolmer, in Hinley,' the Inspector said, ignoring my small joke. 'Come back for me later.'

'Yes, sir,' Sergeant Graves said. 'Hinley it is.'

'Hold on a minute,' I said. 'There's more.'

I carefully pulled one of Feely's embroidered handkerchiefs from my pocket.

'This,' I said, 'might well be a copy of the silver lobster pick that killed Brookie Harewood. Or perhaps it's the original. It's got the de Luce monogram on it. One of the Bull children was digging with it in the Gully. If there *are* any fingerprints on it besides his and mine, you'll quite likely find that they match the ones on the crystal ball.'

I looked round the room to watch the reactions on everyone's faces as I handed the thing over to Inspector Hewitt.

As Mrs. Mullet once said, you could have heard a pin drop.

'Good lord!' Father said, stepping forward and reaching for the thing even as the Inspector was still unwrapping it.

323

I had almost blurted out that the rest of the family silver was on its way to Sotheby's, but something made me hold my tongue. What a bitter blow to Father it would have been had I let *that* slip out.

'Please, Colonel, don't touch it,' the Inspector said. 'I'm afraid this must now be treated as evidence.'

Father stood staring at the silver lobster pick as if he were a snake that had come unexpectedly face-to-face with a mongoose.

Daffy sat bolt upright on the divan, glaring at me with what I took to be hatred in her eyes – as if she held me responsible for all of Father's misfortunes.

Feely's hand was at her mouth.

All of these details were frozen on the instant, as if a photographer's flash had gone off and preserved forever a thin and uncomfortable slice of time. The silence in the room was audible.

'Killed Brookie Harewood?' Inspector Hewitt said at last, turning to me. 'This lobster pick? Please explain what you mean by that.'

'It was in his nose,' I said, 'when I found his body hanging from the Poseidon fountain. Surely you saw it?'

Now it was the Inspector's turn to stare in disbelief at the object in his hand.

'You're quite sure?' he asked.

'Positive,' I said, a little peeved that he should doubt me.

I could see that the Inspector was choosing his words carefully before he spoke.

'We found no lobster pick at the scene of the

324

crime – and none has turned up subsequently.'

No lobster pick at the scene of the crime? What a ludicrous statement! It was like denying the sun in the sky! The thing had been there, plain as day, stuck up Brookie's nostril like a dart in a cork-board.

If the pick had fallen out through force of gravity, for instance, the police would have found it in the fountain. The fact that they hadn't could mean only one thing: that someone had removed it. And that someone, most likely, was Brookie's killer.

Between the time Porcelain and I had walked away from the fountain, and the time that the police arrived – no more than, say, twenty minutes – the killer had crept back, scaled the fountain, and removed the weapon from Brookie's nose. But why?

The Inspector was still staring at me intently. I could see his cogs turning.

'Surely you don't think I killed Brookie Harewood?' I gasped.

'As a matter of fact, I don't,' Inspector Hewitt said, 'but something tells me that you know who did.'

I didn't move a muscle, but inwardly I positively preened!

Fancy that! I thought. *Recognition at last!*

I could have hugged the man, but I didn't. He'd have been mortified, and so – but only later, of course – would I.

'I have my suspicions,' I said, fighting to keep my voice from sliding into an upper register.

'Ah,' the Inspector said, 'then you must share them with us sometime. Well, thank you all. It has been most illuminating.'

He summoned Sergeant Graves with his eyebrows, and went to the door.

'Oh, and Colonel,' he said, turning back. 'You *will* keep Flavia at home?'

Father did not reply, and for that, I decided on the spot, his name would be inscribed forever in my private book of saints and martyrs.

And then, with a rustle of officialdom, the police were gone.

'Do you think he likes me?' Feely asked, making a beeline for the looking glass on the chimneypiece.

'I should say so,' Daffy replied. 'He was all green eyes, like the monster cuttlefish in *Twenty Thousand Leagues Under the Sea.*'

With no more than a look of perplexity, Father left the room.

Within minutes, I knew, he would be submerged in his stamp collection, alone with whatever squids and cuttlefish inhabited the depths of his mind.

At that moment I remembered Porcelain.

It didn't come easily to me to knock at the door of my own laboratory, but knock I did. No point in startling Porcelain and ending up with my throat slit from ear to ear.

But when I stepped inside, the laboratory was empty, and I felt my anger rising. Blast her! Hadn't I told her to stay where she was until I returned?

But when I opened my bedroom door, there she was, sitting cross-legged on my bed like a malnourished Buddha, reading my notebook.

It was too much.

'What do you think you're *doing?*' I shouted, running across the room and snatching the book from her hand.

'Reading about myself,' she said.

I'll admit it: I saw red.

No, that's not quite true: I first saw white – a silent, brilliant white that erased everything – like the A-bombs that had been dropped on Hiroshima and Nagasaki. Only after this deadly burst of flower petals had begun to cool and fade, passing first from yellow through orange, did it at last simmer down to red.

I had been angry before, but this was like something ripped from the pages of the Book of Revelation. Could it be some secret fault in the de Luce makeup that was manifesting itself in me for the first time?

Until now, my fury had always been like those jolly Caribbean carnivals we had seen in the cinema travelogues – a noisy explosion of colour and heat that wilted steadily as the day went on. But now it had suddenly become an icy coldness: a frigid wasteland in which I stood unapproachable. And it was in that instant, I think, that I began to understand my father.

This much was clear: I needed to get away – to be alone – until the tidal wave had passed.

'Excuse me,' I said abruptly, surprising even myself, and walked out of the room.

I sat for a while on the stairs – neither up nor down.

It was true that Porcelain had violated my privacy, but my response had frightened me. In fact, I was still shaking a little.

I riffled idly through the pages of my notebook, not really focusing upon its written entries.

What had Porcelain been reading when I interrupted her? She had been reading about herself, or so she claimed.

I could hardly remember what I had written. I quickly found the spot.

PORCELAIN – *Can't possibly be her grandmother's attacker since she was in London at the time. Or was she? I have only her word for it. But why did she feel compelled to wash out her clothing?*

The answer to that remained a puzzle, but surely, if Porcelain had come back to do me in, she'd have done so by now.

As I closed the book, I remembered that at the time my last notes were made, I had not yet met the Pettibones. I had promised the Queen Bee that I would bring her some papers from Buckshaw relating to Nicodemus Flitch and the Hobblers.

The fact that I had fabricated these juicy documents on the spur of the moment was really of no importance: with a library like Buckshaw's, there might very well be documents lurking that would satisfy the woman's obvious greed.

If the library was unoccupied, I could begin my search at once.

I was feeling better already.

I listened with my ear glued to the door. If Daffy was inside reading, as she usually was, I could swallow a teaspoon of pride and ask her opinion, perhaps under cover of an insult, which almost always resulted in her taking the bait.

If that didn't work, there was always the Solemn Truce. Under these rules, I would, immediately upon entering the room, drop to one knee on the carpet and declare *'Pax vobiscum,'* and if Daffy replied, *'Et cum spiritu tuo,'* the ceasefire went into effect for a period of five minutes by the mantel clock, during which time neither of us was allowed to offer any incivility to the other.

If, on the other hand, she flung an inkwell, then the peace pipe was declined, and the whole thing was off.

But there was no sound from the other side of the panel. I opened the door and peeked round it.

The library was empty.

I stepped inside and closed the door behind me. For safety's sake, I turned the key in the lock and, although it probably hadn't been operated in the past hundred years, the bolt slid home in perfect silence.

Good old Dogger, I thought. He had a way of seeing that essentials were taken care of.

If anyone questioned me, I would claim that I was feeling somewhat peaked, and had hoped to have a nap without being disturbed.

I turned and had a good look round the library. It was simply ages since I'd been alone in this room.

The bookshelves towered towards the ceiling in strata, as if they had been formed geologically in stacks, by the upwards shifting of the earth.

Near the floor and closest to hand were the books that belonged to the present generation of de Luces. Above these, and just out of reach, were those that had been hoarded by the house's Victorian inhabitants, above which, piled to the ceiling, was the rubbish left behind by the Georgians: hundreds and hundreds of leather- and calf-bound volumes with thin worm-eaten pages and type so small it made your eyes go buggy.

I'd had a squint once before at some of these relics, but had found them devoted mainly to the lives and sermons of a bunch of dry old sticks who had lived and died while Mozart was still crawling around in diapers.

If ever there was a graveyard of religious biography, this was it.

I'd work methodically, I thought, one wall at a time, top of the north wall first, then top of the east wall, and so forth.

Books about dissenting clergymen were not exactly kept at one's fingertips at Buckshaw. Besides, I wasn't sure exactly what I was searching for, but I knew that I would likely find it nearer the ceiling.

I dragged the rolling library ladder into position and began my climb: up, up, up – my footing more precarious with every step.

Libraries of this design, I thought, *ought to be equipped with oxygen bottles above a certain height, in case of altitude sickness.*

Which made me think of Harriet, and a sudden sadness came over me. Harriet had scaled these very same bookcases once upon a time. In fact, it was stumbling upon one of her chemistry texts in this very room that had changed my life.

'Get on with it, Flave,' said a strict-sounding

330

voice inside me. 'Harriet is dead, and you've got work to do.'

Up I went, my head still cocked at an uncomfortable angle from reading titles on book spines at the lower levels. Fortunately, at this higher altitude, the older volumes had sensible, no-nonsense horizontal titles stamped deeply into their spines in gold-leaf letters, making them three-dimensional, and relatively easy to read in the perpetual twilight near the ceiling:

The Life of Simeon Hoxey; Notes on the Septuagint; Prayer and Penance; Pew's Thoughts Upon Godliness; Astronomical Principles of Religion Natural and Reveal'd; The Life and Opinions of Tristram Shandy, Gentleman; Polycarp of Smyrna; and so forth.

Just above these was *Hydraulicks and Hydrostaticks*, a relic, no doubt, of Lucius 'Leaking' de Luce. I pulled the book from the shelf and opened it. Sure enough, there was Lucius's bookplate: the de Luce family crest, with his name written beneath it in a surprisingly childish hand. Had he owned the book when he was a boy?

The title page was almost completely covered with dense, inky calculations: sums, angles, algebraic equations, all of them more hurried than neat, crabbed, cramped, and rushing across the page. The entire book was somewhat rippled, as if it had once been wet.

A folded paper had been inserted between the pages which, when I opened it out flat, proved to be a hand-drawn map – but a map unlike any I had ever seen before.

Scattered upon the page were circles of various sizes, each joined to the others by lines, some of which radiated directly to their targets, while others followed more rectangular and roundabout paths. Some of the lines were thick; some thin. Some were single; others double; and a few were shaded in various schemes of cross-hatching.

At first I thought it was a railway map, so dense were the tracks – perhaps an ambitious expansion scheme for the nearby Buckshaw Halt, where trains had once stopped to put down guests and unload goods for the great house.

Only when I recognised the shape at the bottom of the map as the ornamental lake, and the unmistakeable outline of Buckshaw itself, did I realise that the document was, in fact, not a map at all, but a diagram: Lucius 'Leaking' de Luce's plan for his subterranean hydraulic operations.

Interesting, I thought, *but only vaguely.* I shoved the paper into my pocket for future reference and resumed my search for books that might contain some mention of the Hobblers.

Sermons for Sailors; God's Plan for the Indies; Remains of Alexander Knox, Esq.

And suddenly there it was: *English Dissenters.*

I must say – it was an eye-opener!

I suppose I had been expecting a dry-as-dust account of hellfire parsons and dozing parishioners. But what I had stumbled upon was a treasure trove of jealousy, backbiting, vanity, abductions, harrowing midnight escapes, hangings, mutilations, betrayal, and sorcery.

Wherever there had been savage bloodshed in seventeenth- and eighteenth-century English history, there was sure to have been a Dissenter at the heart of it. I made a note to take some of these volumes up to my bedroom for a bit of horrific bedtime reading. They would certainly be more lively than *Wind in the Willows*, which had been languishing on my night-table since Aunt Felicity had sent it to me for Christmas, pretending to believe it was a history of corporal punishment.

With *English Dissenters* in hand, I climbed down the ladder, dropped into the upholstered wing-back chair that Daffy usually occupied, and began flipping through its pages in search of the Hobblers.

Because there was no index, I was forced to go slowly, watching for the word 'Hobblers,' trying not to become too distracted by the violence of the religious text.

Only towards the end of the book did I find what I was looking for. But then, suddenly, there it was, at the bottom of a page, in a footnote marked by a squashed-spider asterisk, set in quaint old-fashioned type.

'*The mischief of Infant-baptism,*' it said, '*is an innovation on the primitive practice of the church: one of the corruptions of the second or third century. It is, moreover, often made the occasion of sin, or is turned into a farce as, for example, in that custom of the sect known as the Hobblers, whose dipping of a child held by the heel into running water, must be understood as no more than a bizarre, not to say barbaric, survival of the Greek myth of Achilles.*'

It took several moments for the words to sink in.

Mrs. Mullet had been right!

TWENTY-SEVEN

Up the east staircase I flew, *English Dissenters* clutched in my hand.

I couldn't contain myself.

'Listen to this,' I said, bursting into my bedroom. Porcelain was sitting exactly as I had left her, staring at me as if I were a madwoman.

I read aloud to her the footnote on infant baptism, the words fairly tumbling from my mouth.

'So what?' she said, unimpressed.

'Mrs. Bull,' I blurted out. 'She lied! Her baby drowned! It had nothing to do with Fenella!'

'I don't know what you're talking about,' Porcelain said.

Of course she didn't! I hadn't told her about the encounter with the enraged Mrs. Bull in the Gully. I could still hear those frightening, hateful words in my mind:

'Gypsy! Gypsy! Clear off!' she had screamed at Fenella. *''Twas you as stole my baby. Tom, get out here! That Gypsy's at the gate!'*

Thinking to spare Porcelain's feelings, I skated quickly over the story of the Bull baby's disappearance, and of the furious outburst its mother had directed at Fenella in the Gully.

Mrs. Mullet's friend had told her the Hobblers dipped their babies by the heel, like Achilles in the River Styx. She didn't quite put it that way, but that's what she meant.

334

'So you see,' I finished triumphantly, 'Fenella had nothing to do with it.'

'Of course she didn't,' Porcelain scoffed. 'She's a harmless old woman, not a kidnapper. Don't tell me you believe those old wives' tales about Gypsies stealing babies?'

'Of course I don't,' I said, but I was not being truthful. In my heart of hearts I had, until that very minute, believed what every child in England had been made to believe.

Porcelain was becoming huffy again, and I didn't want to risk another outburst, either from her, or worse, from me.

'She's that redhead, then?' she said suddenly, bringing the topic back to Mrs. Bull. 'The one that lives in the lane?'

'That's her!' I said. 'How did you know?'

'I saw someone like that ... hanging about,' Porcelain said evasively.

'Where?' I demanded.

'About,' she said, locking eyes with me, just daring me to stare her down.

The truth hit me like a slap in the face.

'Your dream!' I said. 'It was her! In your dream you saw her standing over you in the caravan, didn't you?'

It made perfect sense. If Fenella really *could* see into the past and the future, and her daughter, Lunita, could impress the Air Ministry with her powers, there was no reason Porcelain couldn't summon up such an unpleasant woman in her sleep.

'It was like no dream I've ever had before,' Porcelain said. 'Oh, but God ... I wish I'd never

335

had it!'

'What do you mean?'

'It didn't seem like a dream. I'd fallen asleep on Fenella's bed – didn't even bother taking off my clothes. It must have been a noise that roused me – somewhere close – inside the caravan.'

'You dreamed you'd fallen asleep?'

Porcelain nodded. 'That was what was so horrible about it. I didn't move a muscle. Just kept taking deep quiet breaths, as if I was asleep, which I was, of course. Oh, damn! It's so hard to explain.'

'Go on,' I said. 'I know what you mean. You were in my bed, dreaming you were in Fenella's bed.'

She gave me a look of gratitude. 'There wasn't a sound. I listened for a long time, until I thought they were gone, and then I opened my eyes – no more than a sliver, and...'

'And?'

'There was a face! A big face – right there – just inches away! Almost touching mine!'

'Good lord!'

'So close I couldn't really focus,' Porcelain went on. 'I managed to make a little moan, as if I was dreaming – let my mouth fall open a bit...'

I have to admit I was filled with admiration. I hoped that, even in a dream, I should have the presence of mind to do the same thing myself.

'The lamp was burning low,' she went on. 'It shone through the hair. I could only see the hair.'

'Which was red,' I said.

'Which was red. Long and curly. Wild, it was. And then I opened my eyes–'

'Yes, yes! Go on!'

'And it should have been your face I was

336

looking at, shouldn't it? But it wasn't! It was that face of the man with the red hair. That's why I flew at you and nearly choked you to death!'

'Hold on!' I said. 'The *man* with the red hair?'

'He was beastly ... all covered with soot. He looked like someone who slept in a haystack.'

I shook my head. In a weird way it made sense, I suppose, that in a dream, Porcelain should transform Mrs. Bull, whom she had perhaps glimpsed in the Gully, into a redheaded wild man. Daffy had not long before been reading a book by Professor Jung, and had announced to us suddenly that dreams were symbols that lurked in the subconscious mind.

Ordinarily, I should have written off the contents of a dream as rubbish, but my recent life seemed so flooded with inexplicable instances to the contrary.

In the first place, there had been Fenella's vision – in her crystal ball – of Harriet wanting me to help her come home from the cold, and even though Fenella had claimed that Feely and Daffy put her up to it, the whole thing had left me shaken; wondering, in fact, if her confession was not itself a lie.

Then, too, there had been Brookie's tale about the restless Grey Lady of Buckshaw. I still hadn't decided if he'd been having me on about the so-called legend, but there'd been simply no time to look into it on my own.

I must admit, though, that these nibblings of the supernatural at the base of my brain were more than a little unnerving.

'Why didn't you tell me this before?'

'Oh, I don't know, everything's so confusing. Part of me didn't trust you enough. And I knew that you no more trusted me.'

'I wasn't sure about your clothes,' I told her. 'I wondered why you had to wash them in the river.'

'Yes, you put that in your notebook, didn't you? You thought I might have been soaked with Fenella's blood.'

'Well, I...'

'Come on, Flavia, admit it. You thought I'd bashed in Fenella's skull ... to ... to ... inherit the caravan, or something.'

'Well, it was a possibility,' I said with a grin, hoping it would be infectious.

'The fact of the matter is,' she said, giving her hair a toss, then winding and unwinding a long strand of it round a forefinger, 'that women away from home sometimes feel the urge to rinse out a few things.'

'Oh,' I said.

'If you'd taken the trouble to ask me, I'd have told you.'

Even if it wasn't meant as such, I took this as an invitation to ask blunt questions.

'All right,' I said. 'Then let me ask you this: when the man in the caravan was leaning over you in your dream, did you notice anything besides his hair?'

I thought I knew the answer, but I didn't want to put words in her mouth.

Porcelain knitted her brows and pursed her lips. 'I don't think so – I ... wait! There *was* something else. It was so ghastly I must have forgotten it when you woke me so suddenly.'

338

I leaned forward eagerly.

'Yes?' I said. Already my pulse was beginning to race.

'Fish!' she said. 'There was the most awful reek of dead fish. Ugh!'

I could have hugged her. I could have put my arm around her waist and – if it hadn't been for that curious stiffness in the de Luce blood that keeps me on an invisible tether – danced her round the room.

'Fish,' I said. 'Just as I thought.'

Already, my mind was a flask at the boil, the largest bubbles being: Brookie Harewood and his reeking creel, Ursula Vipond and her decaying willow withies, and Miss Mountjoy with her lifetime supply of cod-liver oil.

The problem was this: not a single one of them had red hair.

So far, the only redheads in my investigation were the Bulls: Mrs. Bull and the two little Bulls. The little ones were out of the question – they were far too young to have attacked Fenella or murdered Brookie.

Which left the obnoxious Mrs. B who, in spite of her other failings, did not, to the best of my knowledge, smell of fish. If she did, Mrs. Mullet couldn't have resisted mentioning it.

Fish or no fish, though, Mrs. Bull had an obvious grievance against Fenella, whom she believed to have kidnapped her baby.

But whoever left the fishy smell hanging about the caravan was not necessarily the same person who fractured Fenella's skull with the crystal ball.

And whoever had done *that* had not necessarily

339

murdered Brookie.

'I'm glad I don't think as hard as you do,' Porcelain said. 'Your eyes go all far away and you look like someone else – someone older. It's quite frightening, actually.'

'Yes,' I said, even though this was news to me.

'I've tried to,' she said, 'but it just doesn't seem to work. I can't think who would want to harm Fenella. And that man – the one we found hanging from the fountain – whoever would want to kill *him*?'

That was the question. Porcelain had put her finger on it.

The whole thing came down to what Inspector Hewitt would call 'motive.' Brookie was an embarrassment to his mother and had stolen from Miss Mountjoy. As far as I knew, he had no connection with the Pettibones, other than the fact that he provided them with stolen goods. It would be odd indeed if those two old curios had murdered him. Without her husband's help, Mrs. Pettibone could never have manhandled Brookie's body into the position in which Porcelain and I had found it. Even *with* her husband's help – old Pettibone was so frail – they'd have needed a motorised crane.

Or the assistance of their friend Edward Sampson, who owned acres of rusting machinery in East Pinching.

'I can think of only one person,' I said.

'And who might that be?'

'I'm afraid I can't tell you.'

'So much for trust,' she said in a flat voice.

'So much for trust.'

It hurt me to cut her off in that way, but I had

340

my reasons, one of which was that she might be forced to spill the beans to Inspector Hewitt. I couldn't have anyone interfering when I was so close to a solution.

Another was that Brookie's killer and Fenella's attacker were still at large, and I couldn't possibly put Porcelain at risk.

She was safe enough here at Buckshaw, but how long could I keep her presence a secret?

That's what I was thinking about when there came a light tap on the door.

'Yes?' I called out.

A moment later, Father walked into the room.

'Flavia–' he began, then stopped in his tracks.

Porcelain leapt from the bed and backed towards the corner of the room.

Father stared at her for a moment, and then at me, then back at Porcelain again. 'Excuse me,' he said, 'I didn't realise–'

'Father,' I said, 'I should like to introduce Porcelain Lee.'

'How do you do?' Father said after an almost imperceptible pause, then sticking out his hand at once, rather than waiting for her to do so first. He was obviously flustered.

Porcelain came forward a couple of halting steps and gave him a single shake: up-down.

'Lovely weather we've been having,' Father went on, 'when it isn't raining, of course.'

I saw my opportunity and I took it.

'It was Porcelain's grandmother, Mrs. Faa, who was attacked in the Gully,' I said.

What seemed like an eternity of shadows fled across Father's face.

341

'I was saddened to hear of that,' he said at last. 'But I'm given to believe she's going to make a splendid recovery.'

Neither of them knowing what to say next, they stood there staring fixedly at each other, and then Father said, 'You'll join us for supper, of course?'

You could have knocked me down with a moth-eaten feather!

Dear old Father! How I admired him. Generations of breeding and his natural gallantry had turned what might have been a sticky situation into a perfect triumph, and my bedroom, rather than the anticipated field of battle, had suddenly become a reception chamber.

Porcelain lowered her eyelids to signal assent.

'Good!' Father exclaimed. 'That's settled, then.'

He turned to me. 'Mrs. Mullet returned not ten minutes ago to retrieve her purse. Left it in the pantry. If she's still here, I'll ask her if she wouldn't mind – I believe she might still be in the kitchen.'

And with that, he was gone.

'Crikey!' Porcelain said.

'Quick,' I told her. 'There's not a minute to lose! You'll probably want to have a wash-up and change into something more ... fresh.'

She'd been wearing Fenella's dowdy black outfit for days, and looked, to be perfectly frank, like a Covent Garden flower seller.

'My things won't fit you,' I said, 'but Daffy's or Feely's will.'

I beckoned her to follow, then led her through the creaking upstairs corridors.

'That's Daffy's room,' I said, pointing, when we reached the west wing of the house. 'And that's

Feely's. Help yourself – I'm sure they won't mind. See you at supper. Come down when the gong is struck.'

I don't know what makes me do these things, but secretly, I could hardly wait to see how my sisters reacted when Porcelain came down for supper in one of their favorite frocks. I hadn't really had the chance to pay them back properly for the humiliation in the cellars. My jiggered looking glass had backfired horribly, but now, suddenly, out of the blue, dear old Fate had given me a second chance.

Not only that but Mrs. M had turned up unexpectedly in the kitchen, which presented a perfect opportunity to ask her the question that might well stamp this case 'Closed.'

I flew down the stairs and skipped into the kitchen.

Hallelujah! Mrs. Mullet was alone.

'Sorry to hear you forgot your purse,' I said. 'If I'd known sooner, I could have brought it to you. It would have been no trouble at all.'

This was called 'storing up credits,' and it operated on the same principle as indulgences in the Roman Catholic Church, or what the shops in London called 'the Lay-away Plan.'

'Thank you, dear,' Mrs. M said, 'but it's just as well I come back. The Colonel's asked me to set a few things on the table, and I don't mind, really, seein' as it's Alf's lodge night, and I wouldn't have much to do anyway but knit and train the budgerigar. We're teachin' it to say "Eee, it was agony, Ivy!" You should 'ear it, dear. Alf says it's ever so 'umorous.'

343

As she spoke, she bustled about the kitchen, preparing to serve supper.

I took a deep breath and made the leap.

'Was Brookie Harewood a Hobbler?' I asked

'Brookie? I'm sure I couldn't tell you, dear. All I knows is, last time I seen 'im slinkin' round the church, I told the vicar 'e'd best lock up the communion plate. That's what I said: "You'd best lock up the communion plate before it goes pop like a weasel."'

'What about Edward Sampson? Do you know anything about him?'

'Ted Sampson? I should say I do! Reggie's half brother, 'e is, a reg'lar bad bun, that one. Owns that salvage yard in East Finchin', and Alf says there's more'n old tin goes through them gates. I shouldn't be tellin' you this, dear. Tender ears, and all that.'

I was filling in the blanks nicely. Pettibone and Company, under cover of a quiet shop, an out-of-the-way salvage yard, and an eccentric religion, were operating an antiques theft and forgery ring. Although I had suspected this for some time, I had not seen, until now, how all of it fitted together.

Essentially, Brookie stole, Edward copied, and Reginald sold treasures removed from stately homes. The ingenious twist was this: after the original objects were copied, they were returned to their owners, so that they would seldom, if ever, be missed.

Or were the originals replaced with the copies? I had not yet had time to find that out, but when I did, I would begin by making a chemical analysis of Sally Fox and Shoppo's metallic content. I had originally intended to begin with the de Luce lobster pick I had found in the hands of Timothy – or was it really 'Timofey' – Bull. But the demands on my time had made that impossible.

With his gob full of sweets, Timofey had been very difficult to understand.

I smiled as I recalled the child mucking in the lane.

'Danny's pocket,' he had replied when I'd asked him where he got his pretty digger. In retrospect, he was almost cute.

'And Mrs. Bull, of course. Is she a Hobbler, too?'

'I couldn't say,' Mrs. Mullet said. 'I've been told Tilda Mountjoy was one of 'em, but I never heard it said that Margaret Bull was, even though them two is as thick as thieves! Them 'Obblers goes traipsin' round to one another's 'ouses of a Sunday to sing their 'ymns, and shout, and roll about on the floor as if they was tryin' to smother a fire in their unmentionables, and God knows what all else.'

I tried to picture Miss Mountjoy rolling around on the floor in the grips of religious ecstasy, but my imagination, vivid as it is, was not up to it.

'They're a rum lot,' Mrs. M went on, 'but there's not a one of 'em would let Margaret Bull through their front gate. Not in a month o' Sundays! Not anymore.'

'Why not?'

'Somethin' 'appened when that baby of 'ers got took. She was never the same after – not that she was much of a marvel before–'

'What about her husband?'

'Tom Bull? 'E took it real hard. Nearly killed

'im, they say. "E went off not long after, and my friend Mrs. Waller said 'is wife told 'er, in confidence, mind, that 'e wouldn't be comin' back.'

'Maybe he went off to find work. Dogger says a lot of men have done that since the end of the war.'

"E had work enough. Worked for Pettibone's brother-in-law.'

'Ted Sampson?'

'The very one we was talkin' about. A foundry-man, Tom Bull was, and a good one, so they say, even though 'e'd 'ad 'is troubles with the police. But when that baby girl o' 'is got took, somethin' 'appened, inside, like, and 'e went off 'is 'ead. Not long after, it were, 'e was up and gone.'

How I longed to blurt out to her that the body of Tom Bull's baby daughter had been found in the Palings, but I dared not breathe a word. The news had not yet reached the village, and I didn't want to be accused of leaking information that the police would sooner keep to themselves – at least for the time being.

'You'd better run along and clean up for dinner, dear,' Mrs. Mullet said suddenly, breaking in upon my train of thought. 'The Colonel says you're 'avin company to supper, so 'e won't want to see dirty 'ands at the table.'

I held my tongue. In ordinary circumstances, I should have lashed out against such an impertinent remark, but today I had a new weapon.

'Quite right, Mrs. M,' I heard myself saying, as I trotted instantly and obediently to the door.

Here I paused, turned dramatically, and then in my best innocent-as-a-lamb voice, said, 'Oh, by the way, Mrs. Mullet, Vanetta Harewood showed me her portrait of Harriet.'

The clatter of dishes stopped, and for a few moments there was a stony silence in the kitchen.

'I knew this day would come,' Mrs. Mullet said suddenly in an odd voice; the voice of a stranger. 'I've been 'alf expectin' it.'

She collapsed suddenly into a chair at the table, buried her face in her apron, and dissolved into a miserable sobbing.

I stood by helplessly, not quite knowing what to do.

At last, I pulled out the chair opposite, sat down at the table, and watched her weep.

I had a special fascination with tears. Chemical analyses of my own and those of others had taught me that tears were a rich and a wonderful broth, whose chief ingredients were water, potassium, proteins, manganese, various yeasty enzymes, fats, oils, and waxes, with a good dollop of sodium chloride thrown in, perhaps for taste. In sufficient quantities, they made for a powerful cleanser.

Not so very different, I thought, *from Mrs. Mullet's chicken soup,* which she flung at even the slightest sniffle.

By now, Mrs. M had begun to subside, and she said, without removing the apron from her face: 'A gift, it was. She wanted it for the Colonel.'

I reached out across the table and placed my hand on her shoulder. I didn't say a word.

Slowly, the apron came down, revealing her anguished face. She took a shuddering breath.

'She wanted to surprise 'im with it. Oh, the trouble she went to! She was ever so 'appy. Bundlin' up you lot of angels and motorin' over to

347

Maiden Fenwick for your sittin's – 'avin' that 'Are-wood woman come 'ere to Buckshaw whenever the Colonel was away. Bitter cold, it was. Bitter.'

She mopped at her eyes and I suddenly felt ill.

Why had I ever mentioned the painting? Had I done it for no reason other than to shock Mrs. Mullet? To see her response? I hoped not.

''Ow I've wanted to tell the Colonel about it,' Mrs. Mullet went on quietly, 'but I couldn't. It's not my place. To think of it lyin' there in 'er studio all these years, an' 'im not knowin' it – it breaks my 'eart. It surely does – it breaks my 'eart.'

'It breaks mine, too, Mrs. M,' I said, and it was the truth.

As she pulled herself to her feet, her face still wet and red, something stirred in my memory.

Red.

Red hair ... Timofey Bull ... his mouth stuffed with sweets and the silver lobster pick in his hand.

'Danny's pocket,' he'd said, when I asked him where he got it. 'Danny's pocket.'

And I had misheard him.

Daddy's pocket!

Red and silver. This was what my dreams and my good sense had been trying to tell me!

I felt suddenly as if a snail were slowly crawling up my spine.

Could it be that Tom Bull was still in Bishop's Lacey? Could he still be living secretly amid the smoke that blanketed his house in the Gully?

If so, it might well be *he* who'd been outside smoking as I crept with Gry past his house in the dark. Perhaps it was *he* who had watched from the wood as Inspector Hewitt and his men

348

removed Brookie's body from the Poseidon fountain – he who had removed the pick from Brookie's nose when Porcelain and I–

Good lord!

And Timofey had found the lobster pick in his father's pocket, which could only mean–

At that very instant, the gong in the foyer was rung, announcing supper.

'Better get along, dear,' Mrs. Mullet said, poking at her hair with a forefinger and giving her face a last swipe with her apron. 'You know what your father's like about promptness. We mustn't keep 'im waitin'.'

'Yes, Mrs. Mullet,' I said.

TWENTY-EIGHT

The household had been summoned, and we all of us stood waiting in the foyer.

I understood at once that Father had decided to make an occasion of Porcelain's presence in the house, perhaps, I thought, because he felt remorse for the way in which he had treated her grandparents. He still did not know, of course, about the tragic death of Johnny Faa.

I stood at the bottom of the stairs, a little apart from the others, taking in, as if for the first time, the sad splendour of the de Luce ancestral home.

There had been a time when Buckshaw rang with laughter, or so I'd been told, but quite frankly, I could not even imagine it. The house seemed to hold itself in stiff disapproval, reflecting only the sound of whispers – setting dim but rigid limits on the lives of all of us who lived within its walls. Other than Father's gorgon sister, Aunt Felicity, who made annual expeditions in order to berate him, there had been no guests at Buckshaw for as long as I could remember.

Daffy and Feely stood with annoyingly perfect posture on either side of Father, both of them scrubbed to disgusting perfection, like the well-bred but rather dim daughters of the local squire in a drawing-room drama. Just wait till they saw Porcelain!

To one side, Dogger hovered, nearly invisible against the dark panelling, save for his white face and his white hair – like a disembodied head afloat in the gloom.

Glancing at his military wristwatch, Father made a slight involuntary frown, but covered it nicely by pulling out his handkerchief and giving his nose an unconvincing blow.

He was nervous!

We stood there in silence, each of us staring off in a different direction.

Precisely fifteen minutes after the gong had sounded, a door closed somewhere above, and we focused our attention upon the top of the staircase.

As Porcelain appeared, we gasped collectively, and Mrs. Mullet, who had just come from the kitchen, gave out a cry like a small nocturnal animal. I thought for a moment she was going to bolt.

Porcelain had not chosen from Daffy's or Feely's wardrobe. She was dressed in one of my mother's most memorable outfits: the knee-length, flame-coloured dress of orange silk chiffon that Harriet had worn to the Royal Aero Society Ball the year before her final journey. A photograph had been taken by the *Times* that evening as Harriet arrived at the Savoy – a photograph that created a stir that to this day has never been quite forgotten.

But it wasn't just the dress: Porcelain had pulled her hair back in the same way that Harriet had done when she was riding to the hounds. She must have copied the style from the black-and-white photo on Harriet's desk.

Because I had rifled my mother's jewel box myself from time to time, I recognised at once the antique amber necklace that lay against Porcelain's surprisingly well-developed bosom, and the stones that glittered on her fingers.

Harriet's – all of them Harriet's!

Porcelain paused on the top step and looked down at us with what I took at the time to be shyness, but later decided might well have been contempt.

I must say that Father behaved magnificently, although at first, I was sure he was going to faint. As Porcelain began her long, slow descent, his jaw muscles began tightening and loosening reflexively. As with most military men, it was the only permissible show of emotion, and as such, it was at once both nerve-wracking and deeply endearing.

Down and down she came towards us, floating on the air like some immortal sprite – a pixie, perhaps, I thought wildly. Perhaps Queen Mab herself!

351

As she neared the bottom, Porcelain broke into the most heartbreaking smile that I have ever seen on a human face: a smile that encompassed us all and yet, at the same time, managed to single out each one of us for particular dazzlement.

No queen – not even Cleopatra herself – had ever made such an entrance, and I found myself gaping in open-mouthed admiration at the sheer audacity of it.

As she swept lightly past me at the bottom of the stairs, she leaned in close upon my neck, her lips almost brushing my ear.

'How do I look?' she whispered.

All she needed was a rose in her teeth, but I hardly dared say so.

Father took a single step forward and offered her his arm.

'Shall we go in to dinner?' he asked.

'Macaroons!' Porcelain said. 'How I love them!'

Mrs. Mullet beamed. 'I shall give you the recipe, dear,' she said. 'It's the tinned milk as gives 'em the extra fillet.'

I nearly gagged, but a few deft passes of my table napkin provided a neat distraction.

Daffy and Feely, to give them credit, had – apart from their initial goggling – seemed not to have turned a hair at Porcelain's borrowed costume, although they couldn't take their eyes off her.

At the table, they asked interesting questions – mostly about her life in London during the war. In general, and against all odds, my sisters were charming beyond belief.

And Father ... dear Father. Although Porcelain's

sudden appearance in Harriet's wardrobe must have shocked him deeply, he managed somehow to keep a miraculously tight grip on himself. In fact, for a few hours, it was as if Harriet had been returned to him from the dead.

He smiled, he listened attentively, and at one point he even told rather an amusing story about an old lady's first encounter with a beekeeper.

It was as if, for a few hours, Porcelain had cast a spell upon us all.

There was only one awkward moment, and it came towards the end of the evening.

Feely had just finished playing a lovely piano arrangement of Antonin Dvorak's *Gypsy Songs, Opus 55: Songs My Great-Grandfather Taught Me,* one of her great favourites.

'Well,' she asked, getting up from the piano and turning to Porcelain, 'what do you think? I've always wanted to hear the opinion of a *real* Gypsy.'

You could have cut the silence with a knife.

'Ophelia...' Father said.

I held my breath, afraid that Porcelain would be offended, but I needn't have worried.

'Quite beautiful in places,' she said, giving Feely that dazzling smile. 'Of course I'm no more than half-Gypsy, so I only enjoyed every other section.'

'I thought she was going to leap over the piano stool and scratch my eyes out!'

We were back upstairs in my bedroom after what had been, for both of us, something of an ordeal.

'Feely wouldn't do that,' I said. 'At least, not with Father in the room.'

There had been no mention of Brookie Harewood, and apart from a polite enquiry by Father ('I hope your grandmother is getting on well?'), nothing whatever said about Fenella.

It was just as well, as I didn't fancy having to answer inconvenient, and perhaps even embarrassing, questions about my recent activities.

'They seem nice, though, your sisters, really,' Porcelain remarked.

'Ha!' I said. 'Shows what little you know! I hate them!'

'Hate them? I should have thought you'd love them.'

'Of course I love them,' I said, throwing myself full length onto the bed. 'That's why I'm so good at hating them.'

'I think you're having me on. What have they ever done to you?'

'They torture me,' I said. 'But please don't ask me for details.'

When I knew that I had gained her undivided attention, I rolled over onto my stomach so that I couldn't see her.

Talking to someone dressed in my mother's clothing was eerie enough, without recounting to her the tortures my sisters had inflicted upon me.

'Torture you?' she said. 'In what way? Tell me about it.'

For a long while there was only the sound of my brass alarm clock ticking on the bedside table, chopping the long minutes into manageable segments.

Then, in a rush, it all came spilling out. I found myself telling her about my ordeal in the cellars: how they had lugged me down the stairs,

354

dumped me on the stone floor, and frightened me with horrid voices; how they had told me I was a changeling, left behind by the pixies when the real Flavia de Luce was abducted.

Until I heard myself telling it to Porcelain, I had no idea how badly shaken the ordeal had left me.

'Do you believe me?' I asked, desperate, somehow, for a yes.

'I'd like to,' she said, 'but it's hard to imagine such ladylike young women operating their own private dungeon.'

Ladylike young women? I'm afraid I almost uttered a word that would have shocked a sailor.

'Come on,' I said, leaping to my feet and tugging at her arm. 'I'll show you what ladylike young women get up to when no one is looking.'

'Cor!' Porcelain said. 'It's a bloody crypt!'

In spite of an occasional electric bulb strung here and there on frayed wiring, the cellars were a sea of darkness. I had brought from the pantry the pewter candlestick that was kept for those not infrequent occasions when the current failed at Buckshaw, and I held it above my head, moving the flickering light from side to side.

'See? There's the sack they threw over my head.

'And look,' I said, holding the candle down close to the flagstones. 'Here are their footprints in the dust.'

'Seems like rather a lot of them for a couple of ladylike young women,' Porcelain said sceptically. 'Rather large, too,' she added.

She was right. I could see that at once.

Distinct footprints led off into the darkness, too

big to be Daffy's or mine or Feely's, which mingled near the bottom of the stairs. Nor were they Father's: he had not come all the way down the steps, and even if he had, his leather-soled shoes left distinct impressions with which I was quite familiar.

Dogger's footprints, too, were unmistakeable: long and narrow, and placed one in front of the other with the precision of a red Indian.

No, these were not Father's footprints, nor were they Dogger's. If my suspicions were correct, they had been made by someone wearing rubber boots.

'Let's see where they go,' I said.

Porcelain's presence bucked up my bravery no end, and I was ready to follow the prints to wherever they might take us.

'Do you think that's wise?' she asked, the whites of her eyes flashing in the light of the candle. 'No one knows we're down here. If we fell into a pit or something, we might die before anyone found us.'

'There are no pits down here,' I said. 'Just a lot of old cellars.'

'Are you sure?'

'Of course I'm sure. I've been down here hundreds of times.'

Which was a lie: prior to my inquisition, I had been in the cellars just once, with Dogger, when I was five, hunting for a pair of eighteenth-century alabaster urns that had been put away at the beginning of the war to protect them from possible air raids.

Candle held high, I set off along one of the black passageways. Porcelain could either follow,

356

or stay where she was in the dark shadows between the widely spaced electric bulbs.

Needless to say, she followed.

I had already formed the theory that the footprints had been made by Brookie Harewood – the *late* Brookie Harewood – but there was no point in mentioning this to Porcelain, who would probably get the wind up at the very idea of following in a dead man's footsteps.

But what on earth could Brookie have been doing in the Buckshaw cellars?

'Poachers know all the shortcuts,' Father had once said, and again, he was probably right.

As we passed under a low brick archway, I let my mind fly back to the night I had caught Brookie in his midnight prowl of the drawing room. It was hard to believe that had been only five days ago.

I still had a perfect mental image of our strange interview, which had ended with Brookie warning me against housebreakers who might have their eyes on Father's silver. 'Lot of that going on nowadays, since the war,' he had said.

And then I had opened one of the French doors and made it quite clear that I wanted him to leave.

No – wait! – I had first *unlocked* the door!

The door had been *locked* when I entered the drawing room. And there was no earthly reason to believe that Brookie had locked it behind him if he had broken into the house from the terrace. He'd have wanted it ready for a quick escape, had he been in danger of being caught.

It was reasonable, therefore, to assume that Brookie had gained entry to the house by some other route: through the cellars, for instance.

And the footprints now before us, disappearing into the darkness – quite clear impressions of a fisherman's Wellington boots, now that I stopped to think about it – suggested that my assumption was correct.

'Come on,' I said, sensing that Porcelain was hanging back. 'Stay close behind me.'

I thought I heard a little whimper, but I may have been wrong.

We had passed the end of the string of electric lights, and were now in an arched passageway lined on both sides with piles of decaying furniture. Here the footprints – more than one set of them, but all made by the same pair of boots – revealed that they had ventured more than once into, and out of, Buckshaw. The most recent prints were razor sharp, while the older impressions were softened slightly by the incessant sifting of dust.

'What's that?' Porcelain cried, seizing my shoulder with a painful grip.

Ahead of us, a shrouded object half blocked the passage.

'I don't know,' I said.

'I thought you'd been down here hundreds of times,' she whispered.

'I have,' I told her, 'but not in this particular passage.'

Before she could question me, I reached out, took hold of the corner of the sheet, and yanked it away.

A cloud of dust went billowing up, blinding us both – making us choke as if we had been caught in a sudden sandstorm.

'Oooh!' Porcelain wailed.

'It's only dust,' I said, even though I was stifling. And then the candle guttered – and went out.

I gave a silent curse and felt in my pocket.

'Hold this,' I said, finding her hands in the darkness and wrapping her fingers round the candlestick. 'I'll have it going in a jiff.'

I dug deeper into my pocket. Drat!

'Bad luck,' I said. 'I think I left the matches in the pantry.'

I felt the candlestick being shoved back into my hands. After a brief moment, there was a scraping sound, and a match flared up brightly.

'Good job I thought to pick them up, then,' Porcelain said, applying the match to the candle. As the flame grew taller and more steady, I could see the object over which the sheet had been draped.

'Look!' I said. 'It's a sedan chair.'

The thing looked like an early closed-in motorcar whose wheels had been stolen. The wood panelling was painted light green with hand-drawn flowers clustered in the corners. The gold medallion on the door was the de Luce crest.

Inside the chair, fleur-de-lis wallpaper had peeled away and hung down in tongues upon the green velvet padding of the seat.

There was an odd musty smell about the chair, and it wasn't just mice.

To think that some of my own ancestors had sat in this very box and been borne by other humans through the streets of some eighteenth-century city!

I wanted nothing more than to climb inside and become part of my family's history. Just to sit, and nothing more.

'This is owned by a woman,' Porcelain said in a slow, strange voice that sounded, more than anything, like an incantation. 'Silk dress ... powdered wig ... white face, and a black spot – like a star – on her cheek. She wants–'

'Stop it!' I shouted, spinning round to face her. 'I don't want to play your stupid games.'

Porcelain stood perfectly still, staring, black eyes shining madly out of her white face. She was entirely covered with dust, Harriet's flame-coloured dress now faded to an ashen orange in the light of the flickering candle.

'Look at you,' she said in a voice that sounded to me accusing. 'Just look at you!'

I couldn't help thinking that I was in the presence of my mother's ghost.

At that moment, a metallic *clang* came from the passageway ahead, and both of us jumped.

It sounded like iron on iron: chains being dragged through the bars of a cage.

'Come on,' Porcelain said, 'let's get out of here.'

'No, wait,' I said. 'I want to find out what's down here.'

She snatched the candlestick from my hand and began to move quickly back towards the stairs.

'Either come back with me, or stay here alone in the dark.'

I had no choice but to follow.

TWENTY-NINE

The flame colour began to brighten as soon as I shoved the material into the beaker.

'See?' I said. 'It's working.'

'What is that stuff?' Porcelain asked.

'Dry-cleaning fluid,' I said, giving Harriet's dress a poke with a glass rod, and stirring gently. 'Carbon tetrachloride, actually.'

I couldn't say its name without recalling, with pleasure, that the stuff had first been synthesised in 1839 by a Frenchman named Henri-Victor Regnault, a one-time upholsterer who had produced carbon tetrachloride through the reaction between chlorine and chloroform. One of the early uses of his invention had been to fumigate barrels of food in which various unpleasant insects had taken up residence; more recently, it had been used to charge fire extinguishers.

'Father uses it to scrutinise watermarks on postage stamps,' I said.

I did not mention that I had recently liberated the bottle from one of his storage cupboards for an experiment involving houseflies.

'Look at the dress. See how clean it is already? A few more minutes and it will be as good as new.'

Porcelain, who had wrapped herself in one of my old dressing gowns, looked on in awe.

I had changed into a cleanish dress and left the dusty one soaking in one of the laboratory's sinks. Later, I would hang it from one of the gas chandeliers to dry.

'You de Luces are a strange lot,' Porcelain said.

'Ha! Less than an hour ago you thought that at least two of us were ladylike young women.'

'That was before you showed me the cellars.'

I noted that our little tour of the Chamber of Horrors had changed her mind.

'Speaking of cellars,' I told her, 'I'm not easily frightened, but I didn't much care for that stuff about the lady who owned the sedan chair.'

'It wasn't stuff. I was telling you what I saw.'

'Saw? You're asking me to believe that you saw a woman in a powdered wig and a silk dress?'

For someone with a scientific mind, like me, this was hard to swallow. I had still not decided what to make of Brookie Harewood's Grey Lady of Buckshaw, or Fenella's cold woman who wanted to come home from the mountain. To say nothing of the pixies. Did everyone take me for a gullible fool, or were there really other worlds just beyond our range of vision?

'In a way, yes,' Porcelain said. 'I saw her with my mind.'

This I could understand – at least a little. I could see things with my own mind: the way, for instance, that trimethylamine could be produced by allowing *Bacillus prodigiosus* to grow on a sample of Mrs. Mullet's mashed potatoes in the heat of a summer afternoon. The resulting blood-red specks – which were known in the Middle Ages as 'Wunderblut,' or 'strange blood,' and which for a whole week in 1819 had appeared on various foods at Padua – would release not only

362

the smell of ammonia, but also the unmistakeable odour of trimethylamine.

When you come right down to it, I suppose, there is no great difference between ghosts and the invisible worlds of chemistry.

I was glad I had remembered dear old trimethylamine: my chemical friend with the fishy smell. I had discussed it with Dogger several days ago and formed certain opinions which I had been prevented from acting upon.

It was time now to pick up the threads and follow them, wherever they might lead.

'I'm tired,' I told Porcelain, yawning vastly.

Five minutes later we were tucked up in bed, one of us drifting rapidly towards oblivion.

I waited until she was asleep, then slipped quietly out of bed.

It was just past midnight when I eased shut my bedroom door and crept silently down the curving staircase.

I remembered that Dogger kept a high-powered torch in the butler's pantry for what he called 'midnight emergencies,' and it took only a moment to find it.

No frail candle this time, I thought: I had at my fingertips sufficient power to light up the Palace Pier at Brighton. I hoped it would be enough.

The cellars seemed colder than I had remembered. I should have worn a jumper, but it was too late now.

I was quickly at the point where the electric bulbs ended: beyond them, a cavernous blackness that led – who knew where?

I switched on the torch and pointed it along the passageway. Far ahead, I could see the outline of the sedan chair. I no longer relished the thought of climbing into the thing and recalling days gone by; in fact, I would be relieved to get past it.

'There is no lady,' I said aloud, and to my relief, there wasn't.

Ahead, the passage took a slight shift to the right. Since I had essentially set off to the right from the bottom of the kitchen stairs, I was heading east – now a little southeast, towards the Visto and the Poseidon fountain.

The Wellington boot footprints were easy to follow now, no longer overprinted with Porcelain's and mine. There were several sets, I noted, three coming and two going. If, as I suspected, they were Brookie's, he had made his first trip to steal one of the firedogs, his second to return it and make off with the second. On his last visit he had left by way of the French doors.

A sudden cold draft swept past me. Good job I'd brought the torch – the candle would certainly have blown out.

With the draft came a dark and a dank odour: an odour I could not at once identify, but one which suggested the reservoirs of neglected water closets: green corrosion with more than a whiff of zinc.

Well, I thought, *I'm not afraid of zinc, and green corrosion is something that has always interested me.*

I pushed on.

When I had been down here earlier with Porcelain, I had heard a definite metallic *clank*, but now the passage – which had begun to narrow – was as silent as the tomb.

364

In front of me was an archway with an open door, beyond which, or so it seemed, was a room.

I took two careful steps down into the chamber and found myself surrounded on all sides with metal pipes: zinc pipes, lead pipes, iron pipes, bronze pipes, copper pipes; pipes running up, down, and across, all interconnected with right elbows and great metal bolts with here and there a huge valve like the steering wheel of a motorcar.

I was at the very heart of Lucius de Luce's subterranean waterworks!

And then I heard it – a metallic clanking that echoed round and round the chamber.

I'll admit it – I froze.

Another *clank*.

'Hello,' I called, my voice shaking. 'Is anyone there?'

From somewhere came another sound: an animal sound for certain, though whether it was human, I could not tell.

What if a fox had made its way into the tunnel? Or a badger?

If that was the case, it would likely run away from a human with a torch – but what if it didn't?

'Hello?' I called again. 'Is anyone there?'

Again a muffled sound, weaker. Was it farther away, or was I imagining things? One thing was certain: it could only be coming from somewhere behind a giant pipe that rose up out of the stonework, levelled off, bent ninety degrees, and headed off towards the far side of the chamber.

I scrambled up onto the thing, straddled it for a moment – then dropped down on the other side.

The passageway into which the pipe led was

lower, narrower, and damp. Moisture beaded on the walls, and the floor, between bricks, was wet earth.

Just ahead, the tunnel was blocked by an iron gate: an iron gate that was chained shut and locked on the other side with a large, old-fashioned padlock.

I gave the thing a rattle, but it was absolutely solid. Without a key, there wasn't a hope of getting past.

'Damn!' I said. 'Damn and double damn!'

'Flavia?' someone croaked.

I must admit that I came very close to disgracing myself.

I shone the beam through the bars and picked out a shape huddled on the ground.

For as long as I live I shall never forget his white face staring up at me, blinded by the torch's beam. He had managed, somehow, to lose his spectacles, and his pale eyes, blind and blinking, were those of a baby mole pulled from its hole and dragged out suddenly into the daylight.

'Colin?' I said. 'Colin Prout?'

'Turn it off!' he pleaded in a ragged voice, twisting away from the light.

I swung the torch away, so that the passage beyond the bars was once more in near-darkness.

'Help me,' Colin said, his voice pitiful.

'I can't. The gate is locked.'

I gave the massive thing a shake with one hand, hoping it would spring open – perhaps by some as-yet-undiscovered magic – but that did not happen.

'Try it from your side,' I told him. 'There might be a latch...'

I knew, even as I said it, that there wasn't, but anything was worth a try.

'Can't,' Colin said, and even in the darkness I could tell that he was on the verge of tears. 'I'm tied up.'

'Tied up?' It seemed impossible, even though I had once or twice been in the same position myself.

'I've got the key, though. It's in me pocket.'

Praise be! I thought. *Finally, a bit of luck,*

'Wiggle yourself over to the gate,' I said. 'I'll try to reach the key.'

There was a painful silence, and then he said, 'I'm ... I'm tied to somethin'.'

And he began to whimper.

It was enough to make a saint spit!

But wait: the padlock was on Colin's side of the gate, wasn't it? I had noticed this but not given it my proper attention.

'Did you lock yourself in?' I asked.

'No,' Colin snuffled.

'Then how did you get in there?'

'We come through the door in the fountain.'

A door in the fountain? We?

I chose to ask the most important question first.

'Who's "we," Colin? Who did this to you?'

I could hear him breathing heavily in the darkness, but he did not answer.

I realised at once the futility of it all. I was not about to spend the rest of my life trying to pry answers out of a captive from whom I was separated by a wall of iron bars.

'All right, then,' I said. 'It doesn't matter. Tell me about the door in the fountain. I'll come round and let you out.'

It made me furious, actually, to think that I should have to ask a stranger about a secret door at Buckshaw – and secret it must be, for I had never heard of such a thing myself. Such mysteries were surely meant to be handed down by word of mouth from one family member to another, not practically pried from a near-stranger who skulked about the countryside in the company of a poacher.

'Simon's toe,' Colin said.

'What? You're not making any sense.'

The sound of sobbing told me there was no more to be got from him.

'Stay here,' I said, although it made no sense. 'I'll be back before you know it.'

'No, wait!' he cried. 'Give me the torch. Don't leave me alone!'

'I have to, Colin. I need the torch to light my way.'

'No, please! I'm 'fraid of the dark!'

'Tell you what,' I said. 'Close your eyes and count to five hundred and fifty. It won't be dark with your eyes closed. When you finish, I'll be back. Here – I'll help you start. One ... two ... three...'

'Can't,' Colin interrupted, 'I 'aven't learnt my hundreds.'

'All right, then, let's sing. Come on, we'll sing together:

'God save our gracious King,
Long live our noble King,
Long may he...

'Come on, Colin, you're not singing.'

'Don't know the words.'

'All right, then, sing something you know. Singing will make me come back sooner.'

There was a long pause, and then he began in a cracked and quavering voice:

'London Bridge is ... fallin' down
Fallin' ... down, fallin' down
London Bridge is fallin' down...'

I turned round and began to pick my way carefully back along the passage, the sound of Colin's voice soon becoming no more than a faint echo. Leaving him there, alone in the darkness, was one of the most difficult things I've ever had to do, although I can't say why. Life is full of surprises like that.

The return journey seemed endless. Time had surely slowed as I made my way back beneath the low arched ceilings to the cellars.

Up the steps I went and into the kitchen. Although the house was in perfect silence, I paused anyway to listen at the door.

Nothing.

Technically, I knew, I was not being disobedient. I had been forbidden to leave home, and I had no intention of doing so. The Poseidon fountain was well within the bounds of Buckshaw, which allowed me to have my cake and jolly well eat it, too.

I slipped quietly out the back door, leaving it unlocked, and into the kitchen garden. Overhead, the stars twinkled like a million mad eyes, while the moon, already halfway to its first quarter, hung like a broken silver fingernail in the night sky.

Ordinarily, even though it wasn't far to the Poseidon fountain, I'd have taken Gladys with me, if only for company. But now, when a single one of her excited squeaks or rattles might awaken the household, I simply couldn't risk it.

I set out at a brisk walk through the wet grass, across the east lawn towards the Visto. Somewhere, an owl hooted, and something tiny scurried through the dead leaves.

Then suddenly, almost without warning, Poseidon was looming above me, odd angles of his metal anatomy catching the starlight, as if some ancient part of the galaxy had fallen to earth.

I climbed up the steps to the base. What was it Colin had said?

'*Simon's toe.*' Yes, that was it – but what had he meant?

Of course! *Poseidon's* toe!

He must have heard the name from Brookie and got it muddled.

I scrambled up onto the fountain's lower bowl. Now Poseidon's giant foot was almost in my face, its big toe curled back as if someone were tickling his tummy.

I reached out and touched the thing – shoved it down as hard as I could. The toe moved – as if on a hidden hinge – and from somewhere below came a distinct metallic *snick*.

'Simon's toe,' I said aloud, smiling and shaking my head, proud of myself for having solved the puzzle.

I climbed down to the ground and – yes! – there it was! One of the large sculptured panels of water nymphs that formed the fountain's decorative base had sprung out slightly from the others.

How devilishly clever of old 'Leaking de Luce' to have hidden the lock's release in one of the statue's feet, where it wouldn't be easily discovered.

The hatch swung open with a groan and I stepped carefully into the fountain's base. As I had suspected it might, a single lead pipe emerged from one of several grottos below and bent up sharply to feed water to the fountain. A large arm-valve was obviously meant to control the flow, and although a heavy covering of cobwebs told me that it had not been used for ages, I was surrounded by the sound of dripping water which echoed un-nervingly in the dankness of the confined chamber.

A dozen precarious steps led down into a wide, rectangular pit at the bottom of the fountain.

They were splattered with blood!

On the edge of the bottom step was a large stain, while diminishing dribbles marked the ones higher up.

The blood had been here for some time, as was evident from its brown, well-oxidised appearance.

This must be the spot where Brookie met his death.

Avoiding the splotches, I picked my way gingerly to the bottom.

The pit was surprisingly spacious.

To one side, overhead, an iron grating revealed slits of the night sky: the stars still shining brightly, giving off so much light, in fact, that even the towering outline of Poseidon himself was visible far above. Gaping upwards at this novel viewpoint, I somehow managed to misstep. I twisted my ankle.

'Damn!' I said, pointing the torch at the ground to see what had caused my injury.

It was a rope, and it lay coiled in the circle of light like a self-contented viper sunning itself after a particularly satisfying lunch.

I can't say that I was surprised, since I had already deduced that there would likely be a rope. I had simply forgotten about it until I tripped on the stupid thing.

What *was* surprising, though, was that the police had not discovered such a crucial bit of evidence: a surprising misstep, not only for me, but also for them.

Better not touch it, I thought. *Best leave it in place for Inspector Hewitt's men.* Besides, I already knew as much as I needed to know about this particular remnant of the crime.

With a couple of halting steps, I limped towards an open tunnel.

But wait! Which of these openings would lead me back to Colin?

The one on the left, I thought, although I could hardly be sure. Lucius de Luce's plan had shown a bewildering maze of subterranean waterworks, and only now that I thought about it did I remember shoving the folded map into my pocket.

I grinned, realising that help was right here at my very fingertips. But when I reached for it, my pocket was empty.

Of course! I had changed my dusty dress for a clean one, and I let slip a mental curse as I realised that Lucius's priceless hand-drawn map was, at this very moment, soaking its way to blankness in a laboratory sink!

There was nothing for it now but to follow my instincts and choose a tunnel: the one on my left.

Here at its eastern extremity, the corridor was not only lower and more narrow, but had fallen into scandalous disrepair. The brick walls and pieces of the roof had crumbled in places, covering parts of the floor with broken rubble.

Careful, I thought. *The whole thing might cave in and–*

Something slapped my face – something dangling from the roof like a dead white arm. I let out a little yelp and stopped in my tracks.

A root! I had been frightened by a stupid root that had been put down, perhaps by one of the long gone borders which had, in earlier times, shaded the walkways of the Visto.

Even though I ducked under the thing, its slimy finger still managed to caress my face, as if it were dying for want of human company.

I limped along, the light of the torch sweeping wildly in front of me.

Here, on both sides of the tunnel, a dusty assortment of ladders, ropes, pails, watering cans, and galvanised funnels had been left, as if the groundskeepers who had used them had wandered off to war and forgotten to return.

A sudden flash of red brought me to a stop. Someone had written on the wall. I let the light play slowly over the painted letters: *H.d.L.*

Harriet de Luce! My mother had been here before me – found her way through this same tunnel – stood on these same bricks – painted her

373

initials on the wall.

Something like a shiver overtook me. I was surrounded with Harriet's presence. How, when I had never known her, could I miss her so deeply?

Then, faintly, from far along the tunnel, there came to my ears the sound of a voice – singing.

'London Bridge is fallin' down ... my fair lady.'

'Colin!' I shouted, and suddenly my eyes were brimming. 'Colin! It's me, Flavia.'

I lurched forward, tripping over fallen stones, feeling the ooze in my shoes from the tunnel's seepage. My hands were raw from clutching at the rough wall for support.

And then, there he was...

'My fair lady,' he was singing.

'It's all right, Colin. You can stop now. Where's the key?'

He winced at the light, then stared at me with a strange, offended look.

'Untie me first,' he said gruffly.

'No – key first,' I said. 'That way you won't run off with it.'

Colin groaned as he rolled slightly onto his left side. I reached into his pocket– Ugh! – and pulled out an iron key.

As he twisted, I could see that Colin's wrists were bound firmly behind him and lashed to an iron pipe that rose up vertically before vanishing into the roof.

The poor creature could have been tied up here for days!

'You must be in agony,' I said, and he looked up at me again with such blank puzzlement that I wondered if he knew the meaning of the word.

I struggled with the knots. Colin's efforts to free himself and the moisture from the seeping walls had shrunken them horribly.

'Do you have a knife?'

Colin shook his head and looked away.

'What? No knife? Come on, Colin – Boy Scouts are born with knives.'

'Took it off me. "Might hurt yourself." That's what they said.'

'Never mind, then. Lean forward. I'll try the key.'

Putting the torch on the ground so that its light reflected from the wall, I attacked the knots with the business end of the key.

Colin groaned, letting out little yelps every time I applied pressure to his bonds. In spite of the clamminess of the tunnel, sweat was dripping from my forehead onto the already saturated rope.

'Hang on,' I told him, 'I've almost got it.'

The last end pulled through – and he was free.

'Stand up,' I said. 'You need to move around.'

He rolled over, unable to get to his feet.

'Grab hold,' I said, offering my hand, but he shook his head.

'You have to get your circulation going,' I told him. 'Rub your arms and legs as hard as you can. Here, I'll help you.'

'It's no good,' he said. 'Can't do it.'

'Of course you can,' I said, rubbing more briskly. 'You need to get some circulation into your toes and fingers.'

His lower lip was trembling and I felt a sudden surge of pity.

'Tell you what. Let's have a rest.'

Even in the half-light his gratitude was hard to miss.

'Now then,' I said. 'Tell me about the blood on the fountain steps.'

Perhaps it wasn't fair, but I needed to know.

At the word 'blood,' Colin shrank back in horror.

'I never done it,' he croaked.

'Never did what, Colin?'

'Never done Brookie. Never shoved that sticker in his nose.'

'He roughed you up, didn't he? Left you no choice.'

'No,' Colin said, managing somehow to pull himself to his feet. 'It weren't like that. It weren't like that at all.'

'Tell me what happened,' I said, surprised by my own coolness in what could prove to be a tricky situation.

'We was chums, Brookie an' me. He told me stories when we wasn't scrappin'.'

'Stories? What kind of stories?'

'You know, King Arthur, like. 'Ad some right lovely talks, we did. Used to tell me about old Nicodemus Flitch, an' 'ow 'e could strike a sinner dead whenever 'e took the notion.'

'Was Brookie a Hobbler?' I asked.

''Course not!' Colin scoffed. 'But 'e wished 'e was. 'E fancied their ways, 'e used to say.'

So there it was: I should have asked Colin in the first place.

'You were telling me about the sticker,' I said, trying to steer Colin gently back to the moment of Brookie's death.

'He showed it to me,' Colin said. 'Ever so pretty ... silver ... like pirate treasure. Dug it up behind your 'ouse, Brookie did. Goin' to make dozens of 'em, 'e said. "Enough for a garden party at Buckin'ham Palace."'

I dared not interrupt.

'"Give it 'ere," I told 'im. "Let's 'ave a gander. Just for a minute. I'll give it back." But 'e wouldn't. "Might stab yourself," 'e said. Laughed at me.

'"'Ere, you promised!" I told 'im. "You said we'd go halfers if I carried the dog-thing."

'I grabbed it ... didn't mean nothin' by it – just wanted to have a gander, is all. 'E grabbed it back and gave it such a tug! I let go too quick, and–'

His face was sheer horror.

'I never done it,' he said. 'I never done it.'

'I understand,' I said. 'It was an accident. I'll do whatever I can to help, but tell me this, Colin – who tied you up?'

He let out such a wail that it nearly froze my blood, even though I already knew the answer.

'It was Tom Bull, wasn't it?'

Colin's eyes grew as round as saucers, and he stared over my shoulder. 'E's comin' back! 'E said 'e'd be back.'

'Nonsense,' I said. 'You've been here for ages.'

'Goin' to do me, Tom Bull is, 'cause I seen what 'e done at the caravan.'

'You saw what he did at the caravan?'

''Eard it, anyhow. 'Eard all the screamin'. Then 'e come out an' tossed somethin' in the river. 'E's goin' to kill me.'

Colin's eyes were wide as saucers.

'He won't kill you,' I told him. 'If he were, he'd

have done it before now.'

And then I heard the sound behind me in the tunnel. Colin's eyes grew even larger, almost starting from their sockets.

"E's 'ere!'

I whipped round with the torch to see a hulking form scuttling towards us like a giant land crab: so large that it nearly filled the passageway from roof to floor, and from wall to wall; a figure bent over nearly double to negotiate the cramped tunnel.

It could only be Tom Bull.

'The key!' I shouted, realising even as I did so that it was in my hand.

I sprang for the lock and gave the thing a twist.

Damn all things mechanical! The lock seemed rusted solid.

No more than a dozen paces away, the huge man was charging along the tunnel towards us, his rasping breath now horribly audible, his wild red hair like that of some raging madman.

Suddenly I was shoved aside. Colin snatched the key from my hand.

'No, Colin!'

He rammed it into the lock, gave it a fierce twist, and the hasp sprang open. A moment later he had yanked open the gate and pushed me – dragged me – almost carried me – through.

He slammed shut the gate, snapped the lock closed, and pushed me well away from the bars.

'Watch this un,' he said. ''Im's got long arms.'

For a moment, Colin and I stood there, breathing heavily, looking in horror at the blood-engorged face of Tom Bull as it glared at us from behind the iron bars.

His great fists grasped the heavy gate, shaking it as if to rip it out by the roots.

The Red Bull!

Fenella had been right!

I jerked back in horror against the wet wall, and as I did so, my twisted ankle gave way and I dropped the torch. We were plunged instantly into inky blackness.

I dropped to my knees, feeling the wet floor with outstretched fingers.

'Keep clear of the bars,' Colin whispered. 'Else 'e'll grab you!'

Not knowing which way was which, I scrabbled in the darkness, fearful that at any instant my wrist would be seized.

After what seemed like an eternity, the back of my hand brushed against the torch. I closed my fingers around it .... picked it up ... pushed the switch with my thumb... nothing.

I gave it a shake – banged it with the heel of my hand ... still nothing.

The torch was broken.

I could have wept.

Close to me, in the darkness, I heard a rustling. I dared not move.

I counted ten heartbeats.

Then there came a scraping – and a match flared up.

''Ad 'em in my pocket,' Colin said proudly. 'All along.'

'Go slowly,' I told him. 'That way. Don't let the match go out.'

As we backed away from the gate into the tunnel, and Tom Bull's face faded into darkness, his mouth moved and he uttered the only words I ever heard him speak.

'Where's my baby?' he cried.

His words echoed like knives from the stone walls.

In the horrid silence that followed, we edged farther back along the tunnel. When the first match burned out, Colin took out another.

'How many of those do you have?' I asked.

'One more,' he said, and he lit it.

We had gained some ground, but it was still a long way to the cellars.

Colin held his last match high, moving slowly again, leading the way.

'Good lad,' I told him. 'You've saved us.'

A sudden gust of cold air blew out the match, and we were plunged once again into blackness.

'Keep moving,' I urged him. 'Follow the wall.'

Colin froze.

'Can't,' he said. 'I'm 'fraid of the dark.'

'It's all right,' I told him. 'I'm with you. I won't let anything happen.'

I pushed against him, but he would not be budged.

'No,' he said. 'Can't.'

I could have gone on without him, but I was incapable of leaving him here alone.

And slowly, I realised that somehow, even in the darkness, I could dimly see Colin's white face. A moment later, I became aware of a growing light that had suddenly filled the passageway.

I spun round, and there, to my amazement, was Dogger, holding a large lantern above his head. Porcelain peered round him, fearfully at first, and then, when she saw I was quite safe, running to me, almost crushing me in her embrace.

'I'm afraid I ratted on you,' she said.

THIRTY

'And Dogger, you see, had already latched the door at the fountain. It only opens from the outside, so there was no way Tom Bull could get out.'

'Well done, Dogger,' Father said. Dogger smiled and gazed out the drawing-room window.

Daffy shifted uneasily on the chesterfield. She had been torn away from her book by Father, who insisted that both she and Feely be present at the interview. It was almost as if he was proud of me.

Feely stood at the chimneypiece, pretending to be bored, stealing quick, greedy glances at herself in the looking glass while otherwise simpering at Sergeant Graves.

'This whole business about the Hobblers is intriguing,' Inspector Hewitt said. 'Your notes have been most helpful.'

I fizzed a little inside.

'I gather they've been carrying out their baptisms in the Gully since sometime in the seventeenth century?'

I nodded. 'Mrs. Bull wanted her baby baptised in the old style, and her husband, I think, probably forbade it.'

'That he did,' said Sergeant Graves. 'He's told us as much.'

The Inspector glared at him.

'She went to the Gully with Miss Mountjoy – Dr. Kissing saw them together. There might have been other Hobblers present, I really don't know.

'But something went horribly wrong. They were dipping the baby by the heel, as Hobbler tradition requires, when something happened. The baby slipped and drowned. They buried it in the Palings – swore to keep the truth to themselves. At least, I think that's what happened.'

Sergeant Graves nodded, and the Inspector shot him *such* a look!

'Mrs. Bull thought at once of blaming it on Fenella. After all, she had just passed the caravan in the lane. She went home and told her husband, Tom, that their baby had been taken by Gypsies. And he believed her – has gone on believing her – until now.'

I took a deep breath and went on. 'Fenella told Mrs. Bull's fortune at the fête last week – told her the same nonsense she tells everyone: that something was buried in her past – something that wanted digging out.'

Only at that instant, as I spoke, did the full force – the full aptness – of Fenella's words come crashing into my consciousness: *'Told her there was something buried in her past; told her it wanted digging out – wanted setting right.'* I had actually copied these words into my notebook without understanding their meaning.

She couldn't *possibly* have learned of the Bull baby's supposed abduction until later – she had been gone from the Gully before the bungled baptism began.

Mrs. Bull, to reinforce her lie, must have been forced to follow through by filing a false report with the police. Tom, because of his shady associations, must have managed to keep well in the background. Hadn't Mrs. Mullet let slip that he'd had his troubles with the law?

How I wished I could ask the Inspector to confirm my conjecture – especially the part about Tom Bull – but I knew he wouldn't – couldn't – tell me. Perhaps some other time...

At any rate, Fenella had almost certainly been tracked down and questioned by the authorities during their investigation of the missing child – tracked down, questioned, and cleared. That much seemed obvious.

So that when Mrs. Bull had wandered unexpectedly into her tent just last week at the fête, it must have seemed as if Fate had sent her there for justice.

'There's something buried in your past. Something that wants digging out ... wants setting right,' Fenella had told her, but it was not the baby she meant – it was Mrs. Bull's accusation of kidnapping!

'Revenge is my specialty,' Fenella had said.

Revenge indeed!

But not without cost.

Surely the woman had recognised Fenella's caravan at the fête? Whatever could have possessed her to enter the tent?

I could think of only one reason: guilt.

Perhaps, in her own mind, Mrs. Bull's lie to her husband and the police was beginning to come unravelled – perhaps in some odd way she believed that a fresh confrontation would deflect any growing suspicion, on Tom's part, of her own guilt.

What was it Dr. Darby had told me? *'People can behave very strangely in times of great stress.'*

'Well?' the Inspector said, interrupting my thoughts. He was waiting for me to go on.

'Well, Mrs. Bull, of course, assumed that Fenella had looked into the crystal ball and seen the drowning. She must have gone home straightaway and told her husband that the Gypsy who had taken their baby was again camped at the Palings. Tom went to the caravan that very night and tried to kill her.

'He still believes his wife's lie, most likely,' I added. 'Even though the baby's body has since been found, I'll bet he's still blaming it on the Gypsies.'

I glanced over at Sergeant Graves for confirmation, but his face was a study in stone.

'How can you be so sure he was at the caravan?' Inspector Hewitt asked, turning to a new page of his notebook.

'Because Colin Prout saw him there. And as if that weren't enough, there was that whole business about the smell of fish,' I said. 'I think you'll find that Tom Bull has a disease that causes his body to exude a fishy odour. Dogger says that a number of such cases have been recorded.'

Inspector Hewitt's eyebrows went up slightly, but he said nothing.

'That's why, as it's grown worse, he's kept to his house for the past year or more. Mrs. Bull put about the story that he'd gone away, but he'd all the while been right here in Bishop's Lacey, working after dark. He's a foundryman, you

384

know, and probably quite handy at melting down scrap iron and moulding it into antiques.'

'Yes,' Inspector Hewitt said, surprising me. 'It's no secret that he was once employed at Sampson's works, in East Finching.'

'And still is,' I suggested. 'At least after dark.'

Inspector Hewitt closed his notebook and got to his feet.

'I'm very pleased to tell you, Colonel, that your firedogs will soon be restored. We found them in the coach house where Harewood kept his antiques.'

I was right! The Sally Fox and Shoppo at Brookie's *had* been Harriet's! Having replaced them with reproductions, Brookie was just waiting for a chance to sell the originals in London.

'There are others involved in what proved to be a very sophisticated ring of thieves and forgers. I trust that, in due time, you'll read about it in the newspapers.'

'But what about Miss Mountjoy?' I blurted it out. I felt quite sorry for poor Tilda Mountjoy.

'She may well face charges as an accessory,' the Inspector said. 'It's up to the Chief Constable, I don't envy him his task.'

'Poor Colin,' I said. 'He hasn't had an easy life, has he?'

'There may be mitigating circumstances,' Inspector Hewitt said. 'Beyond that, I can say nothing.'

'I knew for certain he was mixed up in it when I found the rope.'

I regretted it as soon as the words were out of my mouth.

'Rope? What rope?'

'The rope that fell through the grating at the Poseidon fountain.'

'Woolmer? Graves? What do we know about this?'

'Nothing, sir,' they said in unison.

'Then perhaps you will favour us by taking yourselves to the fountain immediately and rectifying the oversight.'

'Yes, sir,' they said, and marched, red-faced, from the drawing room.

The Inspector again focused his fierce attention on me. 'The rope,' he said. 'Tell me about the rope.'

'There had to be one,' I explained. 'Brookie was far too heavy to be hoisted onto the fountain by anyone but the strongest man. Or a Boy Scout with a rope.'

'Thank you,' Inspector Hewitt said. 'That will do. I'm quite sure we can fill in the blanks.'

'Besides,' I added, 'the rubbed spot on the trident showed quite clearly where the rope had polished away the tarnish.'

'Thank you. I believe we've already noted that.'

Well, then, I thought, *you've no one to blame but yourselves if you didn't think of looking for the rope that caused it. Colin is a Boy Scout, for heaven's sake.* There were times when officialdom was beyond even me.

'One last point,' the Inspector said, rubbing his nose. 'Perhaps you'd be good enough to clear up one small question that has rather eluded me.'

'I'll do my best, Inspector,' I said.

'Why on earth did Colin hang Brookie from the

fountain? Why not leave him where he was?'

'They had struggled for the lobster pick inside the base of the fountain. When Colin let go of the thing suddenly, Brookie's own force caused him to stab himself in the nostril. It was an accident, of course.'

Although this was the way Colin had told it to me, I must confess to gilding the lily more than a little for the Inspector's benefit. I no more believed Colin's version of the story than I believed that dray horses can fly. Brookie's death, in my estimation, was Colin's revenge for years of abuse. It was murder, pure and simple.

But who was I to judge? I had no intention of adding so much as another ounce to the burden of Colin's troubles.

'Brookie fell backwards down the stone steps into the chamber. That's probably what actually killed him.'

Oh Lord, forgive me this one charitable little fib!

'Colin fetched a length of rope from the tunnel and hauled him up onto Poseidon's trident. He had to tie Brookie's wrists together so that the arms wouldn't slip out of the coat later. He didn't want to risk the body falling.'

Inspector Hewitt gave me a look I can only describe as sceptical.

'Brookie,' I went on, 'had told Colin about the Hobblers' belief that Heaven was right there above our heads. You see, he wanted to give Brookie a head start.'

'Good lord!' Father said.

Inspector Hewitt scratched his nose. 'Hmmm,' he said. 'Seems rather far-fetched.'

387

'Not so far-fetched at all, Inspector,' I said. 'That's precisely the way Colin explained it to me. I'm sure that when Dr. Darby and the vicar allow you to question him further...'

The Inspector nodded in a sad way, as if he'd rather suspected it all along.

'Thank you, Flavia,' he said, getting to his feet and closing his notebook. 'And thank *you*, Colonel de Luce. You've been more than generous in helping us get to the bottom of this matter.' He walked to the drawing-room door.

'Oh, and Flavia,' he said rather shyly, turning back. 'I almost forgot. I came here today somewhat as a message bearer. My wife, Antigone, would be delighted if you'd come for tea next Wednesday ... if you're free, of course.'

Antigone? Tea? And then it sank in.

Oh, frabjous day! Callooh! Callay! That glorious goddess, Antigone, was summoning me, Flavia Sabina de Luce, to her vine-covered cottage!

'Thank you, Inspector,' I said. 'I shall consult my calendar and see if I can set aside some time.'

Up the stairs I flew. I couldn't wait to tell Porcelain!

I should have guessed that she'd be gone.

She had torn a blank page from my notebook and fastened it to one of my pillows with a safety pin.

Thanks for everything. Look me up in London sometime.

Your friend,
Porcelain

Just that, and nothing more.

At first I was seized with sadness. In spite of our ups and downs, I had never met anyone quite like Porcelain Lee. I had already begun to miss her.

I find it difficult to write about the portrait of Harriet.

Leaving the painting at Vanetta Harewood's studio with its face against the wall was out of the question. She had, after all, offered it to me, and since Harriet had paid in full for the work, it belonged rightly to her estate at Buckshaw.

I would hang it secretly, I decided, in the drawing room. I would unveil it for my family with as much ceremony as I could muster. I could hardly wait.

In the end, it hadn't been terribly difficult to arrange the transfer. I'd asked Mrs. Mullet to have a word with Clarence Mundy, who operated Bishop's Lacey's only taxicab, and Clarence had agreed to 'lay on transportation,' as he put it.

On a dark and rainy afternoon in late September, we had rolled up at the gate of the cottage studio in Maiden Fenwick, and Clarence had walked me to the door with an oversized black umbrella.

'Come in,' Vanetta Harewood said, 'I've been expecting you.'

'Sorry we're a bit late,' I said. 'The rain, and so forth...'

'It's no trouble at all,' she replied. 'To be truthful, I've been finding the days rather longer than usual.'

Clarence and I waited in the hall until the glowering Ursula appeared with a large object, wrapped in brown paper.

'Keep it dry,' Vanetta said. 'It's my best work.'

And so we brought Harriet's portrait to Buckshaw.

'Hold the umbrella for me,' Clarence said, preparing to wrestle the package from the backseat of the taxicab. 'I'm going to need both hands.'

Shielding the parcel from the slanting rain, we dashed to the door, as awkward as three-legged racers.

I had handed Clarence the fare and was halfway across the foyer when suddenly Father emerged from his study.

'What have you dragged home now?' he asked, and I couldn't find it in my heart to lie.

'It's a painting,' I said. 'It belongs to you.'

Father leaned it against the wall and returned to his study, from which he emerged with a pair of shears to cut the several turns of butcher's string.

He let the paper fall away.

That was two weeks ago.

The portrait of Harriet and her three children is no longer in the foyer, nor is it in the drawing room. Until today, I'd searched the house in vain.

But this morning, when I unlocked the door of my laboratory, I found the painting hanging above the mantelpiece.

I've mentioned this to no one.

Father knows it's there and I know it's there, and for now, that's all that counts.

NOTE TO THE READER

In order to provide sufficiently dramatic lighting for this story, I must admit to having tinkered slightly here and there with the phases of the moon, though the reader may rest assured that, having finished, I've put everything back exactly as it was.

ACKNOWLEDGMENTS

The writing of a book is, among many other things, an extended journey with friends: a kind of pilgrimage. Along the way we have met, sometimes parted, shared meals, and swapped stories, ideas, jokes, and opinions. In doing so, these friends have become inextricably woven into the book's fabric.

My heartfelt gratitude to Dr. John Harland and Janet Harland, to whom this book is dedicated, for many years of friendship and countless excellent suggestions.

To Nora and Don Ivey, who not only opened their home to me, but also saw to it personally that one of my lifelong dreams was made to come true.

To my editors: Bill Massey at Orion Books in London, Kate Miciak at Random House in New York, and Kristin Cochrane at Doubleday Canada in Toronto. And particular thanks to Loren Noveck and Connie Munro, at Random House, New York, my production editor and copy editor respectively, who toil away quietly behind the scenes doing much of the work for which I get the credit.

To Denise Bukowski, my agent, and Susan Morris at the Bukowski Agency, who fearlessly juggle all the mountains of detail with astonishing efficiency.

To Brad Martin, CEO of Random House Canada, for his abiding faith.

To Susan Corcoran and Kelle Ruden of Random House, New York, and Sharon Klein of Random House, Toronto, for their phenomenal support.

To Natalie Braine, Jade Chandler, Juliet Ewers, Jessica Purdue, and Helen Richardson of Orion Books, London, who have relieved me of so much of the worry.

To Jennifer Herman and Michael Ball for making the miles fly by and delivering me safely.

To Ken Boichuk and his Grimsby Author Series, with gratitude for a most memorable evening.

To my old friend Robert Nielsen of Potlatch Publications, who published some of my earliest fiction, and who honestly seemed as happy to see me again as I was to see him.

To Ted Barris, author and longtime friend, whose focused energy is always such an inspiration.

To Marion Misters of Sleuth of Baker Street in Toronto, and Wendy Sharko of The Avid Reader in Cobourg, who welcomed me back to my birthplace and hometown respectively.

To Rita and Hank Schaeffer, who coddled me in Montreal.

To Andreas Kessaris of the Paragraphe Bookstore, Montreal.

To the Random House 'Ladies of Westminster': Cheryl Kelly, Lori Zook, Sherri Drechsler, Pam Kaufman, Judy Pohlhaus, Camille Marchi,

Sherry Virtz, Stacey Carlinia, Emily Bates, Amiee Wingfield, and Lauren Gromlowicz, with whom I shared a ton of books and two tons of laughs.

To Kim Monahan, Randall Klein, and David Weller of Random House, in New York City.

To Tony Borg, Mary Rose Grima, Dr. Joe Rapa, Doris Vella, and Dr. Raymond Xerri, who will probably never realize what a great difference they made. Their many kindnesses and courtesies during the writing of this book will never be forgotten.

To Mary Jo Anderson, Stan Ascher, Andrea Baillie, Tim Belford, Rebecca Brayton, Arlene Bynon, Stephen Clare, Richard Davies, Anne Lagace Dowson, Mike Duncan, Vanessa Gates, Kathleen Hay, Andrew Krystal, Sheryl MacKay, Hubert O'Hearn, Mark Perzel, David Peterson, Ric Peterson, Craig Rintoul, M. J. 'Mike' Stone, Scott Walker, Lisa Winston, and Carolyn Yates, who made it seem easy by asking all the right questions.

To Skip Prichard and George Tattersfield at the Ingram Book Company, in La Vergne, Tennessee; and to Claire Tattersfield, who did me the great honor of skipping school to have her book signed, and to Robin Glennon for arranging a most memorable day.

To fellow authors Annabel Lyon, Michael McKinley, Chuck Palahniuk, and Danielle Trussoni, for sharing part of the journey.

To Paul Ingram of Prairie Lights Books in Iowa City, Iowa, and to Wes Caliger. In spite of having entertained President Obama the day before I arrived, Paul's welcome was the kind that every author dreams about.

To my 'Evil Twin' Barbara Peters at The Poisoned Pen, in Scottsdale, Arizona, who leaves the most astonishing plot ideas on my voice mail.

To the memory of my dear friend David Thompson of Murder by the Book in Houston, Texas, whose shockingly early death in September 2010 has deprived the world of mystery fiction of one of its cornerstones. Known for his encyclopedic knowledge of mystery fiction, David was universally loved by authors and readers alike.

And to David's wife, McKenna Jordan of Murder by the Book, and McKenna's mom, Brenda Jordan, for gentle kindnesses too numerous to count.

To Dan Mayer and Bob Weitrack of Barnes and Noble, New York; to Ellen Clark, Richard Horseman, Dane Jackson, and Eric Tsai of Borders, Ann Arbor, Michigan.

To Barb Hudson, Jennie Turner-Collins, and Micheal Fraser of Joseph-Beth Booksellers, in Cincinnati, Ohio, and to Kathy Tirschek, who got me safely to wherever I needed to go.

With love to the Brysons: Jean, Bill, Barbara, John, Peter, and David, who have always been there.

To the Ball Street Gang: Bob and Pat Barker, Lillian Barker Hoselton, Jane McCaig, Jim Thomas, and honorary member Linda Hutsell-Manning: together again after half a century. Thomas Wolfe was wrong: You *can* go home again.

To Evelyn and Leigh Palmer and to Robert Bruce Thompson, who helped with the chemistry. Any errors remaining are my own.

I must also acknowledge particular indebtedness to the books that inspired the invention of that peculiar sect, the *Hobblers: History and Antiquities of Dissenting Churches and Meeting Houses, in London, Westminster, and Southwark; Including the Lives of Their Ministers, from the Rise of Nonconformism to the Present Time,* Walter Gibson, London, 1814, and *The History of Baptism,* Robert Robinson, Boston, 1817.

And finally, as always, with love to my wife, Shirley, who makes my life easy by cheerfully doing whatever I leave undone, besides doubling as my personal computer technician. No one is more brilliantly adept at rejuvenating worn-out keyboards and, while she's at it, removing the crumbs.

The publishers hope that this book has given you enjoyable reading. Large Print Books are especially designed to be as easy to see and hold as possible. If you wish a complete list of our books please ask at your local library or write directly to:

Magna Large Print Books
Magna House, Long Preston,
Skipton, North Yorkshire.
BD23 4ND

This Large Print Book for the partially sighted, who cannot read normal print, is published under the auspices of

THE ULVERSCROFT FOUNDATION